Rachel,

Sending you love

the form of this grand

tale about looking for it

BURN
BLOW
NOURISH
GROW

Robert Jones

#morelove

1·3·22

LOVE [burns]

BURN. blow. nourish. grow.

the FIRST book of the series

By
Robert Zamees

@zamees
fb.com/robertzamees
zamees.com

Print ISBN 978-1-09833-358-4
ebook ISBN 978-1-09833-359-1

Printed in the United States of America.

Cover design by Whitney Larson, wlarson.com.

I dedicate this novel to my mother, Kathy, who, when she finished reading the first draft said, "I'm sad that my son has lived such a difficult life." And I thought, "That's NOT the story I want to tell!"

So I rewrote it…7 more times. You truly may not know the story you are trying to tell, until you try to tell it.

And, to Promise, wherever and whoever you may be.

Prologue

When time began, the world didn't know love, just as I didn't know it when my life began and you didn't know it when yours began. But we all had the capacity for it—the world, you, and I—as long as we committed to it.

Like I said, we did not know love. It wasn't simply handed to us, as with the ability to breathe. We had to learn *it. And the only place to begin learning love is to first learn to love one's self.*

Some have had great teachers, helpful examples in their lives to follow. But others have not, unfortunately, and over time these role models have become less and less prevalent. A lucky few have self-taught and found true love, but the trial and error process consumes a lifetime of energy. Most never find what they're looking for; they settle for whomever they can stand, and simply end up exhausted, alone, and bitterly unhappy.

Herein lies our problem: as the examples of true love in the world lessen, who is left to teach?

I am. You can call me "Promise."

You don't know me yet, but you will, and soon. I can tell you the story of True Love, from past to present, because it is part of who I am. I can also tell you there are few left in the world who can disrupt the precipitous slide we fight to prevent love from becoming extinct—few who can still learn from my teachings.

Therefore, it's imperative for you to listen, because Love is *dying.*

Love. Is. Dying.

My hope lies in reciting the prayer my mother taught me as a child:

"Promisers, my guardians dear,
To whom True Love commits me here.
Ever this day be at my side,
To light, to guard, to love, and guide."

It was our prayer in the morning, our prayer before meals, and our prayer in the evening. But it seems it was not shared enough, or that it has been forgotten by too many…

Because, like I already said, Love is dying...and we're running out of time.

Chapter 1

I'm older now, but this is how I remember it…

It was always the same when he came to visit; eyes lost in the pain of distant memories. Never did he dress differently from anyone else in the neighborhood, yet there *was* difference in the lines of his face—an aged tome that carried the history of his tribe—and beneath those wrinkles flowed an immeasurably passionate being. All of the kids called him "Grandpa," but my Great Grandpa Walker was a man we knew *of* more than ever *really* knew at all; his life was about coming and going rather than staying.

Great Grandpa had the ability to create special places through his storytelling. In these places, we would forget the tired look of our surroundings: the peaks and valleys of sidewalk slabs powerless against Mother Nature's roots, patchy weeds in front yards acting as grass, chain link fences slumped from years of children scurrying over them, discarded cigarette butts littering tiny porches outside most of the front doors. We cherished the chipped clapboard siding on each small, drably painted house we called home, and understood that our squeaky hinges needed no grease; they served double duty as both doorbell and burglar alarm.

Great Grandpa's raspy, yet soothing voice was familiar to us, making it easy to listen as he created a virtual setting for each story.

Throughout my childhood, he would visit our home for birthdays and holidays, acting as any normal elder would by showering us with praise. He'd bide his time until we were free from our celebratory rituals, waiting patiently for one of us to ask, "Grandpa, can you tell us a story?"

"Yes, of course, my child," he would always reply, a smile upon his face.

Great Grandpa's words never disappeared once they left his lips. We collectively memorized them to be acted out in front yards, backyards, and basements until we had the opportunity to hear his voice again. Each child remembered a tale in a particular way, with his or her own context, but the core of the story never changed—the moral lessons so deeply rooted in the telling. He'd told us stories of his people and their harmonious life. Nature was their home. The sky was their ceiling. The grass was their floor. They knew no walls. Everything had a story that told of its origin, a story that had been passed from generation to generation.

"Have I told you of the place called Autumnnnn?" Great Grandpa asked, drawing out the last syllable to intentionally capture each child's eyes with his own.

"Noooooooooo," we said in unison, perpetuating the bold-faced lies that kids are apt to display. We over-exaggerated, smiling from ear to ear, quite sure we were going to get what we wanted despite the false answer.

He began, "You can see the circular nature of life in Autumn." With both index fingers, he burned a circle into the air like sparklers on the 4th of July. "Where is a leaf born?" he asked.

Children's hands flew wildly into the air.

"Soupy, can you tell me where a leaf is born?" His eyes met mine. I knew the answer, but was nervous to give it. A sparkle in his eye lent me the courage to speak.

"A leaf is born from a tree, Great Grandpa," I said.

"That is true, my grandson, very good. But once born, a leaf desires to be reborn, and cannot do so until it learns the path." He plucked a leaf from an imaginary tree, tossed it into the air, and slowly waved his hand beneath it, cradling it on a cushion of air as it floated to the ground. "It is the same with us. We live. We learn. We eventually learn enough to move on," he smiled as he stood up from his kneeling position. "But most of you children have no need to worry about that just yet." What would you like to name the leaf in our story?" he asked.

"LEAF!" we shouted.

Great Grandpa feigned surprise though we always named the leaf, Leaf. "Very well then, Leaf it is. Can anyone tell me what Leaf prepares for in the fall?" he asked.

Answers could be heard under mumbled breath, but none of the children were confident enough to speak aloud. Grandpa smiled, forcing us to think longer. I remained silent, allowing my friends to partake in the story instead of hoarding it. "Football?" one asked, and Great Grandpa shook his head. "To get raked?" another asked. "To fly away?" asked a third. It wasn't until Great Grandpa heard "To fall" that he smiled and pointed amicably at the bearer of the correct answer.

"Leaf prepares for his crossing by changing his color from green to yellow to orange to red." His finger tapped an invisible line in the air, each tap causing the creation of that color's leaf. "Leaf grows up. As Leaf gets older, Leaf wants to show all the other leaves that Leaf has lived a good and healthy life. Leaf shows this by being the biggest, brightest leaf he can be. When Leaf feels ready, Leaf jumps from the tree and begins his descent to the ground." The imaginary leaves that Great Grandpa had created, now all red, followed his hands as he slowly lowered himself to his knees, his forehead coming to rest on the ground in front of his lap.

We held our breath and waited silently to learn more about Leaf's fate.

When Great Grandpa emerged from his restful pose, I noticed the seasons changing rapidly in his eyes, which were now at the same height as our own; he had brought his world to our level. "If Leaf has not tried Leaf's best through all the seasons, then Leaf will fall to the ground and rot with the other failed leaves." An electric charge formed around Great Grandpa. It zapped the leaves all around us, causing our eyes to widen and our spines to straighten. As the leaves settled back to the ground, Great Grandpa leaned forward and whispered, "Failed and destined to rot on the earth, it will be many seasons before these leaves get the chance to be new leaves again. Like when you are grounded, and it is many days before you can go out again," he added analogously.

We nodded our heads because we all knew what it was like to be grounded, sitting quietly in solace until we'd understood our failure, served our time, or apologized; whatever the reason, in that moment we knew exactly what leaves felt like if they didn't do their best.

Great Grandpa continued to whisper, "If Leaf has been a good leaf, then Leaf will ascend." He then bellowed, "TO THE SKY!" Miraculously, for his age, he popped up from kneeling to standing without using his arms to push off from the ground. His hands above his head and his face to the sky, he continued, "LEAF WILL FLOAT TO THE HEAVENS AND BE BORN AGAIN!" The clouds quickened their route, now jet-fueled and hurried by Great Grandpa's words, and didn't resume their lazy crawl until his hands returned to his sides. He then drew a long breath before bringing his hands together at his chest. His calming smile reminded us to release the collective breath we'd been holding as we watched his gestures.

He brought his face closer to ours and said, "Leaf, having lived a good life, will enjoy Leaf's time in the air making shapes with the clouds. Have *you* seen shapes in the clouds?" He pointed at several of us, inviting answers.

"YES!" we shouted.

"What shapes have you seen?" Great Grandpa asked.

A chorus of mostly unintelligible answers bubbled from our mouths, then formed clouds over our heads in the shape of elephants, horses, rabbits, and turtles.

Great Grandpa laughed heartily. "Leaf will help make all those shapes until Leaf is ready to return to the earth."

A cacophony of neats and cools and whoas and giggles escaped our mouths.

"In order for Leaf to return, though, Leaf must sacrifice himself to lightning, which will turn Leaf into rain." With a quick flick of one hand, a bolt of lightning shot from Great Grandpa's right palm to his left. We jumped when we saw it, blinking instinctively as a form of protection. "It is water that feeds the grass and trees of the earth. It is water that allows them to turn from brown to green again." A steady downpour fell into Great Grandpa's upward palms quelling the smoke that had been left by the lightning. "When it is time, Leaf will choose to return as a raindrop. Leaf will feed the trees, sprout, and slowly return to life as a leaf." Great Grandpa held his arms away from his sides as leaves sprouted all over his body.

One of my closest friends, Faith, raised her hand and asked, "Why does Leaf do this every year? It sounds boring." A few kids followed her question with a smattering of supportive yeahs.

No longer covered in leaves, Great Grandpa took a step back and sat on the porch. "That is a very good question, child. You see, Leaf does not want to be a leaf forever. No-no. Leaf wants to someday grow up and become a tree. Do you want to grow up?"

"Yes!" she shouted. "I want to be a mom and a teacher!"

"You don't want to be a *tree?"* he asked, jokingly.

Faith replied, too young to pick up on his sarcasm, but intuitive enough to recognize his humor, by saying, "Noooooo! I can't be a tree!"

Personally, I wondered if *I* wanted to be a tree.

"Hmmm, I see." Great Grandpa feigned a concerned look. "Well, Leaf has similar dreams. If you promise to do your best year after year, you can accomplish *your* dreams."

Her smile widened at the thought of accomplishing her dreams, as the rest of us entertained thoughts that we could be firemen and astronauts and bus drivers and maybe even presidents.

The captivating energy that Great Grandpa emitted ceased as if he'd lifted the bell jar from the front yard and allowed the noises of the neighborhood to return, which told us that story time was over. Practically all the children begged for another story, but Great Grandpa politely declined by saying, "Be good, children. Thank you for allowing me to tell you a story, but that's all for today. Right now, I need to speak with my grandson." As the children popped up to walk or ride their bicycles home, he motioned to me and said, "Soupy, sit here with me a moment longer. It is time I tell you some very important things about the world." His eyes, once full of glee from telling his story, quickly returned to the dense, black, sorrow-filled ones that more frequently occupied his face. I sat on the porch next to him, our hips touching. He leaned closer and placed his mouth near my ear to make sure others didn't hear our conversation. "There is much to know, both in the world you see and the one you do not, and you can only see one world at a time," he began. "It has been my desire to pass along the teachings of my people, but no one has expressed an interest in learning."

"I'd like to learn, Great Grandpa. I'm really good at school," I said.

Great Grandpa chuckled, "I know you are good at school. So you must listen to what I tell you because I may only get to tell you once."

I blinked, gulped, and tried hard to focus on his words, but I couldn't shake the feeling that they gave me: a fear of never hearing them again.

He sensed the feeling and placed his left arm around my shoulders to comfort me. "Hold your hand out. Like this," he said, holding his right palm flat to the sky. I followed his instruction and held out my right palm. As I did, a warm feeling began in my shoulder and slowly moved its way toward my hand. "There are two worlds. *This* is the world of your body." As he finished his sentence, he placed his palm on top of my own. The warm sensation that was traveling down my arm rushed to his touch, startling me. Great Grandpa smiled, "You feel it, I see. It will not hurt you, at least not while I am here."

"It doesn't hurt, Great Grandpa, it just scared me," I replied.

"As it should, my child, as it should. This heat reminds you of when you first burnt yourself, I am sure."

I nodded.

"You must learn to communicate with your fire."

Puzzled, I asked, "With *my* fire?"

"Yes, your air will control how much you let your fire breathe."

Before I could ask about my air, a warm breeze made the tall weeds dance over the dusty yard. The heat between our palms increased and I felt that tinge of fear return. Great Grandpa lifted his palm from mine, but the heat didn't leave, it remained, burning in the center of my palm as if a magnifying glass was focusing the sun.

"It's getting hot, Great Grandpa. Too HOT!" I said with alarm.

Suddenly, Great Grandpa leaned forward and forcefully spit on my palm.

"HEY!" I said, wiping my hand to my shorts.

"Well?" he asked.

"That's gross," I complained with a wrinkled face.

"And the fire?"

"The fire?" I paused for a moment before the realization hit me. "The fire…it's gone!"

Great Grandpa got up from the porch and kneeled down in the grass. He spit into one hand, then the other, and lowered them both to the ground. "For your thirst," he said.

I mimicked his action, squatting instead of kneeling, spitting into my hands and placing my palms on the ground. "For your thirst," I repeated. I felt the spit sucked away from my palms by the grass. In exchange, I received a burst of energy.

"And this—" Great Grandpa said, leaning toward me until our foreheads touched, "—is the world of your mind.

I was swept into a whole different place. My hands tightly grasped the steering pegs of an ancient, double-masted sailing ship. Our severe cant was forced by a fierce squall that filled the reefed sails and stung us with bullets of rain. I looked at Great Grandpa standing next to me, where he held firm to a line with one hand while the other pointed just off starboard to a light on top of a dark mountain. "GO THERE!" he shouted loudly enough I could hear him over the wind.

"WE'LL HAVE TO TACK!" I shouted in return. I spun the wheel to bring the ship into the wind. When we crossed over to port from starboard, the sails filled with a loud snap and the rigging whined at the stress of the returned pressure. We were now headed directly for the dark island Great Grandpa had spied.

The wind whipped across the deck from left to right, which made it easier to hear Great Grandpa when he shouted, "BEACH IT!"

I set the ship on a course toward the heart of the island, expertly slipped it between two great rocks that served as channel markers, and kept us moving full-powered toward land. A loud crunch threw me into the wheel, which stole my breath. When I got it back I yelled, "DROP THE SAILS!" but Great Grandpa was already on the task. As the halyards holding the sails aloft blew, the tops of the sails themselves floated off to starboard, over the gunnel, and into the dark water. When I looked up, I saw the light on the mountain was no light at all, but a fire.

Great Grandpa was shouting from the forward mast, pointing to his ears, but I couldn't make out what he was trying to tell me. Then, I heard strange voices. They repeated clearly and slowly, "We are the four elements. Burn. Blow. Nourish. Grow. We are the four elements. Burn. Blow. Nourish. Grow. We are the four—"

Suddenly, we'd returned to the world of our bodies and Great Grandpa leaned away from me. The howling wind dissipated in my ears as he asked, "Are you okay?"

"Yes, Great Grandpa."

"Did you hear them?"

"The voices?"

"Yes," he said and nodded. "The voices."

"They said—"

He held his hand up abruptly and said, "Shhh, not here. That was a special place. You must be very careful talking about *that* world when you are in *this* world. Come closer."

I sat down next to him on the grass and he continued, "There are Places of Power in both worlds—in *this* world and *that* world. Very often, you will discover these places while you are dreaming. Do you understand, my grandson?"

"Yes," I replied, but it was a knee-jerk response, and not necessarily true, as I was still thinking about the ship and the island in my head.

"Now listen to me," Great Grandpa said, gently turning my face to his by cradling my chin in his hand, "This is very important—very important. When you find these powerful places, the voices there will say things just like what they said on the island. These things will in some way relate to your life. It will be up to you to figure out what they mean and what you should do."

I replied by nodding my head and gulping at the weight of his words.

"It will be a very long time before you understand that they aren't just talking, but talking to *you*." He placed his hand on my shoulder and I felt the warmth in my body gravitate toward his touch once again. "As you grow, you will learn to think, and learning to think will help you understand. The world of your mind allows you to dream of the things you can accomplish in the world of your body. Repeat that back to me."

"The world," I paused to think, "of my mind dreams about…the things I can do in the world of my body?"

"Yes, very good," he smiled. "I tell you this now, long before you will understand, because it is important for you to find these places soon. Soupy, you are meant to make the world a better place."

I wanted to make a mad dash up the porch steps, into my bedroom, sliding at full speed across the floor as if I was Rickey Henderson stealing second base, the base being my safe place under the bed. I could reach my pseudo suit of armor from under there by tugging on the edge of my comforter, pulling it under the bed, and wrapping it around me. But Great Grandpa's gaze wouldn't let me go. I struggled to find the right words, but said, "Okay, Great Grandpa, I promise to do my best."

"I know you will, my grandson. I know you will." He looked over his shoulder and confirmed that everyone else was inside before he said, "And now, I must go. Stand up with me."

I did, and he gave me a hug, an embrace that felt as protective as any secret hiding place. I pulled back from his hug just enough to ask, "Great Grandpa, when I grow up, will I be able to tell stories like you?"

"Very possibly," he said as he walked toward the side of the house. From there, he grabbed the end of a stick, slung it and the bindle it held over his shoulder, and headed toward the street. I was sad to see him go, as always. After he took a few steps, he reached into his pocket, and said, "To remind you: always do great and honorable things," and tossed a shiny, black rock, slightly larger than the size of a quarter, toward me. I caught it and felt the strength of generations of hands that had grasped it before mine. I closed my fist around the rock and eagerly, but sadly, stepped to the curb and watched Great Grandpa Walker stroll down the street and vanish into the real world.

Burn. Blow. Nourish. Grow. These four words from the island came back to me as Great Grandpa walked away. I felt the urge to look more closely at the rock he'd given me; I saw the sky reflected on its surface. It was then that I noticed my hands had changed; they were now wrinkly. They weren't wrinkly before. They looked...old.

Chapter 2

It happened on the night I became a teenager: a dream that changed the rest of my life. Some say that aging from twelve to thirteen defines a rite of passage into manhood, which might have been true two hundred years ago when we were working the land and contributing to the family at a young age. But in late-twentieth-century America there wasn't much that actually changed; it wasn't like I sprouted body odor or pubic hair or muscles or any such thing overnight.

I was one of the oldest kids in my class—which would eventually mean I'd be the first to drive, vote, and legally drink—but from twelve to thirteen that elder status didn't amount to much. If I was Jewish, I would have been the first of my friends to have a Bar Mitzvah, a celebration to recognize my ascension to an age of responsibility. However, I'm not Jewish and in my single-parent household I already had as much responsibility as I cared to have: doing my laundry, making my meals, cleaning my room—some of those happened a lot less frequently than others.

Nothing changed much in my life on my thirteenth birthday, other than the way I *thought* about my life. And that change came in the form of a voice

I'd never before heard, but *felt* more familiar to me than my mother's. It was a voice that came to me in a dream.

* * *

You must find me.

"Who *are* you?" I asked.

I'm your equal, not now, but hopefully someday. I shine the same bright light as you. But until you can find me—which is the homework I'm about to give you—I'm more apt to be your teacher, your influence, your angel, your female conscious, your lended-ear, your other half, your dream…and someday perhaps your love, but only on such a day when we've become equals. Right now, I'm just your dream.

"I'm dreaming?" I said and looked around slowly, not recognizing the strange setting of this particular dream.

Yes, and for now, it's important to remember that I'm just a dream.

Ever since the day Great Grandpa told me to pay more attention to the world—to look for Places of Power—I'd honed my observation skills. In this dream, I sat in an open-air room shaped like a semi-circle. The curved part of the circular wall stood tall, much higher than my standing height. The wall that bisected the circle, which I faced, was much lower, more like a wall you'd find in a country field built by human hands with lots of stones. In fact, the entire structure *was* built from sleek, black stones. The floor was soft due to a bed of crushed leaves; at least I assumed they were crushed leaves because the air smelled of them. In my seated position, I couldn't see over the top of the half-wall, but I *could* see the outer corona of a glow on the other side. I was sure the voice I heard came from there, mostly because I could *feel* a presence there. After this quick survey of the scene, I said, "I mean, you're right here, doesn't that mean I've found you?"

Yes, but this is the dream world and you must find me in the real world. I know this world—the world of dreams—and I'm here to help you navigate it in order to finish your homework.

"You do know I'm thirteen years old, right?"

Yes, she laughed. *I know you better than you think, and you won't actually be thirteen until the middle of the afternoon.*

The glow on the other side of the semicircle brightened, which revealed more of the room. It was then that I noticed a number of screens built into the rock walls. "TVs?" I wondered aloud.

Not quite, the voice replied.

I blinked and then opened my eyes as wide as I could. The screens weren't televisions, but childhood toys I'd dearly loved: Etch-a-Sketches. Some etched words, others shapes, and some scribbled randomly and seemingly without cause.

Pay no attention to them; they represent all that's going on in your mind.

"My mind is an Etch-a-Sketch?"

Hundreds of them, apparently, it may be my world, but it's your dream.

"All we need is a Lite-Brite and a dark closet, and we'd be set," I added.

The voice continued on a more serious note, *I've been going over this conversation with you in my head for years. And I think the best way to do this is to lecture to you and hope, just hope, that you understand, because I don't know how much time we'll have in this dream. Ready?*

I didn't see any other choice and I was curious to learn more, so I replied, "Ready, but are you—"

Please, the voice interrupted, *let me begin.*

I mumbled, "Just wanted to know if you're a real person."

I could be, but we'll get to that later.

The Etch-a-Sketches began frantically scribbling back and forth, filling up their screens.

Shit, the voice said. *Don't move.*

"What?" I asked.

Shhh.

The glow on the other side of the wall diminished as a hideous scratching noise filled the air. It sounded like several sharp, bony claws on rock, like there were things trying to climb the walls and enter our circle. I immediately threw my hands over my ears. *"WHAT IS THAT?"* I screamed.

Bring your thoughts back to me, Soupy.

"WHAT? WHAT? I CAN'T—"

She repeated, *Soupy, your thoughts, bring them back to me.*

"—HEAR YOU!" It sounded as if things on the *outside* desperately wanted to get *inside*, and that didn't sound like anything I wanted to happen. Because I'd recently learned to fly in my dreams, I flapped my arms frantically for a gradual increase in altitude. As I rose, I looked over the short wall that stood between the voice and me, but saw nothing aside from darkness. There was no longer a light. I did note, however, that it wasn't emptiness, but darkness; it was just too dark to see if anyone was actually there.

Soupy.

It was hard to concentrate with the feverish scratching noise all around me, plus the effort of flapping consumed most of my attention. But another few feet and I'd be able to see the land around the space that hosted our conversation.

Suddenly, the clawing noise stopped, but fear didn't bring immediate relief. I surveyed the land: barren, desert-like, sparsely littered with shrubbery and trees, all of which looked to have been burned at some point in the recent past. I was on the edge of a mesa, the flat land surrounding us on all but one side. Nothing could be seen over the edge of the cliff.

Soupy, the voice repeated.

I looked around the land expecting to see some massive gathering of scarabs or scorpions, some kind of pinching insects stacked hundreds on top of hundreds looking for a way over the rocks. To my surprise, none were found. But from my hovering perch, I could see more of the room than just my half of the semi-circle; it was actually a full circle with a slash—the half-wall—dividing it into two equal halves. It reminded me of a Do Not Enter symbol. "Hey," I pointed toward it, but the act of pointing counteracted my hovering, so I quickly returned to flapping. My initial intent was to point out the obvious shape of the room, but my suddenly greater intent was to avoid an embarrassing return to the ground. *Do not enter*, I thought, *but I just came from there and now I have to go back.*

I briefly scouted the options for an escape and considered them, but curiosity about the voice outweighed fear of the noise. Plus, there was power here, and Great Grandpa once told me to seek Places of Power in both the world of my body *and* the dream world. He told me that voices wouldn't just speak, but speak to *me* in these places, and that was certainly the case here.

Bring your thoughts back to me, Soupy, she said, calmly. *There's no need to be afraid. Things aren't what they seem. You're in the dream world, not the real world. We have much to discuss, so get back down here.*

Landings weren't yet my forte. I hovered a bit longer, thinking through the procedure for a gradual easing back to earth. *At least the ground's padded by leaves,* I thought. First step: flap a little less. As I did so gravity asserted more of its will. There was no stopping it. *Shit.* I succumbed to the downward force and landed with an embarrassing thud. A cloud of leaf dust surrounded me as I picked myself up, coughing and waving at the dust with my hands.

You okay over there? the voice asked, trying to stifle her laughter.

"Fine," I said, though it wasn't true. My young man's ego was badly bruised. I resumed my cross-legged, seated position as part of an effort to quickly change the subject. "What was all that scratching?"

That? Don't worry about it now. I told you, it's not what it seems, and I need you to focus on our conversation. I need you here, so let's get back to our talk.

"Okay."

My family knows your family. We go back a long time, a really *long time, but we'll talk about that later. Right now, suffice to know I know you, not yet as well as I'd like, but it's a start. I've peered into your dreams a few times, that's all.*

"My dreams? You know what I dream about?" I blushed, thinking instantly of my fantasies.

Believe me, there are dreams far worse than any you've likely had. It's my job to peer into dreams, so believe me I know. She paused for a moment. *Sheesh. This is harder than I thought; we keep getting sidetracked and we have so much to cover. Soupy, are you familiar with your family's genealogy?*

"No, but my mom has a family tree somewhere," I replied, happy to know what she meant by "genealogy" even though I didn't know much about mine.

Okay, I'll try to give you the short version. Here we go. It's important to understand where you come from in order to understand who you are…and where you're going. Genealogy is complex, which makes explaining how my family knows your family a long, complicated story. The derivations of complexity have shaped not only our lives, but also the lives of those around us. For now, let's start with your parents and grandparents, you should at least know about them.

I nodded my head because it was tough to keep up with the rapid rate of her words, and then realized she couldn't actually see me, so I replied, "Okay."

Since I know you get good grades, I know you can pay attention. So shut your trap, sit up straight, and listen.

I did as I was told and wondered if perhaps she *could* see me.

Okay, she said, and took a deep breath. *The Heller family, your family, as you know, has always been known as a family of healers. Like many other surnames, healer became Heller much like black smith became Smith, cobbler became Cobb, and tailor became Taylor. In actuality, the Hellers weren't necessarily known for any specific occupation, but were simply the people who lived near a hill known for their fair complexion and bright blue eyes. To this day, "hell" in German means "light" and "heller" means "lighter." Hellers have always been a mysterious bunch, or so the storytellers have said, who have contemplated the world and solved the problems of their neighbors. As a case in point, during the Norman Conquest of 1066, the Hellers were granted vast tracts of land for their problem solving and distinguished assistance…but I ramble. Hellers are known for accomplishing their work through the use of their hands, which has its commonplace origin in the well-known, pious term "healing hands," but which actually dates back to well before the birth of Christianity.*

Your father came from a long line of Hellers who had years ago abandoned the original concept of healing. Spirituality and religion had merged in the Heller family many generations previous when they chose a path to worship God as their one true Healer. When the Bible claimed, in Mark 16:18, that Jesus could "lay hands on the sick and they shall recover," the Hellers instantly accepted a religion they could rally around, no longer in fear of being outcasts for their own spiritual mission of healing. Your father was the breakaway child from his own family. He compartmentalized religion as one part of life, not all of life, and therefore taught you to avoid following the herd or feel the guilt that coloring outside the lines might bring. In other words, he taught you to make your own decisions and live with them.

I nodded my head again, choosing not to speak up for fear of interrupting the story.

Great Grandma Engberg, on your mother's side, is a family mystery. Your mother never knew her, but I've been told she lived in the hills of Scandinavia before making the trek to America. And your mother's mother, also known as your grandmother, died when your mother was a child. Though a mystery, like I said, there's an interesting historical connection between the Engbergs and the Hellers. The Engberg name, literally, translates to "meadow and mountain." What's found between a meadow and a mountain? Often times, it's a foothill, or a hill. Earlier, I told you that Hellers were partly named because they lived near a hill, though we believe the last name was less about the hill and more about the heal, h-e-a-l, the connection is still something to ponder. In kind, while Hellers were known for solving problems, Engbergs were known for helping people get from one place to the next. Your mother's father, Grandpa Walker, heard the call of the nation and served much of his life in the throes of war, attacking and defending hills, a great and honorable deed, totally true to his family's motto.

She paused momentarily before saying, *One second, I'm gathering these last thoughts. There's only a bit left, I swear.*

"No problem. It's interesting since it's *my* family, you know?"

When you were born—a robust, ten-pound bowling ball, I might add—most of your family had no idea what the combination of being the first-born between both lineages might bring. The Walkers, of great and honorable deeds, and the Hellers, always for the state, are the historical mottos for each family. Not that they'd had them embroidered, framed, and hung in their homes, but where you come from and what your family has done has an impact on who you are—or could be, in this case. The connection that had been lost between the two families generations ago was reformed by your birth.

"Okay, okay, okay," I yammered. "I hear you, but why is it so important?

You need to know where you come from because it's your homework to accomplish something great in the world.

I grew suddenly frustrated. "People always tell me that. Why do they *always* tell me that?! I'm only thirteen years old!"

Twelve.

"You know what I mean!"

Maybe they tell you that because it's true. Whether you believe it or not has been irrelevant up until this time. It's your choice to make, but if you're capable of finishing your homework, we believe you'll change the world.

My frustration was still with me, but it abated enough for me to ask, "How do you know all of this?"

You've studied English and math; I've studied you and your family.

"Yeah, you know more about my family than I do. But why?"

Your homework is about more than just Engbergs and Hellers and Walkers, more than just you and me; it's about the world. We're in this together. We can't accomplish what we've been tasked to do without each other. In fact, no one could accomplish this task alone; it will take two. That's why you have to find me.

"So we can save the world?"

She chuckled, *So to speak, but not like you've seen in the movies. The world isn't under attack; the world has forgotten how to love.*

"Love? You know I'm—"

Yes, I know you're only twelve years old and have no idea what love really is, but that's partly why I'm here: to help you learn.

"Can you just tell me where you are?"

It isn't that easy, Soupy. Despite what others believe, life is not mandated, predetermined, or about fate; it's simpler than that. In life you are given homework, some task or tasks to complete, and it's your progress on those assignments that ultimately defines who you are. When they look back on your life, they'll grade you solely on your homework, which is your contribution to the world.

"They?"

Yes, they, but "they" are definitely a conversation for another day.

"Are there instructions for this homework?"

As if you follow instructions?

"Well, that's true, unless you're talking about building all the toys at Christmas—responsibility of the oldest grandchild, you know," I replied.

You've innately got a good sense of what's right. You aren't always vocal about it, but you know how to find the right thing to do.

"No instructions, huh?" I thought for a moment before I added, "So you want a thirteen-year old to commit the rest of his life to a homework assignment he learned about in a dream?"

Several of the black Etch-a-Sketches shook hastily back and forth noting the ridiculous nature of the question I'd just asked.

Don't give me any of that you-suddenly-don't-believe-in-your-dreams business.

"But I don't even know what I wanna be when I grow up!"

Yes, you do. You wrote a paper about it in sixth grade...something about the combination of art as your favorite subject and math being your greatest challenge, I think.

"Dammit," I replied, and then slapped my hand to my mouth.

Soupy, whether you know it or not, you are the ultimate believer in True Love, even at this young age, and you always rise to a challenge. I've presented you with just that, a challenge. There's no map to this destination; it's not that clear. No footprints to follow down a path...no path, actually. You'll have to make your own way. If you want to achieve your ultimate dream, then you'll have to find me and together we'll show the world that True Love actually exists; we'll teach them how to love again.

My posture stiffened. It sounded impossible to teach the whole world *anything*, let alone how to love again. The Etch-a-Sketches reported the nature of my confusion by scribbling so furiously that the ground shook like a low-scale temblor. I thought, *Where would you even start something like that? And how the heck am I supposed to do that when I don't even know what love is?* To address my concerns, I asked, "How do you know I'm the right—"

It's you, Soupy. For the reasons I spelled out earlier: generations of families have prepared for you to be here in this important time...and there's still time for us to succeed.

I wanted to believe her. A noble quest would be a dreamy homework assignment. The Etch-a-Sketches drew hearts. The knobs turned back and forth quickly as they colored in each one. "Are you for real?" I asked.

Only as real as you want me to be.

I repeated her words in my head. Something about them started a question, but I couldn't put my finger on the entirety of it.

And by that I mean, it depends on how you define "real." It also depends on how much effort you put into finishing your homework.

"Homework. Homework. Homework. People in my family have been telling me there's a plan for me—that I'm meant to do great things—for years. I just figured it was the type of stuff *all* parents tell their kids. You know, the 'you can be anything you want when you grow up, like a prince or a princess in a big castle' kind of thing?"

The voice chuckled, *I was told you're more aware than most, must be the hand-me-down soul inside of you.*

My eyebrows raised and I replied with a simple, "Huh?"

This isn't your first time around the block, at least not for all of your parts. Are your hands used?

I looked at my hands. "Used?"

Yeah, are they old?

"What do you mean by old?"

I mean wrinkly.

"Yeah, they are. How do you know?"

It's the sign of an old soul, one that seems to have brought wisdom and a solid intuition into this current life of yours.

"What?" I asked, still confused.

Do you feel like you know me?

I remembered thinking her voice sounded more familiar to me than my own mother's, so I replied, "Yes, I do."

Have you ever met me?

"Not that I know of, but I still don't know who you are."

If you haven't met me, then how can you feel like you know me?

I scratched my head and contorted my face into a bundle of tangled twine.

Maybe we've met before?

"Okay, maybe, but where?"

Maybe in a previous life?

This was getting more interesting by the second. "In a previous life? I guess. I *am* only twelve—"

Don't get me wrong, Soupy, it's not your fault. This night has been a long time coming for me because I've known about it for quite some time, and you're just learning about it now.

"You do sound like someone I've known for a long time. Maybe this 'another life' stuff is true; it's a cool story anyway."

I sensed her thinking about my words, wishing I'd shown more confidence. After a few moments, she said, *Our time is running short, so I can accept that.*

To make sure I understood, I said, "So we *are* doing this homework thing?"

It'd be easy to say we have no choice, but we always have a choice. We're doing it as long as we choose to do it. How's that?

"Sure," I replied. "But how will I know when I've found you?"

You'll know because our togetherness will prove the existence of True Love. We'll be a beacon of light for others; an example to emulate in their lives. The world will once more believe in love and will use this belief to heal itself.

"And how's that supposed to help me find you?"

This is not a simple assignment, Soupy. You might run into me in the grocery store or find out I'm someone you've known for most of your life; we simply don't know where we'll meet, just that we must work together to get there. So let me give you this advice: you'll learn at least one thing from every person you meet in your life. Dating will always be about your head and your heart; don't let anyone tell you otherwise. I know you well enough to know you begin measuring whether you want to spend the rest of your life with a woman from the first moment you set eyes on her. Anyway, make darn sure you learn something from everyone you date.

You're too young to completely understand what I'm telling you. You believe there are a thousand important things to accomplish in life and I've just thrown a monkey wrench into any plan you've ever conjured up. I can't, and won't, sit here telling you what's wrong with your current vision because I know you learn mostly on your own, not from any advice you're given. But I do hope you believe there's a need for love in the world—it's the reason we must accomplish this task. You have no one in the real world to show or teach you what True Love is, right?

I thought for a moment about my own life with divorced parents; the lives of my friends with divorced parents, and struggled to find any examples of true love. Well, unless I could claim my undying love for Cheryl Tiegs on *Charlie's Angels*. Instead, I answered, "Not really."

Listen closely, Soupy. This task I've given you, it's a numbers game, a game of volume. Only by accumulated experience will you eventually figure out who I am and where to find me. Like I said, make sure you learn from every woman because each one will unlock another piece of the puzzle. You'll fail at finding me over and over again. You'll fail with consistency until you succeed. It sounds daunting. It doesn't sound like much fun. In fact, it sounds downright miserable for someone who lives in a glass-half-empty world. But you, Soupy Heller, I know you live in optimism, and I know you'll learn from both failure and success. You'll come off as brash, at times, because you'll know the outcome before everyone else—that's the sense of "knowing" you must draw upon and develop from that old soul in order to keep putting one foot in front of the other. And hopefully, it's from this sense that you'll learn to manage your failure and get more from it.

Believe this, Soupy, and believe in my voice. When you find me you'll have found success, and that success is nothing more and nothing less than True Love—it's the greatest thing in the world.

"Who are you?

Your dream. I told you—

"No, that's not what I meant. I mean, what's your name?"

Until you find me in the real world, call me "Promise."

"Promise?"

Yes, Promise.

"Promise."

That's my name; don't wear it out.

I rolled my eyes. In the distance I heard an alarm. I looked to the stars in an attempt to locate the direction this new sound was coming from, and then

I recognized it. It grew louder, which could only mean it also drew closer. "NO!" I shouted. "Promise? PROMISE?! I HAVE ANOTHER QUESTION! PROMISE? ARE YOU THERE?"

Her voice was fading, but I still heard her say, *Make it quick.*

"How will I know?"

You'll have to ask.

"Ask what?"

Laughter was her reply. She whispered, *Follow your heart for the answer.* Her last word trailed off into the darkness.

* * *

I reached over and punched the button to shut off the alarm clock. Even though I could feel the warm comforter on my body, my eyes could still see the shiny, rock walls filled with Etch-a-Sketches. I lay there for as long as I could, trying to cement the memories and the words from the dream into my mind, not wanting them to disappear once I woke. Too soon the day beckoned and I had to get ready for school. It was my birthday after all, no time to dawdle, which was my way of saying, "It's my birthday, better get up and get it over with, because I can't stand this day."

Promise had just given me the first gift of my thirteenth birthday, and I wasn't sure if it would spring open to scare the crap out of me, or if it'd be something I'd cherish for the rest of my life.

Chapter 3

Never one to waste time in the morning, I showered, got dressed, made two pieces of toast, and scurried out the door to wait for the school bus. My mind was locked into thoughts about the previous night's dream and what it might change about my life.

"Sooooooupaaaaaaaay," they shouted. It was the morning greeting normally accompanied by hand slapping, but today I kept my hands in my pockets.

"Hey," I nodded.

"What's up with you this morning?" a friend asked. "Don't leave me hanging!"

"Nuttin,'" I replied, and then added, "Hey, do you guys know this song?" I pulled the last quarter of my breakfast toast from my mouth and hummed a few bars of a song whose words were evading me. They shrugged their shoulders, not recognizing it. I shrugged my shoulders and considered it a finished conversation topic.

"What's with the humming and no slapping?" my friend asked.

"Why you asking so many questions?" said another friend while landing a backhanded slap to the first friend's bicep.

The first friend feigned a lurch in his direction then backed off, pointed at him, and laughed. "You flinched," he accused.

The lyrics finally came to me, *Arm and arm we laughed like kids.*

"Did not."

"Did too."

"Did not."

"Soupy?" the first friend asked, seeking third-party confirmation.

"You flinched," I ruled.

"Dang," said the friend guilty of the boyhood infraction.

At all the silly things we did.

"You owe me a Coke," said the friend who I'd just granted the right to sentence the other. He then mimicked flipping through a small notepad to the page that kept track of owed Cokes. "And with that Coke you're up to four Cokes." He made a tally on his invisible balance sheet.

"FOUR?"

"Yup."

The high-pitched squeal of the bus brakes ended their debate and we climbed aboard. The first friend flicked the second friend in the back of the ear as we lunged up the steps, "Four Cokes," he repeated. The other friend waved at his ear as if to ward off an annoying fly.

Now that I had the lyrics, they kept coming, *You made me...*

I chose an empty seat, the same one I always sat in, near the back of the bus. In a few stops, my favorite girl would normally get on board. Today, however, she had a dentist appointment, which meant I'd have much needed time to think about last night's dream.

Promises. Promises.

"YES!" I shouted and immediately clamped my hand over my mouth. I was willing to accept the embarrassment for my outburst because I'd finally gotten to the chorus of the song in my head. I ignored the looks of the kids around me because I felt like I'd just unlocked an important command in *Zork III: The Dungeon Master*; which is an obscure reference if you didn't live in the early eighties at the beginning of the war between computers and game consoles. *I'm at the bottom of the endless stairs*, I thought, and a wry smile appeared on my face. But now, I remember the name of the song: "Promises, Promises." *Who sings it...Naked something...* "Naked Eyes!" I blurted out, bringing the stares once more.

Knowing I'd believe.

I grabbed my notebook from my backpack with the intent to write down my thoughts about the previous night. *You want a thirteen-year old to commit the rest of his life to something he learned about in a dream?* It was a silly idea, right? Or was it? Yet she felt so near, so real, so true. I closed my eyes to see the place once again, the warm glow from the other side of the wall, and the voice that came with it. *Promise.* I wrote "promise" at the top of the page, but it confused me, it wasn't right. I scratched it out, because I prefer to write in ballpoint pen instead of pencil, and rewrote "Promise" with a capital "P." I'd never written "Promise" with a capital "P" before; it felt new and exciting.

The bus driver shouted something I didn't quite hear since I was lost in thought. "SOUPY!" she yelled again, more loudly the second time.

I looked up and said, "Yeah?"

She rolled her eyes at me through the oversized rear view mirror, "Where's—" but by the time she got that far, the kid across the aisle from me had already relayed her question.

"DENTIST," I shouted.

"OHHH-KAY." The bus door closed and we lurched forward, one stop closer to school, and I'd only written one word in my notebook, so much for recording my thoughts. Before I went back to my dream, I felt a ping on the radar, so to speak, and instead looked out the bus window toward my girl's house. She was peeking through the curtains of her living room window waving her hand back and forth quickly. I *do* like her energy. She grabbed a sign and slapped it up against the inside of the window, it read: "Happy Birthday!" I waved back, not with the same vigor, but slowly back and forth as the bus drove away. We grew up in the same neighborhood, and although she was one year older than me, we still did most everything together: dances, movies, parties, Scrabble, television watching, and leg wrestling. Next year that might change—probably would change—when she'd be a freshman in high school and I'd still be in junior high. Seems we were rarely alone, but at our age I'm not sure we would have known what to do with alone time anyway. As young teens, there was no "kinda in love," we were either "in love" or "out of love." In our case, we were *in* love, though love was pretty much defined as one big, all-consuming, mind-bending crush, and its biggest responsibility, for me, was to walk her to class and then run to my class before the second bell rang without getting yelled at for running in the halls or being late for class. I was constantly delirious around her, no matter where we were, always processing how to get physically closer and embarrassingly afraid to do it—is it okay to hold her hand, or put my arm around her, or lean in for a kiss? This was my first introduction to geometry and military strategy, and they took up most of my boyhood brainpower. Unfortunately, math and I didn't get along, so I never really got the angles of attack quite right.

As teens, we ask ourselves if our significant others love us practically every minute of every hour, and it can change that quickly. There's no more distilled version of love than that, even if it is just puppy love. A boyfriend today is easily replaced with a new boy who passes an affectionate note in class tomorrow. I don't enjoy that game, which makes it rare for me to put my heart in someone else's hands. As Promise said, "I'm the ultimate believer in true love." But who expects to find true love in junior high school? I guess, all of us. Promise was right. Boy, was she right.

My mind rewound back to the "Happy Birthday" sign. I placed my fingers on the bus window. *Cold.* It erased the memory and reminded me to close my notebook, stuff it into my backpack, and hop off the bus for school.

For the next ten minutes, I heard nothing but questions asking where my girlfriend was that morning. "Dentist," I said. "Dentist," I replied. "Dentist," I passed along. *Dentist,* I thought, while leaning my head back, opening my mouth briefly and then making the sound of a dentist's drill—there were only so many creative ways to answer that question. On a morning when I anticipated the ability to lounge around my own locker instead of hers, I ended up frustrated with everyone reminding me of her absence, but I guess that was better than a barrage of birthday wishes.

It wasn't until third period, which was English class, when I could finally get back to what I *really* wanted to do: write to Promise. As information-packed as my dream was—enough to last for hours, if not days of thought—it still felt like it had passed in minutes. If what she said to me was true, that I must find her for us to be an example of true love in the world—well, that was *way* different from having twenty pre-algebra problems as homework or an essay about *Where the Red Fern Grows*—what Promise asked of me was a term paper, "term" being my life.

Several years ago, Great Grandpa told me that voices would speak to me in powerful places. I understood that Promise was speaking *to* me, despite what Grandpa said about it taking time for me to make that realization, but it was still my choice when it came to actually *doing* something. Should I change the way I act today? Put myself on a course that would, hopefully, allow me to find her? What would be the penalty for ignoring what she said? What would happen in a world without true love? Wait. A world without true love? I didn't have a good example of love in my life...was I already living in a world without true love? Or maybe I'm already doing what I'm supposed to do to find her; that would be ideal, right? Maybe it's this exact process—inquisition, reflection, thought—that's the path to her. I'm already that way so I wouldn't have to change anything. But it can't be that easy, can it? Just be who I already am?

I'd done a lot of thinking in English class and not enough writing, since we were supposed to log a certain number of pages each week. I was in no danger of meeting my minimum since I typically logged more than needed with stories of mythological knights or retractable arms on space satellites, so I simply wrote down a series of questions to ask Promise the next time I was with her:

Have we met before?
What is love?
Why is your voice so familiar to me?
Is this place really my mind?
Are you afraid of the dark?
Who else is here?

Why am I here?
Which of my dreams have you seen?
When will I see you again?
What happens if I fail?

And then I added what I'd learned:

She knows me. She knows my family.
I have homework. Life is like homework (yuck).
I'm supposed to do something great.
Learn one thing from every girl I date.
I'm going to fail. A lot (double yuck).
Her name is Promise. I must find her.

The period bell rang, startling me from thought, again it seemed I'd recorded very little on paper given the amount of information speeding recklessly down my recollection superhighway.

I scrambled to pack up my things and was one of the last to leave the classroom, so I was surprised when I heard the voice of my girl in the hallway.

She loves me, I thought. The sudden appearance of the words in my head surprised me.

"Happy birthday!" she exclaimed.

"Huh?"

"What do you mean, 'huh?' It's your birthday, silly!" she said and wrapped her arms around me.

"Oh yeah," I nonchalantly replied, and poorly feigned a smile while I struggled to keep my balance. "You know I'm not that into birthdays."

"That's dumb. It's *your* birthday!"

"Yeah, yeah, yeah," I shrugged.

"Sourpuss," she said, and playfully frowned.

"Pretty much," I agreed.

My deadpan mood caused her to pause and ask, "Soupy, are you okay?"

"Yeah-yeah, sorry, just deep in thought."

"About me?"

Her expression demanded an immediate response, but I struggled to find the proper one. "Of course," I said, trying to smile. Her question brought me back to *this* world instead of *that* world, which reminded me to ask, "How was the dentist?"

She waved her freshly cleaned whites back and forth like a bleached flag in a changing wind.

I nodded my head and raised my eyebrows to show agreement that they looked well cleaned.

The warning bell for the fourth period rang.

"Gotta go!" She hopped across the hall toward her class. "I'll give you your birthday present later," she said over her shoulder while purposefully flashing her teeth again. I watched her disappear into the classroom and then realized I was in jeopardy of being late to my own class. I scooted around the corner to an adjacent hallway and slipped through the door just after the bell rang, earning my teacher's glance, but no further wrath.

I spent the afternoon in a daze, basically sleep walking from one class to the next, smiling briefly and thanking those who wished me well. I added a question to the bottom of my list in history class: *What would it be like if Promise* is *my true love?* It was a difficult question to grasp because, as we'd discussed in our dream, I didn't yet fully know love. Of course, I wanted my current relationship to last forever. On the other hand, I knew, and ignored, that it wouldn't. *Do I really want to know who I'm going to spend the rest of my life with at age 13?* It's a rather interesting question because a few generations ago I would have known; I would have also only lived about half as long given the rigors of surviving. Thank you, history class and *Oregon Trail.* To a degree, if Promise was telling the truth, then I *do* know who I'm supposed to spend the rest of my life with, I just have to find her.

My thought-consumed mood hadn't changed when the final bell of the day rang. After a brief stop at my locker, I made my way out the front door and stepped onto the bus. My girlfriend was smiling at me from "our" seat. *Are you Promise?* I thought. No way...but maybe? How would I know? I guess I'll just have to ask. There was a lot I liked about her: strong-willed, lovely smile, lived nearby, older woman, and she'd developed physically a bit more quickly than the other girls.

I sat down next to her. She grabbed my hand, squeezed it, and turned toward me to ask excitedly, "How's your birthday going?"

"It's cool," I replied. I loved the way our hands interlocked like they were meant to hold each other; whenever I squeezed hers, she always squeezed mine back.

"Good! Now, what do you want for your birthday?" she playfully asked.

I was smart enough not to give the answer that my teenage, hormonal mind mentally scripted. "I already have you," I stated.

Her head turned down, a blushed pose, and she smiled sweetly at me while batting her lashes. Blonde curls fell across her cheek. I wanted to brush them back behind her ear, but that act—that single act—would change the course of a path I knew I had to take. Nervously, I said, "I had a crazy dream last night."

"Really?" she replied, "About what?"

"True love, oddly enough."

"True love?"

"Yeah, this woman spoke to me about true love."

Sternly, she asked as her upper body backed a few inches away from me, "What woman?"

"I don't know," I responded automatically, but that wasn't quite the case. Her grip on my hand loosened. "I mean…no…I don't know what I mean. I didn't see her, so I don't know if I know her."

"Is this who you've been thinking about all day, this other woman?"

"Yeah," I admitted.

She pulled her hand away from mine and scooted away just enough that our hips no longer touched. The new distance between us wasn't just physical, it was also emotional. I felt a pending loss, but saw no other path forward but to continue the conversation, despite the outcome.

I added, "She told me it's my assignment in life to find her."

"Her? *HER*? What about *me*?"

"Well, that's the thing, she didn't sound like you, but her voice was older, so she could be you, just not this you, maybe a you some time in the future when your voice has matured, you know?" I was just as confused as her. I'd put myself in a situation where I was trying to answer questions for her that I hadn't yet answered for myself.

"Soupy Heller, what on earth are you talking about?"

I shook my head, felt defeated, and looked to the floorboard, "To be honest, I don't have any idea."

"If you don't know, then how am I supposed to know? Are you breaking up with me?" Her tone had escalated from confusion to a tinge of anger.

I looked back to her and quickly replied, "No, no! The exact opposite, actually." I placed my hands on my thighs and felt a warm sensation in my pocket. I ran my fingers along the corduroy lines that formed the contours of the black rock Grandpa had given me, and then retrieved it.

"Why do you always carry that thing?" she asked with disdain.

"To remind me to always do great and honorable things," I replied, just as I'd rehearsed it in my head for many years.

"What does that even mean?" she asked.

I twirled the rock in my palm as I thought about an answer to her question, and noticed we were getting awfully close to her bus stop. If I was going to ask her what I needed to ask, then I'd have to do it now. I gulped, closed my fist around the rock, and asked, "Are you Promise?"

Her response wasn't the response I expected. "Promise? Her name is *Promise*? You know my name, and it sure isn't Promise!" With fortunate timing, we'd reached her stop, so she grabbed her book bag and brushed past me into the aisle. Unfortunately, for me, the entire bus turned to hear our words.

"No, you don't understand," I said to her backside as she walked down the aisle. "She said—," but it was too late for her to hear my words as she bounded down the stairs and into her driveway.

Faces stared at me quizzically trying to figure out what had happened from the bits and pieces they'd overheard. I looked out the window and watched her walk to her front door. She glared at me. I reached toward her and as my fingers touched the window they felt the same autumn chill they'd felt that morning. *What was my birthday present?* I wondered and then looked at my rock, not sure if it had done what it was supposed to remind me to do. I dropped it into my jacket pocket.

She loves me not.

She didn't look back at me like she normally would as she crossed the threshold into her house. Her walk was determined: get inside, grumble, call her friends, and move on. The word would be out about our break up—even though we didn't even speak about it—before I walked through my own front door.

When the bus resumed its course, my best buddy and next-door neighbor slipped into my bench seat pushing me toward the window, a smirk plastered on his face. He nudged me with his elbow and asked, "What's up?" I knew that grin because I'd known him my entire life, so I knew he was about to ask for permission to ask her out. This childish, yet respectful gesture was a precursor to his action whether I gave him approval or not; it'd be less than twenty-four hours before I'd see his arm around her.

"Are you serious?" I asked, turning my eyes away from him and back toward the passing scenery.

"Yeah, man," he said. "Come on, I'll give you two Cokes."

I didn't dignify his response with words. Love was surely worth more than two sodas, which I rarely drank anyway. And if that's the value we place on love, then Promise was right: we don't know anything about it. My friend jumped out of my seat and back into his own.

I got off the bus and purposefully trailed behind my friends, not paying attention to a word of their conversation. At my house, I peeled away from the group, tossed my backpack through the front door, and then headed out for a walk. The end of my driveway presented a decision, left or right? Before making it, I zipped my jacket up to my chin—which somehow always made me feel tucked in and safe—and pulled one glove from each jacket pocket. The glove in my right pocket dislodged my rock. It rattled around on the ground at my feet. I transferred the glove to my left hand and bent down to pick up the rock with my right. It was warm in my hand—generations of hands had held it and rubbed their questions into it, just as I'd so recently done. I pushed my thumb back and forth across its smooth surface and felt my body tingle with the wisdom-to-skin connection we made. "I need your advice," I said. "Maybe you can tell me which way to go?" I stood up, tucked my thumb under one end of the stone, and flipped it into the air like a coin. "Heads I win; tails you lose!" It tumbled end over end, reached its apex, and started its descent. As I caught it, the wind gusted fiercely from my left to my right causing me to wince and turn away. I couldn't tell one side of the rock from the other, but that wasn't the point. The easy choice would have been to walk with the wind, putting it at my back, but I knew this journey wasn't about making the easy choices; it was about learning from the easy *and* the hard ones. Placing the rock back in my pocket, I slipped on both gloves, made an about-face, and started walking into the wind, humming and singing the song that had been in my head all day, *You made me, Promises, Promises.*

Chapter 4

In my dream that night, the night of my thirteenth birthday, I found myself standing on a grassy foothill looking into a valley. The moonlight drenched the valley floor like a stage spotlight, leaving the surrounding hills mostly dark. The entire setting was colorless aside from the black of the darkness, white of the light, and all the grays in between. I wanted to set the moon in motion so it would swing back and forth over the valley like a single, bright bulb in an empty room. From my tiptoes, I reached for the moon but it was too far away. It was a pleasant evening that reminded me of summer nights lying on the hoods of cars staring up at the stars.

It was perfect but for one thing: I was barefoot. I rarely go barefoot in the house, opting for socks without exception, so I very much disliked being barefoot outdoors, even in a dream. Fortunately, it *was* a dream, so I slung my arms out to my sides and flapped them quickly enough to take flight. I hovered down the slope of the foothill and into the valley. My destination was the middle of the valley, but as I approached I noticed a circular structure too small to see from a distance. As I inspected, I recognized it as a lesser version, both in diameter and height, than the circle with a slash through it where I'd met Promise. However, instead of being made from black, onyx boulders, it was constructed of round, gray rocks. The wall across the middle was the same height as the circle, also unlike the previous structure. The grass had been uniformly trampled inside and outside of the circle, like a moat that extended another six feet beyond the stone. I landed with some grace with no one to applaud, ironically. Slowly, I walked the circumference analyzing every stone for some sign to explain why it was here. After one complete loop, I stepped inside the circle. There I stood, eyes closed to heighten my other senses. I noticed no change: the wind still blew across the grass, ruffled my hair, and continued its journey. *Would Promise meet me here?* I thought. After a few breaths, I opened my eyes and walked the inner half of the circle—*pi-r-squared*—but found nothing of interest. I stepped up on the low, rocky wall that split the circle in two. From that height, I saw a book laid open, pages down, on the ground. When I picked it up, it bore great resemblance to my school notebook; the one in which I'd written down my questions for Promise. Carefully, I flipped the notebook over and saw those very same questions. But there were two more words written beneath the questions. I read them aloud by moonlight:

Save me.

It wasn't in the same handwriting as the other words I'd written earlier in the day.

What...if...ssshe...doesssn't...ssshow?

"Who?" I asked aloud.

Promissss.

"I don't know," I replied. The thought hadn't crossed my mind.

Burn. Blooooow. Nourisssh. Grow, the wind said, and then the air went completely still.

I sat down in the trampled grass, assumed a cross-legged position like I had in last night's dream, and proceeded to wait for Promise. I flipped through the pages of the notebook, but realized I only wanted to write more about Promise. I pulled a pen from the spiral wiring of the notebook and wrote at the bottom of the page:

What if she doesn't show?

Chapter 5

She never showed up in my dream that night. In fact, for the next twenty years I had no Promise in my life. Sometimes I felt good when I thought of her and other times I cursed her absence. Like most memories, especially when I had so few about her to draw from, they faded over time; I couldn't stop them from doing so. Some nights I'd lay in bed trying to hear her voice, the one that had been so familiar to me, but over the years it had trailed off as if she was talking but walking away. *If I ever run into her, will I remember her voice?* Surely I would, right? It was familiar when I'd never heard it before, surely it would be again.

Over the course of twenty years, I'd struggled with love immensely and she'd never been there to talk with me about it. I'd been given a promise by Promise that was never fulfilled, and I'd begun to question her existence in any world. Sure, she would enter my mind when I met someone new, or pined over a beautiful woman from afar, but I asked myself, and others, less and less often, "Are you Promise?" And perhaps it was my own fault. Maybe I'd not fought hard enough to finish my homework—I hadn't *earned* another visit from her—or maybe I'd taken a left turn where I should've taken a right. I felt like I'd made good decisions, worked hard, and learned from my actions. Every decision I made—and I mean *every* decision—weighed the pros and cons until I'd racked my brain to see every alternative. Yes, I overthought everything about my life; I especially overthought love because I'd been *asked* to do so. Into my mid-thirties, I had no regrets, but it would've been nice if Promise had shown up like she'd promised.

I sat in my car gripping the steering wheel with flexed forearms and begging to speak with the one woman I needed now more than ever: Promise. I'd recently thrown myself at the feet of a woman, begged her to spend her life with me, and she'd replied with an unequivocal and resounding, "No." It was my most catastrophic failure at love to date. The next few days were about returning the engagement ring, which required an emotional, two-day road trip.

Promise had certainly been right about one thing, at least, I'd failed over and over again at love.

For me, the road is a thinking place. I rarely bother with radio station surfing, cassette tapes, or CDs. I often find a station that has classical music or news, leave it there, and let my mind wander. Other times, I listen intently to the sounds of my car and the road, trying to isolate each individual instrument of the symphony that's created as I drive. It can be meditative, a place where I can unplug from technology more than any other. I was familiar with *this* road and the radio stations along it. Knew them so well that a particular hill or bend in the highway signaled a station change seconds before intermittent static served the same reminder.

On the radio, I heard, *Don't you know that you are a shooting star? And all the world will love you just as long, as long as you are, a shooting star-r-r-r.*

"No shit," I said, in agreement with the lyrics. In a whiny voice, I made up my own lyrics, "Would you ra-ther burn-out or fade a-way? Make a pro-mise and stick-to-it today." Obviously, I was a little punch drunk from my traumatic experience.

I was still creating lyrics that rhymed in my head when the song ended, so I didn't pay much attention to the radio commercial, until I realized it had been going on so long it wasn't actually a commercial. It was religious conversation, which wasn't the format of any west coast radio station I normally listened to. The voice with a southern drawl droned on about being res-*cuuuuuuuuuuued* by the Great Almighty Magnificent All-Around Wonder.

Great Almighty Magnificent All-Around Wonder? I thought. A new name, or at least an acronym was needed for that one. G-A-M-A-A-W. Gamaaw. Perfect. "The GAMAAAAAAW," I said, raising one fist in the air until it thumped the ceiling of the car. "Oops," I said and shook the pain out of my knuckles.

On the radio, she continued, *Have youuuuuu ever felt the powwwwwer? I haaaave. Great Wonder. I haaaave, indeeeed. Have youuuuu ever visited this Place of Power? I haaaaave—*

"Wait. What?" I said, suddenly paying closer attention.

I haaaave becaaaause I have built this Place of Powwwwwer riiiight here on this spot where I firrrst felt love'z touch. Great Almighty Magnificent All-Around WON-der!

"Tell me more about the Place of Power," I urged.

Youuuuuuu can visit meeeeeee in this Place of Powwwwer, yes youuuuu can. Youuuu can doooo it toooday, Great Wonder, today. I'm easy to find, this powwwwerful place is eeeEEEasy to find. Youuuuu just—

The station turned to static. "NO!" I shouted and turned the volume knob up to see if I could still hear her voice beneath the noise. I dialed frequencies to the left and right of the original station, but it was all for naught. *Where was this Place of Power? I need a Place of Power!* "DAMMIT!" I yelled and slammed my palms on the steering wheel. For the next minute, I played with the radio trying to find this voice who claimed to be able to direct me. I needed the power, the energy, the words I might find there to fill up my empty heart. Nothing but static answered. I illegally used one of those between-highway turnaround roads and hammered the gas pedal to return to where I once had the signal. Nothing. I began to cry; it had become a frequent response to many things in my shattered, helpless, emotional state. "You're a wreck, Soup," I said to myself, and then answered, "I know." I shut off the radio and rode with only the steady hum of the engine and the tires grasping the highway.

For several miles, I thought about powerful places and Promise while I tried the impossible: simultaneous tasks of both wallowing in and casting aside self-pity. "Thanks for nothing," I said, which was directed not just toward the preacher, but to Promise and my great grandpa, both of whom had led a gullible little boy to believe there was something else out there, something we don't see, but that's just as important as what we *can* see, touch, taste, feel, and hear. "What a crock of shit," I said, but then shook my head. "I'm sorry. I'm just angry right now." I thought about the irrational fear of being struck by lightning, more likely because I'd just offended a great deity. *GAMAAW!* I *did* believe in something like Promise, just didn't want to believe right now.

I'd tried. I knew I couldn't find true love by wandering aimlessly. So I'd set myself on a path to explore who I am, to understand why I believe what I believe, what makes me happy, and why I use certain words I. Understanding what makes me…well, me…would be the first step toward understanding what type of life I needed to live in order to be happy. *Happiness is a requirement for finding true love, right?* It only made sense that the foundation of who I am should be strong; it's the place I return when I feel weak, the same place I'd offer to my true love when she felt the same.

I believed I had, so far, learned from everything in my life, but without much progress. I'd always asked the most important question in the universe: why? I'd pondered everything from my favorite colors to my emotions, and asked myself that simple, one-word question. *Why?* I'd recorded my thoughts in a journal, so I had a notebook of things about me that I could periodically check to see if I still agreed with them. And if they'd changed, I'd just ask myself again, "Why?" After twenty years, what did I have to show for the answers to these questions? Right now, it felt like jack squat. "Jack squat?" I said aloud. What a funny saying for a way to say nothing at all. Zilch. Nada. No room at the inn. Though I had a notebook of answers, I still didn't know a damn thing. After this recent failure, I was tired of trying. "I give up," I said. "Screw you, why." I laughed and then mimicked the preacher's voice, "Whoooooo the hey-yelllll am I taulking tooooo?"

What was the point of trying any longer? It was over now. I'd put into love everything I had to give. There was nothing else left, nothing else to do.

Should I be mad that I'd failed? No, I'm not the type to get mad often or for very long. I'll hold a grudge for a while, but that flame will slowly burn out. I rarely see the point of anger. If love is the peak, and sorrow is the valley, anger is the avalanche that prevents you from climbing back to the top. Emotion is telling, maybe more telling than anything else because it is *active*. The fact that two things are both blue is less important than when two things both *feel* blue. For me, it isn't about the nouns, but the verbs. In verbs lie immeasurable emotional connections. Until recently, I'd lived my life pouring over the nouns. The difference between wanting a woman who looks a certain way and a woman who feels a certain way is a massive shift in personal ideology. Someone once told me, "If you look for something wrong, you'll always find it; we're imperfect creatures, so focus on what's right." Truer words I may never hear, but truth doesn't come easily. I can't live at one end of the scale or the other. I don't have to be an "all-nouns" or an "all-verbs" guy. There's somewhere in between that's the right balance for me, I just haven't found it yet. Not for lack of trying. Love smashed my heart and pried open my eyes to its importance as a verb. The great fuck-all, love-all of love. *Fuck you, love*, I thought.

Many years ago, Meteorologist Edward Norton Lorenz presented the question: Does the flap of a butterfly's wings in Brazil set off a tornado in Texas? His premise was that small changes in a dynamic system could, potentially, impact the long-term behavior of that system. In layperson's terms, at least for me, he spoke of a theory about something I've come to believe, which is that all things are connected. So when I ask myself, "What's the point?" I know there has to be a point somewhere in the quagmire of wreckage. Relationships exist between things, not necessarily physical connections, but connections that define some invisible relationship between them. The proof is in the pudding, sure, but metaphysical chefs don't make much edible pudding. I'd *felt* the connections, therefore wanted to believe their existence. The verbs. It sounds religious. It sounds like faith. But personally I don't think it's like that at all; it's based more in reality to me than the ridiculous nature of religion.

There's a story my mom once told me…

* * *

"Soupy, sit down. I have something important to tell you," Mom said one afternoon in my teenage years. "Are there any parties this weekend?"

I had a relatively open relationship with her about parties, so I said, "Yeah, there's one on Saturday night." I'd seen what happens to friends' houses after a crew of high-school kids had been there, so my mom and I had a deal; if I promised never to host a party or drive drunk, then she'd let me stay out a bit later if I called to let her know. She'd also come get me if I needed a ride.

"I had an important dream last night. Before I tell you about it, you have to promise you'll actually listen." She knew I wasn't one for taking advice.

"Sure," I said, with an indignant teenage shrug.

"When your friends get in the car to leave, don't go with them," she said.

Her words pushed aside my indifference. "What? Why?" I replied.

"They're going to get pulled over and arrested for drug possession."

My friends smoked pot. I'd tried it and didn't like it; the mixture of smoking and drinking didn't sit well with me. If I had to choose between getting high and getting drunk, I'd choose drunk. My friends pretty much always had a bag of weed somewhere, so it wasn't too hard to believe they might get pulled over for some vehicular infraction and arrested once the officer discovered they were in possession of an illegal drug.

"Yeah right, Mom," I laughed. It was a bold enough prediction that it challenged my belief in her words.

Her tone firmed. "Promise me you won't get in that car. Promise me you'll find another way home or call me and I'll come get you, Soupy Robert."

When she used my first and middle names, I knew she was serious. I looked at her and replied, "I promise, Mom."

She gave me a stern, motherly stare as she calculated whether I'd heard her words. Deciding that I had, she added, "Thank you. I love you."

"Love you, too," I answered.

The parties were always the same; someone's parents had gone out of town and they'd invited a couple of friends over to drink. Of course, a couple of friends exponentially increased to half the school, without fail. I stood in the driveway looking at the car my friends were piling into afterward. We'd followed the normal party pattern: pick everyone up, stop at the park to pass a joint, pound a beer, head to the party, consume as much alcohol as one possibly could in the time we had to do it, look for someone to kiss. I was currently standing between the over-consumption and kissing steps in the process. My dimples played well with the female upperclasswomen even though I was an underclassman—playing varsity sports had its perks—therefore I usually enjoyed an evening of female attention.

"Hey Soup, let's go!" my friends yelled at me from the car. I could see the blunt already forming a small orange glow as it passed from mouth to mouth. The shotgun rider was holding the front seat up for the last spot in the back. He waved at me to take my normal position; no self-respecting upperclassman would allow an underclassman to ride in the front. However, my feet wouldn't move; they wouldn't take a step toward the car.

They're going to get pulled over and arrested for drug possession. Mom's voice echoed in my head. *Don't get in the car with them.*

"SOUP! LET'S GO!"

Out of the corner of my eye, I saw the girl who had been paying the most attention to me at the party. I'd known her for years, so we were close, though we'd never been *that* close. I turned my head to where she was parked, a few spots behind my friends, and watched her walk toward her car.

Don't get in the car with them, mom's voice repeated, blocking out all the other noise as friends tumbled out of the party and into their cars.

My gal pal rounded the front of her car, unlocked and opened her door, and then paused. With her elbows on the roof of her car, she spotted me doing my own, strange thing: standing still and alone in the driveway when the rest of the party was flowing past me. She motioned for me to join her with a point toward the passenger's seat and a tilt of her head.. I gave a nod and a smile to my waiting guy friends and jogged over to her car.

"OHHHHH!" they catcalled toward me. "YOU DISSIN' US?" They all laughed as the shotgun rider jumped in and they took off down the road.

"Want a ride?" she asked with a smile as I walked up. I returned the smile as she got into the car and reached over to unlock my door. I sat down and knew I'd made the right decision, but I was now presented with a completely different scenario than I'd imagined only a few seconds prior: what would I do with *her*. As she started the car and pulled away from the party, she said, "Where to?" My confidence was strong when I stood in the driveway; I knew what *not* to do so it was easy to seek an alternative. Now that I was so close to her, I struggled to find that same ability to easily decide.

My first instinct was to say, "Home," like a good boy, but something in her tone suggested that home would not have lived up to her expectations. Instead, I said, "Wherever you like," and looked at her for the first time since I sat down.

She suddenly screamed, "OH MY GOD!" It wasn't the next thing I expected her to say in our flirtatious foreplay, so I followed her eyes and found that my mom's premonition had come true. At the bottom of the hill, my friend's car was smashed up against a rock column that designated the right side of a driveway entrance. The police had already arrived and I could see that an ambulance was also needed. The shotgun passenger was leaning up against the car holding what looked to be his own severely broken jaw. From what I could tell, they'd approached the T-shaped intersection with too much speed, skidded on the gravel through the stop sign across the road, and crashed. "What do we do?" she asked.

"We keep driving," I answered, not wanting to take the chance that we both had alcohol on our breath and were underage.

The world was in slow motion as we passed, my nose an inch from the glass as I imagined what it would have been like if I'd been sitting in the back of the car. I already knew what was next: the officer would smell the marijuana. Sensing the drug, the officer would have them, and the car, searched. He'd find enough to ruin their nights, but not their lives. Even my friend with the broken jaw would suck his food through a straw for several months and carry wire cutters around in his back pocket in case he needed to snip the wires and puke, but it wouldn't ruin his life.

"Thanks, Mom," I whispered.

A few minutes of silence went by as we counted ourselves among the lucky to not be in such trouble. She broke the silence by asking, "Anywhere I want, eh?"

"Yeah," I replied.

"Then, how about right here?" She quickly pulled the car to the curb in front of a park that was a minute's walk from my house. I barely got my seatbelt unbuckled before her lips were on mine. Having had our brush with catastrophe, we wanted to live, and live passionately in the moment. After several minutes of heated kissing, she said, "Come home with me."

Oddly, instead of throwing caution to the wind, I tried to work out how I'd get back to *my* home if I went to hers, since she lived on the other side of town.

"You'll have to sneak out before my mom wakes up in the morning, though," she added.

"And then what? Walk all the way home?" I asked playfully.

She shrugged. It wasn't the next morning she wanted to talk about.

I placed my hand on her cheek, kissed her deeply one last time, and said, "Thanks for the ride home."

She understood, smiled, and replied, "See you next week."

When I awoke the next morning, it was sometime between breakfast and lunch, though neither sounded like a palatable idea. I groggily made my way up the stairs and found mom sitting at the kitchen table reading the paper, coffee in hand.

"Well?" she asked.

I sat down slowly and with a cracked voice replied, "You were right."

She set the paper aside and said, "Tell me about it."

As she made me a hot cup of tea, I recounted the events of the evening right up to the make-out session; there were some things mom didn't need to know. After I finished, she didn't have an "I told ya so" air. She was surprised and thankful I wasn't in the car, especially since she hadn't foreseen the accident.

"What is it, Mom?" I asked.

"Oh, I'm just trying to figure it all out," she replied.

"And?"

"They're pretty right on," Mom said.

"They? Who are they?"

"The Little People."

"Little People?" I inquired.

"Yes. Not that they're actually 'little people,' that's just what I call them. They show me things in my dreams."

"How do you know the difference between a dream that's real and one that isn't?" I asked.

Mom said, "I've gotten used to their voices over the years, I guess."

"So this isn't the first time this has happened?"

"No, no, not the first time, but it is the first time I felt confident enough about it to say so. I've been getting premonitions about your life for some time now. Typically, they're vibes about your emotional state. Obviously, this most recent dream was about more than just your emotions."

"Well, you sure saved my ass. Thanks, Mom."

"You're welcome," she said, carried the sports section of the newspaper over to my side of the table, and gave me a peck on the forehead. On the way back to her chair, she refilled her coffee mug.

Though my eyes were moving across the words in the paper, my brain was processing something entirely different; our conversation had rustled my mind awake. I said, "Mom, can I ask you another question?"

"Sure."

"Did Great Grandpa Walker teach you how to listen to the Little People?"

She pondered my question for a moment before she replied, "He never taught me, so to speak. I listened to so many of his stories growing up, I began to believe in a world that none of us could see."

"Did I ever tell you about the time he spoke to me about my life?" I asked.

"No."

"He told me about the two worlds, dreams and reality, and how I must understand the ways they work together."

"For what purpose?" she asked.

"To make the world a better place."

"I hope we're all here to do that," she said, matter-of-factly, while looking at me over the rim of her coffee mug. She took another sip and added, "Somehow, I expect he meant something more than just that."

"Who knows," escaped my mouth in the form of a statement, not a question.

I picked the Sports section back up, but I could still sense Mom's wheels turning. "You believe him, don't you?"

"I want to, but I dunno," I replied nonchalantly.

"Soupy, you're not telling me everything." She shifted her posture and squared her shoulders to face me.

I looked up from the paper and into her stare.

She continued, "You can tell me whatever it is or ask me any question you want. I know you know that, but sometimes it just has to be said."

"Well, I've been thinking about what connects us all together; the possibility that dreams and reality *are* tied together. There has to be something there, strings or wires or something, right? Maybe, like, how phone lines connect people anywhere in the world, you know?"

"Go on," she prompted.

My head was fighting me, but I fought for clarity because I wanted to know if Mom had the answers I sought. "Well, I don't have any answers, but I've been calling the connection 'The Network.'"

"I guess the Little People call me on The Network, then," she said with a smile. "I admit, I've wondered about the same thing."

"Really?" I said with surprise.

"Yes, of course. Just because I'm older than you, doesn't mean I've stopped trying to figure things out. We adults don't have all the answers either, you know." She held up one finger to signal a pause as she sipped from her mug. "We always want-want-want when we're kids, and more than anything else I wanted to spend more time in the dream world and not the real world. I guess you could say I'm my grandfather's granddaughter. Growing up was a hard life for us because we didn't have much. I was the oldest of three girls. A childhood for me? Forget about it, I was raising my little sisters."

“Do you think that’s why Great Grandpa never spoke with you? You know, like that’s why he never told you more about the dream world, because you had major responsibility in the real world?”

“Maybe,” she replied, deep in thought.

“Did you ever figure anything out?” I asked.

“As you know, I’m an Engberg and a Walker. If I’m true to my heritage and honor the tools passed down through generations, then my life is supposed to be about helping people get from one place to the next. Raising children can definitely be defined like that,” she smirked in obvious reference to my hangover. “It wasn’t until I gave birth to you that I felt a real change in my ability to perceive. And it’s only been the last couple of years that I’ve realized my perceptions aren’t just about getting people from here to there, they’re also about keeping people healthy.”

“Like chicken noodle soup?” I asked. It was a joke about the origin of my name, which was meant to remind everyone that I’m supposed to help the world heal.

She smiled, “I knew there’d be something different about you, just didn’t know what it would be.”

“If you discover what it is, will you let me know?”

She laughed, “Yeah, of course.” She got up from the table, ruffled my hair, and asked, “Hung-over boy, what do you want for breakfast?”

“Ungh. I need the magic healing power of Mom’s biscuits and sausage gravy,” I replied.

“Coming right up,” she said.

* * *

It was a great story to remember as I drove; the memory got me to my stopping point for the night: a small, coastal, college town where I’d spent nearly a decade of my life. It wasn’t my destination, only a pit stop on the way north to return the engagement ring.

The town hadn't changed much since I'd left, aside from experiencing a bit of name-brand, retail infestation. I descended from the mountain range that cupped the town and headed to the same cheap motel I always stayed in. It's a place close enough to the local bars and restaurants that it allowed me to stumble home on foot instead of driving.

I checked into my room and proceeded directly to the sink where I turned on the hot water, allowed it to warm up, and splashed it on my face. Looking in the mirror, I saw someone I didn't recognize. Haggard. Ashen. Emaciated. Exhausted. Pallid. Worn. Weakened. The thesaurus in my head rumbled through all the words I could use to describe how I looked and felt. There was no fuel left in my emotional or physical tanks. I needed help, and help was to be found down the street and around the corner in short order. I walked away from the sink to set out a change of clothes for the evening. When I returned to the now-steamy mirror, I squeakily used my finger to slowly draw eyes where I imagined I'd see mine if the hot water hadn't turned the mirror opaque. I backed up to ponder my art, then once again reached for the mirror and drew Xs through both eyes. A word came into my mind, *Burn.* I spelled it out below my art. Satisfied, I went back to the task of washing my face. "SUMBITCH!" I shouted as my hands met the scalding water. Reaching for a hand towel, I added, "When are you going to learn to *listen* to those voices in your head, Soup?" I sat on the closed toilet lid, buried my face into the damp hand towel, and listened to my own breath for a few seconds. I moved the towel over my mouth and let out a harried scream of defeat, then slapped myself hard across the right cheek. From my seated perch, I noticed the aged contrast between the yellowed linoleum, wallpaper, and the shower curtain, and compared them to the stark white color of the towels. Defeat resonated in everything but the towels, and I imagined the stories that this bathroom could tell about occupants who came feeling as defeated as I, probably with drugs, sex, or suicide in tow. *That's not your solution.* The towels weren't new, of course, they still had a dirty soul, but they constantly received a new bleach on life. I needed the same thing, some bleach, because drugs, sex, or suicide were *not* my answers. Experience is important, but addiction and death aren't experiences I was ready to endure.

One thing *was* for certain: motel rooms are about the loneliest places in the world, which makes them terrible places for lonely people to visit.

Chapter 6

From the motel, I walked straight to a bar; home of many memories. Getting there carried me back in time. I passed a Mexican restaurant that was our Thursday night happy hour watering hole. Our bartender, like the rest of us, had moved out of town many years ago. Above me ran the train trestle that, on many nights, provided my path home when I'd had too much to drink—shortest distance between two points being a straight line and all that. A tavern strangely nestled among several car dealerships once served pitchers of beer for a quarter each during certain hours of the day. There were only a limited number of pitchers to go around, so if you wanted to keep drinking you had to hold onto your pitcher like it was your life. Down the street sat the town's centerpiece; a beautiful theater marquee that drew patrons like moths. The cinema was a remarkable attraction, inside and out, ornate and adorned with red velvet, but the only memory I could recall involved a first date to see a movie, *Philadelphia*. Good movie. Bad date movie.

It was a weeknight, so the town wasn't abuzz with students hopping from one bar to the next, which meant I found a seat in a mostly empty barroom. A sticky, worn floor greeted me, as did centerfolds taped to the lower glass cabinets behind the bar along with the fake IDs that'd been confiscated and plastered to the wooden styles of the bar's cabinetry. I looked up and saw, with pleasure, the ceiling tiles my friends had purchased, decorated, and returned to the bar as an eternal memorial to our many hours spent there. On Friday nights, back then, my first drink was free if I could get there by a quarter after midnight. Such a feat required kicking patrons out and locking the doors at my job early since we closed *at* midnight, but I usually made it. The layout of the bar had changed frequently over the years from booths to tables to standing room only, but the jukebox never moved, and it always played Johnny Cash's "Ring of Fire" to a roomful of people who knew the pantomime to go with it. It was here that the only shot I took on my twenty-first birthday required the entire bar to chant, "SHOT! SHOT! SHOT!" and despite my claim that doing so would make me puke, which it did, I put back the house shot, a Bull's Sweat, which was a devastating mixture of sloe gin and Tabasco sauce, and made a beeline for the bathroom. In *my* opinion, if you never had the house drink then you never *really* stepped through the doors of the bar. It was also the place where the head-shaving game between my college roommates came to its bald-headed end. Of my three roommates, one would always start by saying, "Dude, I'll shave my head if you shave your head," and someone would always reply, "No way!" On one particular night, with massive over-consumption to blame, none of the four of us negated the act, so all of us shaved our heads; there should have been a ceiling tile to commemorate *that* event.

The bartender brought me a beer in a glass mug. *Nice.* Glass mugs were reserved for regulars. My show of comfort in this place—or perhaps my age—must have been a sign that I'd once been a regular…more likely my age. The first beer went down quickly, so I raised my finger to ask for another. When I did, I noticed two patrons at the other end of the bar playing Liar's Dice; a game we'd also played with regularity. Some things *don't* change.

* * *

On Sundays, when I was a teenager, my family would visit Grandma and Grandpa Heller's house for games—board games, card games, dice games, games on television—you name it and we probably played it, watched it, and bet on it. We were a Catholic gambling, drinking, game-playing, sports-watching, betting, smoking family, for sure. There were typically so many people in the house it was rare to play someone head-to-head at anything. As soon as a deck of cards rustled or dice rattled—Uno, cribbage, or Yahtzee, Scat or Pitch—the rest of the family would gather around the dinner table to play. Spare change would emerge, the ante would be set, and the trash talking would begin...although the trash talking should probably be listed first since it never really began, so to speak, it rarely ever stopped.

It was rare on one Sunday, then, to have Grandma Heller all to myself, but we'd arrived before the rest of the family on this particular day. Therefore, I challenged Grandma to her favorite game, Yahtzee, which was my first mistake since she rarely ever lost. "She went to church enough that God was on her side," we said, and she really did. Within the first three sentences of seeing her she'd always ask, "Have you been going to church?" I replied "no" practically every time, which would earn me an authoritative eye, and a promise that she'd say some "extra prayers" for me the next time she attended. My goal was to get through that portion of the conversation as quickly as possible so I could enjoy the rest of my visit.

We'd been playing the game for several minutes, and I was already behind, when I decided to ask, "Do you know Promise?"

"Promise? The only promises I know are the ones I make and the ones I expect others to keep," she said, as she blew her charmed breath on the dice in the leather cup. Grandma's voice was in my head repeating, *Yahtzee-Yahtzee-Yahtzee,* as the dice played leapfrog over each other in the cup. *Come'on Yahtzee!* she shouted in her thoughts before tumbling the dice across the shiny, plastic tablecloth.

Unbelievable, I thought, but only showed her a big smile. Her dice showed five threes. *Perhaps there is something to the power of positive thinking.*

"Yahtzee," she said, as if it was no big deal, though her smile gave her excitement away and her hand didn't hesitate to mark her scorecard accordingly.

"Throwing a Yahtzee never gets old for you, does it?" I said as I scooped up the dice and tossed them back into the leather cup for my roll.

"No, Soupy, it doesn't. Why would it?" she said from over the top of her sacred glass of Coke. It wasn't a Coke and a smile; it was a Coke and a smirk. "Once you've played this game as much as I have, you'll throw your fair share of Yahtzees, too," she added, as if experience played a large part in a game heavily decided by chance.

"Now would be a *great* time for that!" I threw the dice and ended up with a one, a two, two threes, and a six. Obviously, I'd either been distracted or my thoughts hadn't near the impact on the dice as hers.

"Got your threes, yet?" she asked.

"No," I answered and grabbed all of the dice but the two threes. As I shook the tumbler, I thought, *Threes-threes-threes,* but I got a one, a two, and a five.

"Nope," she said, "One more try."

I rolled my eyes at her and said, "As if I'll ever come close to beating you."

"That's not the Soupy Heller I know," she said as I threw a two and a four. Grandma grabbed the dice, put them in the cup, and said, "Optimism, that's you. Smart. Competitive."

"Yeah, well, I guess I've been trying too hard to figure it all out lately," I admitted.

She looked at her scorecard, knew she needed her threes, too, and set her mental machine to work. "Trying to figure *it* out, huh?" She tossed two threes, two fours, and a six. "Threes," she said, and scooped up the other three dice.

I didn't reply to her question, it seemed rhetorical. She got another three on her second roll. Grandma grabbed the dice and shook the tumbler, but before she threw she stopped. "I forgot to blow on the dice," she said. "Never forget to blow on the dice when you really need them to work for you." As she did, I felt a whisk of wind blow through the room like someone had opened the front door. The smoke from her cigarette changed direction briefly before resuming its normal upward course. Grandma smiled. Two dice landed on the table, one her fourth three and the other took a last turn, teasing us both with a fifth three, but showed a six. "Dang it. You can't always get everything you wish for," she said. "But I'll take four threes and a six any day."

"I bet you will," I said sarcastically.

"Grandpa!" she shouted into the next room.

"Yes, Mother?" he replied.

"I think it's time," she said.

"Soupy, come here!" he shouted back to us.

I had no idea what was going on, but I got up from the table and made my way to the living room where I stood next to his recliner. "Yessir?"

"Go downstairs, get me a beer, and get one for yourself," he demanded.

I never questioned his orders, and definitely wouldn't question one that might result in my first beer with him. I walked downstairs, as ordered, and returned with the goods. I handed him a beer, which he placed on the end table, and then held out his hand to shake. For as long as I could remember, we'd had our own sacred shake: regular handshake to thumb lock shake to cupped finger shake to wrist shake with a slide down the forearm, and finally a finger gun that we'd use to shoot each other. Without fail, Grandpa would act like he'd taken a bullet to the chest, and we'd both laugh. When I was a kid, it was hilarious that he'd be the one to take the fake bullet, and as I got older it just became part of the routine; an expectation that he'd do just as he'd always done...and he never failed to do so.

"Soupy," he said, while adjusting his recliner. "You're old enough now to have a beer when you're here as long as you aren't driving. He popped the tab on his beer and gestured for a toast. After struggling to get my can open, and accepting his assistance, I eventually clinked my can to his. "Now, go ahead and get back to your game."

"Yessir," I repeated. By the time I returned to the table, Grandma had refilled her own drink, but this time the Coke had a familiar white tinge floating on top. Kahlua had been added to the dark soda.

Grandma raised her glass for a toast, "Always for the State," she said, and we touched glass to can. She savored her beverage by smacking her lips, but

I nearly gagged as the carbonated alcohol burned my throat for the second time in minutes. "No need to take a big swig," she said. "Take another one; a smaller one."

I did as told, then set down the can to ask, "You know that thing you just said, what does it mean?"

"Always for the State? It's been our family motto from the beginning of time, but that's not what you're asking, you want to know *what it really means*, don't you?"

"Yes," I replied.

She pulled her eyeglasses gently from her face and let the chain that held them go taut against her neck. "The best path is not necessarily the one you see first; the best path is *always* the one that will teach you the most about who you are, despite the outcome."

She'd emphasized "always," which meant it was an immutable fact, which I understood. However, the "state" required more thought. She watched me as the tumblers turned over in my head. *Always for the State. For the State?* The ice jingled in her glass as she took another sip of her drink. I could hear the golf tournament's television announcers in the other room; a room where I'd served as the channel changer long before we'd had remotes to do that for us. There were two soundtracks perfect for a Sunday afternoon nap, a golf tournament and a car race. Today the former distracted me from this important conversation, so I pushed it out of my mind. *The State, like the fifty states?* I thought.

Grandma shook her head back and forth, straightened up, took a big breath, and then exhaled.

The State of the Union? That made more sense.

She cleared her throat, and then said, "Your temperament impacts the temperament of the world." With another quick pull from her drink, she continued, "And we Hellers are always for the state of the world; the love in the world is what we strive to improve or better said, what we strive to maintain. It is our mission, and your path."

"Always for the State," I repeated. "The greater good?"

She nodded her head, and then continued, "Our ability to heal doesn't come from a magical elixir or a pill of any color. Hellers carry only what can be found on or within their person. Pay attention, and you will know. You don't need to promise me that you'll follow your path, it will be difficult not to. So you don't have to make me any promises; the promise is built into who you are," she said. Grandma picked up the dice, put them in the tumbler, and slid the cup across the table to me.

Before I took my turn in the game, Grandpa walked in and added, "Mother, did you remind him that he's the last?" he asked.

"No, Father," she answered. "That's your job."

"Soupy, you're the last one," he said while walking up to Grandma and placing his hand on her shoulder. "You're the last male in the family who can carry on the Heller name," he repeated, though he didn't need to double up on the point. My uncles either didn't have children or they had girls, my aunts had already or would all take on someone else's last name, and I had only a sister. I *was* the last one with the family name. I gulped and nodded my head in understanding.

Grandpa left the kitchen table to return to his television. Grandma pointed at the Yahtzee tumbler, and while grinning said, "Your turn."

* * *

The gentleman at the bar blew on his dice, but I felt no accompanying breeze like I had so many years ago in Grandma's kitchen. *Learn from everyone you meet,* I thought. It reminded me of a college professor in this very town telling me there was always one thing you could learn from someone. "In order to see the good guest lectures, you need to see *all* the guest lectures," he'd tell me.

Grandma and Grandpa both died many years ago, and unfortunately I'd only applied some of their teachings: I'd paid attention and I'd learned from as many people as I could, including the ones I'd dated, but I'd done nothing about maintaining our lineage or contributing to the greater love. All things in due time, I suppose. It wasn't like I could start working on the lineage without having first found love, right?

Several beers and a couple hours later, I'd had enough of my old haunt, plus the irresistible drunken-hunger had set in. Like many a college town, this one had one of the greatest solutions to my stomach's problem: a twenty-four-hour burrito shop. "Burrito de pollo asado, por favor. Unicamente el queso y la salsa. Para a va," I requested, and it was practically the only Spanish I knew.

I walked more quickly back to the motel than I had on the way out even though it was uphill. My mind was blank, too tired to think, and satisfied with what I'd accomplished with one night on the town: memories of what used to be, a true distraction from what is, and no worry about what might be. I walked on autopilot, which was maybe the best use of my memory the entire night: the memory that knew the way to my temporary motel room home. There were only two things left to do, inhale the burrito and pass out.

Chapter 7

That night, I dreamt.

I could hear before I could feel.

I could feel before I could move.

I could move before I could see.

I heard an engine running in the distance, but in the damp, dark setting, it was impossible to determine the direction of the sound. One side of my face was pressed to the cool, wet earth. My body was losing the warmth it had just gained from the motel room bed. I tempered my breath, not wanting to stir, but I sensed a nearby, ominous presence. I moved my hand slowly across my clothes and heard the grating sound of rough fabric against rough fabric, like two pieces of sandpaper being rubbed together. I must be wearing my foul-weather sailing gear; it would be impossible to move quietly.

Everything was wet: the ground, my clothes, the air. Breathing for a few minutes was the equivalent of taking a gulp of water in this thick, dewy fog. But I had to move; I was too prone to the presence by laying here. As quietly as I could—admittedly, about as quiet as dragging a dead body through the underbrush—I managed to bring myself up to my hands and knees, vigilant for any movement other than my own. There, I paused, listening to be sure the only sound in the night was the idling car engine.

A light suddenly appeared.

Shit! I yelled in my head as my heart reached its highest gear. I raised my right arm reflexively to cover my eyes from the glare. When brave enough to peek, two headlights in the distance lighted a surreal scene of tree trunks impaling a diaphanous ground mist, as if the gods above had flung their spears downward trying to slay the creeping, white beast.

Considering my options, I decided to stand, which improved my ability to fight or flee. With this thick, low-lying fog creating a mysterious layer about twelve inches above the ground, my fire engine red, foul-weather attire stood out like a channel marker buoy on the sea—all I needed was a clanging bell on my head to alert all ships of the proper course. *Red on right returning.* It was time to move.

I heard Promise's voice in my head, *I shine the same bright light as you.* Followed by *Poltergeist's* Zelda Rubinstein, *Cross over children. All are welcome. Go into the light. There is peace and serenity in the*—I cut off the overplayed-in-my-head movie quote. Obviously, the voices in my head agreed on the same course of action.

My first step squished like I'd stepped on ten sponges of water. The bubbling, oozing sound may as well have been a rolling crack of thunder in the quiet forest. I paused. There were eyes on me. The forest exhaled; its hot breath pushed the fog toward the headlights, then inhaled to bring it back in my direction.

A few moments passed. Nothing moved. I took a second step. Squish.

Again, the forest breathed, this time adding a low growl. My own breath became labored. I slowly turned my head. I didn't truly want to know, but just *had* to know if the beast I envisioned, its massive jowls open and hanging over the top of me, was waiting to see the whites of my eyes before it took me in one giant, excruciatingly-bone-crushing bite. *No, Steven!* Again, a scene from *Poltergeist* with Carol Ann's dad pulling the rope so early he brought a nightmarish evil into the bedroom. I quickly turned to look. Nothing but darkness. Bottomless pit kind of darkness. The breath I'd been holding escaped and fell like a dying balloon to join the listless collective of dead breath on the forest floor.

I fled.

SQUISH. SQUISH. SQUISH.

The ground fog resisted me like it'd magically turned from shallow swamp to rip current river and I was running against the flow. Each step angered the forest—I could *feel* it—its palpable emotion dialed into the sound of my movement. I picked up the pace, from cautiously running to sprinting carelessly across a ground surface I couldn't at all see. The presence closed the distance between us. I slammed my right fist into my chest to urge my heart and lungs to work harder. "COME ON!" I screamed, motivating my body to continue its flight, but foul-weather gear wasn't made for running. I pushed off a tree trunk to keep from slamming into it and felt the frigid temperature of the bark. I'd covered only a third of the distance to the headlights, but I'd burned more than half my energy. The trees became mile markers. *Just make it to the next tree.* I made it. *Just make it to the next tree.* I made it. *Just make it*—I wasn't going to make it. There was no other choice but to stand my ground. I slid to a stop behind the next tree, using it as a shield by throwing my back up against its lighted side, then gathered my courage for another look backward. *One. Two. THREE!* I turned, looked and felt the apex of gravitational intent, as if day and night aligned to support the strongest tide's mission to carry me away from the light. There was no movie-like beast, only the bottomless darkness moving toward me and consuming the holes in the white fog where I had stepped. To hold my position, I dropped to my knees and cradled the tree, then leaned over backwards to look at the headlights, could I make it? Maybe if determination could best gravity and luck grace each step. The darkness touched me; I felt my arms and legs meld to the trunk of the tree. No longer could I pull away. I screamed, "NOOOO!" and looked one final time toward the headlights, mentally reaching out to them as desperately as I could. In that instant, a gale-force wind charged into the forest, agitating the fog and causing the darkness to retreat, thereby releasing me from its grip. Astounded, I rolled away from the tree and peered into the wind looking for a path to safety. The wind was so strong I had to close my eyes for protection. *See the forest despite the trees.* I frantically scampered toward the next closest tree. The wind in my face. The darkness behind me. I found myself in the eddy of the tree, which reduced both the pull of the foggy stream and the strength of the wind. *Think, Soupy.* On my knees, and with the wind howling in my ears, my mind raced to find a solution as my upper torso rocked back and forth. I let out a great, deep breath, and made myself as small in the shadow of the tree as I could. It was then that my forehead touched the cool, wet earth.

There it was; the map was suddenly in my head. I visualized the route from my spot to the headlights. The fog revealed eddies of swirling, reverse current behind each tree—a path of least resistance. Like sailing upwind, I needed to move in angles just off the direct wind heading, tacking back and forth from tree to tree, using the eddies behind them to cover distance with less resistance. I gathered up my strength, inhaled greatly, leapt up and charged into the flow, head down, shielding my face and churning my legs until I was close enough to dive into the eddy behind the next tree and crawl into its shadow. The forest roared angrily. I drew energy from the shadow of the tree, it only took a few seconds to recuperate, and I was back into the fray, determined to survive, each segment exhausting every ounce of fuel, each tree refilling the tank. From the last tree, I dove headfirst into the clearing, scurried to my feet, and ran the short distance to the open door of the idling vehicle. On instinct, I pulled the door closed, pushed down the lock, gripped the steering wheel, and stared intently, without blinking, into the forest, my breath coming and going in enormous, heaving exchanges of oxygen for carbon dioxide.

Nothing moved. No imminent eclipse. No creeping black hole. No river of fog. No beast from the closet.

The scene had inverted. I now saw the opposite exposure, instead of dark tree trunks on a white background, white trunks on a black background.

As I accepted safety and relief, my forehead collapsed to the steering wheel and my hands fell from the wheel to my thighs, bumping the lever that controlled the headlights.

YESSSSSS! a voice from the returned darkness hissed.

Frantically, I searched for the knob and pulled the lights back on. So frantically, in fact, I pulled the knob right out of the dash. I held it up, looked at it, and shook my head.

* * *

Outside the car, the forest had changed to a setting in the living room of my childhood home. "Turn off the TV and go to bed, Soupy," Mom said from the top of the stairs.

"Okay," I replied. Despite parental warnings of it "being bad for my eyes," I often watched television in the dark and sat far too close to the screen. Add that to the nonsensical world that television exposed—dream realities, sports gods, and superheroes—and very little benefit was gained from the hours I spent there. Because I watched it in the dark, once I pressed the power button on the TV—long before the days of remote controls—there was no light left to see the ground I'd have to cover from where I stood to the stairs. Therefore, the process of getting from the living room to the kitchen proceeded like this: check carpet for trip-hazards, turn body toward stairs, reach backward, push the television off button, bolt across the room, vault up the stairs three at a time, *and* the most important step in the process: avoid dark hand reaching for collar of my shirt with the intent to chain me in the living room darkness forever. At the top of the stairs, I'd turn the corner and bound up another flight to the security of my bedroom, where I'd pump my fist in the air having expertly evaded the grasp of the darkness again, close my bedroom door, flip off the light and slide safely into bed.

* * *

I slinked down in the driver's seat, eager to catch my breath in a place that, for now, felt safe.

Chapter 8

The back door of the car opened. *The beast?* I was afraid to move. *If I don't move, it can't see me.* The door closed. *Did someone get in? Did something get in?* I held my breath not wanting to risk the chance of being discovered. *Did I remember to lock the doors? Yes. Shit. Back doors. Didn't lock those.*

A bright, golden light filled up the inside of the car.

A voice from the back seat said, *Are you awake, or what? You know your light is on; that means you're available.*

I whispered, "What?" and realized I'd whispered it. "What?" I repeated more loudly.

Your light. It's on.

I inched up in my seat slightly because I was curious. *My light?* The dome interior light wasn't shining, which added to my confusion.

What'll it be, Soupy? There's never enough time. Let's not waste it.

Suddenly, the voice struck the chord of a twenty-year old memory. I sat up in the seat and turned to look at her—to see her for the first time in my life—but the rising sun blasted through the rear window with such intensity I had to shield my eyes and turn away. I could only see her silhouette.

It's not that easy, she said.

My elation turned instantly to anger. "Easy? EASY? You think I don't already know it isn't *that easy*?"

Soupy—

I cut her off before she could continue. It *was* easier to be angry not facing her. "Do *you* know how hard it was to have one night with you? A night when you told me my whole life had some purpose—some *fucking homework*—to find true love, or you, or whatever it is that I'm supposed to be doing…and then…and then to have you completely disappear? DO YOU KNOW HOW HARD THAT WAS?!" My hands gripped the steering wheel so tightly they turned white. I looked at the door to see if it was still locked, considering flight, not from fear, but from anger. "You never came back. *You never. Came. Back.* Where the hell were you? I was *thirteen years old* and you deserted me."

I never said—

"I KNOW WHAT YOU SAID! I've replayed it over and over in my head for twenty years. Okay. OKAY?!"

You're angry, that's understandable, but let me ask you one question: what are you going to do if it's another twenty years before you meet me again?

"WHAT?" Her question angered me even more. "ARE YOU KIDDING ME?!" I wanted to turn around again, badly, wanted her to see the anger on my face.

I'm just asking: what kind of conversation do you want to replay in your head for the next twenty years?

My anger was not ready to be put aside. I wanted *my* moment—my *fucking* moment—to curse her out for not fulfilling her promise. *How many times had I begged for her guidance? How many? Hundreds? Thousands? Shouldn't I deserve the opportunity to say my piece, sleep on it, and wake up with a fresh perspective? Doesn't she owe me that? YES! She does.* I gripped the lower portion of the steering wheel and slowly applied more and more force with the intent to rip it from the column and fling it out the window. "Give me a second," I said, between gritted teeth. I closed my eyes and took three deeps breaths, but the emotional cauldron inside of me was boiling over like pasta left on high heat for too long. *In through the nose. Out through the mouth,* I urged myself in thought, but the outer rim of my vision started to blur. I reached for the door handle, pulled, but it didn't open. *Locked.* I pulled up the chrome-painted door lock, yanked the handle, threw my left foot out and planted it firmly on the gravel. A blast of arctic air caused me to wince. My body shivered, a strange collision of the angry heat inside and the frigid cold outside.

Soupy? Her quaint voice found its way from the back seat to my ears.

As much as I wanted to ignore her, I replied, "Hold on. Just. Hold. On. Let me think." My right foot joined my left. I ran my fingers through my hair as I suffered over what to do next. "I can't," I said, and walked away from the car toward the grass. When I reached it, I dropped to my knees and thrust my hands into it. *Cool my fire*, I thought. It was as if icy stalagmites shot through my palms and into my bloodstream. "AGHHHHHH!" My scream felt like it woke the forest. My eyes darted toward the woods.

I was no longer hot, but I wasn't fully cooled either. A fuse inside of me had been blown, shutting off the electricity to run the machine. I willed my fingers to straighten, reaching toward the sunlight—*the shortest distance between two points is*—fully stretched, my fingers closed the circuit to the sun and warmth flowed through me. *Mmmm, mmmm, good*, I thought.

With energy, came humility. Embarrassed, I stood up and turned toward the car. *A cab? I'm driving a cab?* The sun's glare on the backseat window obscured my view inside. *Had I lost her?* A chill ascended my spine and I sprinted back. Within a few feet, I tripped and bounced heavily on the rough gravel, nearly rolling under the cab. "FUCK!" My elbows, knees, and palms had taken the brunt of the impact, but my foul weather gear had protected everything but my hands, which were badly skinned. I grimaced, rolled onto my back to stare at the blue sky, and whispered to myself, "Idiot." With effort, I sat up, pulled off the red jacket, and cast it aside. Then, from my seated position, slowly wriggled out of the coveralls before I reached out to open the bright, yellow car door. *A cab? Really?* I crawled my way back into the driver's seat.

You okay? Promise nonchalantly asked.

"I don't know. I did a little thing my grandpa taught me years ago. I thought it might cool my jets, if you know what I mean," I replied.

Better?

"Yeah, I guess, but it totally didn't work the way I figured it would."

Did you do it right?

"I don't know." I didn't feel like talking about it anymore.

Are you okay?

"Yeah, aside from a bruised ego and rocks permanently embedded in my palms. No big deal."

Did you have a nice trip?

"Funny."

Enjoy the fall?

"What are you, twelve?"

What was the big hurry?

"Honestly?"

Yes, of course.

"I thought I'd lost you."

There was silence in the cab for a moment, awkward enough for me to change the course of our conversation. "Hey—" I started as I twisted my upper body around slowly to speak with her face-to-face.

SOUP! You can't look, it's not that easy.

Facing forward, I sharply retorted, "You already said that." The gas lighter on my emotional stove began to click repeatedly as it relit the flame I'd just extinguished.

Yes, and I didn't explain it because I haven't yet had a chance, she said, smartly. *You can't see me because it would make finding me in the real world easier. And like I said, you must learn from your failures, not sit around looking for someone who looks like me.*

"It's been twenty years, Promise. I've already failed a crap-ton of times. Are you telling me this, right here and now, isn't the point in the future I've been working toward?"

You're in the wrong world.

"Okay, okay," I said and waited for her to change her mind. She said nothing, so I continued, "Not that I like it—I've been ticked at you for two decades—but I *do* realize the importance of this opportunity. And you're right, it *has* been twenty years, and if our time together ended right now, what would I have learned to help me through the next twenty? Nothing."

Look, are you sure? Because I can get out.

"No-no, stay." Her change in temperament from explanatory to actionable activated my sense of guilt. "My need to talk with you is greater than my desire to bark at you," I admitted.

It's better for us both, she said.

Her reply reminded me of all the unanswered questions I once wrote down. This time, I wasn't the twelve-going-on-thirteen-year old struggling to figure it out in the presence of his supposed dream girl. I also knew not to succumb to the flood of words bombarding my brain, but to focus. "How does this work?" I asked, because understanding the rules would help me get my mental house in order.

We just talk. Do you need to go back over our last conversation?

"Oh no, I've got that one fairly well memorized. But you just told me I can't look at you, so it's more than 'just talking.' Are there any other rules?"

Hmmm. I don't think so, but I reserve the right to change my mind.

In truth, I was struggling to remember our last conversation. Her presence was helping, but accessing the list of questions I'd written down years ago was still buried somewhere in the cobwebs of my head. "Are you—" I started…

Yes?

"That wasn't the right question, sorry. It's on the tip of my tongue. Give me a second." *That list. THAT LIST. What was on it? Dammit.* I closed my eyes. *Ask something.* I forcefully pushed the scribbling of words and lines and shapes into the margins of my mind and surprisingly found one obvious question. *It's not, where did you go?* It's, "Where have you been?"

Start the meter and ask me again.

"Do what?"

Start the meter.

"The meter?"

You mean you haven't realized you're driving a cab?

I laughed. "A cab? Yes, never done this before." I reached over to the mechanism atop the dashboard, as I'd seen many cab drivers do, and intended to start the meter but discovered a plethora of buttons to decipher. “Hmmm,” I hummed as I leaned in more closely to read the tiny words on the buttons. After reading them once, I pushed “Meter” without much thought and a “Hired” light lit up on the little box.

Now, ask me again.

I played along, “Promise, where have you been these twenty years?”

Since she already knew the question, her answer was queued up and ready to go. *You'd be better off asking me where I haven't been. Spending most of my time in the world of dreams takes me everywhere. I've had to earn my way back to you.*

“Are you saying you can't just come visit whenever you'd like?”

Right. I can't. I go where I'm needed.

“Seriously? Like, I didn't need you?” I was torn between feeling selfish and apologetic, now knowing that it wasn't in her control. “Would have been nice to know that the first time we spoke.”

I didn't know twenty years ago. I don't have all of the answers, Soupy. You and I, we're the same. We're both looking for answers to questions most people never think to ask, because the answers will help us find each other. You have your questions; I have mine.

Until now, I had thought of her as a password-protected computer I had to hack to steal the answers to my homework. Apparently, that's not the case, and this new reality was scrambling my mind. I felt like I'd walked through a door she'd opened, and as soon as I stepped outside a piano fell on my head. “I never thought of it that way. I just assumed you had all the answers.”

I may have had more answers than you twenty years ago, but I assume there's a reason I'm here now. And in my experience, I've learned there's no telling if I'm here to answer your questions, or you're here to answer mine...could be both.

“I still feel like a kid. Like, you know this shit way better than I do.”

Spend a lot of time in the dream world and you'll get used to it, believe me. My hope is that I'm not waiting for you to catch up as much as I was the last time. Meaning, I truly hope our paths are converging.

"Converging? But you once said that *I* needed to find *you*," I said, emphasizing the pronouns because I'd thought for twenty years that she was sitting around somewhere and I was doing all the work.

It was an easy way for you to understand your assignment. Remember, you were *only thirteen years old.*

"Twelve, technically," I'd never forgotten her point that it was the *eve* of my thirteenth birthday when we first met.

Twelve, yeah. Touché. This isn't one of us trying to find the other; we're trying to find each other. I must work at getting to the place where you'll be, just as much as you getting to the place I'll be. We don't know when we have to be there or where that place is, yet.

"When I met you, I thought you were going to hold my hand through it all; that's not what has happened," I said. "Was I wrong to have that expectation?" I was feeling more comfortable, more organized in thought, more like myself.

Would you have preferred it that way? Do you think it would've been easier?

"Easier? Hell, yes!" But then, I hesitated, because I knew that easy is the enemy of experience. "Though, I probably wouldn't have learned what I've learned—the hard part is the learning part, so I don't want shortcuts. I don't know how many times I've told others this, but the world, with all its lawsuits and lotteries, is in constant pursuit of the earning without the learning," I said, and smiled. The axiom, a so-called "Soupyism," was one of my own.

She laughed. *I can see that one thing is true: in twenty years you've given life a lot of thought.*

"As directed, ma'am," I replied sarcastically.

Don't give me all the credit. You probably weren't selected for your task based on—she paused—*I was going to say based on who you will become, but that's probably just as important as being selected because of how you're built.*

"Which came first, the man or the mission?" I asked.

Good question. Let's just keep asking it and stay ready for an answer.

"Deal." Despite my practiced ability to stay aware of my surroundings, the scenery outside of the cab had changed, and I'd only just realized we were now parked in the middle of a street. "Hey, this is my old neighborhood. What are we doing here?"

You tell me; it's your dream.

"Lots of memories from this neighborhood." I said as I looked around. "Is that what we're supposed to talk about?"

If you like.

Our cab was parked up the street from my childhood home, so I drove a block and stopped in front of it. No one was outside. Too early, I suppose. The tree across the street that was supposedly on its deathbed from errant Frisbee throws, by owner's decree, was alive, well, and oddly the same size as it had been when I was a kid. The grass in the neighbor's yard directly next to my own was still ten times as luscious as our own and much preferred for any tackling games. It was as if nothing had changed since I left; yet the houses and yards felt half the size as when I was a kid, maybe because I was now twice as big. Active memories from here all had a soundtrack, the lack of noise made it feel claustrophobic.

What's on your mind, Soupy?

"It was never this quiet when I lived here." I flipped my thumb over my left shoulder and said, "Those neighbors were always arguing." I pointed to several other houses. "Those neighbors were always tending to their yards." I pointed to my own house. "I was always throwing some kind of ball against the garage door, stairs, or roof. Down there, at the end of the street, we played games in either that back yard, that side yard, or see that basketball hoop down there, on that driveway. There were a lot of kids in this neighborhood, so there was always something going on." I paused for a moment before I continued, the uncomfortable quiet suddenly reminding me of the more haunted aspects of my childhood—times when I *had* to be quiet to avoid some looming danger. "Even with so many kids and open doors there were still a lot of mysteries in these houses."

Promise asked, *Mysteries?*

"You know how a young, creative mind operates." I was sure she did since she'd jumped in and out of so many dreams. I took the cab out of park and let it roll down the street. "We rarely saw anyone go into or come out of that house," to which I pointed, "the shades were always drawn. On the other side of the street, we saw *lots* of people going in and out of that house. If you could sneak through unseen by the old, grouchy owner of *that* house, then you had a shortcut down the hill to the backside of the grocery store. When the owner of that house was out mowing his lawn we wouldn't go anywhere near him so as to avoid his scowl. He worked odd hours and spent lots of time in his immaculate, well-tooled garage, which we knew because we'd peeked through the curtains drawn over the garage glass on days when we were sure he was away." I touched the brake to stop the cab, pointed between two houses and asked, "There. Do you see the roof peak of the A-frame clubhouse there in the back of that yard?"

Yes, she replied.

"I think just about everyone in the neighborhood had their first kiss there."

Including you?

"Nope, not me. Mine was while listening to some record I don't remember the name of, with a girl who moved away a few months after it happened."

I'll bet she remembers it all.

"Well, that's the difference between girls and boys now, isn't it?"

For some girls and boys, anyway.

With my foot once more lifted from the brake, we coasted down the rest of the hill and came to a stop in front of another house. Promise noticed my prolonged stare at the house and asked, *Something to tell me about that house?*

"That's a loaded question if ever there was one. *Plenty* to tell you about things that happened in and around that house." I smiled.

Good things, it sounds. Spill it.

"Where to begin? I lived back there up the street, but I *grew up* in this house right here...in more ways than one. I probably spent every weekend here from fourth grade to high school. Not only did my best friend live here, but my dream girl did, too. If I was Squints Palledorous from *The Sandlot*, then she was my Wendy Peffercorn." I laughed. "I would have faked drowning in a pool every darn day if I knew she'd jump down from her lifeguard chair to give me mouth-to-mouth."

Promise joined in the laughter before she added, *Dream girl, eh? This sounds like a long story! Maybe you should park this thing somewhere other than the middle of the street?*

It was an odd request since the street was empty, but she sounded like she knew what she was talking about so I complied. "Good idea." I backed the car into the driveway across the street from the storied house and turned off the engine. "Promise, this is the house of my *first*."

I don't mean to sound dense, but first what? Are we still talking about first kisses?

"Not that first, the *other* first," I admitted. The sun had followed us down the street and had now retired behind the western horizon.

Chilly, Promise said, and then added, *Gotta put on my hat and gloves.*

"Want me to turn on the heater?"

Yes, do that, too!

I restarted the car, set the heater vents to blow toward the back of the cab, and slid the lever on the thermostat from cold to hot. In the dark we could see light from the television in the living room flickering on the curtains, abruptly and continuously. "In that room right there, the one with the television, I spent Friday nights building forts, eating chips and frozen pizza, and watching *The Three Stooges* and *Friday Fright Night*. That routine didn't change for what seemed like forever, and neither did my crush on my best friend's older sister. Although, I must admit, I don't recall her being around much on Friday nights; always had a date. But one hot summer night, before I entered high school, she came home early. I adored her—*absolutely* adored her. Though she was a couple of years older than me, we could always find things to talk about since we were genuinely interested in each other's thoughts and often surprised at the answers we received. I guess that's why we'd stay up late at night talking and drawing unicorns."

Unicorns?

I brought my hands to my heart, batted my eyelashes, and claimed, "Magical beasts."

Dork.

"I'll take that as a compliment. Seriously, we could have drawn trees or popped zits or cleaned the kitchen and I would've been happy, as long as she was there. Do you have any idea what it's like to be able to smell and touch your dream girl even when you have no idea what you'd do with her if she'd let you do anything?"

Believe me, we girls have our fair share of crushes growing up.

"I'll bet you do." I winked at Promise. The wink would have needed a boomerang to reach her so I doubt she saw it. "I was never disappointed when she wasn't there because my friend and I enjoyed time together; it was a bonus when she was. On this particular evening, she simply walked into the house, changed clothes in her room, and returned to watch a movie with us."

That must have made you happy.

"Very happy. My friend was lounging on the floor and I was on the couch. The living room was dimly lit by the television and the candle we'd burn in front of the TV's light sensor to brighten the picture. You remember having to do that?" I wondered if Promise even had a television growing up, but I was too involved in the story to wait for an answer. "When she walked into the room to join us, I was torn between the excitement of her presence and the desire to hide any outward sign of that excitement.

Soupy Robert Heller, Promise said in a motherly tone.

I realized Promise was referring to a state of excitement that I'd not at all intended. I laughed. "No! That's not what I meant! I'm just trying to say that the only thing in the room I was focused on, object or person, was her, my dream girl. Where's your mind? Hello? The gutter called, it wants its mind back."

Okay, you got me...and now you know a little bit more about how my *mind works.* I could sense that she'd blushed. *Point for you.*

"Promise me you *aren't* going to keep score," I said. Another thing I'd learned about relationships: keeping score wasn't a sustainable tactic because there was always a winner *and* a loser.

I promise, she replied.

"As my dream girl and I had gotten older, we'd gotten busier. You know, sports, plays, clubs, friends, dates, and whatnot. So I'd not had any quality time with her in a long while. Damn the irony, she was free for the evening and we were stuck watching a movie in the living room instead of actually doing something with each other. I liked my friend to pieces, but we're talking 'dream girl time' here. I desperately wanted him to call it a night and go to bed."

I'll bet you did.

"Not for what you might be thinking, Promise. I just wanted to talk with her without giving him the idea that I was overly enthralled by her presence. I never wanted him to think I was there simply to spend time with his sister. Never. First of all, it wasn't true. Second, even though it wasn't true I knew it'd be tough to convince him otherwise. It was better to simply avoid giving him the notion."

I'm with ya.

"Okay, here we go. Ready?"

As ever!

"The greatest movie ever made is called *My Tutor*. Released in 1983, the main character, Bobby, failed French class during his senior year of high school and had to take a summer class in order to gain admittance to college in the fall. His parents hire a beautiful, French-speaking woman to tutor him for the summer. They also let her live in the family's guesthouse. See where I'm going with this?" I giggled. "Perhaps needless to say, she taught him more than a foreign language that summer—*that* was the benefit of growing up with cable television."

Now whose mind is the gutter calling for? Promise humorously accused.

"One point! Gospel Girls!" We both laughed.

Hello? Scorekeeping?

"Couldn't help myself, sorry. Meanwhile, back in the living room, my friend got up and said he was going to bed. If you'da been there you might have heard a 'Night, dude,' but inside I was screaming, 'OHMYGOD-OHMYGOD-OHMYGOD,' because my wish had come true. It wasn't more than a few minutes before she asked if she could join me on the couch. "Uh-huh," I replied and inched my horizontal body forward so she could slip into the space between it and the back of the couch. I wanted her to hold me, though that's easier to say now than it was back then because I honestly had no idea what I was doing, just so happened there was more room behind me than in front of me."

You gave her the outside spoon?

"Yes, Promise, I gave her the outside spoon. Feeling the immediate warmth of her body, hearing each breath she took, letting her arms slowly make their way around me, and her touch—my goodness, her fingers, her touch—she slowly caressed my arms and ran her fingers through my hair. And her scent—my how I love an intimate scent—filled up my head and rushed its way to my heart." I inhaled deeply, as if I could pull her scent inside me all over again. "Before long, she asked me to turn around and face her—"

* * *

Soupy's voice tailed off as I lost him to some other place in his head. He wasn't that familiar with the intricacies of this world, my dream world—at least, not yet. There were things he would learn, and learn quickly if we were both going to get something from this night together. So I simply watched and listened, trying to glean as much as I could from his dream-within-a-dream experience.

His head slumped to his chest. I leaned forward in my seat to see if he was still breathing. It was the closest we'd ever been to each other. I wanted to reach over the seat to stroke his hair but I feared it would immediately end this "mission" to find me. I wanted to, but I couldn't; I was bound by—

"Yes," *he said aloud, surprising me. It was a very timid answer to a question I didn't know because I didn't hear it asked, but I could guess since he did tell me that this was his first. I leaned away from him so as not to disturb his dream, or to be truthful, jeopardize our mission.*

He gulped, it was plain to see, and then squirmed uncomfortably in his seat before lying down across the vinyl bench, face down, as if his lover had just invited him to occupy the intimate, skin on skin, position on top of her.

I leaned forward again from the back of the cab to watch him more closely, just not close enough to once again tempt my desire to end it all. I wondered, Could we accomplish our mission if we started it all in the dream world? *He wasn't breathing. He didn't dare move. A bead of sweat formed in the space above his ear, poised to run down his cheek at any moment. I knew, both now and then, his mind's processor was working overtime. I willed for the suspense to be over; for him to relive the first moment, a moment he'd played out in his head for a countless number of years afterward, the way young boys are apt to do—I know because I'd been in enough of their dreams. Then, as if he was aware of my thoughts, his body began to move in a slow rhythm, his shoulders fell from their hunched, tense state, and his breathing, though heavier than normal, returned. A deep breath escaped his lips, and on them rode my name,* "Promissssss." *I grabbed the headrest barely resisting the urge to pull myself far enough over the seat to wrest him awake.* What? *I thought.* What is it, my love? *I wanted so badly to touch him, but I couldn't disturb his heaven or destroy ours. He began to moan, quietly and sporadically at first, but then more softly. The hairs on the back of his neck stood on end pleasantly, in response to someone's virtual touch. Under his clothes, his muscles tensed in a rhythm that was sure to bring one thing, probably sooner rather than later if he was truly reliving his first experience.*

His back arched upward. I leaned into my seat and into the darker shadows of the cab, aware of the inevitable, and watched as his eyes opened in surprise to stare blankly out the passenger's window. In them, he showed the immaturity of a teenager farther along a path than he'd before been: vigilant, accomplished, and confused all at once—so malleable at the will of whim. For better or worse, party to luck's roll of the dice, the young Soupy could now make the first notch on his mental bedpost. I chuckled briefly at the irony of my first time while watching his first time. Mine just so happened to be in a car, which was likely where most people his age were conceived. Slowly, his body turned one hundred and eighty degrees as he laid down on his back to stare at the beige-colored fabric of the cab's ceiling. In unison, his breathing slowed with his heart rate—the moment of afterglow.

"She told me to close my eyes, and—" *he mumbled.*

I again resisted the urge to lean forward and stroke his bangs; the risk was just too great: if his eyes were open, he would see me. Dammit. *I heard the leather crinkle and assumed it was his body settling into its post-coital comfort until I heard a voice, not Soupy's, say,* "Kiss me." *I tensed up and checked every corner of the cab for another person, even dared to look into the front seat, but no one could be seen. I peered through each window, starting with the front windshield, then the driver's side and passenger's side. No one. I spun around in my seat quickly to look at the back window—still no one.*

"Look at him," *it added.*

I didn't trust the voice. I replied, "I can't."

"Your loss, because I can."

I sensed the attitude in her voice.

Soupy's lips pursed and then relaxed. I wanted to believe it was the ecstasy of his first after-sex kiss with the woman of his dreams—the equivalent of saying "that was amazing" and lighting up a cigarette to share with one's partner—but I was concerned by the unfamiliar voice. If he'd kissed his dream girl, then this particular kiss—this was his real first kiss, the one he'd played out in his head a million times before it happened and would always remember, probably to the same tune of a million times, or more. And by watching him, I could see how much he enjoyed it, both audibly and physically. Yet the question remained: whom was he kissing? I felt overwhelmed with the weight of this passion that was an important part of his education. Again, I wanted to reach out and touch him, especially now that he'd shared this moment with me, and wake him to see if he could tell me who else is here.

The voice filled the inside of the cab once again, this time with more desperation than confidence. "Save me," *it said, tailing off at the end as if someone had turned down the volume.*

"Save you?" I replied, but she didn't respond.

"What?" *Soupy whispered. I snapped into a more rigid position, wary, as always, of the rules of our relationship.*

"Hm?" I said, the sound escaping my lips before I realized I'd made it.

"Nothing," *he whispered.*

What's going on here? It was the first time I'd experienced a voice that seemingly came out of nowhere. Unsure of what to make of it, I double-checked the exterior of the cab, making sure my eyes scanned every inch of possibility. I didn't want to move. I didn't know what to do. I sat as still as possible, measuring my breath, hoping that some explanation might instantaneously arrive.

"He was chosen for a reason," *the original voice added.*

"Wha—" before I could finish my question, Soupy sat up in his seat.

* * *

Before I realized what I was saying, I heard myself speak, "She asked me if I'd respect her in the morning." I felt dazed, as if I'd been woken from the deepest part of sleep. I struggled to recognize my surroundings. Out of instinct, I rubbed my eyes with balled up fists trying to force the fuzzy areas out of my peripheral vision. A rush of memories flooded back: a cab, Promise, face forward, my first, all a dream. "What just happened?" I asked, not sure if Promise was still in the back seat.

I wish I knew. You left, went somewhere else, and you've just now returned.

"Did you—," I wanted to ask if she'd jumped into my dream, but was embarrassed about the relatively short length of time anyone would have been there to witness the entire act.

No, Soup, I wasn't there with you, but I could hear your breathing.

Relieved, I said, "Okay."

Who else was there?

Confused by the question, I answered, "My dream girl, of course."

Yes, of course. Anyone else?

I chuckled knowing that I wouldn't have been able to handle any more pleasure in that single evening if another woman was present. "Not that I recall, Promise, no." Sarcastically, I added, "Do you *really* think I could have handled that?"

That wasn't my point. There was—no, I don't really know what to say about it. Anyway, you said she asked if you'd respect her in the morning, what was your answer?

"I said 'yes,' of course. A timid yes, but yes just the same given how nervous I was."

I know exactly what that yes sounds like, Promise said, because she'd heard it.

Her voice was farther away than it had been previously, as if something else was on her mind. "Promise, I sense that something's amiss. What just happened?"

The best way I can think to explain it is, you had a dream within a dream.

"Is that common?" I asked.

Let's just say it's not uncommon.

There was something more, I could sense it, but not place it. "What else?"

I don't know, Soupy. Something I've never experienced before; a voice, but no one present who spoke it and I didn't recognize it.

"What did it say?" I asked.

Save me, she replied.

I thought about that for a moment—we *both* thought about it for a moment—before I asked, "Was it a female voice or a male voice?"

Hard to say, it was a whisper, but I think it was female. Someone you have in mind?

"No," I started, then paused. "At least, I don't think so," but the faces of several women, from relationships I hadn't yet gotten around to discussing, flashed through my mind.

The silence between us was slightly uncomfortable as we both tried to figure out a reason for what had happened. Finally, Promise broke it by stating, *You haven't yet told me her name.*

Confused by the environment, namely this dream state, and who among all the women I knew might need to be saved, I replied, "Her name?"

Yes, the first woman you slept with. What was her name?

"Desire," I replied.

Desire. She repeated, *Desire. How appropriate since she was your first experience; the one who filled your dreams since puberty, the one who got it all started.*

"No, Promise. That's not altogether true. "Yes, she filled my fantasies, but you filled my dreams."

Promise replied, "You're too sweet."

I just smiled. There was no need for an additional response. And sometimes simply accepting a compliment is the best course of action.

What was it like? For a guy, I mean.

"Honestly, I was in such a state of disbelief that I barely remember the specifics, just that it actually happened."

Fairly different for a girl—like our first kiss, we have a pretty good memory of our first time. Do you think your experience with Desire shaped your life? In other words, what did you learn?

"Shape my life? Well, I went back the next night for Round Two."

You what?! Promise said, and laughed.

"Yup, but her father, who normally worked nights, was home the next night, so we simply sat around on her bed talking."

That *father?* she said emphasizing the first word more than the second.

"Huh," the emphasis set alarms off in my head as I quickly searched the streets for his presence. "Is he here?"

There's a station wagon pulling into the driveway right now, Promise said.

I hunched, abruptly hiding myself but for the ability to peek over the dashboard. "Shit. We gotta go."

Wait. If you go now he'll notice us.

"Oh, he's already noticed us," I said. "It's his job to notice things."

He backed his station wagon into the driveway and got out to manually open the garage door. Upon his return to the driver's seat he stopped, stood, and stared at us. His eyes pierced the windshield as he calculated whether a taxicab parked in the driveway across the street equaled a threat.

"Gotta go," I stated, threw the cab into drive, drove us briskly out of the driveway not breaking for the curb at the end of it, sped up the hill, and swerved the cab into the grocery store parking lot. I chose a parking space several rows removed from the storefront and centered among the various exits that were available. "Sorry Promise, that man *always* scared the shit out of me."

No need to apologize, Soup. I know the type. Just from the look in his eyes, I could see the storm of voices inside his head. They're usually only quieted by the command of careless indifference.

I heard a virtual clock ticking the seconds away as I stared at the entrance to the parking lot. *One Mississippi. Two Mississippi. Three Mississippi. Four Mississippi.* One hand tightly gripped the steering wheel while the other held the transmission control in case we needed to change gears and high-tail it out of there. *Five Mississippi. Six Mississippi. Seven Mississippi.* Though I was taught to drive with one foot alternating between the gas and brake pedals, I employed the two-footed technique used by racecar drivers for faster response. The sky turned from black to deep blue. *Eight Mississippi. Nine Mississippi. Ten Mississippi.* No station wagon entered the parking lot. In fact, no cars at all entered the lot. *Relax,* I thought, *He's not the type to react publicly.* It was true, and that's what scared me the most about him; he wouldn't react, but he also wouldn't forget. He'd filed the experience away for a later date; one I hoped would never come. I relaxed my grip and expressed false confidence in front of a woman I adored, "Fuck that guy." I rapped my fingers on the steering wheel and lightly added, "Like I said, lots of mysteries on the streets of my childhood."

Forget him, Soup. That was almost twenty years ago. Besides, I'd much rather talk about love, not fear, in the time we have left.

She spoke like a woman I still needed to learn much from, despite what she'd said about us potentially being equals. She'd surprised me, maybe because I simply wasn't used to being around someone who *could* teach me something, but the wisdom in those particular words of hers, I intuitively knew, could change a world that spent far too much time making decisions based on fear—especially when fear is disguised as faith. *What an odd connection to make: fear and faith.* It was true, however, that this grocery store would eventually be converted to The International House of Prayer. In fact, the whole neighborhood would be converted. *What kind of fear drives someone to give an entire life to faith?* It wasn't a topic to discuss now, Promise and I had enough to talk about. Obviously, there aren't enough Promises in the world, so I had to make sure I learned from one when I had her near. The sun announced its arrival with a ray of light that landed on the corner of my right eye. I turned my head toward the passenger side front windshield to confirm whether it was friend or foe, daylight or flashlight. It posed no threat, so I relaxed and said, "Love. Yes'm. I agree," I said, and then added, "Where did we leave off?"

The start of a new you. The post-Desire you. You loved her, I'm sure, as best you knew how, which makes her a very significant person in your life. You couldn't resist the lure of lust. For you, likely a function of learning; gaining and experiencing something you'd never before experienced. And for her, quite possibly, the necessity to educate someone she also cared deeply about.

I struggled to refocus after the near-father experience, so I said, "Holy crap, you just came up with all that right now?"

Yes, and this conversation just went serious, so get onboard, Soupy, she said with a more forceful tone.

"Okay, okay." I interlaced my fingers and stretched them outward to make my knuckles crack. "Yes, I can see both sides of what you're saying. We were friends for years before that night, and in fact have been very friendly each time we've seen each other since—which isn't exactly fair or accurate—we have this wonderful tendency to fall right back into our own little world when we see each other; it's natural for us to burn through a few hours talking regardless of who else is around."

I can sense the deep connection between the two of you. Another time. Another place. Who knows what might have been?

"I've thought about that often. After those two nights we spent together, she moved away to pursue her lifelong dream, her life's passion, and it was many years before I saw her again."

Seriously? She left a few days later? That must have crushed you!

"Actually, it didn't. Believe me when I say I rode the high of having my first time with the girl of my dreams for months—no, that's not nearly true—it was a lot longer than that."

I see it now, yes. It was risky of her to give you that. She probably waited until a time when she knew she was about to leave—waited because *of your connection with her; then passed along something—a gift, so to speak—to someone she cared about before she left.*

I asked, "Why do you think that?"

Finding True Love is like an equation, at least this is my current theory, it's an equation that helps me keep track of all the things that are important to me. One important variable in the equation is sex. You began to define that variable with Desire. It's impossible for you to solve the equation without either experiencing it or choosing to make it irrelevant, which comes with its own additional challenges. She gave you the experience to analyze, improve upon, and compare to; she gave you one piece of the puzzle needed to complete your homework.

"My experience with her was intense and hilarious. As a young boy would, I spent *many* occasions reliving it. In fact, I didn't sleep with another girl throughout my remaining high school years."

WHAT?! Come on. Really? Most boys would jump in the sack with any female who had a heartbeat after their first taste of sex. You must be joking.

"No joke."

Why were you so different?

"I'd slept with the most incredibly desirable woman who'd ever been in my life. What would an immature high school girl have to offer me?" I said with a smile.

Promise laughed. *True, I suppose. I'm surprised you didn't sleep with another girl for a totally different reason, though.*

"What reason is that?"

More experience.

"You're getting to know me very quickly, Promise, but Desire asked me to respect her, and lying down with just anyone after her, well, it just didn't seem respectful. Hell, I didn't even tell anyone it happened for several years."

Respect is an important part of the sex variable, and it takes too many people too long to figure it out. There's something to be said for your integrity, especially at such a young age. I'm guessing you were a rare commodity in your age group. And you never told anyone about it? That's impressive, but how did you resist bragging about your conquest?

"For the same reason: respect. I knew she was leaving, but she might someday come back and then, well, who knows. I didn't want to screw up any potential future, for what, bragging rights?"

Well, yeah.

"It's twenty years later, Promise. What would those bragging rights have gotten me?"

Probably an ex-wife and a couple of kids.

"How pessimistic of you!" I lauded, but then added, "But you're probably right."

I usually am.

Instead of challenging the ego of that remark, I asked, "Where to?"

Just drive. Let's keep talking, she said. *It's been too long.*

I thrust the cab out of park and said, "Sounds like a great idea."

There's a road near my childhood home that makes the list of my favorites. Covered by trees on both sides, it winds along a fledgling river to the west and a rocky hillside to the east. It never has much traffic, which prompted us, as teenagers, to maneuver it at high speed at night without any headlights just to see if we could do it—risking life to feel more alive.

Promise had finally come back to me, and though tough at first it hadn't taken long to forgive her absence. Isn't that partly what love is about—being able to forgive and be forgiven—providing the benefit of the doubt for what happened, instead of assuming something was done intentionally to offend? I was happy to have her back, but I was haunted that I might not see her again for a long time. *Is that it?* I thought, and then shook my head to come back to the present; the last thing I needed was to get into an accident with Promise in the back seat.

I made a right turn and said, "This is one of my favorite roads." It passed a secluded neighborhood as it bent to the right and then made a more severe turn to the left, which was followed by a gradual curve back to the right that passed a relatively blind intersection. I let my intuition drive and my mind wander through memories. "Ooops," I claimed calmly, yanking the wheel to the left as the right front tire nudged the gravel on the side of the road.

What are you doing up there? Promise asked. I could hear the concern in her voice.

And then, the engine died.

I put the cab in neutral to keep up our momentum and tried turning the ignition key: nothing, not even a click. I reset the key to the off position and tried it once more while pumping the gas pedal. Still nothing. I pumped the gas once, all the way to the floor making sure the carburetor had fuel, and tried again, which only resulted in flooding the cab with the smell of gasoline.

What's the matter?

I didn't answer until I guided the cab to a stop, leaving the wheels on the right side just off the pavement on the soft shoulder. "The cab won't start," I said, and avoided adding the word "obviously" for fear she'd think I was pointing out that she'd asked a stupid question, which she had. "Fucking cabs," I added, and tried to crank it over again; the result was the same. With a sigh, I sat back in my seat trying to figure out what to do next.

Have you—

A loud crack, like that of a falling tree limb, interrupted Promise's question. It was followed by a splash in the water. I jumped in my seat and felt that spine-tingling sensation so often associated with an unexpected surprise. We both stopped breathing. It was a means to listen for any follow-up noise. Follow-up noises typically incite more action than the initial alert, but it's those who take action first who most often survive—interesting irony between human reaction and non-reaction. It was with this in mind that I began to reach for the ignition once more, and then a single cicada began its song. I overreacted by snapping my neck toward the sound. It seemed to come from under the front of the car. I unbuckled my seatbelt as I slowly, but deliberately, reached over to lock the passenger door. "Lock the doors," I instructed Promise. I heard the back door locks descend as I locked the driver's door.

What—

"Shhh," I quieted Promise.

The cicadas' song increased in volume exponentially as brother invited brother to join the chorus. Large drops of rain began to fall, making hollow metallic sounds like hundreds of acorns falling on the roof of the cab. As the rain intensified, it drowned out the sound of the cicadas; a welcome change from living things to elements. The storm passed quickly—maybe thirty full seconds of rain—leaving it eerily quiet. The change in humidity caused the windows inside the cab to fog up quickly. I wiped my hand over the windshield, but it only stayed clear a few seconds before it fogged up again.

"I think we need to get out of here," I whispered.

Why?

"It doesn't feel right."

I tried the keys in the ignition again. Nothing. As I contemplated what to do next, my hand knocked the keys to the floor. "Shit," I said aloud. My fingers tapped the floor mat, essentially trying to dip into the space like a crane's bucket to retrieve what had been lost. I didn't want to look down for fear of taking my eyes from the foggy windows. Finally, frustrated with my own failure, I looked to the floor mat to find the keys.

A few moments passed before Promise asked, *Um, Soup?*

"What?" I replied a little too forcefully.

It's getting darker.

She was right; the cab had grown much darker. The keys clinked together when my fingertips brushed them. *Finally.* I grabbed them into my palm and found that the windows had become fogged again. With a rapid wipe of my hand, I discovered leaves, tons of them, pasted to the glass. "What the hell?" I flipped the lever to activate the wipers but nothing happened. I toggled it up and down a few times before Promise made me aware of the problem.

Don't the wipers need the keys in the ignition to work?

I rolled my eyes to the left and bit my tongue to keep from saying anything I'd regret, and then jammed the keys into the ignition. There was no response, of course, because the entire car was dead.

The wind rocked the cab slightly as a gust whistled past. *Blow,* I pleaded in my thoughts, as if the word might clear the leaves from the glass.

Promise said, *I don't think I like your dreams.*

Another gust lifted the cab and I began to bounce in the seat yelling, "Come on. Blow, baby, blow!" As if Velcro was being ripped apart, the leaves were eventually peeled from the windows. "Later, suckers!" I yelled.

Soup, look ahead.

Surprised, I saw an old tow truck sitting in front of us. I rolled down the window and flagged the driver. Strangely, I thought of Richard Dreyfuss stopped at the railroad tracks reading a map in *Close Encounters of the Third Kind*. He waved a vehicle behind him to go around never seeing that it went over his truck instead of around it.

The tow truck flipped on its flashing lights and slowly inched its way past the front bumper of the cab until it stopped even with my door. The driver's window dropped jerkily, evidence of an old fashioned crank, just like the one in the cab. As it opened, I heard the faint sound of a very recognizable song:

> *"Second time around,*
> *I'm still believing words that you said.*
> *You said you'd always be here,*
> *'In love forever,'*
> *Still repeats in my head.*
> *You can't finish what you start.*
> *If this is love it breaks my heart."*

A bright, orange circle of light intensified as the driver inhaled through his cigar to reveal his chubby, stubbly face for the first time. Upon exhale, he said in a thick, country accent, "Whut—uh—seems ta be the pro'lem 'ere?" If ever Stephen King was going to play a bit part in one of his movies, this was his character.

"Cab won't start," I answered.

"You try pumpin' the gahs?" he asked.

"Yes," I replied, pushing aside the need to explain that I wasn't a complete idiot.

"You akchally *got* gas in 'er?"

"Yessir," I answered.

He chuckled. "You'd be sir-prised." He took a long puff from his cigar as he thought.

"I bet," I added, as the smell of his stogie finally reached me.

"Let's say," he said. The sound of "say" was actually the word "see." "You got laights?"

"No lights," I said, as I pulled the plunger for them in and out quickly a few times, deftly not *all the way out* again, to prove my answer. He looked over his shoulder to see if I was lying.

"Hmmmph." Another long pull from the cigar lit up his face. I noticed a cock-eyed "CAT" ball cap sitting on his head, the kind that still had mesh on the back half. He shook his cigar at me from between his fingers as if he'd finally figured out the problem. "I cud git out 'n look, but it's-a gonna caust ya."

"I've got money," I said, having no idea whether I had money or not.

"Money?" He laughed. "MONEY?!" The whole truck bounced up and down like he was jolly St. Nick in his rust bucket of a sled. When his laughing ceased, he said, "Fer shits 'n giggles, give 'er anudda craink."

I shrugged and figured, why not. Nothing happened, not even a click. I looked back to the truck and its jovial driver.

He frowned at me. "You know eneethang 'bout magnats?"

"You mean, like, opposites attract?" I asked, my own frown replicating his.

"Yep," he said. "Now, fergit it."

"Forget what?" I was unsure whether he meant "fergit it," like, forget what he was about to say, or "fergit it," like, forget that opposites attract.

He gestured by making a circular motion with his cigar to suggest that I give the cab another try.

I did nothing but stare straight ahead. I knew, if I turned the key I'd get the same result. And I'd already fallen to the bottom of the list of Men Who Know Something About Cars.

He hmmmph'ed again. "I kin feel that from hare. So kin they," he said as he flashed his cigar in an upward direction indicating a "they" out there somewhere. "Gitcher head straiyht."

What the hell was this guy going on about? Get my head straight? I just wanted this damn cab to start.

Try it, Promise whispered, so as not to be heard by the tow truck driver.

"START!" I thought as I turned the key, and shockingly the engine roared to life. At the same time the headlights flipped on, the wipers scraped across the windshield, and the radio blasted the same tune as his tow truck—all in all, scaring the shit out of me.

"WHOOO-WHEEEE!" he cheered, chuckling hard enough to make his shock absorbers squeal.

"I guess," I said, smiling, but not quite sure what had changed other than luck.

He leaned forward and flipped off his flashing lights. As he straightened up, he turned back toward me and said, "Happens a lot in 'nees parts." He stuffed the stogie back into his mouth, reached for the gearshift, and before he drove off said, "Watch aut fer the purdy gurl."

I watched his taillights disappear through the side view mirror. "The pretty girl?" I asked aloud as it started to rain again. In his dialect, I asked Promise, "He talkin' 'bout chu?"

I have no idea, she said, totally baffled by the whole scene. *But I hope not. Can we get out of here before something else totally fucking weird happens?*

"You think *this* is weird? Hang around a little while and watch what my mind can do."

Is this some passive aggressive attempt at getting *me to leave?*

"No-no, I like having you here."

If you like it, then let's get out of here. Your favorite road is far from my favorite.

"Is there a road you prefer?" I asked.

Pick another favorite; a less creepy one this time, please.

"My favorite, aside from this one, would be a long drive from here."

No problem. Remember, you're in my world; things are much different here. Time is under your control; we can skip through years in the blink of an eye or rewind to look at things in slow motion. We can also jump from place to place; you're the one who holds the remote control.

"And where is this remote control?" I was a creative man, so I had no trouble accepting the parameters, but I didn't quite understand the way it was supposed to work.

It's in your head, she replied.

Confused, I failed to find an acceptable follow-up question to her answer.

Soupy, you started the car. Just believe.

"Believe in what, a flying car?"

If you want, but that wouldn't be the quickest way to get where you want to go.

"What's faster than a flying car…a flying car with turbo jets?"

Minutely better, I guess.

And then I had it. Many of my memories are tied to music, having had a musically inclined father, so I immediately started singing. "Ventura Highway, in the sunshine." Promise joined in for the next verse. "Where the days are longer, the nights are stronger, than moooonshine. You're gonna go, I know-ooo-ohh-ooo-ohh-ooo-ohh." Before us, like photographic slides in a carousel changing from one to the next, the outside switched instantaneously from a tiny road in the woods to a beautiful, ocean-side highway on a sparkling summer day.

"SHA-ZAM!" I exclaimed, feeling proud of my maneuver.

Shazam?

"Didn't you have a television growing up?"

I'm not going to answer on the grounds that—

"It might give me too much info? Yeah-yeah."

On a highway I'm always checking the mirrors around me. If ever I need to make a lane change, emergency or otherwise, I know which way I can go. However, with Promise in the backseat and the rule not to "see" her, I adjusted the rear view mirror so it would only give me a view of the cab's ceiling. I also maneuvered into the slow lane of the highway. No rush to get anywhere.

"You know, you could've told me about this little trick earlier."

With so much to cover, we'll just have to learn as we go.

"There's no manual in the glove box?" I asked, and reached for the compartment.

'Fraid not. Nice place you picked, by the way, she added.

"Love it here. Always have," I replied. "Who wouldn't?"

I agree.

We enjoyed the drive until a red sports car zipped past us well above the speed limit.

So many cars driving past this awesome scenery, yet no one ever stops and everyone's in such a big hurry. Have you ever stopped?

"Yeah, I have a thing for highlighting roads on a map. And the best roads for stopping aren't usually these big ones with four or five lanes in each direction. I like to get off the road and stop where everything's moving a little more slowly. I glanced back and forth between the road and the ocean for several seconds and wondered if we should stop. Instead, I asked, "Anything in particular you'd like to talk about?"

Yeah, actually there is. What the hell happened back there?

"Car died." I continued the sarcasm by adding, "Like, literally, dead, but then, it just started again, like it was waiting for me to *really, really want* it to start again."

No shit, Soupy, I was there. Does that happen often?

I shrugged and said, "It's my first time as a cab driver. I wouldn't know."

Of course, she added.

"However, the tow truck driver said that it happens with regularity in 'nees' parts, whatever that means."

What do you think it means?

"No idea. You?"

No idea, either.

"How about we take a breath, smell the ocean air, and talk about something else, then?"

I heard her roll down the rear window a few inches before a roar of wind filled the cab. She took a deep breath before she rolled the window back up.

"Better?"

Yes, thank you.

"Okay, then let's talk about something else. This thing right here, this whole enter my dreams thing—so tell me how you do it?"

Billy Ocean's hit song entered my head and immediately began playing on the radio:

"Get out of my dreams;

Get into my car.

Get in the backseat, baby!"

Though relevant, I still rolled my eyes at the lyrics because it would take at least an hour to get it out of my head.

As if she didn't hear the song, Promise answered, *It's what my family does; we've perfected the skill of communicating in dreams. When I was very young, my mother would visit my dreams and talk to me. At first, so I could hear her voice and sleep more soundly, but eventually she taught me the way.*

"That's cool. Can you teach me?"

Ancient family secret, she said in a poorly executed Asian accent, which was a blatant rip off from the detergent commercials from our childhood.

I playfully growled at Promise before asking, "Was it hard to learn?"

I definitely had my challenges.

"How so?"

Not everyone's dreams are pleasant. Only through experience can you learn when to stay and when to leave.

"So you can choose when to leave, but not always when to return?"

Yes, thankfully, it would be torturous if that weren't possible.

"Did you find yourself close to leaving *this* dream when the cab stalled?"

No, she quickly replied. *We're in this together.*

"Good answer." I smiled. "What might prompt you to leave?"

You don't really want to know.

"Come on!" I pleaded.

No, really. Just use your imagination.

"You have a confidentiality agreement or something? Like a doctor or a lawyer?"

No, but maybe I should.

"Is it always like this?" I asked wagging my finger back and forth over my shoulder between the two of us.

Like what?

"Like you and I driving around in a cab having a conversation about whatever?"

Yes and no. Sometimes I talk and sometimes I don't. Sometimes I just listen and other times I only watch. The context can be really strange or absolutely normal, and like talking, sometimes it's important and other times it's not.

"Alright then, so let me ask this, how often do you actually interact?"

Not as often as I'd like. Believe me, I can see the solutions or I know exactly what to say about a particular problem, but most people aren't listening.

"Do you think that's the demarcation?"

The line between those who want to listen and those who don't?

"I don't know about 'want,' maybe more like 'don't even realize it's an option,' but yeah."

Hmm. I don't know if there's a reason why some people engage and others don't. It's not really up to me. If the host recognizes me or hears me, then I typically engage. It doesn't always happen that way, though. I used to freak out when I'd talk on and on and no one would respond. I'd eventually shout to try and get someone's attention. It took a long time to know when I was supposed to shut up and learn something important about that person, and when I was actually supposed to engage. I never know when a dream is meant to teach.

"Have you revealed who you are to everyone?" I asked, not sure if I wanted to know the answer.

No. For everyone else, I'm like a figment of imagination. It's my job to figure out what someone needs from a dream—criticism, compliment, kick in the ass—and help resolve whatever issue exists in their real world.

"And your parents?"

I don't know much about them. I left when I was old enough to take care of myself. It's hard to be close to someone else who also has my ability; things get all crossed up and confused.

"Why?"

We jump from dream to dream so frequently, it's hard to have someplace called "home" when you're rarely there. Better making anywhere you go someplace you can call "home."

"I'm with you on that one, but was it tough to leave your parents?"

Not as much as you might think. It wasn't a surprise decision; it's the way for us. My father prepared me for the harsh reality of the world and my Mother gave me the compassion to live in it. I wanted to see as much of the world as I could before it was time for me to find you. And when I say "see," understand that I can see more of the world by looking into dreams than I ever could traveling on my own. It was my way of becoming more worldly and worthy of True Love. I knew I had to leave, so when it was time to go, it was no problem to do it.

"Does the line blur betw—?"

Between the real world and the dream world, yes, I thought you would get to that question eventually. And yes, I do exist in the real world, but I have to work very hard at marking the difference between my real world and someone else's dream world.

"But aren't some dreams better than the real world?"

For some, but never for you...or for me. Soup, you can't have it.

"Have what?"

Have what you are about to ask me for. Go ahead, just ask.

"Can we just start our lives together right now, right here in the dream world?"

You'll wake up at some point.

"So what? Then maybe I'll just start sleeping more than I'm awake."

You've forgotten that part of our assignment is to be an example to the rest of the world—the rest of the real *world.*

"Dream world doesn't count?"

Nope. Real world, Soupy.

"Stupid rules." I paused for a moment before adding, "I could live with my life if you were in my dreams every night."

But you'd be a failure, she chided.

"You ruin all the fun," I said.

Promise prompted, *'Bout time you told me about another love, don't you think?*

"You're the customer," I said, tipping my head in respect.

We'd just left my hometown for this coastal drive and we now had to go back. I felt cocky, so I closed my eyes and imagined the street just outside the house where I met my first love. When I saw it in my mind, I yelled, "GO!"

BRAAAAAAAAKE! Promise screamed as I opened my eyes and jammed both feet down on the brake pedal. The cab wheels locked up, making a tremendous racket. My front and the rear bumper of another cab in front of me came within an inch of each other, maybe even air kissed like the cheek-to-cheek greeting of two foreign friends, before our speeds equalized and our cab skidded sideways to a stop while the other kept heading down the street..

"DUDE!" I yelled and raised my hands at the cab in front of me though, technically, I'd been the one not paying enough attention. "Forgot to account for that when we made the hyper-jump. My bad," I admitted to Promise after taking a deep breath. I flipped on the blinker for a right turn into a driveway, which I was perfectly positioned to make despite nearly killing everyone.

Yeah, so much for beginner's luck. You might want to work on the transition thing.

I thought it best not to offer a response.

We drove up the long driveway through a stand of trees that provided the house with visual privacy from the road. As we got nearer, Promise squealed, *IS THAT HER?!*

"Shhh," I quieted her. "Geez, how do you know they can't hear you?"

Female intuition, she answered. *Ooo! And that's you!*

I parked the cab twenty feet from the persons she referenced and rolled down my window in an attempt to hear their conversation.

If you want to hear what they're saying, try the radio.

"Seriously? Wait. Forget I asked." I reached for the radio volume and turned it up enough to hear every word.

* * *

"Hey," she said, her shoulder length, straight, blonde hair flitting in the breeze.

"Hey," I replied.

"In my country, 'hej' means 'hi.'" It was the first time she'd ever been to the United States.

I giggled lightly and scratched my head with my index finger. "Yeah, in mine, too."

She let out a hearty laugh and I joined her. "What I mean is, 'hej,' h-e-j, is short for 'hejsan,' h-e-j-s-a-n, which means 'hello.'"

"Ahhh, I get it." I was still smiling. "Well, 'hey,' h-e-y, which is kinda short for h-e-y-space-y-o-u, is one way we greet each other here in the States."

"Okaaay," she said with a raised brow, a smile, and a slight hop.

I waited for small birds to land on her shoulder and start a song—she was that perky—and the thought prompted a slightly larger smile to appear on my face.

"Jes?" she asked. For her, Ys came out sounding like Js.

"Nothing," I said, trying to quell the pending outburst of laughter driven wholly by the fact that I was totally smitten with her presence, both physically and socially. "Some Disney cartoon entered my thoughts," I said, brushing the air with my hand to wave the thought away.

Her face showed that she didn't understand, but that was my point.

"You got a nice day for your arrival," I said, pointing to the blue sky.

She looked about and agreed, "Jes."

I stared at her face as she looked around, sneaking a peek as they say, but her eyes came back quickly. Mine darted away, but I'd already been caught. I slowly faced her once again, fully blushing. We both smiled.

"Do ju come here often?" she asked.

I couldn't contain myself anymore, laughter exploded from me. Doubled over, I held up a finger to indicate that I'd explain. When I could speak again, I placed a hand on her upper arm and said, "That question is usually reserved for us as a pick-up line." Hurriedly, I added, "Not that I would know, except for the fact that I've seen it in movies."

She put on her biggest smile and shrugged.

"Yes," I added. "I come here very often."

She hopped again, and said, "Then I will see ju soon." She turned and walked inside.

"Yes, I think you will," I whispered and waved.

* * *

I touched my index finger to mid-air, said "Pause," and the scene in front of us paused. "Cool," I added, and then rewound the picture by circling my finger in the air in a counterclockwise direction until I had a frame of her smile.

Spill it, Soup! What's the deal? That was practically the simplest, sweetest first conversation I've ever heard!

"We said what needed to be said, I guess."

More with your eyes than your words, I think.

"And smiles," I said and admired the beauty of hers frozen in front of me. It had been too long since I saw it; I blushed and felt light hearted. "Honesty was a foreign exchange student during my senior year of high school. Just so happened she lived in a house where I spent nearly as much of my high school upperclassman years as I did at my own. As times change and we grow up, so do those we spend our lives with, you know? We had cars now; it was easier to travel and I didn't have to walk everywhere or get a ride from my parents."

Understood.

"From the first moment I saw her, I dropped what I was doing and forgot what I was thinking, as I'm sure you can imagine after watching that clip. Seriously. Wow. I mean, just seeing her like this again makes my heart melt. Everything I'd dreamed of *you* being was suddenly right there in front of me."

Too cute! Promise was bouncing on the back seat with excitement, making it squeak like an old mattress.

"What on Earth are you doing back there?" I asked, laughing.

I need popcorn for this movie! I'm excited!

It struck me as odd that she was excited about some other relationship in my life, which obviously hadn't worked out or we wouldn't be here. Before I could say more, Promise added in a terrible accent, *I get to learn about juuu!*

"What's with you and the accents?" I asked, chiding her.

Puh-lease, like you don't do it, too.

She had me there. "Whatever," I said, playfully. I took my index finger, and like touching a tablet, swiped it across the air and flipped through a bunch of frames to the next conversation. "We had a few weeks at the end of the summer before school started. Like this one."

* * *

"What do ju like about me?" Honesty asked. We were sitting outside, cross-legged, facing each other on a blanket.

Immediately embarrassed, I replied sheepishly, "Your smile." It caused her to smile and I brushed a thumb across her cheek then tucked a strand of hair behind her ear that had been blowing across her face.

"Kiss me," she said, and I happily obliged.

* * *

I paused the frame on our kiss.

Well played, Mr. Soupy.

"What can I say? 'Twas no lie. In fact, I gave her that answer every time she asked; it was the honest truth. I loved talking with her."

And kissing her.

"Well, yeah." I flipped through the frames again until day turned to night and a car pulled up next to us. "At that age, we didn't have a place to hang out in private—you know, to make out—so we'd drive around talking about whatever came to mind."

That was probably unique to her—spending that much time in a car—it's such a big part of the culture here in the States.

"Indeed, it was. We often lost track of time," I admitted. "We'd get lost in our own world of conversation talking about what this means and what that means and how things are different between her country and mine."

Bliss.

"However, we always made sure we got back to her house well before her curfew."

What? Why would you do—

"To make out. Duh." I said "Play" and the scene set into motion once more.

You set me up for that one.

"Sho' 'nuff," I admitted. "Mom—we all called her that—would flash the outdoor light when we'd reached her curfew."

Promise laughed aloud.

I shook my head and said nothing, allowing Promise to have her moment. With my thumb, I motioned to have her look out the left window where Honesty and I were embraced in a lengthy kiss in the car next to us.

Awwwww, Promise cooed.

"Enough," I said, but enjoyed watching just as much as she did.

The light over the garage flashed and Honesty jumped from the car. She was close enough for me to reach out of my window and touch her. I fought the urge to do so as she pushed the car door closed and bounded off into the house. Watching her go, I reminisced of the innocent afterglow, and then realized I could look to my left and witness it. My younger face was satisfied, happy, unblinking, elated—those were the words that came to mind—it had been a long time, in the real world, since I'd felt that way, a very long time.

"Honesty and I quickly fell in love. I was her first love and she was mine. Each tender moment together became the first impression of that moment—etched into our memories as the first we'd ever shared so deeply. Any outsider who looked at us would roll their eyes immediately and claim, 'Lovebirds.'"

I forwarded to a scene where the two of us were holding hands. Honesty and Soupy walked past the front of the cab from right to left, and each time they reached the far left I'd rewind the video to roll them back to the other side, forcing them to walk past again.

Lovebirds. Les inseparables.

"Say what?"

In French, "lovebirds" are often called "the inseparables."

"Oui. That we were." I pondered our inseparable nature before I continued, "As I said before, we just wanted to be together. I helped her master English while she taught me a few phrases in her own language. Her voice was music to my ears; it was a song I'd listen to as long as she was willing to sing."

Toootal lovebirds, she said, drawing out the long "o" in "total."

"When I introduced Honesty to my family, they loved her—*absolutely* loved her."

Duh. Who wouldn't? Look at her!

"I didn't have a family member who *didn't* want to talk with her. Hell, it was like they were lined up to keep her sitting in the living room for hours while they all took their turns. Afterward, each one would come tell me how wonderful she is—Honesty this and Honesty that—and all I could do was smile and nod my head. 'I know,' I'd say."

Her smile must have been contagious, just look at her! Your family caught it, too!

"And vice versa with *my* smile, her mom even caught the contagion though she was thousands of miles away. She wrote a letter to Honesty saying I sounded like a dream come true."

I dragged Honesty and Soupy back, in reverse, to the far right and let them walk past again. "My dad, creative man that he is, started calling me Mr. Mild."

Mr. Mild?

"MILD, an acronym for Mother In-Law's Dream," I admitted.

Cheekily, Promise repeated the name and giggled.

"At this point, you'd think everything was roses, right?"

Absolutely!

"We've got to mosey down the road a few blocks—mosey back home to show you how things stopped being so rosy."

Soup? What did you do? she said. I could hear her foot tapping against the back of the seat in anticipation of scolding me.

After reversing the cab, I drove down the driveway and headed back toward the neighborhood we'd visited earlier. We drove in fast-forward. The sun raced below the horizon to usher the night into our theater. "Several months into our relationship, like any right-minded teenagers, we decided to get intimate while my parents were out of the house."

I feel worried.

"Wait for it," I said.

I parked the cab in front of my house. Raising both hands, I touched my index fingers together and then pulled them apart, creating a cinema screen on the garage door in front of us.

* * *

"I want to sleep with ju," Honesty whispered in my ear with her enchanting accent.

I kissed her and moved my hands to the buttons on her shirt. With a smile, our eyes met, and I looked down to focus on the clasps, snaps, and zippers we'd have to overcome to reach our goal. Each breath of hers landed on my forehead, and as each hurdle was leapt, the pace of her heart and breath increased. Heat radiated from her naked body, and she picked up where I left off, overcoming the hurdles that my clothing presented. For the first time in our lives, we were naked together, her on top of me, all hurdles behind us. We paused to take in the moment. I slowly ran my hands up from the base of her back, across her shoulders, caressed her neck, and then, with her cheeks in both of my hands, we kissed. No words were exchanged, simply a knowing look, and with that came the beginning of a feverish intimacy we'd thought about frequently, but never entertained.

Nerves returned as she was poised to lower her body onto mine.

"Are you okay?" I asked.

"Jes," she replied. "I'm not nervous, I yust want it to be the right time."

"I know," I replied, smoothing her arms with the gentle touch of my hands. "Is it?"

She nodded, indicating that it was, but her body didn't respond to her decision. Her hands on my chest were supporting her weight that, in order to make love, would have to transfer to her torso. We were frozen in the same position for only a few seconds, but they felt like lifetimes.

I sensed her fear in the dark. "We don't have to do this yet, Honesty," I said as I pulled her face close to mine, moving her body away from its precarious position.

"But I want ju, Soupy," she replied, and tears came to her eyes.

"I know you do. And I want you, too." I stroked her hair as she laid her head on my chest.

"Promise me we'll try again soon," she pleaded.

"Only when we're both ready." We lay there holding and caressing each other for a while longer. I'd never felt closer to her than I did in that moment, bare to the world and in each other's arms. In the dark, where many people find their fears, we'd confronted one we both shared. Though we didn't conquer it, we were more familiar with it from that day forward.

* * *

You are a good and perceptive man, Soupy Heller.

"Thank you, Promise." I closed the cinema screen I'd created on the garage and sat there in the dark. "Things didn't get any easier after that."

Do you mean sexually, or—

"Just everything, Promise. It all went to shit. Though my friends were great guys, they grew weary of Honesty's bubbly demeanor. They complained to me about it constantly. She was *always* asking questions about this, that, and the other."

She was curious! Promise said adamantly.

"I know! But I felt torn—torn between this budding love and these guys I'd known for most of my life." My hands pounded the steering wheel in frustration. A car pulled up behind us, blocking the driveway, and honked its horn. "Carpool to school," I said, just as the younger me bounded out the front door of my house, down the stairs, and into the car. "It was every morning, every afternoon, *every damn minute* I spent with my friends that they complained about how often Honesty smiled." I threw the cab into reverse and followed the other car to school.

Let me get this straight, your friends didn't like it when a girl smiled?

"Nope."

Did they not realize that making girls smile is key to keeping them around?

My heart took on two states: it hurt as I relived this immaturity that defined my relationship with Honesty so many years ago, and it swelled in yearning for Promise. I felt like an idiot, just as I'd felt every other time I'd thought back on how I treated Honesty.

Promise asked, *How did you deal with their complaints?*

"I shrugged them off initially, with a pop on the shoulder or a 'Come on, dude' meant to tell them I wasn't taking them seriously. But like I said, it became the topic of every minute I spent around them." In a whiney voice, I mimicked, "'She smiles too much. She asks too many questions.' They drove me nuts with it! Feeling torn between love and friendships, I started to believe them, to agree with them. It makes me sick to admit it. When her and I were alone, it became hard *not* to hear my friends' voices in my head."

We sat at a stoplight. I stared out the side window with my chin on my elbow, unable to shake the sullen feeling.

It had to be difficult to feel the pull between a woman you'd just met and two friends you'd known your entire life. Don't beat yourself up too much, Soup.

"One night, when I couldn't take it anymore, I asked Honesty to leave a party with me even though I told my friends I'd drive them home. Her and I left without telling everyone goodbye. I needed, *just needed,* some alone time with her away from all the bullshit. Imagine a rare, beautiful flower that you've decided to stop watering because you'd rather watch it wilt before your eyes; that was our love, a little more brown on the edges each day."

The light turned green, but I'd not noticed. Several cars behind us honked, which woke me from my contemplative state. I raised my right hand inside the cab, not caring if they saw my apologetic wave through the back window. My foot hammered the accelerator and the cab lurched away from the light and up the hill, putting as much distance as I possibly could between us and those I'd offended.

Goodness, Soup, Promise said, calmly, even though I heard the sound of her hands reaching for something to hold onto. *I think you need a break.*

Chapter 9

I woke from my slumber, fully clothed, in my motel room and didn't feel at all rested, but resting and drinking don't often sleep in the same bed. I'd fallen asleep leaning against the headboard with my head to one side, which was the reason for the crick in my neck. Remains of the burrito, brown paper bag and balled up aluminum foil, slept on the cheap motel carpet. For the umpteenth time, I heard how the Yankees came from behind in extra innings to win, which was confirmation that this wasn't a dream; the Yankees would have lost by at least a dozen runs if I were still dreaming.

Bladder alarm. I *really* had to pee. Gravity carried me to the bathroom like the floor had suddenly tilted downward in that direction. I unzipped, placed a hand against the wall over the toilet, and let it flow. For a man, there is this moment between action and relief when we hold our breath, waiting, until the stream emerges, often bringing forth a sigh as we're satisfied by the comforting flow and splash of liquid. There's a reason the sound of water makes you want to pee.

"A maaaan's bladder," I said, gruffly, after I'd been standing, and peeing, for nearly a full minute. A hiccup followed my exclamation, and that was cause enough to giggle at how drunk I still was. As I laughed, my stream shot over the side of the toilet and onto the floor. “Whoa. Buckle up, hombre. Check ya-self before ya wreck ya-self, this is an eight-ball piss.” With refocused determination, I finished the task, or so I thought. I began to tuck and turn, but then quickly turned back to urination position, re-aimed, and returned to the task. “EIGGGGGGHT BALLLLLLL,” I exclaimed, wobbling so much I was forced to reach out and grab the towel rack over the toilet for balance.

Bladder empty, I stumbled away from the stool and left a trail of clothes from bathroom to bed before flopping into it and wrestling with the bedspread and sheets beneath my weight. With enormous effort, I kicked all the covers and pillows away but for one covering sheet, and instantly resumed my previous sleeping state.

Chapter 10

As soon as I'd fallen back to sleep, my eyes opened again.

Promise broke the silence by saying, *Welcome back.*

"Snow?" I asked.

Yep. You act like you're surprised to see it.

"I guess." I paused for a moment, then added, "it *is* the next step in my story about Honesty." Our cab was idling in the middle of the street, perpendicular to the flow of traffic should there have been any, pointed in the direction of a duplex. "Happy New Year, Promise."

Happy New Year?

"Yep."

Well then, Happy New Year to you, too, Soup.

"I'm not a fan of New Year's Eve. Too many crowds. Too many people drinking. Too many people driving. And besides, I never have anyone to kiss. Even when I do—oh, I'll just tell the story."

Out with the old and in with the new.

I thought about what Promise had just said, *Out with the old and in with the new,* and replied, "What's wrong with something old?"

Between you and me? Nothing. Too much of the world likes everything shiny and new.

Promise's reply rammed home the emotional moral to Honesty's story as if she already knew the end. I pointed at the figure standing in our headlights and said, "Should I stay or should I go now? That's me, perhaps hard to tell with all the winter gear on." My hands were stuffed in my jacket pockets as I rocked back and forth on my Nikes to keep my body moving in the frigid air. "This was a moment of decision: stop in at the New Year's Eve party or walk over to Honesty's house and spend the evening with her."

Why wasn't Honesty at the party?

"Sick."

That sucks.

"I'd walked to the party even though it was chilly, since I didn't want to drive home after a few drinks. It would have only a few more minutes to walk down the street to Honesty's place."

As Promise and I watched, Soupy reached into his pocket and removed a small, flat, black stone. He ran his thumb over the smooth sides of it, obviously contemplating his choices. Something wasn't right because he looked at both sides of the stone repeatedly before placing it back into his pocket.

"It was cold," I said.

What does that mean? Promise asked.

I shivered, not from the temperature inside the cab, but from watching Soupy walk into the house. "I didn't remember that stone ever being cold before; it always held warmth."

Why did you have a stone in your pocket?

"Oh, sorry. I haven't explained that, have I? My great grandpa gave it to me when I was a child. Oddly, it sort of has a tendency to be around when I'm faced with a difficult decision. And when that happens, I flip it."

You flip a rock?

"Yep."

Does it have a head and a tail?

"Nope."

Then, how do you know what's been decided?

"I just know," I replied.

Promise answered with silence.

"I decided to stop for a drink at the party, say hi to friends while I warmed up a bit, then walk the rest of the way to Honesty's house. Several drinks later, I was still there."

Two friends tumbled out of the house and started wrestling on the front lawn; a ritual that they'd formed—though neither of them could tell you how or why it started—and the end result was always the same: grass stains on their jeans, nothing more. Soupy followed them out, drink in hand, watching as they grappled.

People walked in and out of the party. Each time they passed Soupy, someone would ask, "Where's Honesty?" and Soupy would reply, "Sick," and they would add, "Sucks," and he would say, "Yeah."

Everyone was used to you and Honesty being together.

"Yeah."

You two really were inseparable. Lovebirds.

"Do you think I made it all up?" I asked.

Oh no, Soup. Third-party confirmation is always nice to have, though.

"People asked so often I couldn't actually carry a fluid conversation. I should've taken it as a sign to go see Honesty."

Why is that?

"Another girl at the party had been a crush of mine for many years."

No.

"Yes," I said, guiltily.

Show me.

"Who she is isn't important; not to take anything away from her, but her role is ultimately only a bit part."

You need to explain yourself.

I sighed audibly and then continued the story, "Every girl I've ever dated has had a sparkle about her, or I never would have dated her for very long. This girl was very cute, but that was only part of my interest. My quirky attraction came from her totally, without a doubt kooky character combined with her off-the-charts book smarts. We'd known each other for many years, but I was surprised every day by the random things she said."

She arrived at the house, hugged me while I stood on the porch, and then continued into the party. As she walked away, her hand grabbed mine, tugging it gently, but firmly, to coax me inside. I shook my head, not with any real resistance, only to make her beg more intently. Still holding my hand, she pressed her tall, thin frame against mine, ran the fingernails of her free hand over the back of my neck, and whispered into my ear. After that I didn't resist any longer.

"There are a lot of excuses I could use to explain why I went back into the party: beer, the attraction, hanging with friends—"

But?

"Hormones? A calling? Experience? I don't know. There are nights when I just can't make sense of myself, and I guess on this night I stopped making decisions and let someone else make them for me."

Was she American?

"Yeah," I answered. "But what's that got to do with anything?"

She was a better-known quantity to you than Honesty. You didn't have to tell her everything about you because she already knew you well. With all of the struggles you were feeling in the tug-of-war between your friends and Honesty, this girl provided a comfort zone, or place for you to rest. After you'd put so much into teaching Honesty about you, maybe you were just worn out?

"You might be right, but it's still no excuse."

I'm not try—

save her.

—ing to give you an excuse.

"What?" I asked.

I said, I'm not trying to—

"No, I heard that part, but what did you say in the middle of it?"

In the middle of it? What on Earth are—

save her.

—you talking about?

"THERE! It happened again! Are you saying 'save her' in the middle of your sentences?"

Save her? What? No.

"Well, someone is. If it isn't you then who is it?"

I still have no idea what the hell you're talking about.

save her.

"Did you say it that time?"

Say what?

"If you're fucking with me, just tell me now. Seriously. If this is payback for the dead engine thing, I'm telling you, I didn't do it on purpose!"

And I'm not saying anything like "save her!" Save who?

"HOW SHOULD I KNOW?!"

I don't know what—

"SHHH! Wait."

A few seconds passed as the scent of the girl on the front lawn took over Soupy's senses.

yessssss. save her.

"Oh shit. OH! SHIT!" I shouted, straightening up in my seat and pointing at the house. "THAT'S THE VOICE I HEARD THAT NIGHT!"

Promise grew more frantic in my ear, *What voice?*

"THAT ONE!" I shouted and forcefully tapped my finger on my head. "I REMEMBER!"

I turned up the radio's volume as far as it would go, loud enough to hear the white noise from the speakers. Suddenly, a snake-like hiss filled the interior of the cab as the voice again whispered, *now kiss her.*

"THERE!" I snapped my fingers at the radio, "THE—"

SHHH! Promise demanded.

A few moments of silence passed, and then it yelled, *KISS HER!*

Promise and I jumped so fiercely the cab rocked. "LOOK! LOOK, PROMISE!" I pointed to the porch, "THERE I GO BACK INTO THE HOUSE! SHIT!" I reached for the door handle to jump out of the cab and stop myself from doing what I'd done so many years prior.

Soupy.

After throwing the door open, I put my bare feet down on the cold, icy road—

SOUPY.

"Promise, I need shoes. I don't have shoes. Do you have my shoes?" I searched the passenger seat, floorboards, and glove box.

SOUPY!

"SHOES!" I retorted.

Promise screamed my name, *SOUPY!*

I continued to rummage around in the front of the cab for anything that could protect my bare feet from the cold pavement.

Promise screamed, *YOU CAN'T CHANGE IT!* The radio picked up her frequency to amplify her scream as she kicked hard against the back of my seat. *I DON'T WANT TO LOSE YOU!*

That got my attention. I froze before whimpering, "But that was the voice. The voice I heard that night. The voice that drove my appetite for affection. That voice, Promise." I was defeated, and in defeat I watched as the door to the house closed behind Soupy. It was too late now anyway.

You can't do anything about it, Promise sternly said, but I could sense the empathy behind it.

"I know, but I really fucked up that night," I said on the verge of tears.

I can see that, and I feel for you, and that's why I'm here.

"If I could just—" I threw my hand at the house as a gesture to throw the memory away, but then pressed the inside of my forearm against my eyes in an attempt not to cry. "That voice. That fucking voice. That—"

Talk to me.

"That's the voice I heard in my head that night. The one that said 'save me.'" Just saying those two words brought anger and sorrow to their boiling points.

Yes, I heard it.

"It confused me, Promise. I'd never heard it before, and I'd forgotten about it until now."

Breathe, Soupy. I'm right here.

I just stared at the house.

Do you know the voice?

I thought for a moment, “No, at least I don’t think so. I don’t know, Promise, it’s kind of hard to think right now.”

Because it sounded an awful lot like the voice I heard when you were, you know, having your dream within a dream.

“It did?” I wanted to turn around, look her in the eyes, and *know* she was telling the truth.

Yes, it did.

“What the hell is going on around here?”

Your dream, Promise said.

“Yeah, my dream. My fucking reality.”

There’s more to this story, isn’t there? Maybe telling it, getting it over with, will help us both get through it.

“Yeah, okay,” I gathered myself before I started by exhaling deeply. “Unable to find any privacy at the party I followed her downstairs, sat on the couch, and kissed her. I forgot that anyone else was there. I wanted all of her, every inch of skin, every fiber of her being, every yelp, moan, and exclamation that intimately signaled to keep going. I let her pull my body into her chest and between her legs. I didn’t care if anyone saw us, and since it was a small house everyone saw us. She kept telling those who walked downstairs, ‘We’re just talking!’ How she found the breath to speak between kisses, I’ll never know. Those who saw us turned around and went back upstairs, embarrassed for me, I suppose. As you know, they all knew how inseparable Honesty and I were, and being witness to my infidelity was too much for them.”

Soupy, you loved talking with Honesty any hour of the day, or so you said, and “just talking” with this other girl was your excuse? If I could reach over this seat and smack you upside the head, Soupy Robert, I’d do so in a heartbeat. You, of all people, YOU ARE NEVER JUST TALKING.

“I know. I fucked up. I can’t argue with you. It’s not enough hook to hang a hat on, but Promise, I swear to you that ‘just talking’ never materialized into anything beyond ‘just kissing.’ I’m sorry to admit that it would have been a different matter in that driven state of mind if we’d actually had privacy. I wish I could say differently, but I gave myself to her and followed wherever she wanted to lead. I *am* thankful, so very thankful, that it didn’t progress beyond lips. I simply can't imagine the guilt being any heavier than it already is…or was…or is…whatever."

You were, what, eighteen years old? You can go a little easier on yourself. Not much, but a little.

"I awoke the next morning in a terrified haze. You know that feeling when you can't sleep any longer and if you lay there you'll just stare at the ceiling until you drive yourself crazy?"

Ummm—

"Never mind. When I woke up, I knew what I had to do. *Knew it* like I know my, my what, I don't know…the back of my own hands or the contours of my face or the mole on the side of my neck that I always knick when shaving, Hmmm, I guess if I knick it I don't know it, but you know what I mean: knew it like I *know myself.* I *knew* I had to get to Honesty's house and tell her what happened before anyone else did."

Yeah, you better, she said, flatly.

"At that moment, I didn't think much past the express need for pouring it all out. I was just a kid, you know?" I put the cab in drive, cranked the wheel to the right, and drove us away from the house. "We're going to Honesty's bedroom." We returned to the driveway where Promise had last seen Honesty and I kissing before curfew. I quietly said to myself, "This is going to hurt."

As it should, Promise added, though I didn't realize she heard me. *I don't care that your conscience got the best of you; it decided to show up several hours too late, Soupy.*

I created a screen on Honesty's two-car garage door and pressed play.

With the shades drawn, her room was completely dark. She was lying on her side under a thick blanket; her sinuses were clogged by the sound of her rough sniffling. By the light from the hallway I could see her disheveled hair, tangled every which way, unlike her normally well groomed, golden mane. Her nose had stolen the rosy glow that usually lived in her cheeks.

"I couldn't breathe when I walked in and saw her," I said to Promise, "and neither could she, though for two very different reasons. The entire room was flooded with darkness. Carbon and oxygen bloated like they were crowded elbow-to-elbow in a rush hour subway train, and the smell wasn't much better.

We were both sick, her with an illness and I with guilt. Yet she smiled when she saw me. *She smiled*, Promise. I didn't deserve it, and she didn't know it, but I still didn't deserve it. That smile pierced me. For her to feel so terribly sick, yet still find the energy to smile, I just can't find the words to explain how deeply that smile challenged my resolve to tell her the truth. What I'd known so firmly just an hour ago—to spill my guts—was now shaky, at best."

On the screen Soupy sat on the floor next to Honesty's bed. He stroked her hair once, let his hand rest on her shoulder, and laid his cheek on her thigh.

* * *

My heart was beating too rapidly. *Could she tell?* There was so much love, so much, but there wasn't enough last night. The piano was swinging back and forth over my head…again, it seemed. It confused me, but there was no other way. None. I began to feel selfish that I was savoring these moments of being close to her heart before I dropped a bomb on the places I'd just made feel so warm. "I have to tell you something," I said, softly.

"Jes, what is it?" she replied, a sniffle following the end of her question.

I took a deep breath, remembered I had no choice but to admit my fault, and said, "I kissed another girl last night."

Her eyes opened wide. She sat up in bed and pushed me away, crushing my heart instantly. My words gave her emotions: confusion, anger, concern. Her brow furrowed. Her hands clenched. I watched as she fought through the sludge of sickness to find the right words. Each second, I felt the piano raise itself and repeatedly come crashing down on my chest. I couldn't handle the look on her face, and I didn't know how to make it go away, so I said, "I don't know why. I stood in the driveway of the party last night—"

Despite what I'd just said, she asked, "Why?" in a voice that pleaded for an answer.

I reached for her hand, but she pulled it quickly out of my reach. My eyes rolled to the dark ceiling, as if I might find an answer written there. "I—," I started, but struggled to know what word was supposed to come next. She waited. I didn't know. It was true. "I…I don't know why, Honesty." I looked away from her in an attempt to gather any tinge of additional strength. "I don't. I really don't." Forlornly, I looked back toward her. "I wanted to walk here and spend the evening with you, but I went into the party—"

"WHY?" she asked again, more assertively this time, confusion bubbling to anger.

"Honesty," I paused while I clenched my own hands in frustration with the fact that I couldn't find any words that could both admit dishonesty *and* return us to happiness. "I don't have a good excuse." I looked at her, but her gaze was too much. Regret drowned me. I dropped my head in shame. My chin fell to my chest forcing my lungs to collapse.

She grabbed her blanket and pulled it into her chest as if she was suddenly a young child raising her shield against the monster that had crawled out from beneath the bed. A deep coughing spell racked her body and forced her to groan; the fog inside of her prevented her from seeing clearly into what had happened and what should happen next. She didn't have to say so, I knew the timing for my words couldn't have been worse.

I didn't try to touch her again, just placed my hand nearer to her on the mattress. It gave me the temporary fortitude to look her in the eyes and say, "I'm ashamed of my actions and I'm very, very sorry."

A voice inside my head screamed, *WHAT THE FUCK ARE YOU DOING?*

Another voice replied, *I HAVE NO FUCKING IDEA!*

I'd admitted what I had to admit. I felt no relief from it and hadn't expected to. I hadn't thought beyond this point, so I didn't know what to do next, but I didn't want to leave her. I waited for something, anything, some idea, some words, some strength to simply get up and leave.

She broke the silence. "What does this mean?" The tone of her voice was equally fierce and fearful.

I nearly said "What?" in surprise, but caught myself. I'd not anticipated this question even though it was the most obvious next step, obvious now that we were right in the middle of the situation. Confused, I repeated her words, "What does this mean?" My mind was exploring and evaluating all the different replies, searching for the right one. *What do you want? Who do you want? How do you want? Where do you want?* The questions in my head were coming too quickly for me to answer them. I stuttered as if that might force the right words to come out. “I d-don’t want, um—”

She grabbed a pillow, held it tightly to her chest, and slid down to the floor bringing her eyes to my level. I started crying, confused about how to answer; my tears matched those already streaming down her face.

“I don’t know, Honesty.” Again, I lowered my head.

“No,” she leaned forward and tilted her head sideways as if the angle would capture my eyes and hers. “Ju have to know because I don’t know. Ju did this. Ju tell me what it means,” she said, making sure I understood. Her grip on the pillow loosened as she finished, though it didn’t diminish the protective boundary between us.

save yourself.

I’d been hunched over, but the voice caused me to straighten, and before I thought about my words, I said, “I want to date her, too.”

Honesty’s face twisted in surprise from words she hadn’t seen coming. It was a direction I wasn’t really sure I wanted to go, but it suddenly felt like the only option. Once it was out there I saw no way to retract it.

“Was it because we didn’t have sex?” she asked.

It was my turn to be surprised by a conversation path I hadn’t seen coming. *Was it?* Her question punched me in the gut, completely, breaking apart my insides, making them as weary as hers. Had I started a relationship with someone else—someone I wanted to keep—because I thought she was “easier” than Honesty? *Are you a man or a boy?* I would never have done that intentionally, not consciously anyway…would I? I didn’t have an answer. I mean, I had an answer, but for some reason I was questioning it because the last thing I wanted to do was lie. I *believed* that sex had *not* been part of the equation, but something had driven me to act in that manner. “Sex?” I asked, and saying that one word made me feel instantly more like a boy than a man.

“Jes,” she confirmed simply and powerfully.

save yourself.

I couldn't lie, but I also struggled to answer. "Maybe?" As soon as I said "maybe" out loud, I *knew* it wasn't the right answer, not because it wouldn't help my situation with Honesty, but because it wasn't at all true. "Maybe" or "yes" was the way to save myself, as it would end everything right here and now. I didn't want the easy way out; she deserved more than that. She deserved the truth. "No, I'm sorry, it was *not* about sex, Honesty. I hadn't thought about whether it was or wasn't until you'd asked, but it most definitely was *not* about sex. I quit listening to my heart for a night and my head went on vacation and nothing was left but this shell of me—it's no excuse—it was me, but I wasn't myself."

She looked at me, completely confused.

"I'm sorry," I said, shaking my head to show my equivalent state of confusion. "The words—emotions are interfering with the words. Did sex have something to do with it? Yes. Was it about sex? No. I think it started that way, but I realized what was happening before it ended that way."

She stared at me.

"And I wish I could raise that realization as a proud banner of great decision-making, but it doesn't change the fact that I kissed another girl. I'm so very sorry." Emotions swept the remaining jumbled mess of words from my throat as I began to sob uncontrollably.

She laid me down on the floor and then followed suit, like when two swans face each other, mirror images without touching, both curled into the fetal position, her pillow still the barrier between us. Our eyes were open, looking at each other, blinking when needed. My heartbeat slowed until I could only hear the sound of her raspy breath.

In great confidence she said, "I want all of ju or none of ju."

My eyes widened and my heart raced once more. *All of me or none of me?* The words separated us, like when Laverne taped off half the apartment from Shirley and declared it to be her space, or like when Les Nessman of "WKRP in Cincinnati" taped an outline around his desk to pretend like he had an office. There was my side and her side. Two choices: all of her or none of her. *I dare you to cross this line.* I wanted to choose her. Wanted it badly, but something stopped me from making that choice. I wanted to reach through the words and pull her into my chest; my actions would be my answer, but my arms wouldn't budge. I didn't like the choices. They were clear, but limited. Black or white. Light or dark. Yes or no. All of her or none of her. There was no choice of all of her, and all of the other *her*, too. She knew what she wanted and made a move to get it. I didn't, unless wanting my cake and eating it too was truly what I wanted. I felt backed into a corner—by no one's actions but my own—but backed into a corner nonetheless. I'd grossly failed at life and underestimated the situation. I was broken down on the road without a gas station for hundreds of miles in any direction, and the sun was setting into a moonless night. *Fight.* Fight? *Fight your way out of the corner.*

I started verbally swinging.

"I can't give you all of me," I said, speaking like the voice in my head.

"Then ju don't get any of me," she said. Honesty got up, returned to her bed, burrowed under the covers, and audibly sobbed.

Her words on the carpet between us had been flattened by my own. I was alone in the ring and everyone had left the building. I knew it was over. She made sure I knew it was over. She left on a brisk gust of wind that had tumbled hope across the road and into the desert, lost in the night. The room started to spin. Somewhere I found the strength to push up from the floor and onto my hands and knees. *Don't puke.* I wanted to throw up, and that possible outcome got me to my feet with an urgency I hadn't expected, and a magnetic pull to leave the room quickly. But I couldn't leave without witnessing what I'd done to the most beautiful, pure woman to ever enter my life. As I looked, my chest locked up again, my heart and my lungs ceased operating, and I was overcome with the desire to run from not just her room, but from the entire house. My body wouldn't cooperate. I latched onto the doorframe, one foot still in her life while the other had left. I couldn't move; afraid I'd never experience the purity of love again, *any* purity of love again. Never. My stomach warned with a tumbling like a drenched towel in a dryer. Honesty stirred under the covers. She was alive, not dead. We were alive, not yet dead. Like a freeway pile up in the fog, words collided bumper-to-bumper in my throat. The first word refused to speak, and without it the others would never be heard. My heart crawled up into my throat, forcefully ramming into the back of the pile up in an effort to push out the first word. At the same time, I could taste the acidic warning from my stomach. The wet towel tumbled and I doubled over, barely able to resist the splurge; only my grip on the doorframe kept me upright. In that moment my heart lost the fight; it could no longer stop my motion toward the front door. I took one last look at her tired figure, then bumped heavily into the doorjamb as I tried to leave. She stirred, but I couldn't risk hearing any more of her words; couldn't have them chasing me from her personal space. I moved into the hallway where I could no longer see her. I was in the living room and someone asked me if Honesty was okay and then if I was okay. I was in the kitchen and the wet towel tumbled more purposefully. I was in the garage and the driveway and at my car where the wet towel ejected from the dryer and onto the driveway. Then, I was at my house. I was in my foyer and my hallway and down my stairs and into my room and into bed. I mimicked Honesty's last pose and spoke to myself. *I puked. I didn't die. I wanted to die. I* want *to die. I'm sorry, Honesty, so sorry. No, I don't want to die. I have to cry. I can't cry. I have to cry.*

I cried. I cried myself to sleep.

* * *

I couldn't stop tears as I sat in the cab watching one of my most difficult and hurtful memories unfold again.

Is Soupy going to be okay? I mean, he doesn't do anything stupid, right? Promise asked.

"Well, I *am* still here if that's what you mean," I answered, doing as best as I could to wipe the tears from my cheeks and regain my composure.

I can tell that was hard for you.

"Ya think?" I chuckled, but my heart wasn't in it. "It *was* hard for me. When I woke up, I walked to my former elementary school, which was a block behind my house, found my favorite swing on the empty playground, watched the sun rise, and set in motion thoughts about simple things in life, like swinging, for instance, and kickball and sending notes in class and flying a kite and being the first one done with lunch so I could put my name on the chalkboard."

All good moments.

I wiped my eyes as I continued, "During that introspection, I realized more truth about Honesty's beauty than I had ever before known." Shaking my head, I added, "Why is it always after the fact, Promise? Though sick and barely able to form words, the confidence in conviction she showed, despite her vulnerability, was the mark of a wondrous and unique trait. We were so young. She knew so little about my country. Yet there she was, being more mature and unique and wonderful than I'd ever been at any time in my life, and I had just crapped all over it, not listened, not understood, not heard what—" The second onslaught of tears hit me.

Let it out, Soup. Let it out.

I did, for quite some time. When the worst of the crying was past, I said, "There was no doubt, Promise, my first love was my first loss. Had I done the right thing? I still don't know."

I don't have an answer to that question for you. But you, Soup, you showed sincerity by telling the truth.

"Thank you...I think," I said, solemnly.

It pains me to ask this, but there's always a question of time, and I never know how much we have left, especially when we get toward the end of a story. So I have to ask, did you pursue the other girl?

"Barely, like a month or something like that."

And, how were things with Honesty?

"We didn't cross paths or speak much of a word to each other. For a whole month after we broke up, she didn't leave the house except to attend school. No social events. No experiencing America. I destroyed her."

I know. I know. You did hurt her, and if she didn't leave the house for a month, then you spoiled quite a chunk of her year abroad.

"You don't have to remind me, Promise."

I'm sorry, Soup, I didn't mean to poke at your wound. Just, well...I don't know about you, but I can't get the picture of her sobbing in bed out of my head.

"There's nothing that rightfully defends my actions. I took this amazing love, this beautiful flower, this wonderful song, and crushed it in my hand. I didn't know lonely until I left Honesty."

I don't think you can truly know loneliness without togetherness; you can't know one without the other.

"Yeah, I learned that."

Then, you learned something.

"I guess so."

Is this helping you, Soupy? Shall I go?

"No Promise, please stay. There's just a bit more. It won't take long. Just give me a moment." I reached into the glove box, grabbed a box of tissues, and took care of all the needed tear-wiping and nose-blowing. "Okay, sorry. Like I said, it was several months before we spoke again, and by that time she only had a few months left in the States. We learned to co-exist, but it wasn't anything like friendly. At her going away party, I did as I'd been doing for months and stayed out of her way; that is, until our eyes met. The burden I'd been carrying—guilt at having destroyed our love—lessened its weight on me when she smiled."

Her eyes let you out of it.

"And her smile. She nodded her head to the side, non-verbally asking me to join her on the couch."

I changed the frame on the garage door and pressed play.

* * *

"Hey," she said.

"Hej," I replied. "That's h-e-j, and it's short for h-e-j-s-a-n, which means 'hello' in your language."

"Jes," she said with a smile.

"I'm sorry for—"

She stopped me with a finger to her lips and said, "I know."

The silence between us was an equivalent effort to set aside the past several months and move on with our lives: more smiles, less sorrow.

"It's nice to be next to you again," I said, turning toward her.

She turned toward me, as well.

Our moment ended abruptly when our friends piled into the room. One of them sat down between us and said, "What'r you two doing on the couch?"

"Just talking," I said, which was the absolute worst thing to say. Maybe she'd never heard that story. Maybe everyone had forgotten. Maybe. I didn't ask.

"Let's party," my friend said and grabbed us both by the hands to lead us into the kitchen.

* * *

"I had no idea what I wanted to say to her; I just wanted one last chance to say something. The more I thought about it, the more nervous I became. I left the party and found a bench in the backyard to be alone with my thoughts; to sit and reflect on the past year."

* * *

"Soup?" It was Honesty's voice.

"Yes?" I replied.

"What are ju doing back here?"

"Remembering," I replied.

She sat down next to me and said, "Time to stop thinking and start talking."

She held her hand out to mine and I accepted her grasp. I could feel her warmth. There were things we both wanted to say. It was the end of the evening, the party was basically over, so we had privacy. She led me to her room; the first time I'd been inside those four walls since the infamous day of love's first loss.

"Here?" I asked, nervously.

"We have to say goodbye. For us, it's not yust a hug and a peck on the cheek," she added.

I nodded in the dark as we sat on the bed. Skipping idle chatter, I pulled her close to me and held her in my arms as we both laid down, her back to my chest, spooning. Our embrace eliminated the clock that had been counting down the hours, minutes, and seconds until we'd be thousands of miles apart. Listening to her breath, I once again felt close to her heart—close enough to feel it beating in her chest—and took in the aroma of her hair, that clean smell of a spring day that begs life and love to blossom. *We fit*, I thought. Instantaneously, we both took a long, deep breath.

On this last night of her time in my country, we didn't find bliss—time would have to stop for that—we found satisfaction; permission to forgive.

"I have an idea," I said.

She turned her head to look at me. "Jes?"

"Let's start at the beginning," I suggested. "Tell me what you remember about us. I want to know what this year looked like through your eyes. Let's laugh and cry and joke and rib and smile and give all the memories we've shared the goodbyes they deserve, and make sure we never forget what it felt like to love."

Honesty rolled over to face me, placed both of her hands on my cheeks, and gave me a long, slow, passionate kiss; the type that leaves one's face savoring the touch as the love moves from lips to heart to soul. I didn't open my eyes again until that kiss touched every part of me.

"Jes, let's do that," she said, with one of the most sincere smiles I'd ever seen.

And, for hours, that's exactly what we did. It was the perfect goodbye.

* * *

You touch my heart, Soupy.

"Can't stop showing and telling now, Promise." I changed the scene on the garage door. "The next day I felt plagued by lost opportunity. I couldn't keep from looking at my watch and wondering where she was on her journey home. At eight in the morning, I knew she was loading her luggage into the van and heading to the airport. At nine, the family would be carrying bags from the curb to her airline ticket counter. Nine-thirty would start the long, hard goodbyes between them. I asked myself why I left her last night. I asked myself why I didn't go to the airport with her. I asked myself why I didn't latch onto every single second we had left and refuse to let them go, and I had no answers for my desperate questions. By nine-thirty, I was sitting on the lid of the toilet in my bathroom, crying as hard as I'd ever cried in my life. It hurt to know she was leaving, maybe even already gone. The distance between us had been too great while she was here, and it was only going to become greater once her plane left the ground."

Oh, Soup.

"By ten-thirty, everyone would have said their goodbyes, done their own crying, and those who lived here would be piling back into the van to drive home. By ten-thirty, I'd also done all the crying I could handle, so I got up off the toilet, splashed water on my face, wiped my eyes, and forced myself back into my life. Mom was waiting in the kitchen with a hug and a warm cup of tea."

I would expect you to take it hard. You're the type who spends a lot of time reviewing what you've done right and wrong in life, aren't you?

"Yes, practically every night, often at the expense of sleep."

I'm glad you're built that way, Soup. It certainly helps our cause.

"Her departure was a helpless moment; there wasn't *anything* I could have done to change it," I said. "I thought of you, Promise." *What?* I wasn't sure why I'd just said that. It definitely wasn't a planned part of the story. "I—"

Did you think she might be me?

"Do I think *that* with every girl I'm interested in?" I asked, rhetorically.

Point taken.

"If we hadn't made it better at the end, I don't know how I would have felt when she left, probably worse, definitely burdened with regret. But we both learned lessons about resilience, virtue, truth, sincerity—I'd crushed her heart, and in return felt equally as crushed, yet we found a way to rebuild from the dirt and ashes and crumbles of that emotion. I admired her growth, her strength. Honesty's foundation was strong. We both lived through the pain and learned from it."

What did you learn?

"Personally, I vowed never to cheat on *anyone* ever again."

Having experienced great loss, you better understood the potential of great love, and you wanted it.

"Yeah, I mean, who wouldn't?"

You'd be surprised, Promise said, and then repeated herself, *You'd be surprised.*

Drained, I wiped the tears from my face and felt how swollen my cheeks had become. "Criminy, I'm sure I look like hell."

I wanted to sleep. I didn't want to spend any more time in the cab.

Chapter 11

A buzzing sound woke me. My phone was ringing. Vibration mode. I lifted my head and looked around the motel room, but couldn't place the location of the noise. It stopped.

Text messages started. Someone knew I rarely answered the phone, but would respond to text.

Knowing my body would loathe to cooperate, I had to make a plan for getting out of bed. Having surveyed the room for my phone, I was fairly certain it was still in my jeans. With my right hand, I threw the sheet across the bed, went down on all fours, reached for the waist of my jeans, pulled them back into bed, and threw the sheet back over my body. Done.

"where u at holmes?" read the text message. *In bed. Asleep. In the dark. Crying over Honesty. With my dream girl.* All of those responses would start a conversation I'd much rather have tomorrow than tonight, so I didn't answer. Instead, I put my phone on the nightstand and noticed the time: midnight. I'd only been in bed for a few hours—a few dreamy, but restless hours.

Chapter 12

Mobility is key to any journey. It's rather hard to take one unless you're moving, present dream world excluded, I suppose. After Honesty returned home to her country, I graduated from high school, which made it time for me to leave, too.

In my dream, Mom leaned into the window of my cab, kissed me on the forehead, and said, "You must travel to know yourself," while holding up one finger to make her first point. When she added a second finger, she also said, "You must know yourself to know true love." And finally, she completed the logical conclusion, "Therefore, you must travel to know true love." I looked at her, nodded my head, leaned up for a kiss, gave her a wave, and drove off. As I did, she added a loving addendum, "Travel safely." Tears formed in her eyes. I left her standing there—oddly, alone in the middle of a four-lane interstate—while I went in search of answers. With a look in the rearview mirror, I said one last goodbye and then focused forward.

We're a mobile culture, especially in the States; if we're moving, we're alive. Horace Greeley urged us to "go west," so we did, and still do, though we're not so picky about the direction anymore. We learn how to drive before we learn how to drink, vote, live away from home, or marry. We despise hospitals because they, by rule, keep us immobile, but we love doctors and nurses because they help us regain our mobility. When old age takes away our ability to drive, we often slip quickly into death. Even at a young age, I knew I had to keep moving to feel alive.

I lost. Yes, I'd failed at love. Failure wasn't something I was used to experiencing. Now, the faster I drove the farther from failure I'd be. *What has he won, Jim?* As a loser's sunny side bonus: no one I'd meet on this journey would know of my failure unless I shared it. "You've also won," I said, and paused for effect, "A NEW CAR!" I waited for a moment, wondering if my cab would instantly upgrade, and felt an additional tinge of failure when it didn't.

The sun slipped over the western horizon and darkness came on fast, more quickly than normal. It zoomed up from behind and overtook my cab, the highway, the landscape, and the sky—like someone spilled a gallon of dark ink on an uneven table; it seeped across more rapidly than one could sop it up or channel its flow. Within seconds, the only lights were the headlights and interior lights of the cab. I felt the darkness, and along with it came weariness; the road is a hell of a lot more boring when there's nothing to look at. I flipped on the radio, tapped on the steering wheel, and sang along to Willie Nelson's "On the Road Again," which had been our family vacation song whenever we left town. After that hit, "Pancho and Lefty," and then "They All Went to Mexico," and then "Blue Eyes Crying in the Rain," and then "Angel Flying too Close to the Ground." By that time, my weariness had manifested itself into some serious, full-body yawning. I cranked up the air conditioner and directed all the vents toward my face. *Nod.* "Tic-tic-tic-tic-tic," I said as the painted lines on the highway passed beneath the cab wheels. *Nod.* I tried, but failed, to successfully slalom the Botts' Dots, those little reflectors that mark the lanes. *Nod.* None of it could keep me awake. I finally fell asleep while driving.

"SHIT!" I said, jerking my head up and opening my eyes. The vibration of the carved notches in the breakdown lane roused me and I swung the wheel quickly to the left. "Wake up, Soup." Driving with my knees allowed me to use my hands to pull upward on the lids of both my eyes, as if that would magically stop them from closing again. *Toothpicks.* Toothpicks? Ah yes, to prop the lids open, of course. "Did you see that?" I said to no one in particular, and then leaned forward to peer more intently out the front windshield. "Whoa. What the fuck? The trees, dude. Wake up. DUDE! THE TREES," I said excitedly, intending to slap the arm of a passenger who wasn't actually there and never had been. The back of my hand only made contact with the back of the passenger's seat. "THE TREES!" I shouted. "THEY'RE BENDING OVER THE ROAD!"

Pull. Over.

A white light flashed inside my head. Awareness returned. No one was in the cab with me. The trees over the road were gone. It was time to stop driving. I pulled over. It didn't matter where. I didn't care where.

"Tha—," I began to thank the non-existent passenger for advising us to pull over. "Whatever. That's all, folks." I rolled up the windows, turned off the engine, and lay down across the front seat bench. It was extremely quiet, totally uncomfortable, and very disconcerting to sleep on the side of an empty freeway. To distract myself, I counted: *one, two, three, four, five, six, seven, eight, nine, ten, eleven, twelve, thir*—an 18-wheeler rumbled past, loudly blowing its air horn. The blast of air and sound rocked my cab, causing me to sit up immediately. Oddly, the sky was already showing a bluish tint of new daylight. I watched the truck's tail lights disappear over a small hill.

After I rubbed my eyes, I surveyed the surroundings. "Imagine that: no trees. WAIT! One tree!" I pointed toward a large fig tree—one of the largest I'd ever seen—that stood monolithic on the flat, grassy plain about three hundred yards perpendicular to the highway. I could feel its energy, so I slid out of the passenger door, stretched, and walked toward it.

I thought, *This is the middle of nowhere.* With each step, I put distance between where I had been and where I was going—and I liked it. The waist-high wheat rustled in the wind, bending toward me, welcoming me. I walked with hands stretched outward, allowing the brushy spikes to tickle the undersides of my palms, as if I was shaking their hands, patting their heads, wishing them well, thanking them for their company. *Asking for their votes.* I plucked one constituent stalk from the flock and trimmed it down to chewable size; a few inches between the teeth so the husk could bounce with each step.

As I approached the tree, I saw that the area around it was expertly manicured, plush, green grass. As I expected, it was a very, very large fig, one that'd beaten the odds against those who had clear-cut this land for farming. Its canopy shaded a circle at high noon that would have been about twenty yards in diameter. The mowed area extended beyond that shady circle an additional twenty yards. At the edge of the branches sat a white, wooden desk and two empty chairs. The chair was a simple four-legged, wooden table chair, one corner of it tucked under the desk. A brown, leather chair-and-a-half sat on the "visiting" side of the desk.

After crossing the wheat field onto the grass, I strolled past the desk, dragging the tips of my fingers along the top of the wooden chair as I continued toward the fig tree; I had to touch the tree, to feel it, maybe even hug it. The air freshened as I approached, so I took in great, deep breaths. The leaves, much like the grass, showed a deep, healthy color that was atypical for any tree in an early, Mid-western autumn. The leaves announced my arrival by applauding lightly. I smiled in thanks, partly because I appreciated their warm welcome and partly because I wanted them to know I meant no harm. It was warm for a day so late in the year, but as soon as I entered the canopy of the tree, it became a breezy, cool, fresh, spring day—that's to say, in other words, it felt *new*, like the beginning of life instead of the end. The lowest branches of the tree were out of my reach; I admired their strength as they spanned from the trunk; a massive trunk, to say the least. I touched and stroked it gently, and then closed my eyes to see if I could sense a heartbeat; it hummed. I rolled the wheat stalk around in my mouth letting the husk switch from one side to the other. And in this place, this middle of nowhere place, with a tree where no other tree could be seen, I felt new again.

It felt good to be engaged in the next phase of my life's journey.

I nestled into a nook formed by the massive, above-ground roots. With my back resting against the tree, I twirled the wheat stalk with my fingers, rolling my tongue over its stem. There, I thought about life, about who I have been, am, want to be, and would someday become. I thought about what made me *me*. Days passed to nights and nights passed to days as I sat under the tree completely comfortable, secure, and lost in thought.

I missed Promise. She hadn't been gone long, but I already needed her back. There was still so much to tell.

A familiar voice called to me, "Grandson."

I opened my eyes to see Great Grandpa Walker motioning from the desk and chairs for me to come join him. "Grandpa!" I shouted, and ran to him.

Smiling, he asked as we hugged, "How has your walk been?"

"Pleasurable. Always. And this tree is beautiful."

"That it is, my grandson, that it is." We sat down, he in the leather chair and me at the desk. While pointing to the tree, he said, "It's been a long time, but do you remember what I told you about places like this?"

I thought for a moment. "Places…of Power?"

"Yes. And?"

"And…powerful places where I will learn things," I added.

"Well done," Great Grandpa said. "Anything else?"

I tried to recall something I was missing, but my memory didn't comply.

"That's okay," he smiled. "I never told you anything else." His laugh spread across the plain.

"Awww, shit!" I said, then immediately clapped my hand over my mouth.

His laugh blossomed into a deep, hearty, knee-slapper. "Soupy, I dare say you are old enough to swear now."

I laughed with him. It was nice to be in his company, real or dream world.

He pointed to the tree once again. "This tree, it has learned to live with the elements—it has mastered their languages. That is why it has prospered."

"Yes, I can see that," I said, recognizing the tree's accomplishment. Motioning Great Grandpa to look around at the rest of the treeless landscape, I then added, "And it's also been lucky enough to convince the right people that it needed to live."

"Luck? No, no, no," he shook his head. "They are not called 'Places of Luck.' They are called 'Places of Power.'" With a serious look on his face, he raised his palm toward the tree. "Do you feel it?"

I turned in my chair to face the tree and raised my hand to it. *Yes.* A tingle of energy centered in my palm. "Yes, I do."

"Stand up," he said, and I obeyed. "On one leg." I raised my left leg and extended my hands out for balance. "No, put your hands back at your sides." Again, I obeyed, but now struggling to balance. "Trust in the place," Grandpa added. After a pause that allowed me to establish better balance, he said, "Close your eyes and reach for the tree, not with your body, but with your fingers, like you are plucking a small fruit." I did so for several seconds, repeating the act of plucking fruits. "When I tell you to do so, stand again on two feet, but leave one hand raised high. Bring your other hand to meet it over your head. Got it?" I nodded. "Then, in one motion, exhale and wash your hands across the front of your body from head to torso." I nodded again to show that I'd understood. "Now." I followed his instructions. As my hands traveled from my head down my body, a flood of energy surprisingly filled me.

"Incredible," I said, afraid to move and disrupt the flow.

"You just understood the language of the tree," he said.

I turned toward him before I asked, "Really?" He nodded. "But how?"

"Well, to be truthful, *I* spoke the language of the tree through you. I asked it, as nicely as I could, if I could borrow some of its energy."

"Borrow?" I asked. "Do I have to give it back?"

"All things in balance, always. Someday, you will," Great Grandpa said. "The next time you need energy, Soupy, you must remember to ask."

"Yes, Grandpa. No problem." I returned to my chair emblazoned with new knowledge. "How do you know all of this?" I asked.

A smile bent his face into a mass of sun-formed wrinkles; an opportunity to tell a story had presented itself, and he was the master storyteller. "I have walked the land," he said, and stood up from his chair. "All of this land, every mile, every inch. To know it, I had to see it, touch it, feel it." In one fluid motion, he swept his hand through the air down across the blades of grass until he looked as if he'd just thrown a bowling ball down an alley. "We are Walkers, after all," he added, holding the pose while turning his head to look me in the eye. "We belonged to none, and were accepted by all. Our tales preceded us, though we were rarely ever seen in the same place twice." Grandpa reenacted the energy request from the tree so gracefully that he never once wobbled. With newly gained energy, he pointed east and continued, "Walkers of English descent came to the States with centuries of family tradition to apply to these vast new lands." His arms spread wide and then embraced the world. With fingers interlaced, he made the motion of a snake wiggling back and forth, "During their journey, they encountered a very wide and powerful river. Since it was growing dark, they made camp instead of braving a ford." With deft rotation, he spun one hundred and eighty degrees to face me, then raised his hands above his head in the shape of a teepee. The mid-morning sun was placed perfectly at the apex of his body-formed triangle and I suddenly felt warmth on my face. "My people—those who make up the non-Walker half of me—were camped nearby, natives to this land, the smoke from their fires marking their place." As if he'd captured a piece of the sun in his closed fist, he showed me his palm shining like the light of an oncoming train. Closing his palm, white smoke escaped from between his fingers. "For many long nights, these two peoples shared histories and pleasantries." He wafted smoke toward his nose and inhaled deeply; he was channeling memories of his lineage. From his back pocket, Grandpa revealed a small square of bright red cloth. He unfolded it until it was three by three feet, then waved it like he was spreading a picnic blanket; it hovered flat at the level of his waist, only the breeze rippled its form. "The English-born Walkers were known for improving the quality of cloth by trampling and scouring it in water to improve its thickness."

As his fingers walked across the surface of the cloth, I humorously asked, "Do you mean to say they walked on water?"

"It was their job to do so," he replied stoically, no acknowledgment of my joke. His hand waved across the surface of the cloth to smooth it out. From his pocket he pulled another small square, this one canary yellow, which he unfolded atop the other, and the two merged into a thicker, now orange, square. "Walkers were said to lead richer and fuller lives—perhaps a function of their trade becoming their legacy—but they taught their young to focus on the important things in life: to live more fully with a focus on what matters."

A strong gust of wind caught hold of the square cloth and carried it up into the sky like a kite that's string had been cut. "Grandpa! Your handkerchief!" I exclaimed, pointing as it floated away.

His finger politely waved back and forth at me indicating that it was of no importance. Grandpa looked over his shoulder, and then said, "There is a storm coming."

I looked to the right and saw a darkening sky.

Grandpa asked, "Do you believe in fate?"

I thought for a moment before I answered honestly, "I don't know." His right eyebrow rose.

"It was fate that my families met on that day and in that time. Once they understood the past they began to focus on the future. There was change blowing on the wind from every direction." Across his cheeks blew wispy lengths of hair that had escaped his ponytail. "The idea that man could own the land made it more difficult for Walkers to walk freely. Each year, travel was forced more frequently to the roads between the lands." He brought his arms across his chest to form an X, closed his eyes, and tilted his head back. Grandpa followed his head's momentum and fell back into the leather chair.

I started to stand up to see if he was all right, but he opened his eyes before I was more than a few inches out of my seat. "The roads were death. The land was life," he said.

Though no cloud or airplane existed in the sky above us, a dark shadow crossed the plain, wilting the tall grasses as it came. Fortunately, they sprang back to life after the shadow passed. I started to ask a question, but Grandpa's wrinkled old hands clapped, as loud as thunder, instantly bringing my thoughts back to him. He glared at me, without blinking, until he knew my attention had returned.

"To preserve the legacy of their peoples, each family knew that sons and daughters had to co-mingle, leave the group, and find new ways to travel among society." His hands, still with palms pressed together, now interlocked as his fingers laced. Grandpa brought his thumbs to his lips. Strands of hair wrapped around his wrists, binding them. "No longer could such large groups roam lands that were owned by others. Landowners believed it was the land that made them free, but ownership of land made them a slave to it." He took a deep breath and blew into the hollow between his thumbs and the once-bound locks fell to his shoulders. "Walkers knew they must separate—to remain together they must fracture—a nation bound by land and seasons would find itself imprisoned more than ever before. As per their plan, these two peoples merged. Some were sent into society—deemed an invaluable experience because of its inevitability—while others continued to walk the land."

I nodded my head to show I understood.

With his elbows on the arms of the chair, he rested his chin on the knuckles of both hands and looked me in the eyes. "This is your time to walk," he said. "You are part Walker, but you are also part of someone else's family. You will discover, in time, the traits you inherited from both. Pay attention now, so you may figure it out later."

"Grandpa," I said while motioning to the vast landscape, "I'm not really sure where to go."

He replied, "It won't always matter which way you go. Your intuition will guide you."

My thigh grew steadily warm until I reached across my jeans to feel the lump from the piece of onyx in my pocket. I looked down to remove it and show Grandpa I still had it, but by the time I did so he was gone.

As if the barrier that had been holding back the weather evaporated, ominous clouds tumbled across the sky in attack formation. The point of the attack burrowed into the calm blue sky, parting it for conquest and making its flanks susceptible. Two companies of troops departed the main advance, one on the left and one on the right, while the initial attack made a straight line for the fig tree, which was my location. The lead cloud conquered the sun, and everything turned from full color to black and white.

The wheat and fig leaves sounded the alarm that trouble was coming as the strengthening winds ran through them. Since I was a kid, a change in breeze and temperature inherently triggered a response to quickly seek shelter. However, my childhood instinct failed as I watched, mesmerized, by the advance of the storm. With each second, more of the blue sky turned light gray as it disappeared behind the front. Sheets of rain falling in the distance blurred the horizon. The nearer the storm came, the more an unending, rolling thunder replaced the sound of the wind.

CRRRRRACK!

A bolt of lightning connected the clouds to the land and stood my arm hairs on end. That was all the motivation I needed to seek shelter. I grabbed the desk chair and carried it several yards until it was under the canopy of the tree. From there, I watched the grass turn a darker gray, flattened by the force of the falling rain. It approached at a startling pace, like a steamroller with performance exhaust.

CRRRRRACK!

I jumped and winced, covering my eyes as lightning struck the desk and blew it into a million pieces. "DAD!" I screamed, as I noticed my dad sitting in the leather chair, a look of complete surprise on his face. "DAD!" I repeated, and stood up to wave my hands in the air to get his attention. He looked lost. He wasn't hearing my shouts, the sound of the approaching rain was too deafening. I ran toward him until he noticed my movement. "COME ON!" I yelled and pointed to the canopy of the tree. The first few drops of rain pelted his face. He lowered his chin to his chest and placed his hand over his eyes to shield them from it. I slid across the darkening grass, nearly clamoring into the leather chair as he stood up. "GRAB THE OTHER END!" I shouted while pointing first to the chair and then again to the shelter of the tree.

Dad mumbled something I couldn't make out. My quizzical look prompted him to shout more loudly, "I KNOW THAT TREE!"

"LET'S GO!" He copied my motion as I bent down to grab the leather chair and we made our way toward shelter. The wind and rain now hammered at our backs, which, fortunately, drove us toward our destination, but the walk was growing more slippery by the second. We stumbled under the tree and clumsily dropped the chair to the dry ground. Each of us shook our arms back to life once they were freed from the weight we'd carried.

Something was different. Very different. *Silence.* The storm raged like a stampede of wild buffalo, but we couldn't hear it under the tree, it was completely silent. I raised my index finger and motioned around as if to say, "Do you notice it, too?" but didn't speak, so as not to disturb the peace.

I flipped my chair around and sat in it, straddling the back and facing my dad. He sat down in the leather chair. The scenery remained a muddy black and white; a strange silent film feeling as the rain continued to fall, but made no noise. We didn't make eye contact, simply surveyed our set. I leaned forward, which was actually backwards for the chair, balancing on its hind legs.

"You're going to break that chair," he said.

Ignoring his statement, I instead replied, "So this is where you went when you left us?"

"Told you, I know this tree."

Since my parents had divorced when I was in grade school, time with Dad had been filled with shopping sprees in convenience stores where he'd tell my sister and I to grab whatever we wanted to eat for the weekend. We'd salivate at the thought of chips and donuts and sodas, and then come home with terrible stomach aches. Perhaps fortunately, we'd only had to endure the joy and pain of these health-toxic weekends for a few years until he moved away.

I asked, "Has it been an adventure?" I'd always thought Dad had left us for an adventure, while Mom stayed behind to raise and teach us how to take care of ourselves.

He just stared at me.

I returned all four legs to the ground and started to get up, but then he asked, "Do you dream?"

Strange question. We're in a dream, I thought, so I sat back down, ran my fingers through my hair, and contemplated my response, "Yeah. You?"

He answered, "Definitely. Like watching a movie."

Just like me. "I must get that from you," I said.

"Why?"

Confused by his question, I asked, "What do you mean?"

"Why do we dream so vividly while others don't?

"I don't know."

He answered his own question confidently. "Because we're in touch with our souls."

I added, "My dreams usually come after I'm fully rested, but fall back to sleep again. Each night, I go into a deep three-hour sleep and the next three hours are about waking up. It totals a nice six hours of sleep. But if I go back to sleep, the next three-hour segment kicks in and the crazy dreams begin."

"Then you're groggy when you wake," he added. "I remember that about you."

"Yeah," I concurred. I leaned forward on the back legs of the chair before I said, "Dad, she's back."

He knew who I was referring to, so he said, "Oh, is she now?"

"Yes, she told me my assignment in life is to find her."

"For what purpose?"

"True love," I claimed.

His eyes met mine; his interest was piqued. We sat there while Dad ran his fingers up and down his chin like he was stroking an invisible beard. "I see…" he said. After an audible hum, he added, "There is something…no…what am I trying to say here…" He leaned forward in his chair making the leather creak, and placed his hands on his knees, his thinking posture. "I remember something my Grandpa Heller said to me when I was a boy."

Now *my* interest was piqued.

"Mind who you're with, not where you stand," he said. "I don't know why I remember it or how it's relevant here."

"What do you think it means?" I asked.

"When I was a kid, I thought he was trying to tell me to respect my elders. As in, 'mind' my elders. And if I did what I was asked to do, then I wouldn't be standing around so much. But as I got older, I decided he was telling me to be careful about the company I kept; that trouble can be found anywhere, in any place and at any time, so where you stand is irrelevant."

"Trouble, or opportunity," I added.

Dad smiled. "Tell me more about her."

"Not much to say, I haven't seen her." To address his confusion, I continued, "She won't *let* me see her; something about cracking the foundation of our potential love. It was strange at first, but I'm getting used to it."

"Maybe she's not real," Dad said.

"Maybe not, but maybe so."

"That's not what I meant…maybe *she's* not *real*," he said again, stressing two of the last three words.

My face twisted quizzically.

"You'll figure it out," he said. "You always do." Dad looked off into the distance.

"Dad, do you believe in true love?"

He thought for a moment before answering, "Depends on what you mean by true love."

"Yeah, I guess it would, but that's kinda the point. Is it objective or subjective? Is true love the same thing for everyone, or—"

He interrupted, "No, I doubt it's the same thing for everyone, but you asked me if I think true love exists. I think you're really asking me whether true love is just a dream."

"I *know* it's a dream, I've met her."

"Point taken. So you want to know if it exists in the real world?"

"Yeah."

"Then, I still think it depends on how we define it." Dad smiled. "True love between people, right?"

Sarcastically, I replied, "No between bars of chocolate, Dad."

He laughed, "People do love their chocolate, possibly even claim it to be their one true love."

"Yeah, it doesn't talk back, it's fat-free, it's there when you need it, or if not, you can run out to buy more of it. Perfect true love," I joked.

"Yes, but if you don't work at it, then it'll turn to fat," he said with a smirk on his face.

"Good one, Dad."

"I hoped you'd like that one," he said.

I licked my finger and then raised my hand to gesture that I was making a mark on a scoreboard in his favor. He pumped his fist silently in the air to celebrate his score.

"Romantically?" he asked.

"True love?"

"Yes, true love, as in romantically?"

"Yessir."

He frowned. Dad never liked it when I called him "sir," but it was a respectful habit that I often forget to tamp when he was around.

"I can't say I've ever felt it, but I do believe in it," he said.

"But how can you believe if you don't know?"

With a simple word, he said, "faith."

The silent rain ceased to fall.

"Faith is a concept I struggle with, Dad, and I think it's partly because we weren't a very religious family. I mean, our extended family had avid churchgoers, but our nuclear family stayed out of the chapel—"

"We were holiday Catholics."

"Yeah, and religion is so synonymous with faith. I never understood what faith was supposed to feel like."

Dad asked, "Do you believe that one day you'll find success?"

"Yeah."

"Then you have faith."

"It's that simple?"

"Yes, faith is your trust in something: a person, an idea, a place," he said, and looked at the tree.

"So you trust that true love, as an idea, exists?" I asked.

"Right," he answered. "When I was a boy, my father took me down to the basement—the basement was where the punishment was administered—because I'd taken the Lord's name in vain. He asked me if I believed in God. I told him I wasn't sure. Then, two things happened: I got one hell of a whipping and I stopped worshiping ideals. If believing in God meant I wouldn't get whipped, then I could do that. But as for ideals, I never tried to find true love because I was too afraid I'd get the belt."

"Are you saying your challenges with God challenged your belief in other ideals?"

"Yes, I built an impenetrable layer around myself to keep everything out—I didn't want to get hurt anymore. There's one thing about not letting anything in: nothing gets out. I never learned to express feelings or show love. I'm always happy to see that you're better than me with emotion, which is why I like to introduce you as 'the new, improved version.' As I've gotten older, my beliefs have changed; *something* is watching over us. God? Maybe. Guardian angels? For sure. There have been too many times when I've thanked my lucky stars for an averted disaster, so someone must be watching over me for some reason."

"Thought about the reason?" I asked.

"Yes," he paused. "But I already accomplished it."

"Accomplished what?"

"Bringing you and your sister into the world," he said.

I had to think about his response, so I stood up, placed my right foot on the seat of the chair, used my knee to support my elbow, and then said, "So you're telling me you've accomplished your life's homework?" With my own assignment having been underway for twenty-something years, I was interested in what someone might say about completing his own.

Dad answered, "Yes, I think I have."

I scratched my head. "So now what?"

"What do you mean?"

"What do you do now that your homework is done?"

"Nothing," came his simple reply. "I'm just happy to watch you both grow up."

I looked away to think for a moment. Promise's mention of our lives being graded based on our homework came to mind. "I don't mean to sound rude, but do you think your homework will get a good grade?"

He laughed, and then said, "What do you think, Soup?"

"Yeah-yeah-yeah," I replied. "I ask because your skepticism about God is similar to the skepticism I have about my own homework: to find true love and show it to the world—"

The chair broke under my weight and I fell down on top of it.

"Dad popped out of his chair and asked, "You okay?"

"Shit. That's pretty fucking funny," I said.

"I told—"

"Yeah, you told me so," I said to complete his sentence.

A voice came from afar and said, "Cab 13? Cab 13, you there?" We both looked toward the source of the voice.

Dad asked, "You drive a cab?"

"You wanna reconsider whether your homework will get a good grade?"

He reached down and grabbed my hand to help me up. I asked, “Care for a ride?”

“Sure,” he answered. “Do I have to ride in the back?”

“Nah, plenty of room up front.”

We walked toward the cab. When we left the tree’s canopy, a cool wind touched us. The weather was no longer silent, nor was the highway. The sunlight came racing across the sky directly toward us, pushing the clouds over our heads and returning color to the world. I braced for impact as the light shined on us, but felt nothing apart from its warmth.

“Cab 13? Come on, Soup, I know you’re out there,” the static-laden voice said.

While we walked, Dad continued the conversation, “You were talking about skepticism, but I know you’re one to always consider all outcomes. As much as you’ve considered failure, I know you’ve also considered success.”

“Yeah, but what if skepticism is the reason for failure?” I asked.

“We’ve come full-circle and back to faith, haven’t we?” he said while clapping me on the shoulder.

“Seriously, I’ve been wondering if maybe she’s just my feminine voice.”

“Is that her on the cab radio?” he asked, smiling.

“No-no, she’s usually in the back of the cab, not on the radio.”

“Hmmm,” he said. “Maybe I *should* ride in the back.”

“That’d just be weird,” I said.

Dad and I hopped into the cab and I picked up the radio. “Cab 13. Over.”

“Cab 13, where have you been?” the voice asked.

“Breaking furniture with family,” I replied, smiling at my dad.

“I see.” The authoritative tone in the voice noted that permission for a break, any kind of break, hadn’t been given. “Well, you’ve got a call for a pickup. Airport. Woman named Honesty?”

“Honesty?” I said, and then held down the transmit button to reply. “On my way.”

Dad waited for me to hang the transmitter back on its hook, and then asked, “Honesty?”

“Honesty. Yeah, you know—”

"I remember who she is, but how does she know how to find you?" he asked.

I'd already asked myself the same question and found no answer. "I don't know. Up until now I've only had Promise in my cab."

"Promise?" he asked.

"Yeah, that's *the* dream girl," I replied.

Dad's wheels were still turning, "Do you ever get any other fares?"

"So far, not yet."

Dad continued, "And what happens when you pick Promise up?"

"We talk."

"That's it?"

"Yep, she helps me work things out in my head."

"And you do the same for her?" he asked.

I hadn't thought about that much, but if Promise were my true love I would hope it's the case. "Yeah, I think so." I started the cab and put it in drive. After a look in the mirrors and over my left shoulder, I pulled out onto the highway.

"Promise. I like her name," Dad said. "She sounds like an angel."

"Yeah," I agreed.

"Or a devil."

"A devil?" I looked at Dad, but he was no longer there. I shook my head and said quietly, "Damn, I'm tired of people disappearing on me all the time."

Chapter 13

The next chronologically important event in my past was my reunion with Honesty, so it made sense that she had called me back into action. Though I'd already lived it once, I was reluctant to reach my destination. The suburbs ticked passed as I drove the highway. Droves of human drones sat in front of their televisions, by choice, feeding off whatever the media had cooked up for breakfast. "Better you than me," I said aloud, long since frustrated with a country of people who watched *hours* of television each day. It was dawn, and I knew most households would have already turned on their boxes for weather, or traffic, or cartoons—the television made them sedentary, like starting the day by eating a bowl of concrete. *Sedentary.* Yeah, sedentary. They'd stopped moving, so they were dying. I was glad not to be one of them. I was moving.

The sun popped over the horizon behind me like it had put both hands on the land and pulled itself to "Kilroy was here" height, though it didn't stop to peek over the wall like the drawings often conveyed, simply pushed itself up into the morning sky.

Morning, Soup.

I jumped in my seat and grasped my chest, which barely contained my beating heart. "Damn Promise, you scared the shit out of me."

Sorry, darlin.'

"Is there any way to ease that transition?"

You mean the same way we need to ease the transition when you jump from one road to the next?

Not fighting her criticism and instead accepting it, I replied, "Yes, *exactly* like that."

Not that I know of.

"I suppose I'll get used to it, hopefully sooner than later."

Tell me what's up?

"We're on the way to pick up Honesty," I said.

Oh reeeally, she teased, drawing out the word. *Didn't she just leave?*

"She did, and so did I. We've skipped forward about a year, and over that time I moved to the west coast to explore new people, places, ideas, and thoughts. You know? I grew up a lot in that year by spending great swaths of time thinking about how I'm built. My mom said to me before I left, 'You must travel to know yourself. You must know yourself to know true love. Therefore, you must travel to know true love.'"

Promise thought about that for a moment, and then replied, *Hard to argue with the simplicity of it.*

"Yes, she knew me best, and knew that by seeing the world I would see more deeply into myself."

Do you think that's true for everyone?

"I'm not big on platitudes, but I *do* think it's true that more people should follow that advice."

That's definitely *true.*

"Honesty and I also traded a lot of letters over that year, actually filled a shoebox with the words and gifts we sent across the miles."

I can imagine, but what brought her back after only a year's time?

"A friend's wedding," I replied. "Promise, I know all of this already happened, but I'm getting nervous about picking her up, to watch us go through it all over again. Back then, I wondered if we would kiss, laugh, if there would be magic. Was this another chance?"

Promise mumbled playfully, *Such an optimist. It's cute.*

"What's that?" I asked, rather lost in the memories.

This is what I think: After the way you two parted—a reconnection of two hearts before they separated again—I wondered…or, I hoped a reunion might happen; it had *to. The desire was there, you know, but life too often has a way of getting in the way.*

"If second chances exist, then, in my eyes, this was a big one. So big, I spent weeks rereading her letters. My goal was to give her a gift: the anthology of us from past to present. In a beautiful, fabric-covered notebook, I rewrote and pasted song lyrics, poetry, and quotes that reminded us of what we had, and hopefully could have again. Together, I dreamed we'd flip through it, relive all those good feelings, and seek answers about ourselves, both old and new. For the great, grand finale, I wrote a speech—a speech? No, not really a speech—a statement of purpose with emotional overtones that covered the past, present, and future. Do you have any idea what I'm talking about?"

I hope I'm about to find out.

"Yes, I think you are. And if you know me, then you know I'd prepared for any outcome, as much as I could, from rejection to packing a bag and moving to another country, you know how—"

Yes, I know how you consider all of the possibilities when you prepare.

"Are we already completing each other's sentences?"

I already told you that I did my homework on you.

"Yeah-yeah. It's true. It's what I do. The day she arrived, I knocked around my house as if I'd lost my sense of balance: stubbed my toe on the bed frame, knocked my hip on the doorknob, drooled toothpaste on my shirt and had to change it, cracked my forehead on the medicine cabinet mirror when I bent over to spit into the sink after brushing—it was a ridiculously distracting day."

Like I said, cute.

"Cab 13. Cab 13," came the call over the radio.

"This is Cab 13," I replied. "What's up, dispatch?"

"Just got a call from one of our cabs at the airport. She says she picked up your fare."

"Seriously? What? Why? That was *my* fare!" I said, angrily.

"Not there? No fare," the dispatcher replied. "I gotta keep my cabs moving."

"Shit!" I yelled, and then added, "Now what?" I pressed the transmission button and said, "Fine. Over and out."

You do *know where she's going, right?*

"Yeah, and I guess that solves that problem."

What problem?

"How to get both of you into the cab at the same time without screwing up our future."

HA! she exclaimed, *I was actually kind of wondering the same thing.*

"Hold on, I need to reroute us," I said as I swerved onto a highway interchange and then fast-forwarded our way home. We pulled up to the driveway, the same one where we'd watched the final night Honesty and I had shared together. I created another video screen on the garage door for our viewing purposes. "Ready?"

Ready? I was born *ready!*

"Several friends gathered at the house to greet her. Sound familiar? When she walked in, it was the first time I'd seen her for a year, as you know. And *when* she walked in, her smile exploded my emotions as if every firework in the world went off at exactly the same time. Honesty smiled and hugged everyone as I nervously hopped back and forth, from foot to foot, at the end of the greeting line. I didn't care, *really* didn't care, how obvious it was that I still had very strong feelings for her. She hummed when we embraced, and I reciprocated. The reverberation between us was powerful and not at all surprising. We said nothing to each other; body language was our language."

I flipped through the video to skip most of the party, stopping only after everyone else had gone home and we were sitting together in the backyard.

* * *

"I've missed you, Honesty," Soupy whispered in her ear.

"I've missed ju, too," she replied.

He wanted to kiss her, longed to feel her lips on his once again. She sensed his desire and broke the moment with words, "How about a walk?"

"Of course," he smiled, and offered her his arm as escort, which she gladly took.

After they'd walked far enough into the woods to have some visual privacy from the house, she stopped, turned him toward her, and repeated, "I've missed ju, too." With both her hands on his cheeks, she delivered what he so desperately wanted from her only a few minutes prior: a brief, but loving kiss. Soupy left his eyes closed, her kiss lingering on his lips, and etched the feeling into his memory. She giggled, placed her hand to her mouth, and turned her cheek, happily embarrassed; she'd been overcome by emotion just as much as he had.

* * *

I paused the picture and said to Promise, "I would have lived in that moment forever."

A smile crossed my face as I stared at the afterglow a second longer before fast-forwarding our walk back to the house.

"Here. This is the moment I've been looking for," I said, and returned us to normal speed. "It's after the party ended."

* * *

Soupy asked Honesty, "Will you stay up and talk with me for awhile?"

"Jes," she replied as they sat down on the couch next to each other.

"I have something to give you," he said as he laid a small, fabric-covered book on her lap. "These are the things that remind me of us."

She opened the book in her lap and a huge smile appeared on her face. They flipped through it laughing and crying and adding to the colorful stories that the quotes, quips, and lyrics in the book brought back to them.

When they reached the end, Soupy said, "I have more to say and it might take me awhile to get it all out, so please bear with me."

Honesty nodded and smiled while closing the book. She set it on the couch beside her.

He cleared his throat before he began. "I've reached the point in my life when I long to know if my search is over or just beginning. I've rested my head in hotels, hammocks, and houses, both with and without pillows, many nights trying to decide if the woman sleeping next to me was the right one. A single night of satisfaction never turns to true love, so I've continued to travel light in search of that place—that place called home—where a woman takes me into her arms and allows me, even wants me, to unpack my thoughts and share them with her: no remorse and no reservation, just a lifetime of memorable returns. I've been listening to what everyone says about us: you, your parents, and our friends. I've heard all of it," he paused, and then corrected himself, "I mean, I've heard everyone's thoughts about how I treated you. Yet I can't resist what I hear inside of me, it speaks more loudly about my feelings for you now than it did back then. Within me is truth—and I've learned how to better listen to it—truth about the deep feelings I have for you." Soupy stopped to catch his breath, sat up a bit more, and took a moment to mentally check his place in the speech he needed to give. "I can still hear what you said to me that New Year's Day—all of me or none of me—your slumbered body beside me on the floor of your bedroom, so much pain I caused you. I never, ever want to hurt anyone like that again. Never. I know I struggled to tell you my true feelings that day, but since then I've made it my duty to be open and honest."

Soupy adjusted his position on the couch and turned toward her. She reciprocated by turning toward him, as well. "I was afraid to watch you leave me. I feared a commitment that was going to get severed by the thousands of miles between here and there. I was too young and stupid to realize what we *really* had. You've always joked about how American women have a plan for their lives—a plan that will go wrong because that's exactly what life does: it happens. Well, I had a plan too, a plan that didn't involve moving to another country right out of high school. I'd been groomed by friends and family to go to college here in the United States; it was so ingrained in me, I never considered any other alternative. So, instead of choosing you, I chose my plan, even though you were teaching me more about life and love than I'd ever learned about anything else." Soupy took a deep breath. "Am I still scared? Yes, of course, but I'm not scared of you leaving me here in the States again—in fact, I know that's the most likely scenario—I fear that you'll never come back. I mean, not in a physical sense, I fear that we'll never get back to each other no matter where we are in the world." He placed his hand on her knee and said quietly but with confidence, "Honesty, I believe we're right for each other. Life has changed for both of us so much, but I still believe it. I believe we were right for each other back then, and now we've walked two different paths to the same place—this place right here on this couch—hopefully, both wanting the same thing from our lives at the same time." He quickly took another breath and gulped. "Therefore, I have to tell you this now because I don't know if I'll ever get another chance to do so: You alone know the way to my heart. I'd be the happiest man in the world if you choose to walk this path together with me. In other words, Honesty, I believe we're meant for each other." Her hand grabbed his and then he added nervously, "Do you?"

She sat there, a tear in her eye and a smile on her face, looking as if more loving words had never been spoken to her.

He couldn't stand the pause between his question and her answer. Words were coming straight from his heart, so he added, "With all the letters and feelings that have crossed the miles between us, maybe you know I never stopped caring for you. I've longed to pour out these feelings, waiting for an opportunity to do so in person to convey the depth behind them. Everyone in my life, friend or family member, knows exactly who you are to me—they all know how I feel about you, how much I love you, and how much I've desired to tell you all of this in person. The time has come—I believe and hope—to do something in my life that's more important than anything I've ever done. There are no more ties or anchors or beliefs to hold me back from my dreams. I'm young and free and curious. I want to experience true love and—"

Soupy saw words starting to form on her lips. "P-p-please Honesty, please let me finish. I beg you. I need to get through this—despite whether you already know your answer—I need to, have to, say this out loud in order to move on to the next stage of my life, no matter what path it takes."

She touched Soupy on the shoulder and nodded for him to continue.

Tears flowed from his eyes. Breathing had become nearly impossible. Though difficult, he surged forward. He had to. "You've thought about being with me, I'm sure of it. If not, then I must resign myself to the fact that you once thought such things, and accept that I'll only remember, but never again experience, squeezing your hand and feeling you squeeze mine back."

She gently squeezed his hand and he squeezed hers back, which gave him the confidence to complete his thought.

Soupy was long-winded and emotional, but living in the moment and letting the words flow directly from his heart. "I've allowed the music, flowers, and letters to speak for me, but none of them have been able to perfectly say what I'm going to say to you now." He collected himself. "I love you, Honesty. Jag älskar dig hemskt mycket, och kommer alltid att göra så," he said, struggling through her native language. "I've been waiting so long to say those words to you in a way that gives you no doubt, absolutely *no* doubt of their validity. Honesty, I'll follow you across the boundaries of any nation and over the depths of any sea if that's what it takes for us to be together. I'll do this, hopefully, hand-in-hand with you, trading squeezes and learning from love." He looked deep into her eyes. "You *are* my dream."

They were both openly crying. Honesty wanted to speak, but could only wipe her eyes, nod her head, and beg for him to keep talking, never wanting this emotional moment to end.

"Tack så hemskt mycket…for being you. Thank you…for being you," he said, and she laughed.

"Ja ja," she said, still crying.

Soupy continued, "I want to hear about your dreams. I want you to teach me more of your language. I want to show you all the wonders I've discovered in my country during my travels and I want you to show me the beauty of yours—places I've yet to see, but you already know so well. I want to hold your hand. I want to see you smile. I want to fall asleep with you on my mind and in my arms. I want to sit across from you and tell you stories until you laugh so hard you're begging for a timeout to wipe your eyes with a tissue. I want to spend my days telling you how much I want you and need you. I want to play with your hair. I want to skip barefoot on beaches leaving a path of love in our wake. But all that said, there is one thing I'd like to say to you more than any other." He paused for effect, placed his hand under her right cheek, and tilted his head before he said, "Hej."

They both laughed loudly, but their hands quickly found their mouths so as not to wake everyone else in the house. When they'd calmed their laughter, she looked at him to ask, "Hey, h-e-y, or hej, h-e-j?" and their laughter once more filled the room.

Soupy shrugged his shoulders and replied, "Does it really matter anymore, as long as we keep asking it?" He pulled his palms together and finished his long speech by opening them up to her and saying, "This is what I have to offer you."

Honesty grabbed his hands and held them in hers. She said, "No one has ever done anything like this for me—the book, the words, the emotions—and I don't know that anyone else ever will."

Soupy shook his head in affirmation, barely able to contain his anticipation.

"These are very special to me and always will be," she said as she took a breath, "But I'm with someone else; I've been with him since I returned home and I think he's the one for me."

Even though he'd considered this outcome, Soupy's heart disintegrated with the last letter of her last word. He wasn't angry with her; he had gotten an answer and could now move on with his life, but he couldn't yet actually move—not a word or a smile or a shrug.

"Thank you for all of this," she said through a fountain of tears. She held him in her arms for a few minutes though he was barely capable of holding her back, then she simply got up and went to bed. Her arm trailed across his chest as she left the couch. Honesty walked out of the room wiping her eyes, not looking at him. Soupy had no idea what to do next. There was no will to act. Everything inside of him screamed with the clarity of her intent to be with someone else. It was over so quickly, too quickly, though it took so long to prepare and deliver and now…now…what was he supposed to do?

The path in front of him had been revealed; it was the path of loneliness.

Chapter 14

I opened my eyes quickly—a reaction born from intense fear—and pressed my hands against the hard plastic wall in front of me, which forced my back to slide across the floor and into a cushioned wall. It was dark and I was in motion; it was then that I realized I was lying on the back seat of a car.

Other than the road, the first thing I heard was a familiar song on the radio, and an unfamiliar voice singing the words.

You made me promises, promises…

It was the familiar voice that kept me from sitting up; I didn't yet want to be discovered as awake because I felt the overwhelming need to first understand my surroundings. Numbers and letters were only inches from my face, visible only with the passing of each streetlight. 0-1-5-dash-1-5-1-5. They made no sense to me. I backed away from them and could see the entire sign: COMPLAINTS? 888-015-1515.

You knew you'd never keep.

It was obvious when I sat up that I was in the back of a taxicab, but was it a cab in the real world or the dream world? I shook my head back and forth furiously in an attempt to make some sense of it. There wasn't much legroom in the backseat of this cab; it was built for an end-of-shift, high-pressure hose down with its plastic seats, floorboards, seat backs, and of course, rotating pay slot in the Plexiglas.

Promises, promises.

We were speeding down a highway at night, similar to the empty one I'd recently driven in my own cab. And likewise, the driver was trying to slalom the Botts' Dots, with much the same result as I'd had in hitting them more than missing them. The combination of speed and steering made it difficult to avoid sliding back and forth on the plastic bench seat; a torturous amusement park ride that wouldn't stop.

Why do I believe?

The driver jumped on the brakes with both feet causing my head to smash into the Plexiglas, and I blacked out.

Chapter 15

"SHIT!" I screamed and yanked the cab into the ditch on the side of the road. Promise screamed. Gravel ricocheted off the undercarriage as I dropped both feet simultaneously on the brake pedal in an effort to stop the car as quickly as I could. The cab bounced across the culvert and continued its sideways slide up the other side of the ditch for a good twenty yards before coming to a stop. A rear tire bounced playfully into the woods, as if freed from capture, before a cloud of dirt billowed over the back of the cab to obstruct my view. I hulked over the steering wheel, gasping, my forehead resting on it, staring at the speedometer. "Shit," I repeated, more calmly than before.

Tell me about it, Promise said in agreement.

Without moving my head, I asked, "You okay?"

Fine. You?

"I'm alive. I think."

When your heart stops racing and you pull your head away from the wheel, can you tell me what the hell that was all about?

"Yeah, hold on." We had stopped in front of my friend's house, where Honesty had lived for a year, and we were lucky to have avoided any nearby trees. "Promise, I—," but I was too confused to find the words to explain what had just happened. "Where were you?"

What do you mean, 'where was I?'

I put my forehead back down on the steering wheel and tried to think.

Are you okay? Promise asked.

I shook my head back and forth, an implied no. "There was—," I winced as I talked into the center of the steering wheel. "There was another cab."

Another cab?

"—but I wasn't driving. I was—"

You weren't driving?

"Someone else was driving. Someone was singing. Someone else was—"

A car horn sounded right in front of us, and when I looked up I saw a cab identical to ours idling on the road, no driver and no passengers. On instinct, since our cab was totaled, I opened up the door to head for the other cab.

Soupy? Soup, where are you go—

I didn't reply, as soon as I stepped out of this cab I could no longer hear her voice. This new cab was pointing the opposite direction, toward the driveway. *Convenient.* I dragged my left hand smoothly from the front headlight of the cab along the yellow paint of the right front quarter panel, up the front windshield, and over the roof until I reached the end of the front door. I pulled the door open and glanced briefly and thoughtlessly into the back seat as I sat down. Luckily, Promise wasn't in my new cab.

Everything was the same. In fact, this cab was an exact replica of the old cab. I looked back at the wreckage of the old one and realized I didn't need to assess the damage; I'd actually had that car accident in real life. The rear axle was severed and the exhaust was filled with mud. It would be a while before that cab was put back into service. I pulled the transmission handle down into drive and slowly made my way up the driveway to park in what had become a familiar spot. I then relaxed and ran my fingers over the steering wheel for several minutes.

The back door opened, closed, and Promise complained, *I can't believe you made me walk up the driveway.*

I didn't answer her. Instead, I drew a screen on the garage door and allowed it to play. Soupy sat on the couch just after Honesty had left the room. He didn't move. He barely breathed.

Soup? Wake up, Soup, I heard from the back seat.

Yes, wake up, Soup, I thought. I didn't know if she was talking to him or me. I didn't have anywhere else to go. He didn't have anywhere else to go. What reason was there to wake up?

My seat shook as Promise tried to rouse me from my catatonic state.

SOUP!!!

"He's rebooting," I said.

Is that what you're doing, too?

"I don't know…maybe. Maybe I'm just thinking."

I don't like it when you go away.

"I don't have anywhere to go, neither does he," I said as I pointed to the screen.

What's he thinking about?

"Everything. Nothing. All I can really say is that his mind is working a mile a minute rewiring itself to figure out what's next."

But I thought you said you'd already considered all the possibilities that could come from your conversation with Honesty?

"Well, yeah, but I hadn't figured out what to do about them, I just expected any of them could occur, not which one *would* occur and what I'd do next."

After a moment, she said, *What* was *next?*

"I honestly don't remember."

Why do you make every decision such a thought-laden process?

"When I think, I'm comparing the voice in my head to the voice in my heart. For most of my younger life I'd lived in my head, but Honesty gave my heart a voice. She made it audible and *important*. She added an unfamiliar complexity to my decision-making process, as you can see.

Yeah, that's obvious.

"I'd be a better man for it, but I hadn't the slightest clue how to consume it."

What do you mean?

"I mean I'd never used my heart to make a decision. Never. I'd always, *always,* used my head. It operated in the rational world, cataloged my everyday experiences with people, and understood the physical connections between things. My heart, on the other hand, was my center of pleasure, definitely not a trustworthy place to put any real-world decision-making."

That probably defines a difference between you and your friends; the voices in their hearts drove their predilection for risk and pleasure. But look at you, your heart went from your center of pleasure to your center of pain. Know what I mean?

"Yeah."

So if we're learning something, then don't forget that part.

I raised my finger in the air to note that I'd heard her, but didn't confirm it audibly.

Soupy, do you think love resides in the head or the heart?

"It's a great question, but I dunno, Promise."

Venture a guess.

"Really? Now?"

You said you didn't have anywhere else to go, neither does he, so talk.

"Alright." After a few seconds, I answered, "I'd say that love *should* reside in both the head and heart because it *should* fill the mind and the body, you know, fill the intellect and the soul."

Yes, it should. I agree, but does it?

"No, I don't think so. So few people learn to listen, first of all, and second, people have a tendency to hone in on one voice, one source, and trust what it says without verifying it against other sources." After a moment, I added, "Shit, that happens in politics and business and news; that shit happens everywhere. Too many are blind to thought."

Blind to thought, yes. Don't think, just act.

"That works great when you have to survive, but our lives aren't threatened every day."

Failure to evolve?

"Exactly," I agreed. "Please find me another woman who uses her brain."

We sat briefly in silence, watching as Soup continued to sit on the couch.

I'm sad he's so blue.

I chuckled. "Blue? It's my favorite color."

Why?

"You're lookin' at it," I said as I pointed to the screen. "Blue is the color of deep things. The color of things I love to ponder: the blue sky, the ocean blue, blue jeans, and am I blue, so blue."

Blue jeans?

"A nice ass in a pair of blue jeans is certainly something to ponder," I added.

Promised hummed in agreement.

So tell me, you're supposed to learn something from every girl you date. What did you learn from Honesty?

"The obvious answer…hmm…I don't *always* get what I want. Is it that simple?"

Well, it's true: people don't always get what they want, and sometimes it's hard to admit. We make mistakes and we learn from them. As long as we apologize and strive not to repeat them, they are forgivable and valuable lessons to us. Besides, who wants to be perfect anyhow?

"Perfection is boring."

Exactly, if something is perfect then there's no room for improvement, but I think you learned more than that; I'd say you learned something equally as simple.

"What's that?"

You learned how to love.

"Yes, I'd definitely say that's true. I'd never cared for anyone like I cared for her. She made me *think* about love."

I'm not saying she made you 'think' about love; she made you feel *it.*

"The heart. Yes, the heart versus the head. I'm with you."

Exactly.

"I learned that I still had a lot to learn," although brief, a smile crossed my face. "But I think all that thought created more questions than answers."

As it should at such a young age, Soupy. You're not going to get all the answers the first time around.

"But I don't like doing anything twice."

Get over it. You'd never loved before you met Honesty, and you'd never lost either.

"Is it possible to understand one without the other?" I asked.

It's a good question, one that I don't have an answer for.

"What is love anyway? I mean, we just watched part of my life where I had it, but only for a few months. I certainly couldn't define it yet."

I don't think there's anything wrong with that. You didn't have many examples in your life to point at prior to loving Honesty. It's kinda why we're on this mission, remember?

"I certainly think the head and heart are linked. Maybe there are two kinds of love: one for your head and one for your heart. It's never easy, but it's easier to find one or the other, and difficult to find them both in the same person. Hell, it's hard enough for me to find *one* of them in one person. People find love in the head or love in the heart and then hold fast to it, shorting themselves of a fuller love that would make them much happier."

Maybe.

"What if we think of love as a language? The right woman speaks to my head by filling my days and nights with witty banter, exploration into thought and opinion, so we can enjoyably and respectfully converse about the ways of the world. The right woman also speaks to my heart to fill it with passion, literally making my heart smile inside my chest each time she walks into the room."

For you, which one wins, the head or the heart? With which do you lean on to make the right decision?

"I don't think like that because I'm not so black and white; not so one or the other. You gotta have both. My head and heart must communicate with each other. Up until I dated Honesty, I'd never had a reason for my head and heart to talk with each other." I motioned to Soupy sitting on the couch. "Even now, I don't know if they speak the same language. It's a journey, as you know, and I don't know if, or when, it will end, but it was in this moment on the couch that I knew it had really started."

Honesty was your first love and you learned a lot with her, but there's a lot you haven't yet noticed. Did you notice how energized you were when teaching her about your world and learning about hers? That's a major part of what makes you who you are. You know?

"That I'm a teacher and I crave learning?"

Yes, but that's not exactly what I'm saying. You're a Healer, and sometimes being a Healer means being an educator. Your conversations with Honesty about your world helped her become part of it.

"Yeah, I can see that."

And, she was willing to forgive you. She let you back in. Forgive and hope for forgiveness, that's part of how you should live. Sure, it's a simple thought, but it has large implications because its roots are founded in the desire and effort to be a good person, not just for yourself, but for the greater good. In other words, don't offend someone intentionally. When you realize you've offended someone unintentionally, then work hard to explain why you did it and understand why it was considered offensive. Hope to be forgiven, and then remember what you learned to avoid doing it again. I look at those moments as learning opportunities. I'm here. You're there. Between us lies what we can learn.

"I like it as a mantra: do good in the world, forgive, and hope to be forgiven."

It works, doesn't it? At least, I think it does.

"It could. Now, if we can get everyone else to buy into it," I said.

Let's not tackle the whole world just yet. Let's stay focused on you. Honesty was your first love, numero uno, and the number "one" is a spiritual symbol of a new beginning. It is pure, indivisible, and comes from nothing else. Therefore, your experience with Honesty was just that: raw, primal, fresh, and new. You could compare nothing to her, yet she became the basis of comparison for the rest of your life. She's now a source, an experience you can draw upon to evaluate your feelings in the future. She represents the beginning of your capacity for love, as well as the start of your journey.

"I'm thankful to her for that."

Finally—and I need you to understand this, Soupy—you didn't break her as much as you think you did. It takes quite a bit of gumption to leave everything you've known in life and decide to spend a year in a foreign country with people you've never met. She had strength to begin with, and it probably helped her recover more quickly.

"Thank you for saying that, Promise." Worthy or not, some guilt lifted.

She was the brightest light ever to shine on your life. She did that for everyone, not just you.

"Yes, she did."

It's good for you to know this so you can recognize it in the future. Okay?

"Yes ma'am."

Chapter 16

I sat on the exact same couch as I'd just watched Soupy and Honesty sit on, while a cicada started a song outside. His mates were soon to join in, as they are known to do, to attract females. And then, the lights in the house went out.

A voice in the darkness said, *They're not singing for mates. They're calling out in distress.*

My head snapped toward the direction of her voice, but I couldn't see her figure in the darkness. "Distress?" I asked.

Yes, cicadas also use their tymbals to note distress. Inquiring minds want to know, what do you *sing when in distress?*

I asked, "Who are you?"

Step outside and you shall see.

I wasn't sure I wanted to do that based on the way she said it. "Why?"

You'll have to get off the couch at some point.

She was right.

Well?

My conundrum was between curiosity and fear: I was curious to know more about her, but I feared what knowing more might reveal.

The volume of the cicadas increased. I closed my eyes and listened. No longer could I hear where one cicada ended and another began; in unison they played one continuous tone.

I've called them here to convince you.

"Convince me?"

To get up.

"I don't need any help with that."

I beg to differ.

"Who the hell are you?" I asked again, more confused and frustrated this time.

You don't have time to repeat yourself.

"Apparently I do since you haven't answered yet!"

The volume of the cicadas grew uncomfortably loud. I put my hands over my ears, but it didn't help.

Ready?

I didn't answer her question, just rose and started toward the door. As I neared it, I reached out and flipped the light switch, an attempt to discover whom the voice belonged to, but the lights didn't cooperate. I forced the switch up and down several times, but the only thing that changed was the song of the cicadas growing louder.

It's not that easy, she said. *I'll show you.*

My back arched in pain as something icily cold pierced my shoulder. I felt the tendril moving inside of me, making its way through my neck and into my soul, where it tapped it like drawing sap from a maple tree. A drip-drip-drip into a metal bucket on the floor began, and there was nothing I could do.

As my soul dripped away, the cicadas rejoiced.

Outside, the sun rose, night had already slipped away.

You won't recognize the light without knowing the dark.

I turned around and saw Honesty and Soupy sitting on the couch again. Except, this time her image wasn't vivid, it was ghostly. She got up and left Soupy sitting there. Then, she repeated the act. It happened over and over, a five-second clip replaying the end of us. I screamed in frustration hoping Soupy would hear me, and save me, to no avail.

I grunted, and the dripping stopped, then started again. *Save your soul? Who will save your soul?* "Okay, here we go," I said to myself, then forced my internal pressure as high as it would go, as if I'd just landed in an airplane and needed my ears to pop. The intravenous tendril slid out, slightly. I took in a massive breath of air and built the pressure again. The tube released and slithered away.

I could move again. I'd been in this house so many times, it was easy to move in the dark. Behind me was the door from the kitchen to the garage. The two-car garage door was almost always open, so it would provide an easy escape. Except, when I crossed the threshold I was somewhere else; someplace unknown to me entirely. The only link back to where I'd left was the song of the cicadas, which wound down until a few stragglers ceased droning. It was chilly and crisp and dark, not like a garage should feel. And there was...sky.

My eyes adjusted.

I'd transitioned from a known horror to an unknown one.

This is The Bind, the voice said.

"The what?" I asked.

The Bind. No one can find you here. Stay as long as you like.

"The what?" I repeated.

Her silhouette moved across the ground and disappeared among a covey of trees not too far from where I stood, maybe fifteen or twenty yards. *Make yourself at home. Explore as much as your heart desires,* she said, and then followed up her words with a disconcerting cackle.

I took my first steps in The Bind and my body tensed up. A well of emotional anger grew inside of me. *Where is this coming from?* I clenched my hands into fists. I closed my eyes, crumpled up my face, curled my toes, and tensed my muscles. I was a snake coiling up prior to a strike. All of my negative emotions coalesced--when I'd been ridiculed, taken advantage of, disrespected, fooled—all those emotions released in one Herculean scream, "AGGGGGGGGHHHHHHHHHHHHHHHHHHHHH!"

Afterward, I doubled over, exhausted, and breathless as my body heaved.

Use it, the voice said.

No longer chilly, I felt the heat of a steam boiler—my pilot light was lit and radiating warmth—an internal fire, a new fire, a fire I'd never before felt. It came with a deep desire to speak my mind, to say all the things I'd always wanted to say to those who thought they knew me, but who didn't know the first damn thing about me.

A circle of boulders existed on the ground inside the surrounding covey of trees. The round stones were different sizes, protruding from the ground six inches to, maybe, two or three feet. In each case, most of their masses were buried in the ground. I stepped up on a boulder that was about a foot in height, and let my hands drop to my sides as words bubbled ever closer to my lips.

"The bullshit of the real world doesn't matter here; it's irrelevant in here. No longer will I let it bombard me without battling back. No! No longer will I keep it all inside until it eats me alive."

Yes, she said, *that's right.*

"Those who speak *only* in a filibuster of bullshit have taught me well, little do they know, for I have listened, I have seen, I can stack bullshit into layers upon layers of total bullshit to completely cover up the truth. I bid you farewell, truth. Anyone want to oppose me? I'll shove this bullshit back down your throat before you ever realize where it came from."

A few cicadas sang the refrain of their song. She coaxed them, *Gather around, friends, gather around.*

I continued, "Here, here—RIGHT HERE—," I said as I stamped my foot on a stone. "I will self-actualize without the bureaucracy of hierarchy. HERE—," I stomped again. "I will find my own relevance: relevance as *reason*, relevance for *action*, relevance in *response*."

More things moved in the darkness. More things came to listen. More of them applauded in their own way.

I was singing my mating song.

"Do you want to hear more? Do you want to *know more*?" I didn't wait for a response. "What we are taught is nothing—NOTHING—more than a recipe for cutting to the front of the line. CUT. CUT. CUT." I said as I mimicked scissors with my fingers. "We are taught to be quicker. We are taught to be stronger. We are taught to last longer. HOO-HOO and RAH-RAH. What does that get us? I said, WHAT DOES THAT GET US? I'll tell you what it gets us—," I hopped from one boulder to the next. "It gets us stale bread. Who wants some? WHO WANTS SOME?" I feigned crumbling up stale bread in my hands as I hopped from stone to stone, flinging it outside the perimeter of the circle. The ground moved as something, a lot of somethings, fed.

"I'm saving you, yes, just as you asked." I smiled as I stepped past the place where the silhouette of the female voice sat. Calmly, I added, "What we are taught is nothing as soon as everyone knows it. So let me tell you what I'm going to do for you; I'm going to reinvent education. Yes, you heard me right. I'm going to reinvent *your* education. They, those bullshit bastards, they think they know what's best, but what's best is always changing; that's what we know, what *WE KNOW!*" I clapped and thunder sounded across The Bind. My tongue drew across my lips, moistening them, before I wiped my forearm across my face to dry them off again. "They don't have any examples of what's best anymore. NONE. Their ideals are forgotten, their textbooks don't teach, and their storytellers are dead-dead-dead-Dead-DEAD." I was now on a roll, walking casually from rock to rock while I continued my speech. "New techniques will be found. Where?"

Here, she said excitedly.

"Yesss, here. In The BIND!" I jumped and landed on a boulder with both feet as I said it, raising my arms out to my sides and looking up into the sky. I shouted to The Universe, "DOOOO YOUUUU HEARRRR MEEE?" Thunder slowly tumbled into a great crescendo as the sky quickly filled with angry-looking clouds, which provided an excellent answer to my question. There was applause all around, on land and in the sky. As I bathed in it, a drop of rain landed on my cheek. I wiped it up pleasantly and sucked the liquid from my index finger. "Mmmmmm, *we* will respect experience, not titles, no, never titles. We wait in line for titles. NO MORE. This democracy of lines that make up life? NO MORE. My life izzzzz *not* a democracy, NO!" I screamed, "I AM AN AUTOCRAT. AUTOCRAAAAACY! I AM THE ONE WITH UNLIMITED CONTROL OVER OTHERS!" The rain came heavy and wet, but no one moved. They were mesmerized.

I caught the rain in my mouth and then spit it out. "GROW, DAMMIT!" I squatted down to direct my yell at the things on the ground, encouraging them. "GROOOOOOOOW! SATISFYING YOUR SOUL IS YOUR OWN RIGHT!" The applause came once more, and much louder than before. I stepped slowly from stone to stone, enjoying my glory as I rubbed my chin in thought.

"Yes, I have it," I said, shaking a finger back and forth in the air. "We will get out of line. Yes, get out of line. We will not do things the way they've been done—those ways are dead. If we trample the toes of the distinguished, then so be it." Suddenly, with a great rush of energy, I shouted, "ARE. YOU. WITH. ME?!" Applause.

"*WE*. WILL NOT. DO AS THEY SAY. *WE*. WILL NOT. REGURGITATE." Applause.

"PROCREATE." Applause.

"PRAY." Applause.

"OR OHHHH-BEY." Applause.

"IF THEY FORCE US TO MEMORIZE THEIR SO-CALLED FACTS, THEY WILL *BURN*." As I clenched my fist in the air it began to glow a deep, hot red. "SATISFYING MY SOUL IS MY OWN RIGHT!"

Yes, she agreed.

"I WILL LOSE MY REALITY."

Yes.

"GETTING LOST WILL MAKE ME FREE!"

Yes.

"THE BIND WILL MAKE ME FREE!"

Yes.

"IMAGINE, FRIENDS, EEEEE-MAGINE HOW WE WILL FEEEEEEEEEED!!!"

Imagine, she said as she waved her hand across the darkness.

The Bind erupted with noise, part applause, part somethings scurrying away. I collapsed on a boulder, utterly exhausted.

You've made quite the first impression.

I didn't answer. The crash from an utterly amazing adrenaline rush had begun.

This, all *of this, is what you can discover when you empty your mind.*

Chapter 17

The motel room pillow under my head was wet with sweat. The sheets stuck to my body as I rolled to find the drier end of the pillow. My eyes opened. I could feel the wetness on my body, confirmed by my hand. Out of instinct, I smelled my fingers expecting the acrid scent of urine, but was happy to find it absent. *Rain*, I thought. Too tired and too drunk to do anything about a wet bed, I scurried over to the dry half and went back to sleep.

Chapter 18

I sat once more in my cab, hands on the steering wheel, staring down the middle of an empty four-lane highway. It was a scorcher outside, easily above one hundred degrees. My brow was wet, as was every other body part touching the leather seat. The radio was playing the one song that had triggered more questions for me than any other in my life.

> *"Never had a doubt,*
> *In the beginning,*
> *Never a doubt.*
> *Trusted you true,*
> *In the beginning..."*

I switched it off, trying to retain as much as I could from my first visit to The Bind, but it was slipping away from me quickly, too quickly. It was dark, that much I recall, and I was...*giving a...speech? Walking on rocks, and talking to...who was she, this voice?* I closed my eyes trying to lock down the memories, but they were already too faint.

"Okay, now what?" I asked myself aloud. Heat radiated from the sunbaked road, which prompted me to turn on the car, and subsequently the air conditioning. As the cab cooled off, I thought back to my life after Honesty. I chose to focus more on who I was, than the women I could have loved. *Yes, let's drive to those times,* I thought. I shifted into drive and began rolling away when a whistle pierced the air.

HEY, CABBIE! came Promise's recognizable voice as she knocked on the trunk of the cab.

Instinctively, I looked into the rear view mirror, but only saw a gloved hand trail across the top of the trunk. The rear car door opened and I turned the mirror away as Promise slid into the back of the cab. "You almost missed the train as it was pulling out of the station," I said.

Damn, it's hot, she said. *Glad the train is air-conditioned.*

"Tell me about it, but what can ya do about the weather?"

I always say, "There's no such thing as bad weather, only bad clothing choices," but I could go naked in this heat and not cool off.

"Prove it," I added, desperately needing something to take my mind off the mysteries that had been left in The Bind.

Keep your eyes on the road, cabbie.

"We're just sitting here, in case you hadn't noticed, no real need to look at the road. Someplace you need to go?"

Yes, wherever we'll find the next story.

"Super, but I need to talk to you about something on the way."

Oh?

"Yeah, I was just somewhere else, like, somewhere in this dream world, but nowhere I'd ever been."

That doesn't really narrow it down much, she chided.

I wasn't in the mood for playfulness. "I'm sure, but this was no ordinary place; it was *dark,*" I added.

Believe me, every possible place you can imagine exists in the dream world.

"Ever heard of a place called 'The Bind?'"

The Bind? No.

"That's where I was."

What happened, Soup?

"Well, therein lies the rub, I can't remember any of it aside from being there with someone else, some female voice, and I gave this rousing speech, and…cicadas? Yeah, lots of cicadas…and stones, you know, like, really big, buried stones."

Cicadas and stones?

"I dream like I'm watching—"

Yeah, I know.

"—a movie, right, sorry, I forgot."

Was it an important place? I mean, do you think it's relevant to our story?

"Yeah, I do, and it scares me to feel that way."

Was there anyone there other than the voice you mentioned?

"I don't think so. I didn't see anyone. It was pretty dark and I didn't feel the presence of anyone else. About all I distinctly remember is the sound of her voice."

Anyone you know?

"I'm not sure I know-know the voice, if you know what I mean, but it was comforting to hear, maybe even familiar, though I just can't place it."

A black Honda Civic flew past us on the highway in the slow lane startling both of us, and disappeared over the other side of the hill. A few moments later a highway patrol car rocked the cab with a burst of wind as it rushed by in pursuit of the Honda. As I watched the police car disappear, Promise said, *Whaddaya say we don't sit here in the middle of the road?*

"Good idea," I said and checked the side view mirrors for more traffic before stepping on the accelerator.

As we drove, farms and grasslands gave way to foothills, as mountains became visible in the distance. Promise asked, *Where are we headed?*

"After Honesty, I spent several years focused on understanding who I am. My mom said it before I left, "In order to know love, you have to know you," and I took it to heart. It made sense, logically.

What did you learn?

"I learned more about the importance of the four elements in life: air, earth, fire, water. You know, in high school you don't have much choice about what you study, most of what you're doing is making your resume look good for whatever is next. Once I got to college, I was free to explore, and when I say that, I mean free to explore some profession, sure, but also free to explore who I am. And though many other things have been hard to hold onto, or trust, or have faith in over the years, the things my great grandpa showed me when I was a kid—burn, blow, nourish, grow—I've never forgotten them."

Burn, blow, nourish, grow?

"Yeah, verbs for the four elements. My great grandpa gave me a glimpse of them when I was a kid. He told stories, and he could do the most amazing things with his hands, totally leading us to believe he was an incredible magician, but after the magic show, he once showed me that his tricks weren't magic at all; he knew the language of the four elements."

He did this in the real world? I've seen it in dreams; I've seen a lot of things in dreams, but never in the real world.

"Yes, in the real world, Promise," I replied. "He showed me his techniques when I was a kid. Though, I've never been able to replicate any without him. I've assumed his presence lent me some skill, but I believed I *could* learn, and that was one of my priorities in those years we're now talking about."

Did you?

"No, but I started understanding what my mom was talking about when she said, 'to know love.' She wasn't just talking about the word love, per say, but about all things, to *love* all things. You see, it wasn't that my great grandpa, her grandpa, could control the elements. No, he could communicate with them. He could understand their languages, and I believe interpret what they needed and what they could give."

Yes.

"But I knew, knew it as fact, that I could never understand the elements without understanding myself. I've often tried to communicate with them over the years; never gotten a response."

Do you still believe?

"Yes, I do."

So you think you need to learn this elemental language in order to find me?

"Yeah, I think that's a big part of it."

Why?

"Because I don't think I'm worthy of true love until I prove my love for these most basic, fundamental building blocks—learning their language is a sign of love. We always talk about what they do to us and then fantasize about a world where we can control them. The heat's too hot. The wind's too strong. That's totally wrong, Promise. You just said something about there never being bad weather, just bad clothing choices, and that's exactly right. When you love them, you understand them: what they need, why they burn, blow, nourish, and grow."

I think there's something to your philosophy, Soup.

"There has to be. It simply can't be that love has been lost. That if we look under the bed, or in the closet, or under the front seat of the car we'll find it. It hasn't been lost because we misplaced it last week; it's been lost *over generations.* In other words, it hasn't been lost, it's been *forgotten.*

It's definitely been forgotten, and at the same time, it's been placed way up on this pedestal. We expect it, take it for granted, think it should come easy, and that, once found, it should be around forever.

"People assume they know what love is at a young age, find a mate, get married, and start a family. This process in youth—almost to a couple—is a terrible idea; almost cultish in the freakishly, so-called normal way society casts this pressure on young couples to get married. Girls want to get married because they've dreamed about it since they were eight years old, and at some point all their friends are doing it. Boys are too oblivious to make intelligent decisions. Parents want to become grandparents. Mind you, none of this is wrong. In fact, they're wonderful changes in life for those who wish to make them, but it doesn't have to happen at such a young age, not anymore. Marriage should be a celebration of love, not a love for celebrations."

Marriage does too often turn into a hateful institution when it isn't done for the right reasons. I've seen it in thousands of dreams; the 'want' to get married overshadows all the problems in a relationship, but those problems don't go away with a party, a vacation, and definitely not once kids become part of their lives.

"Instant gratification. We all want instant gratification and assume it'll work itself out. No one takes the time to earn love, or even to learn love. Too many don't understand the major building blocks of love, which is exactly what I'm trying to learn."

The elements of love.

"Exactly," I agreed. "I'm still learning about them."

You better be. What have you learned so far?

"I started with myself; what am I made of?"

Hot air?

"Funny, but true," I replied. "I *am* made up of air: the intellectual, the overthinker. I think and reason in the abstract, leaning on curiosity and creativity to solve problems. I've been called eccentric or strange because I desire to figure out how the world works, not the mechanical inner-workings, you know, but the order of all things. I see all sides, all paths, in order to know my options before I choose one of them."

Endless supply of hot air, too, it seems.

"Do you wanna learn more or ride in silence?" I asked, playfully.

Learn more, always!

"So once I learned more about myself—and just know this conversation doesn't do justice to the work I put into it—I tried to understand the other elements and how they manifest themselves in other people. When I say there were different women in my life over these years, I really mean to say I was testing particular combinations of my air and their own dominant elements."

What did you learn?

"If I spend time with earth, then we create a dust storm. If I spend time with water, then we lose the light and flood the land. If I spend time with fire, then we burn hot, but quickly burn out. I didn't date much, but I dated enough to recognize quickly when a relationship wasn't going to work."

Didn't you leave out an element? Earth, water, fire...air, did you date someone with a dominant element similar to your own?

"Unfortunately, I didn't. I don't want this conversation to sound as if I knew what I was doing the whole time, by no means is that the truth. I was fumbling and tripping over my own feet and making silly decisions based on faulty logic—failing fast and learning as much as I could from those failures."

Yes, good for you, maybe not so much for them.

"Not always good for me either, lots of carnage with women who I probably would have been better off keeping as friends, and who might have still been in my life today if I'd not been so hell-bent to learn and so arrogant about what I already knew."

Youth, Soupy. Don't forget, you were young.

"What I focus on remembering is exactly what you told me to remember: I will fail over and over again, but I must learn from those failures. I guess I was trying to fail my way to you as quickly as I could."

Nice idea, but how did that work out?

"Look around, I'm still up here and you're still back there," I said while flipping my thumb over my shoulder. I don't want to talk about all the girls who were part of my life in this phase of it, but there's one we should quickly discuss, largely because she was the impetus for reminding me of my homework."

Bring it on.

"I ran into a high school friend at a party and our reunion turned hot very, very quickly. We jumped into the moment, feet first and holding hands, though the moment didn't last more than a summer. It was torrid, but not without substance. I'd known her for years. In fact, we'd dated briefly in high school, and I genuinely loved her as a nice, caring, beautiful person. We were young and brash and foolhardy, we didn't care about what would happen; we only cared about what *was* happening. We packed a year of emotion into a few hot summer months, spending every spare minute together. It was easy to fall in love when we'd already known each other for eight years. The time and place and combination of her fire and my air started a flame that burned very brightly. She knew she could catch my eye and get a wink in return… and she loved to do so. But I would soon have to return to school. If I close my eyes, I can still see the two of us sitting on the street curb in front of her house talking and crying about the fact that I had to leave, had to, because somewhere inside of me I knew I hadn't yet learned what I had to learn. I couldn't articulate it then, much beyond pursuing this dream I'd had since I was a kid, and the best place for me to pursue it was where I'd started this phase of the journey. That 'someplace' wasn't where she wanted to be. But dammit, having her on my arm, holding her hand, looking into her indescribably deep, blue eyes, feeling the heat of her radiating next to me, calling to me, it was hard to get up and walk away."

You left her?

"Yeah, it wasn't easy."

Like Honesty left you?

I thought about that for a moment. "Yeah, I guess. Interesting, isn't it? The way we act to keep things balanced. I put love fifteen hundred miles behind me just as Honesty put it three thousand miles behind her."

Long distance relationships suck, unless you've got one really big... travel budget.

"Dear, me," I laughed. "I thought for a second you were going to say something really risqué."

Did you now?

I could sense a temptress' smile on her face. "I left physically, but it was hard to leave emotionally. We'd agreed to try the distance thing; it was just too hard to remotely fan the flames of our heat. For a month, the letters and phone calls were enough, but it all came crashing down on her birthday. I called her the morning after she celebrated and a guy answered her phone, though she didn't have any male roommates."

Oh, dear.

"When she came to the phone, I asked about her evening and she said it had gone from fun to drunk to, now, hung over. She told me she got so drunk she passed out on the floor of her living room. I told her I wished I could have been there to celebrate with her. Promise, what I really wanted to hear back was her wish for the same. Just tell me that she wished I'd been there, too. Give me something to hold on to, you know?"

Yes, Soupy.

"But she was silent. So I asked her who had answered the phone and she said a friend who'd helped her home, and then passed out on the living room floor."

Oh, shit. Busted.

"It was awkward. I could feel the tension through the phone. There could have been many reasons for them both sleeping next to each other on the floor, sure, but the combination of my intuition and her lack of explanation, well, it was all right there on the floor for me to see."

The heat from your fire was extinguished.

"Burned out. *Flamed out,* is how it felt that day, like being drenched by a bucket of freezing-cold water. But the truth, in hindsight, was that our fire started cooling as soon as I left, since neither of us could physically stoke it any more."

How did you take it?

"I spiraled quickly into an emotional depression, and questioned who I wanted to be in life. I considered going to her, staying near her, and relying on some magical ability to figure it all out later. I thought perhaps a life of dating, marrying, and parenting at a young age suddenly wasn't all that wrong."

Wow, what a test she put you through by challenging all that you'd come to believe.

"Yes, and that's exactly the point of this story," I added. "I called my mom, and she provided the voice of reason."

I dialed in Mom's voice on the cab's radio.

* * *

"Hey, Mom," I said when she answered.

"Are you alright?" she asked.

"Well...no, not really."

"What happened?"

"I'm single again," I said through tears.

"I *knew* something was going on with you; I could feel it."

"Yeah."

"Look, Soup, I know it was tough to leave her last summer. You love her. We love her, too. But the reasons you left are the same reasons why you have to stay where you are."

"I know," and I did, but hearing it was what I truly needed.

"You might know, then again you might not, so I'm reminding you that you're pursuing this dream you've had ever since, what, junior high?"

"Yeah."

"It's about the type of man you want to be. You're feeling a lot of emotions right now, I can hear them in your voice, but don't be rash in your decision-making."

"Yes, Mom, I hear you. I just thought it was *her.*"

"You *know* who you want to be…don't forget that," she said.

"Okay."

"And don't forget to call me on Sunday mornings," she said.

"Okay, Mom, I will."

"I love you."

"Love you, too."

* * *

I love your mom! I can see where you get your insight. I wonder if her 'Little People' told her you were struggling.

"I bet they did. Promise, do you know these Little People?" I asked.

I could, you know, but I'd never know it. Those who do what I do can take any form they wish in someone else's dreams, whatever form will lend the most credibility to what we need to tell the dreamer.

"I see," I said, filing away that knowledge for future thought. "Anyway, Mom saved me on that one. Hearing her say it gave me the strength to see the right path again."

That's the second story you've told me about your mom.

"True, but at this point in my life we were growing more apart than closer together. I was so focused on learning the things she didn't learn, basically because she never left home. I still loved her, of course, and wanted to talk to her about what I was learning, it just didn't come up with all the distance between us. And let's be honest, it took the whole family a few years to recover from the collective heartbreak that ensued after Honesty left."

Now, to be fair, her leaving wasn't the whole story.

"Yes, yes, true, and I didn't mean to say it that way. You know what I meant."

Yes, just making sure you know it, too.

"Believe me. I know it."

Okay then, let me say this: a boy who loves his mother is incredibly attractive.

"Yes, and a girl who gets along with her mother is a wonderful thing, too."

You appreciate a woman's opinion, don't you?

"Yeah, I was raised around a bunch of women."

Do you think that's why you need a feminine opinion in your life?

"Need? Do I think I *need* a feminine opinion in my life? You know, yeah, I don't just *need* them, I want them. I almost always bond with mothers, no matter whose they are. If I'm traveling and I'll see one of my 'moms,' then I can say I'm 'going home.'"

Cute.

"Back to the story. After that difficult end to another relationship, I refocused on who I wanted to be. I admit, it took some time, but when I made that first step, as usual, the world stepped up to assist."

What did you truly think was your burden?

"My burden? Unhappiness."

Why?

"I didn't like being part of the herd, where everybody and every day were the same. I realized how close I'd come to doing what everyone else was doing, and that wasn't what I wanted to do."

What did you want, then?

"I didn't know *what* I wanted, but I had a better idea of what I *didn't* want."

So you were back to being a man of discovery.

"Yes, totally. No more *wan*dering around all day *won*dering if I was in the right place. I wrote a scathing op-ed about the educational system in the college newspaper, which prompted one of my professors to reach out to me for a conversation."

Were you trying to reinvent education?

"Well, yeah, I was frustrated with the system. Wait, how did you know?"

Like I've said; I know you.

I wanted to look her in the eyes, but I remembered the rules. "Well, okay. So I spoke with him about my life, how I didn't want to be quickly processed along the assembly line with the rest of the student body from orientation to graduation. That I needed to *know* more, to learn more about myself. That I needed to have some freedom to explore and discover."

What was his reply?

"'This,' he said, 'we can work with.'" I smiled. "For three months, he gave me homework assignments that involved writing, writing, and more writing about my thoughts. He set up appointments for me to interview professionals in a ton of different industries to basically ask them 'Why?' And in those homework assignments, he asked me to create art from their answers. Most of the time, that art was in words: poetry or journaling. Once in awhile, it was pencil or marker on whatever scrap of paper or cardboard was laying around. Then, we'd talk about it. The goal, of course, was to understand why people do what they do, choose what they choose, and live how they live."

Right. Everyone has a value system used to set priorities and make decisions.

"Some of the professionals I interviewed absolutely loved their jobs and relished opportunities to learn and improve. Others considered their work a necessary distraction from time with family, so they looked to leave their jobs each day as soon as possible. There wasn't anything wrong with either value system; they were just different. In my writing, I loved the passionate professionals, as I'm sure you can imagine. There were long days in their lives, but those days weren't burdensome. Their longs days were about learning and teaching; being part of something that was thoughtful or tangible or helpful to the world. They didn't bear the weekdays only to live on the weekends. They loved to shape minds. They loved to create new technologies. They loved to make life easier for others. They were all 'givers' first, not 'receivers,' and what they gave put a lot of healing into the world."

You know, parents do all of that too, but with their own children. It's just another 'profession,' if you know what I mean.

"Yeah, I guess they do, don't they?"

Mmmm hmmm. You do recall that you have them, right? Parents.

"Yeah, yeah."

But it seems, you learned that you wanted to heal like a professional heals, not *like a parent heals.*

"Yes, exactly. That my job should satisfy my pocketbook *and* my soul. For me, healing is what would satisfy my soul, so I had to look for an occupation that would allow me to work hard, discover, excel, and do good. There was this one particular conversation with my professor after I'd done several interviews, we were talking about what I'd learned and he was pressing me to make another connection-—a theme, if you will—that I should take from the interviews."

This sounds like our conversations.

"Yeah, it kind of was. Anyway, my professor was waiting for me to make the connection, but I was struggling. I scratched my eyes, squinted, and smiled, which prompted him to pick up a red colored pencil and draw an object on a piece of onion skin paper. It was a heart. I traced the heart he'd drawn with the tip of my finger hoping that his thoughts would transfer into my mind. He slowly tapped the pencil several times near the heart, not to add to the drawing, but to simulate the beating of an actual heart. 'A heart beating?' I asked him, and he asked me what makes a heartbeat. I replied, 'Love?' 'Yes,' he said, 'by interviewing them, you saw how they defined love. Now, go find your love.'"

Now, go find your love.

"Yes, ma'am."

Our drive had taken us down the western slope of a mountain range to reconnect with the sight of the ocean. I rolled down my window and took in deep breaths of air. "Can you feel that, Promise?"

The air?

"Yeah, the air." I said, as I drove the cab toward the beach. "To answer your question from earlier, it's my assumption that if I spend time with a woman made of air, then we'll both breathe deeply and happily, and do so often."

If air is good, then let's find some incredibly good air to breathe!

"Yes, let's," I replied.

We drove out onto an empty beach and parked the cab, watching in silence as the sun set over the ocean. Our background music was the sound of waves crashing on the shore.

"Ever see the green flash?" I asked.

Yes, Promise replied.

"People say it doesn't exist, but I think if you *want* to see it, you will."

I agree.

The half-circle of the sun drew to a sliver and showed us that elusive green spark as it disappeared below the horizon of the blue sea.

Beautiful. Did you see it?

"Yes," I replied.

Sometimes it's the little things, isn't it?

"Yeah, but maybe more than just sometimes. Maybe most times," I added. "I love the little things, the attention to detail that shows you care."

Any woman will love that you love the little things, and those little things will make you a fine romantic. If there are givers and receivers in the world, then you're a giver. Your satisfaction comes from giving or helping people find what they need.

Sarcastically, I said, "Duh, isn't that what a Heller does? Seems an obvious trait for someone birthed from a Walker and a Heller."

Sure, that's obvious, but on a serious note, it's also quite obvious you need to learn how to receive, and you can start by learning how to take a compliment.

"What do you mean?"

Do you feel strange when people do things for you or say nice things about you?

"Yeah, I do. Matter of fact, when it comes to compliments I either brush them off or feel the need to compliment in return."

Quit it.

"Why?"

Okay, when I say that, I mean you don't have to do this complimentary return complimenting every single time. Accept that you deserve the compliment, don't deflect it.

"Again, why?"

Because you should bathe in all you *are for a moment. Accept that you did something good or nice, and simply learn how to say, 'Thank you.'*

"Hmmm, but—"

No buts! Jeez, are you ever listening to me? I just complimented you!

"BUT—"

NO BUTS! Promise and I both laughed. *You won't settle for less than remarkable, this much about you, at least, I know is true. So whether you're taking steps to accomplish your dreams or helping someone else accomplish theirs, just learn how to thank anyone who pats you on the back.*

"Speaking of dreams...Promise, do you dream?"

What if I'm dreaming right now, just like you?

"Well, that'd be a trip, wouldn't it?

What if I'm some other woman—tens or hundreds of other women—dreaming about this conversation with you right now, and you're my *Promise?*

"Ummm, interesting thought."

Are you asking because my answer would be further proof I exist somewhere in the world?

"Well, yeah, I guess. Sometimes you're a little too far into my own head, but at least you accept my doubts that this is real."

Doubts are rational, and of course I accept you for who you are.

"Do you dream?"

Yes, Soup, I dream.

"Do you dream of me like I dream of you?"

Yes, I dream of you, but not quite like you dream of me, unless there's something you're not telling me about yourself.

I started singing, "Ooo-OOO-OOO, dreaaaam weaver—"

Oh, Lord, Promise said, which stopped my singing.

"WHHHAT?" I asked.

It's your personality, I guess, to love and to laugh at.

"Laugh at? Laugh *with*, Promise, laugh *with*."

Sure, okay, whatever, she agreed, jokingly.

"Whizzywhig."

Whizzy what?

"Whizzywhig. W-Y-S-I-W-Y-G. What You See Is What You Get. It's an acronym. I'd write it down for you if I weren't driving."

Why on Earth are you saying whizzy-whatever?

"What you see," I said, and pointed to myself, "is what you get," and pointed back at her.

That's such bullshit, Soup. What someone sees with you is maybe a thimbleful of what's inside.

She caught me by surprise with that statement, and I'm not fond of surprises, so I stiffened up a bit behind the wheel. Fact was, she was totally right.

"Promise, have you ever taken the Myers-Briggs personality test?"

No, but I assume you have and you're about to tell me about it?

I ignored her response and continued, "Myers and Briggs, through their exam, would say that I'm Introverted, Intuitive, Thinking, and Perceptive, I-N-T-P."

I'd say that's pretty right on. Do you agree?

"I do, but the balance among them is a question I often consider. I'm definitely an extroverted introvert. I revel in the opportunity to tell stories in public, but it drains my battery. In situations where extraversion is required for long periods of time—every dang time I end up sick. Recharge only comes from quiet isolation, like through reading a book or watching a movie."

No one ever believes that about you, do they? They all see this outgoing guy and think you love to be the life of the party.

"Yeah, I'm a real enigma, eh?"

Sure are, but I like puzzles.

"Intuitive? Yes. Thinking? Yes. Perceptive? Yes."

To find me, you're going to have to feel *something.*

"I've wondered about that. My 'T' for Thinking is so much stronger than my 'F' for Feeling. Although, I'm pretty sure who I was then—this thinking guy—has been changing as I age."

Change? That would make you the only man on Earth to ever accomplish change.

"Yeah, whatever," I replied, weakly defending my gender.

And, that would make you unique! If you're doing what everyone else is doing, then you're not likely to discover something great.

"Well, then these glorious abstract, pragmatic, tough-minded, ambitious, and hard-working traits should help me achieve great success."

Um, Soup, I said 'feeling.' Those all sound pretty thinker-focused.

Moving my forearms up and down like a robot and speaking in a robotic voice, I said, "Head. Rules. Over. Heart."

Definitely not a fan of Mr. Soupy Roboto Heller.

"No more robot, then. Back to work. So I knew I needed to focus on this 'feeling' stuff."

Feeling stu—

"Oooo, I've got a really good spot for our next story, it's up the road a little ways. When we get there, I'll start my next one."

Good.

As I fired up the engine and put the cab in drive, I also started butchering the Tony! Toni! Tone! hit, "It feeeeeeeeeeeeeels good, yeah. It feels good," but by the time I got through the chorus I was sure Promise was no longer with me because there was no way she'd sit through that rendition without saying something.

"Promise?"

There was no answer.

"PROMISE?!"

Still no answer.

As if I was playing a video game, I drove my cab up over the sidewalk, past the boardwalk and straight onto the beach, which was surprisingly firm under tires, though spitting sand wildly about. About halfway between the boardwalk and the sea, I slammed on the brakes with both feet and felt the cab slide to a stop.

With hands at ten and two on the steering wheel, I let out a loud, emotional groan, tried to push both feet through the floorboard without success, then thrust the transmission into park.

The light of the day was fading.

Chapter 19

No one else was around: no sunbathers, surfers, runners, or beach walkers. I stepped out of the cab and took a deep breath as I stretched my hands above my head and arched my back. *There's no place like home,* I thought, and considered clicking my heels together, but this place seemed homey enough for now, so it wouldn't make much sense.

A black car approached from far down the beach. It drove parallel to the water, fish tailing as it accelerated toward me.

"What the hell?" I said aloud, and briskly walked to the other side of my cab to put a protective barrier between us. It made no evidence of slowing as it approached, so I took a few steps away from the cab, giving it room to roll should it be the target. The black car fishtailed a few more times, spitting sand every which way, then slid to a stop at a forty-five degree angle to my car, the two front bumpers only a few feet apart. The sand settled.

It was an old world, black cab like you might find in London, with tinted windows. They were too dark to see inside.

For several minutes, I waited for someone to exit the vehicle, honk the horn, or flash the lights, but nothing happened. I could only hear the idling engine and the waves on the beach. With courage, I moved closer. Like a police officer might, I rounded the rear of the visiting cab and crouched stealthily alongside it, expecting the driver's door be thrust open at any moment. Nothing like that happened. I cupped my hands against the rear driver's side window, which was another failed attempt to see inside due to the tint being far too dark. I backed away and sidestepped in an arc toward the front, minding a clear distance from the outswing of the doors. Also a fruitless task, so I moved back around to the trunk of the car. As I neared the passenger side doors, the rear door opened. It surprised me, of course, so I backed away to shelter behind the cab. When no one got out, I moved swiftly away and to an angle that would allow me to see inside. It was empty. And I couldn't see if there was a driver because the "taxi" glass between the back and the front was also tinted.

"Should I stay or should I go now?" I sang in a whisper as I tried to think. "If I go there will be trouble. If I stay there will be double." I inched closer to the open door. *Curiosity or fear?* Explore and discover. *Exactly.* I quietly slipped into the back, leaving one leg hanging out in case a hasty escape was needed. In the back, there was a familiar sign, "COMPLAINTS? 888-015-1515."

I whispered once more, "If I go there will be trouble. If I stay there will be double," I paused, thinking, for a few seconds. "Screw it," I said. "It's just the dream world," and yanked the door closed.

The engine revved and the brake released. We did a half-donut on the packed sand, then bounced through the looser portion of the beach...or so I assumed since I couldn't see outside. The cab bounced up onto the asphalt from the beach, throwing me into the ceiling before it bottomed out on the road and screeched sideways to a halt. "Shit, man!" I said. Without missing a beat, the driver cranked the wheel to the left, punched the accelerator, and laid rubber on the road until we were speeding away. I banged on the window between the front and the back. "HEY!" I shouted, but got no response. The door handles were useless; not that I would have exited the cab at this speed, but I surely wanted to know if I had the option.

With nothing else to try, I settled in for the ride, wherever it might take me.

Minutes passed, and it got darker inside the cab, as if the sun had set and night had come. The cab slowed and bumpily made its way from what seemed like an asphalt to a dirt road, and eventually stopped. Then, the door opened.

Outside I saw a dark field, lit only by the cab's headlights. The lights revealed a path. After I closed the door, I rapped on the driver's side window and flipped the driver the finger, holding it behind me as I walked away. The engine revved, but showed no further threat. It was chilly, so I thrust my hands into my pockets and made my way down the path. Soon, I was guided less by the headlights and more by the moonlight. The cab reversed, in the same hurried manner as before, then shifted to drive and accelerated away.

"Hit the road, Black Jack, and don't cha come back no more-no more-no more," I sang.

At the end of the path, there was a circular clearing that was home to a stand of boulders.

There came a voice, *Welcome back.*

"Hey," I said in response.

Isn't one of these stones yours?

"My stone? I dunno." I walked toward the circle of rocks.

Look, but don't touch, she said.

"Huh?"

It's just you and me this time, none of our friends.

A flashback memory of thousands, if not millions, of cicadas returned to me, stunning me with their noise for a brief second. "What the—?"

He remembers.

I didn't, and didn't, so I wasn't sure how to reply. Instead, I picked a stony perch and sat down, cross-legged.

He touches, once.

She was on the opposite side of the stone circle. It was too dark to make out anything more than her shadow.

What do you think of this place?

"What *is* this place?" I asked.

It's The Bind.

I was pretty sure I remembered her telling me that the last time I was here. "Yes, but what is The Bind?"

It's your *constraint, so you tell me.*

"My constraint? What do you mean by 'my constraint?'

She didn't answer.

"Like, when I want to get out of a cab, but the doors are locked? Or—"

Sometimes.

"Like, when I'm having a nightmare and can't wake up?'"

Yes, like that, too.

"So it's just 'The Bind."

Your *bind, but yes.*

"And who are you?"

I'm the voice in your bind.

"Do you have a name?" I asked.

I am the Nectar.

"Nectar?"

Hot, sticky-sweet, from my head, to my feet.

"I get it," I added while looking around cautiously. "By the way, your cab driver sucks."

She laughed before she added, *So I've heard.*

"What do we do here in The Bind?" I asked.

We talk.

"What do we talk about?"

Whatever you want.

This conversation reminded me of the first time I met Promise. "Okay, you know how I got here, but how did *you* get here?"

This is my home.

"You're here *all* the time?"

Mostly.

"How do you see anything?"

Your eyes get used to it, she answered.

Neither of us said anything for several seconds. If it was a game of Who Could Be Quiet the Longest, I was sure Nectar would win.

"We can talk about anything I want?"

Yes.

"Then, how to do I get out of here?"

She laughed. *Find yourself in a bind?*

"Very funny."

How do you think?

I thought before I answered. "I survey the scene for my options." Looking around, I didn't see *any* options that amounted to anything other than getting lost in the dark. Aside from knowing there's a dirt road that leads to a paved road that leads to a beach, I didn't know much at all.

Your options here?

With my best English-accented, Hawkman's voice from the movie *Flash Gordon*, I said, "Flying blind on a rocket cycle at the moment."

My accent didn't elicit the humor I'd intended. Then again, I'd only just met Nectar and hadn't any idea how to unwind her.

Flying blind on a rocket cycle? she replied.

This made me chuckle, since it actually followed the script of the movie.

Pardon?

"Never you mind," I said. "Options? Aside from knowing this clearing and that road," I said as I pointed over my shoulder, "I don't know much."

The Bind, she said.

The most knowledgeable person I knew on this new topic, that being The Bind, was sitting in a stone circle with me. "I suppose you're my best option," I stated.

I thought you might think so.

"Now what?"

We talk—

"Fuck-sake, I know we talk—"

Or, we don't.

She had me there, since I didn't have many other options.

That's not what I meant, she said.

"The only *thing* I can *see* here is you, but I can't see you far well enough." I slowly stood from my cross-legged position.

Don't touch, she repeated.

I stepped one stone closer to her.

He touches, twice.

"I'm thinking about my options," I said.

Your future?

"It's hard not to."

It seems you're running away with yourself.

"Exactly," I said, as I stepped onto the next stone.

Tsk-tsk. Where does he run to?

"I'm trying to find options. Options have answers."

Breaking the rules is an option.

"Yes, it can be." I was now about ten stones from her.

Once you are here, being bound is not a choice.

It was a strange statement, one that made me pause before taking the next step.

It's wonderfully sticky.

Those two words, "wonderfully" and "sticky," weren't words I'd heard used together that often, if ever.

He listens, but does he hear?

A choice crossed my mind: bolt for the road and try to find my way back to the beach, or continue toward Nectar, who I hoped might unlock more options.

Will he touch again? she coaxed invitingly.

I stepped to the next stone.

She purred. *He does. There's good and bad inside of you.*

"Yes, I suppose there's good and bad inside of everyone." There was no longer a desire to delay between stones. I walked them until only two stones separated us.

He touches and touches and touches sum'more, despite being warned.

My breath was labored, not from the effort, but from the proximity of her presence.

When you lay in bed, you're both reading the story you've lived and writing the story you've yet to read.

I replayed her words in my head to make sure I understood them. My reply was intimately simply, "Yes."

What makes for a good story?

"Drama," I quickly answered.

She laughed and said, *Definitely.*

My mind was racing, so I waited for her to continue talking.

Some try to avoid it, then they're unprepared when it arrives.

"Why avoid it when it's inevitable," I somewhat meekly said. "It's better to have a plan for it."

Is that what's going on here? You have a plan?

No good, or even plausible, answers came to mind.

What, not going to tell me your secrets?

"Not unless you can read my mind."

So you think, she said as she stepped one stone closer to me.

"Huh?" escaped my lips.

If this is a dream, maybe we are *in your mind.*

"Promise would probably agree with you."

Promise? Did you say 'Promise?'

Nectar leapt onto the stone adjacent to mine. I felt an invisible wave of sudden anger that caused me to shift my feet to strengthen my balance.

"D-d-do you know her?" I stammered.

I know her. Nectar slapped her hands together in front of my face, then spit on the ground beside us before she continued, *Has she been promising you sugar plum fairies and trueee looooove and all that nonsense?*

"Well, yeah."

I hope you can live with broken promises.

"Why do you say that?" I asked, my anxiety turning from trepidation to defense.

Look around. Do you see true love?

"Not mine, no. Is it yours?"

She ignored the question. *Don't just look around here. Look at your life. Do you see it there?*

"No, but that's why I'm supposed to find her. *We* will be the example of true love in the world that everyone else can see."

She's been saying that for years. Do you know how many years?

"No, how many?"

Years. YEARS! To every Gullible Gus who comes along. Let me ask you this: how many of these true loves do you think she's found?

"I don't know."

NONE! Nectar shouted, and a chilly breeze rolled through the clearing.

"But I'm the one."

In a whiny voice she repeated my words, *But I'm the one.*

"There's no need for that."

Everyone is the one. Why? Because there isn't one.

"I don't believe you."

Don't believe me, then, and waste your life looking for something that doesn't exist.

"It does exist. It *has* to exist," I stated.

She laughed aloud. *Why? Isn't the world a more interesting place with all the drama, as you said?*

"Yes, of course it is. Your assumption is that dramatic is synonymous with traumatic."

And, it's not?

"No, not at all. Love is romantic, which is also dramatic."

And traumatic.

My anxiety was now anger.

If you survey the world they WILL NOT agree with you— too many people listen to their bind. Always have. Always will.

"Maybe too many people don't have a good example to follow."

She shouted to the surrounding field, *'SCUSE ME, PLEASE. WHO LET AN IDEALIST IN HERE?*

"I still think it's possible. Screw you if you don't."

She leaned in until her face was right before mine. *You've no idea yet what is possible,* she said, firmly. *Close your eyes.*

"Why?"

Close. Your. Eyes.

"W-w-why?" I said, less resistant than before.

She passed a hand slowly in front of my face, as if closing my eyes post-mortem, and repeated, less forcefully and in a voice that sounded eerily like another, *Close your eyes for me, Soupy.*

I did.

Step down into the circle.

I slowly followed her instructions.

Good, she said. *Now, be bound.*

I was afraid to move, but I felt an inherent trust that hadn't been part of our conversation or presence until now. A scent of lilies filled my head.

Her hands grabbed me by the wrists, pulled them toward her and placed them on her body to each side of her breasts.

I reacted strongly to pull away, shouting, "YOU SAID WE COULDN'T—"

WHAT DO YOU FEEL? Her words held me as firmly as her grasp. When I stopped struggling, she asked again in that all too familiar voice, *What do you feel?*

"Y-y-you," I whispered.

She urged my hands downward and I heeded the command to explore more of her body. Her hands on mine, she guided me over her hips to her thighs, up across her navel and then to her breasts. There, she directed me to cup them firmly.

Yessssss, she cooed and hissed simultaneously.

My breath stammered as much as my words.

Don't you just love the first time?

"Y-y-yes," I moaned.

You want to ride with me, don't you?

Her question caught me off guard because it felt incredibly out of context. I didn't answer.

You do. I know you do. I can feel it and *I can see it.*

And then, a question came immediately to mind—the one I'd been asking women who got anywhere near my heart—and I couldn't stop from saying it, "Are you Promise?"

Nectar said, *You're a fucking idiot*, then slapped me across the face. Confused and shocked, I opened my eyes and she was gone.

Chapter 20

Still in shock, I stood in the dark clearing as the sun raced up into the sky. "Okay then," I said aloud while stretching my hands out away from my chest. "Nothing else to see here," I added, and then slowly stepped out of the circle and walked toward the road.

A car horn sounded in the distance. *Great*, I thought, *return of the crazy cabbie.* However, when I reached the road I saw it wasn't the black cab, but my own dated, yellow cab, which was a welcome sight. "Hello, old friend," I said, as I slid my hand along the hood, opened the door, and sat in the driver's seat. I changed direction via a three-point turn, and drove away.

A few miles up the road I came to a four-way stop. *Which way?* There was a road sign at the intersection. To the left was Faith, 44 miles down the road. A right turn would take me 15 miles to Possibly. Straight was Gravity, only 12 miles ahead. "Gravity it is," I said, and proceeded through the intersection.

As I drove, an approaching road sign stated, "Road May Close During Severe Weather. Chains Required." Someone had painted the word "ALWAYS" under and between "chains" and "required," so I pulled over, pulled 4 tire chains out of the trunk, and put them on the tires. Technically, I knew there was severe weather ahead in Gravity, might as well prepare now. No sooner had that thought crossed my mind, large flakes of snow began to fall. They blanketed everything quickly, bringing an eerie silence to the land. The crunch of my footfalls on the snow felt like an intrusion, like the creaky step that gives away your return after curfew.

I stopped what I was doing, caught a snowflake on my tongue, and said, "Once per year." With a deep, cool inhale of breath, I got back into the cab.

I was so enthralled by my love of the snow, I didn't sense her presence..

Beautiful snow, isn't it? Promise said.

"Incredible. I love snow like this."

Even though you have to drive in it?

"Sure, let's drive," I said. "It's what we do, and we're only a few miles away from the next story. You in?"

Of course, start the meter!

"Great," I slapped the box on the dash not caring if it started or not, then put the car into drive.

Gonna charge me for this one? Promise asked.

"Maybe."

I see how you are.

"Worth every penny; that's how I am." We weren't more than two miles up the road when I pulled over near a group of people building a snowman on top of their car. "See that group over there?"

Yes.

"Those were my friends in college. We did everything together—work, drink, play sports, listen to music, take road trips. My college family."

Why are they building a snowman on top of the car?

"That's Jimmy."

Jimmy?

"Jimmy the Snowman. He didn't live long, except as legend, but that's not why we're here, to talk about snowmen. The girl in the pink sweater is Gravity."

Promise's seat squeaked as she leaned forward to get a closer look at Gravity.

She's cute!

"My friend was dating her and the rest of us just shook our heads about it—she was too immature, much younger than the rest of us, and very impulsive, reckless...she didn't fit our social culture."

Immature? You're building a snowman on top of a car, Soupy.

I laughed, "True. Present case excepted, I guess."

Gravity leaned over the back of the car and started puking. She'd had way too many margaritas. "Look. There. Case in point. She couldn't keep up with our drinking!"

Will someone please go hold her hair, at least?

I took my foot off the brake, drove past the scene, and toward the town of Gravity.

Love finds its way to you in the future, eh?

"Over several months of getting to know her, we all actually grew to love her, despite the fact that she broke up with our friend. She'd become family and there wasn't much he could do about it. Besides, we'd learned she *wasn't* actually dating our friend, he just had the hots for her, and she *did* have a boyfriend who was studying overseas for a year. Despite all of that, her and I were soon feeling the beginning of a desirable connection, fueled by long conversations about life and love. She had a lot more to say than I ever thought her capable of saying. Surprise! I guess you don't judge a book by the pink sweater and puking, you know?"

Yeah, I know. How much younger than you was she, Soupy?

Not as young as you might think: six years.

No big deal as you get older, but probably a pretty big maturity gap when you were both in your early- to mid-twenties.

"Indeed, I had a lot to teach her," I added. "I hadn't planned on dating anyone, and I don't think she'd planned on dating me, but the more time we spent together the more it just sort of fell into place. She helped me learn how to be a better listener and thinker—prerequisites, really, for my Heller family name—and this teaching drove a strong desire for intimacy despite any boyfriend elsewhere."

If you could see me, then you'd see me shaking my head.

"I didn't intend on picking her: she was there and we hit it off and things just kept moving in that direction. I didn't ask for it initially, but I was sure asking for it the more we were together. And when I say it, I mean 'love.'"

It's fair to say, sometimes we pick love and sometimes we don't. You know, sometimes it slaps you in the face and other times it grows on you.

"I'm not sure we know the difference," I said.

What do you mean?

"I mean, if it grows on us we were lucky for it, and when we pick, it often seems that luck is a huge part of our wish. Like, twenty years from now we'll say, 'We sure were lucky to have met,' or 'We've been lucky to be together this long.' Everyone bets on being the luckiest mother sucker on the planet."

Too many, I'd say.

"We want luck, instead of effort, to do all the work to maintain something so few have, then live miserably because we never get it."

Where'd Soupy the Optimist go?

"This is Soupy the Realist."

I'd driven us into the small town where Gravity and I met, and intentionally parked us too far for the naked eye to see into the house where the action was taking place.

"I brought binoculars for you," I said and handed them back to Promise.

Binoculars?

"See the house at the top of the hill, first on the left with all the lights on?"

Yes.

"The dimly lit room on the far left of the house is my bedroom."

Got it.

"Friday nights became wine-chat nights and we didn't stray from the weekly event: a bottle of wine (or two), Dave Matthews, Sarah McLachlan, lit candles, and incredible conversation that walked us farther down a path of togetherness. Each week, I'd fall more deeply in love with her, and it was driving me crazy not to express it. On this night, I'd opened a bottle of syrah just as the doorbell rang. When I opened the door, she was wearing a lovely, lightweight sundress that flowed around her body in ways too wonderful to describe with words. Buttons down the front of the dress revealed the pathway to a passion that I so desperately wanted to experience. I strategically undressed her in my head, then filed the instructions away in an easily accessible place."

You never miss a beat, do you?

"Rarely," I smiled. "Live in the now while seeing the path of options in the future. I kissed her on the cheek as I hugged her, paid her a deserved compliment, then simply grabbed up the bottle and the glasses and led her to the bedroom, which wasn't atypical, with roommates it was the only place in the house that guaranteed privacy."

Sure, Romeo, sure.

I picked up my own pair of binoculars…

* * *

"I've been looking forward to seeing you all week," she said with a smile.

"It's always like that, isn't it," Soupy said with a confident air. "We see each other on campus and we do things with our friends, but what we look forward to most is being alone together."

He opened the door to a bedroom softly lit by candles; words from Dave Matthews Band's "#41" welcomed her. It was their favorite Friday night song.

> *"Come and see.*
> *I swear by now I'm playing time against my troubles.*
> *I'm coming slow but speeding.*
> *Do you wish a dance and while I'm in the front,*
> *The play on time is won.*
> *Oh, but the difficulty's coming here."*

"Yes, our song! Pour me some wine, pleeeeeeease!" she stated as she kicked off her flip-flops and jumped onto the bed, her effervescent smile proudly displayed on her face.

One thing that attracted Soupy to her was the ability to switch from serious to playful without skipping a beat. As he poured her a glass of wine, he noticed she wasn't too concerned about revealing what she'd worn beneath her dress as she sat casually on his bed. She might have had plans for them that night, but she might also have been so deep into her playful mode that it simply didn't dawn on her that she was revealing the sexy nature of her undergarments. Soupy wasn't sure, but he was sure to find out. The combined mixture of candles, music, aroma, and wine—revolving around this lithe female he wanted so badly to love—created a magnetism that pulled them together and prompted conversation in close proximity, close enough to kiss.

"Hi, Soupyheller," she whispered with a wry smile as she looked longingly at his lips. It was her habit to call him by his first and last name together as if they were one. As she continued talking, she drew out each phrase clearly, "Tell me. What's on. Your mind."

"If I did that, I'd get in big trouble. Have you seen what you're wearing?" Without giving her a chance to respond, he said, "How 'bout I change the subject?" Every ounce of passion inside of him wanted to dive into her obvious invitation to kiss, but he forced himself to resist because she was dating someone else. And as much as he wanted her, longed for her, dreamed about her, she *had* to make the first move, or what would love really mean? If he didn't respect her "other" love, then he couldn't call himself her friend, let alone anything more. He'd told her this on many occasions, out of respect.

Her smile got even larger, "Sure!" came the slightly too silly reply. Her silliness sometimes came at the most surprising and frustrating moments.

"You realize your man comes back in a couple of weeks, right?" Soupy asked.

The humidity of intimacy, which had been begging for less clothing, whisked out from under the bedroom door and disappeared along with her playful mood. He knew it would happen, but they had to have this conversation.

"Sounds like I should down this glass of wine before we continue," she said playfully while backing a few inches away from him.

"What are we going to do?" he asked. "Wait. Hold on. You don't have to answer that yet." He squinted while putting his index finger on his temple.

"There are so many things in my head. Give me a few seconds to line them up. I'm gonna ramble, but you're kinda used to that."

She smiled and they both took a large gulp of wine as Dave continued his serenade.

> *"I will go in this way,*
> *And find my own way out.*
> *I won't tell you, so be,*
> *But it's coming to much more.*
> *Me.*
> *Come down all the ghosts come back,*
> *Reeling in you now.*
> *Oh, what if they came down crushing?*
> *In the way I used to play for all of the loneliness that nobody notices now.*
> *I'm begging slow, I'm coming here."*

"I never anticipated that I'd enjoy our time together as much as I do." She looked confused, so Soupy hastily corrected himself. "Nice start, Soup. That didn't come out the way I intended," he said and took another deep breath. "When I first met you I didn't see the woman I see sitting on my bed right now. I've never felt this closeness before; I'm entwined with you in a way I've never been woven to another. And as you know, I haven't dated anyone for several years; haven't even *wanted* to be with anyone over those years because short-term relationships simply seemed ludicrous and ultimately harmful to my goals as a student."

He held up his index finger to indicate he was in dire need of wine, but wasn't yet finished rambling.

"But you, you've released this rush of emotion that's been locked up inside of me for years. Because we talk so often, you know practically everything about me. You know that dating hasn't been my priority. And if you know that, then you must also see that you," He placed his hand on her knee, "You've smashed my priorities."

She set her wine glass down on the nightstand. Soupy followed suit and allowed her to put both of his hands into her own.

"Only waiting.
I wanted to stay.
I wanted to play.
I want to love you.
I'm only this far.
And only tomorrow leads my way."

Soupy continued, "I know I get wordy when I have something to say, so I'll simply tell you what I've been dying to tell you for weeks. I don't know what the future will hold. We've been more about these 'now' moments than being in a committed relationship together, and there are definite unknowns in a few weeks. Before we get there I have to tell you face to face that I'm in love with you."

She leaned forward, took her hands from his and placed them on his cheeks. The polar magnetism of north and south met at the collision of their lips for the first time since they'd met. After a nervous, yet passionate and slightly forceful beginning, their kiss slowly tapered off allowing their lips to more softly part from each other.

She whispered as she looked into his eyes, "I don't know what's going to happen in a few weeks, but let's not talk about the future when there's so much between us right here, right now."

Her lips returned to his as he eased her down onto the bed.

"I'm coming waltzing back and moving into your head.
Please, I wouldn't pass this by.
I wouldn't take any more than
What sort of man goes by.
I will bring water.
Why won't you ever be glad
It melts into wonder?
I came in praying for you.
Why won't you run in the rain and play?
Let the tears splash all over you."

They became one—his hands on hers, her hands on his, his body into hers, her body into his—slowly, but purposefully.

"I haven't done this in a long time, Gravity," he whispered.

"Me either," she replied.

* * *

Promise let out a deep breath, as if she'd been holding it during the whole episode. *I love the way you love. It's your words, Soup, my God, your words.*

I blushed. "They're just there when I need them. What can I say?"

Say more. They're beautiful.

"We don't have time for that right now. Sorry to spoil the mood, but this incredibly beautiful moment, in hindsight, was more like a goodbye or a thank you, an end, than it was a beginning."

Boo. Hiss.

"The overseas traveling boyfriend returned."

Promise growled before she said, *Did she regret the act?*

"Gosh, I hope not, that would take away from the beauty of our first time together. I suppose it was possible, but I wouldn't say likely…actually, I take that back. Not likely at all. It was her desire to live in the moment without much regard for the future, beautiful and untarnished, for her at least. But it was like she'd had a goal to make love to me, and once that box was checked she had to go back to the returning man."

And for you?

"Well, for me it was difficult because I'd waited so long for this unanticipated connection to blossom. Once I'd seen it in all its flowered beauty, my heart longed even more to keep it alive."

So, that serious-playful switch flipped back and it left you feeling lonely.

"Lonely and angry. I wasn't mad at myself for falling in love with someone who was with another, no, I was mad at her for not being able to make a decision, stringing us both along, and acting like it was no big deal. LOVE IS

A BIG FUCKING DEAL!" I shouted as I slammed my hands on the steering wheel and then gripped it until my knuckles turned white. The wellspring of emotion surprised me.

Soupy, you have to learn from it. I know you're passionate about love because I've seen how these memories take you back to the same deep emotions you had when you first experienced them. But this is the learning moment, not the living moment, the learning—

I interrupted as if I wasn't hearing Promise speak. "She crushed it. SHE CRUSHED IT." The heat that had bubbled up from my heart turned my face beet red. I slammed my fists on the steering wheel again, then threw the transmission into drive and hammered the gas pedal to the floor.

SOUP! WHOA! WHAT ARE YOU DOING?! We careened toward a busy intersection as my knuckles stayed white on the wheel. Promise screamed, *INTERSECTION! INTERSECTION! SLOW DOWN!*

"EVERY GOOD MOVIE HAS A NEAR DEADLY COLLISION, YES?!" I screamed back at her. Promise continued to shout. I was a focused, uncaring man willing to accept whatever fate befell this ludicrous, suicidal act of mindfully plowing through a busy intersection. I yelled with the clarity of a sensible lunatic, "IF WE BREAK IT, WE'LL BUY IT!"

Promise screamed. It was likely the loudest sound ever to escape her lips.

Our cab hit sixty miles an hour, and in a blaze of yellow, leapt through the intersection with the horn blaring and somehow, maybe by luck, avoiding a crash.

"That woulda been ugly," I said laughing and allowing the uphill slope on the other side of the intersection to naturally kill our speed.

Promise was pissed. *WHAT THE HELL IS WRONG WITH YOU?!*

"Hey, chill out, I was tempting fate...and changing the subject," I admitted.

TEMPTING FATE? Dammit, Soup, It doesn't work that way. IT DOESN'T! AND IF YOU WANT TO CHANGE THE SUBJECT JUST SAY SO!

"Geez Louise, fine. We're alive, okay? It's just a dream anyway."

You THINK you know it all? You THINK you have all the answers. I'm just telling you, it doesn't work that way.

I didn't care how it worked, especially because we'd reached the top of the other side of the valley, made a left turn, and parked just a few feet away from Soupy and Gravity sitting on the street curb.

What's going on? Promise was still pretty steamed by the sound of her voice and just starting to catch her own breath, but saw that the story continued.

"We were burning letters written by her overseas-now-returned lover."

The letters he wrote while he was away?

"Yeah, she would read them to me and then laugh while they burned. We'd tried using the bathtub, but they scorched the porcelain. Oops, sorry, Mr. Landlord."

And this was your *idea?*

"Oh, hell no, it was hers. I thought it was another sign that she was going to choose me, this symbolic act of erasing those memories so we could write new ones."

I punched the accelerator past the house of the burning letters, hit the bottom of the street, made a sharp right, a sharp left, and then slammed on the brakes a half-block from Gravity's house."

You don't listen, do you?

"I'm one badass driver in my dreams, Promise. What can I say?"

Look, I don't even know all the rules in the dream world and I've been in and out of it since I was born. Don't go acting like you're a god; that shit will catch up to you. I've seen it happen. Acting like a jackass in your dreams is NOT how to find me.

Gravity and the back-from-overseas guy walked up the driveway and into the house holding hands. As he held the door for her, she tiptoed up for a quick kiss. It evolved into a more passionate one, and she reached for his jeans buttons while pulling him into her house.

"It was my turn and then his turn and then my turn and then his—"

I get it.

"It drove me crazy."

As it would anyone.

"It drove me crazier that she would tell me all about him, but he knew nothing about me. Once he returned they resumed their routine, whatever that was. Meaning, they were spending time together again, but her life and my life were so intertwined with our social groups that I couldn't avoid shit like this. Over time, Gravity became really annoying and secretive around me. She'd once kept me up-to-date on each minute of her life and now that connection was gone. I didn't know what to do about it, so I tried to avoid her."

She reverted back to the immature girl you first met, not the one you'd helped her become.

"I couldn't stand it. I don't like doing things twice. The love we discovered just—poof—vanished. It was sad, but I didn't have time for sad when I kept seeing them together on campus. I admit, I just needed to be pissed off about the way she handled it: telling me one thing and doing something completely different. Why should she get both ends of the bargain?"

Well, she shouldn't, but she could only get what you both would give her.

"I'd grown both personally and professionally, but I knew there was nothing left for me to learn here. In a town I loved—a town where I'd discovered love and loved with my entire heart—the unintended sight of one kiss killed my desire to be there any longer."

I retraced the route back to the house because I knew exactly what I was about to show Promise: my departure. I parked the cab across the street from the house and shut off the engine. "I wanted out of town so badly I dropped out of school four weeks from graduation, bought a car, and moved to another city."

Four weeks from graduation?

"Yep. Well, I kinda dropped out six weeks prior, but I gave myself two weeks to let *almost* everyone know and plan my departure."

But four weeks from getting what you'd prioritized for years?

I didn't answer her because Gravity drove up and parked in front of the driveway, blocking the car that I'd packed with my things. She walked briskly toward me with a concerned look on her face.

* * *

"Are you going to leave without telling me?" she asked. It wasn't quite friendly, but it wasn't quite angry either. She realized she didn't have much of a leg to stand on no matter what emotion she approached with.

He *nearly* retorted with, "You mean like you left me?" but instead chose, "I haven't really figured that out yet."

"I would want you to say goodbye, Soup," she said.

She'd only called him by his first name, not his first and last as if they were one word.

And again, Soupy choked back a similar retort and opted for something that would incur less potential wrath. "Yeah," he said, and then turned away.

"Do you want my help?" she asked.

He didn't stop or turn around, just mumbled, "Not really."

"What?"

"Not really," came out, but only slightly louder.

"Soup, I can't hear you," she said calmly, but sternly.

"Not. Really."

He walked from the garage into the house and looked out the window briefly to see her standing alone in the driveway with one hand on her hip, perplexed about what to do next. As he returned with an armful of clothes, she asked if she could help once more, and again he refused.

"Okay, I can tell you aren't interested in a conversation right now and I'm not going to push you into one. I stopped by because I heard you were leaving. I just want to apologize and give you this."

When his head emerged from the trunk of his car, he saw her holding a keychain. The ring of it was around her index finger, which caused the idol to swing back and forth in the sun. Attached to the ring was a flat, black rock. A symbol of the many times they'd walked along the beaches and rivers nearby. She embraced him, though he didn't reciprocate, and whispered an apology into his ear. As she backed away she grabbed his wrist, turned his palm open, and dropped the keychain into it.

"To remember someplace we love," she said, and walked back to her car. When she sat down, she raised her hand to show a similar keychain.

Awash in conflicting emotions, Soupy watched her drive down the street and out of sight. In his pocket were the keys to his new car, still using a twisty tie from the dealer as a keychain. He undid the tie and put the only two keys he owned in his life, both for his new car, onto the ring she'd just given him. He held the flat, black rock in his hand to see if it was warm; it was cold. And before it heated up again, he knew he had to leave for good.

* * *

"I had to get out of there or I might never have left," I admitted to Promise.

I understand, she said.

Soupy closed the trunk, the passenger door, and then stood outside the driver's door taking one last look around the neighborhood.

"You're gonna be alright, man," I whispered from the cab to him as he stood there.

Soup got in the car, pulled the door closed, buckled up, started the car, then killed it trying to get out of the driveway.

I chuckled, having forgotten that I'd lied about being proficient with a manual transmission when I bought the car. "I couldn't drive a stick, Promise. I barely made it through the test drive."

We both laughed, though my heart wasn't in it.

He'll figure that out, too.

I shook my head back and forth while starting the cab. "Promise, I have to make this part of the trip alone. I'm sorry."

She didn't ask questions, just said, *Goodbye for now, Soupy. I love you.*

I waved at her to signify I felt the same, but I didn't have the energy for words.

Chapter 21

In two cars, with Soupy leading, I followed him as he took the long way out of town to drive past our most memorable spots. More than anything else, these were the memories he needed to drive away from, but he couldn't do so without one last goodbye. It wouldn't be forever, but it was goodbye, for now.

From the freeway, the wind blew through all four of my cab's windows, airing it out. The sorrow of loss would hang with me for a few miles until there was enough distance between Gravity and myself to allow momentum to steer.

It was about a five-hour drive to my next home, not long enough to require a stop for gas, or anything else for that matter. Therefore, I fast-forwarded through the trip and slowed it only briefly on those segments of the drive when the ocean could be seen. We didn't break any laws getting down the road. In fact, we kept at the speed limit, which meant a lot more cars passed us than we passed ourselves. Soupy didn't feel reckless; he was contemplating all that had happened, right and wrong, and thinking about what was next. I did the same, despite these few years after the initial drive—

—and that's when it struck me: I had kissed someone behind Honesty's back just as Gravity had kissed someone behind mine. "Shit balls," I said, shaking my head. "Damn karma." It was an important revelation, not because there was anything I could do about it. What comes around often does go around, so they say.

"How do I win?" I asked no one in particular. There's always something…

I like the ones who don't like me.

I don't like the ones who like me.

When we both like each other something comes along and fucks it all up—*but it's the homework Promise gave me.*

Friends and family say, "You're too picky?" or "What's wrong with you?"

There's nothing wrong with me; I want to be happy. I'm picky because it's important to be picky. The problem is that people aren't picky *enough.* Isn't the world full of too many non-believers and non-starters as it is?

There's always those who go against the flow. Some live. Some die.

It's okay for a child to dream of being a professional athlete, even though the chances of it happening are practically nil, but dreaming of true love is just plain silly.

"SILLY!" I shouted.

We school our children in algebra, the periodic table of elements, we make them memorize dates and places in history, and to what end? To score well on a test? How does that help with life?

Sure, knowledge is important—learning how to learn is important—but what of learning how to love? If school were a song, we'd all get straight As. There are plenty of love songs, why don't we learn from those?

Few gather opinions anymore, aside from those supporting whatever conclusion they'd like to make—that's not the truth, that's an assumption.

I mumbled, "Ass out of you and me."

Pretty stupid, if you ask me.

I was arguing with myself, and it was only getting worse. I knew it, and I didn't care. *Oh, you didn't ask me?* Well, you won't get answers without asking questions. I'd assumed that the quality time I'd shared with Gravity was enough; that the words I'd said and the feelings I'd shared were enough. *They weren't enough.* Why weren't they enough? *But they were enough.* I looked at the keychain dangling from the ignition, heard her words in my head and said them aloud, "To remember someplace we loved." Someplace we loved? Loved. *Past tense.* We don't love it anymore? No, but that wasn't what she said, "Love." She said it without the "d" on the end. "To remember someplace we love." There was only one place we could love, the place I just left, unless she meant someplace more than the physical places in the world. *The heart?* Did we love in the heart? Yeah, I'd miss that place and would like to remember it, but I don't feel it right now, and didn't feel it when I left her, either. I felt heartless. *True loss, not true love.* Being together made me feel alive. *And now I feel dead.* It was an adventure, an exhilarating adventure. Exhilarating enough to kill me? I didn't fight for her because I didn't think I had to. Would it have killed me if I *had* fought for her and lost? *I don't know.* We both have to fight for it, not against each other but with each other. *Not just one of us, both of us.*

She cut out my heart and I cut her out of my life.

Gravity still had much to learn, and she had to learn by doing, not talking. Even though he couldn't hear me, I spoke to Soup in the car up ahead of me, "Don't worry, man. She'll be back."

WHAT?! a voice from behind me said.

I turned out of instinct to look over my shoulder but didn't see anyone there. The motion caused me to steer the cab wildly to the right and into the breakdown lane where the tires threw dirt, gravel, and dead rubber around until I slammed the brakes to a stop. "WHO'S THERE?" A tractor-trailer rocked the cab as it blew past us pulling its air horn for an unnecessarily long time. "FUCK OFF!" I yelled at the trucker, and saw Soup's car disappear down the highway.

It's me, Soupy. Promise. I'm down here on the floorboards.

"Why THE FUCK are you here? I asked you to give me a moment, and YOU JUST NEARLY KILLED US!"

I assumed this was an important drive for you and I didn't want to miss it.

I mimicked her earlier tirade, and did so in a whiney voice, "It doesn't work that way. It doesn't work that way. IT DOESN'T WORK THAT WAY!" I turned back around to face the road hoping that Soup had seen us stop and pulled over himself. Nope. Didn't work that way.

Stop. That's just rude.

"Not giving me privacy WHEN I ASKED FOR IT is rude."

I have our greater good at heart—

I was about to say, "FUCK OUR GREATER GOOD," but that would not have been representative of my belief, only of the heightened emotion of the moment. Instead, I took deep breaths until I felt my heart rate resume a more natural rhythm.

"Promise, I'm having a hard time forming the right words with my head so full of the wrong ones, so pardon my silence."

I understand…and I'm sorry.

"I know you're sorry. The 'mission' is the mission, right? You have homework just like I do, and you don't change the world by following the rules, right?"

Right.

"Might make it right. Might not make it right. I'm so scrambled right now, I don't even fucking know."

Then let's focus on what you do know: your past.

"This isn't easy," I admitted, probably for the one-thousandth time.

I know.

"I meant to say, 'this isn't *going* to be easy.'"

I know that, too. Changing the world isn't supposed to be easy.

"You're about to ask me about Gravity, aren't you?"

Yes, what's this about her coming back?

"Yeah, not like, tomorrow, but several months down the road she asked if I'd talk with her again."

And you said yes? Of course you said yes. Never mind the question.

"The was *so much* potential with us before she regressed back to the I-don't-know-what-the-fuck-I'm-doing girl. She still had my heart, Promise. It wasn't in my chest. It wasn't on that keychain. I wanted the woman from Friday nights to come find me and be the woman on every night. So we started talking again."

Talk then.

"Yes, I do." I fast-forwarded the remainder of the drive south, and through many months, which brought us to the airport."

Don't tell me we're picking up Gravity?

"Yup. Better make some room back there."

As soon as I saw her standing in the cab line, my heart skipped many beats. She was always so incredibly cute—whether in a sundress or running shorts or dirty, ripped up sweats. It was an important quality to me that I'd learned from Honesty: love *her*, not what's on her.

There she is.

"Yes, I see her, Promise. Thanks."

Just trying to be helpful.

The cab pulled up next to her and I jumped out to load her small roller bag into the trunk. "That's okay," she said, "Precious cargo, so I'll just keep it in the back seat."

"Yes, ma'am," I replied, as I closed the door behind her. She didn't recognize me, which was a concern I wasn't sure I'd know how to handle if she did.

She is *cute,* Promise said, seemingly knowing that Gravity wouldn't see or hear her, either.

"Where to?" I asked, and she gave me the address to my own home. As I drove, Gravity mumbled under her breath as if practicing a speech.

She's nervous.

I shook my head, not wanting to speak to Promise for fear it might confuse Gravity. "What brings ya here?" I asked Gravity.

"Pardon?" she asked.

"What brings you to town?" I repeated.

"A chance," she replied, "to start over."

"Second chances. You've earned one?"

She replied, "I hope so."

"I wish you luck."

"Thanks," she said, and went back to mumbling and staring out of the window.

We pulled into the driveway and Gravity let out a deep, nervous breath. She was building the courage to head to the front door. She opened the door to get out, then remembered she had a fare to pay. "I'm sorry, what do I owe you?"

"Don't worry about it," I said. "I believe in second chances, too. Just consider this my good gesture. Pay it forward someday."

"Thank you," she replied, "I might need it."

Good luck, Promise added.

Gravity carefully stepped out of the cab with her bag and rolled it toward the front door. She took another deep breath, quickly primped, then unzipped her roller bag. She pulled out something, placed it carefully in one hand, then reached for the doorbell.

"I knew she was coming," I told Promise. "Well, I assumed she was coming because I could feel my heart nearer. Who else would have it?"

We watched as Soupy opened the door before Gravity had a chance to ring the doorbell.

* * *

Soupy opened the door. Though he knew she was coming, he hadn't the time to prepare like she had, minutes instead of days or weeks.

"I need to talk to you, Soup," Gravity said. She revealed her keychain with the flat black rock. "Do you still have yours?" she asked.

He looked toward the hook near the door and her eyes followed his to see it hanging there. They were stones they'd found on a beach walk; round, flat, black stones the size one could close a palm around.

"Will you talk to me?" she asked.

He answered her question with an affirming nod.

"I've traveled many miles, my own journey, if you will, that took me away from you, but the farther away I went the more I knew I had to return. Your heart grows cold when the distance between us increases, and so does mine," she said as she held her rock toward him. "I made a mistake. I'm sorry. I've learned a lesson. Maybe I needed to make this mistake to realize what kind of woman I am and what kind of man you are. I'd be grateful if you'd let me back into your life. If not, then this is yours." With that, she held her rock out to him.

Soup accepted her rock, grabbed his own from the hook, and held them both to his ear.

In his hand he could feel them growing warm, and as they warmed their rhythmic chorus resumed. He motioned for her to come inside and she accepted the offer, her luggage rolling in tow. But instead of walking into the house as a guest, she walked into his arms for a hug, letting her luggage fall to the tiled foyer.

"Please kiss me," she requested, leaning into him.

"Yes," he replied.

Chapter 22

Someone banged heavily on the motel room door and yelled, "LET ME IN, MAN!"

Clothes were still flung around the motel room. I wasn't coherent or sober enough to either ask who it was or tell him to hold on for one damn second while I got dressed. The clock read 1:11 A.M. I opened the door leaving the chain intact.

"Yeah?" I asked.

"Oh shit, dude. Ummm, you're not Joe," the drunken door-banger stated.

"Nope."

"Is Joe in there?"

"You've got the wrong room." I closed the door without waiting for an answer. After about ten seconds of silence, the entire motel received a serenade to Joe.

"JOE! JOE! JOOOOOOE-JOE. WHERE ARE YOU? I NEED TO PISS AND PASS OUT! JOOOOE!"

Fortunately, the noise didn't last long. The motel manager quelled the fuss about the same time as someone opened his door and said, "Dude, get in here." I presumed it was the notorious Joe. For me, the damage had been done. I was awake and hung over, so I sat on the bed staring at the closed door and wondering whether I should pee, puke, or pass out again. A belch of burrito mixed with beer worked its way up through my esophagus, escaped, and left a terrible taste in my mouth.

"Fuck," I said, for no reason at all. I scratched my head and crawled back under the covers.

As soon as I closed my eyes I was dreaming.

I saw an image of Gravity curled up in a red, velvet wingback chair. She was completely naked, wide-eyed, and shivering, with her knees tucked up under her chin and her arms wrapped around them. The chair was inside of a stone circle, not in the middle, but off to one side. I shouted at her, "GRAVITY!" but she didn't reply. I hurried over to her, got down on one knee, and felt her forehead before I grabbed her hands. She was cold, and she didn't respond to my touch. All she did was shiver and stare over my shoulder.

Burn. Blow. Nourish. Grow.

I knew those whispering words. I turned to see what she was staring at and saw the mountain with the fire on top. "What the fuck?" I whispered.

Burn. Blow. Nourish. Grow.

I turned back to Gravity, put my hands on her cheeks and tried shaking her awake. She didn't even blink. I brushed the hair away from her face, tucked it behind her ears, and looked into her eyes.

Burn. Blow. Nourish. Grow.

Options? Carry her? Where? Shake her? Ineffective. Kiss her? *Yes, kiss her.* It had been known to work in certain fairy tale circles. I gently pulled her chin upward, closed my eyes, and pressed my lips to hers. She awoke from her catatonic state and fiercely slapped my cheek.

Chapter 23

"THE MOUNTAIN!" I shouted, suddenly sitting up in the driver's seat.

Catch your breath, Soup. Promise said, then asked, *What mountain?*

I touched my hand to my left cheek and winced. "A dream. A mountain with, with fire on top, and these voices that kept repeating, 'Burn, blow, nourish, grow.'"

The four elements your great grandpa told you about?

"Yeah, and the mountain where I first heard them. But Gravity was there, sitting in a chair naked and afraid."

Afraid of what?

"I'm not sure. I couldn't get her attention, couldn't get her to look away from the mountain. She was all knees-to-chest and unresponsive."

You tried to help her?

"Yes, I did, but I wasn't there very long. Didn't seem like I had many options, so I kissed her," I said.

That fairy tale remedy doesn't always work, and sometimes it gets you slapped.

"Yeah, tell me about it," I said as I pointed to the handprint on my cheek.

Then what?

"Then I woke up here in the driveway again. What the hell? How long was I gone?"

A few minutes, maybe. I've seen this before, dreamers can black out suddenly. You're working so hard to learn from your memories it drains you; you aren't getting rest.

"Yeah, I don't feel rested, but then again, all the alcohol in my system isn't helping."

No, it isn't. In fact, it might be hurting.

"Hurting," I asked?

No inhibitions to keep you from the places you might have never intended to go.

"The Bind?"

It's a theory.

"Yeah, maybe. I doubt there's anything I can do about it."

Sleep it off.

"Thanks, Mom." I thought for a few seconds before I motioned to my condo, "Have they come out yet?"

No.

"They will."

A call came in over the cab radio, "Cab 13. Cab 13. Over?"

I replied, "Cab 13, over."

"Pick up at The Mountain. You know the place?"

"Yeah, on the way. Out."

Looks like we're headed to The Mountain.

"Well, Gravity and I had a mountain to climb anyway."

What do you mean?

I backed the cab out of the driveway and drove toward the highway. "Our reunion, the one we witnessed earlier, felt so perfect. We finally lived under the same roof, and we didn't leave very often, if you know what I mean."

Yes, I know what you mean.

"I was building a career. She was finishing up school and doing the same. We just…I don't know how to say it best, we just saw each other, basically, in the bedroom. Both of us put in long days and weekends away from home, so there weren't many opportunities for our relationship to grow. So you know what happens when you grow but don't grow with each other?"

You grow apart.

"Yeah, we grew apart. But we didn't *want* to grow apart, so we forced ourselves into taking trips out of town away from all the work. Those trips were to some of the most beautiful places on the west coast. We'd take them with a goal in mind, let's 'think' about this or let's 'talk' about that while we're away. We did a good job with those goals, the thinking and talking, but the outcomes weren't as aligned as we'd hoped. Gravity and I wanted different things at different times. Our hearts were good and we *really craved* each other, but those things that drove us to succeed outside of love—the things we wanted to be when we grew up—we had different rates of getting to those places."

And when two hearts aren't working together for the same goals, they start working against each other.

"We were both running, sprinting really, to that next place in life, but when I looked beside me she wasn't there, and when I turned around to find her she was way behind. I felt like I was always waiting for her to catch up."

I'm not making a statement here, just asking a question: is that fair to her?

"No, not really. I wanted her to run at the same rate and in the same direction. She just wanted to run in a totally different direction."

Do you think she was overly focused on loving you because she'd emotionally left you once?

"Maybe."

Do you think you wanted to run from her because she'd run from you in the past?

"Maybe that, too."

We exited the highway and drove a few miles to a drive-in theater at the base of The Mountain. We were early, meaning we were there a bit before sundown, but the pay gate was open.

The attendant at the gate said, "Don't get many big city cabs here, Mister."

"Big city? I guess," I replied. "How much for me and my fare lady in the back?"

The attendant ducked down to check the back seat and then looked confused as he pushed his glasses back up the bridge of his nose.

I said, "Believe me, she's there, just a little shy."

"I can't charge you for someone I can't see," he said, and stood there blinking.

"Well—"

He interrupted, "Unless you've got someone in the trunk; that wouldn't surprise me 'cause we get that here all the time. My manager told me to keep an eye out for that sort of thing, but I have a sixth sense."

"Really?"

"Yeah, I can smell stowaways," he said, pushing his glasses up the bridge of his nose once more. "I think you're okay, mister, I don't smell anyone in your trunk."

I laughed, "Nope, no one in the trunk, and since there's no one in the back seat you can see, what do ya say it's a two-for-one night?"

He stared at me, bent over to look into the back seat once again, and finally said, "Yeah, okay, I can go for that."

"Great," I said, and handed him a few bills.

"You, um, two, enjoy the show."

I thanked him and entered the drive-in.

Did you just call me your fare lady?

"My fare lady, of course. The meter is running, you know, but between you and me, I don't think he got the joke."

I'm not sure many would.

A few cars had already entered and parked at the drive-in. I chose a spot in the middle of the lot and began to roll down the window when I realized there wasn't a speaker to hang on it like the old school drive-ins.

Try the radio, smarty-pants.

As I turned up the radio, I heard, "...this story about a man's journey to find true love."

"Hey, just in time to catch the previews." I deepened my voice and said, "Promise, I give you...The Mountain."

* * *

On the movie screen, a man and woman hiked up the switchback trail of a mountain foothill. He was several paces ahead of her and seemed motivated to reach the top; she was struggling to take each step and stopping to rest with frequency.

"HEY!" she yelled up the trail. "CAN WE REST?!"

He stopped, looked back at her, and without saying a word set down his backpack and pulled out his water bottle. He held *her* bottle up as incentive to make another ten strides up the trail for a drink. She closed the distance and snatched the bottle from his hand as he turned to look up the trail to the top of the mountain.

"What's the hurry, Soup?" she asked.

He pointed to the top of the trail, "Can you imagine what we can see from up there?"

She looked at him sternly to express that she didn't really care.

"Ready?" he asked.

Her arms dropped loosely to her sides as a vote for prolonged rest, but she caved and waved him on up the trail. He flipped the pack onto his back and put one foot in front of the other until she shouted out for him to wait once again.

When she caught up, she said, "I'm right here, not up there." She added, pointing up the trail a bit farther, "Can we make it to the shade of that overhang and sit for a while?"

He squinted into the sun, looked at the overhang only a few switchbacks ahead, glanced up at the peak, and then to her, "Sure." He now knew he wasn't making it to the peak with her, not on this day.

They sat down once they reached the shade, opened their bottles of water, and leaned up against the rock. She looked at him, but he was looking out over the valley. He could feel her stare, but refused to acknowledge it; she was keeping him from his goal and he was frustrated with her because of it.

Finally she spoke, and spoke as if she'd been formulating the words all the way up the trail, "I need to share some of my thoughts with you." She collected herself and continued, "Have we really been dating the last few months?"

"Why, what else would you call it?" he replied.

"Cohabitating? Screwing? Being friends with benefits? We don't go anywhere unless it's the bedroom," she said.

"What do you mean, we're *somewhere* right now." He spread his hands to showcase the amazing view of the valley below.

"Do we really have to go this far in order to go somewhere? We don't go anywhere when we're at home. We have to get out of town to be together. What's wrong with that picture? We say we want to be with each other and we show up, packed, and ready for a life together, but the trip never starts. You're always running off somewhere, I'm waiting for you to come home. Sure, we come back together around bedtime completely exhausted and maybe we find an intimate moment together, but where is that going? We're not going backwards, but we never take steps forward together either." She wiped sweat from her brow and continued, "Should we just accept our friendship as-is and stop trying to make more of it?" she asked.

He didn't have an answer for her, so he kept looking out at the valley.

"Do you remember what it was like when we were just friends? How comfortable we were with talking, and now, now we never talk, Soup. If you ask me, we need to be friends again in order for us to figure out what's next. We need to get back to the place where we started, when it was just the two of us talking and learning about each other."

He thought for a moment before he said, "That place is where I fell in love with you the first time. I already *know* that I love you. I can't start all over again. I can't wonder about when I might see you or whether you actually love me. I need to know it's already there."

"I don't know what you expect of me and I don't know what to expect of you." She continued, "I *do* know that I've put a lot of strain on myself to figure us out, and that strain impacts you, too."

Soup said, "A lot has changed for us since the day we met. I'm trying to figure out who I am, and I can see you are, too. Who are *we*? You know? I want to become this and you want to become that; doesn't that mean we *aren't* who we were back in college, that couple talking and listening to music?"

"Do you remember the day I gave you the keychain?"

He nodded his head in affirmation.

"Do you know how much I've grown since then? I'm so much better at making decisions about things that make me happy. I loved and I lost and I learned, but I don't know what I'm supposed to be learning right now—I'm *not* learning right now."

"What else can I do to make us feel right to you?" he asked.

"You can walk next to me instead of in front of me," she said. "When you know I'm home alone, sometimes choose our life over yours. I sit there and fume because we're not together and you're out with friends."

He looked at her and asked, "Why aren't you working on you when I'm working on me?"

"That's not why I moved here. I moved here to be *with* you not to be there *for* you. Something is missing; it's you," she claimed.

As he stood up, frustrated, he said, "I'm RIGHT HERE, GRAVITY!"

"BUT YOU'RE NOT," she stammered back, standing up to equal his frustration. She pointed down the mountain and said, "You just RAN up that trail! How many times did you leave me behind?" Tears started to form in her eyes. "Dammit! I get frustrated when we do this!"

His heart longed for her when she cried. He closed his eyes so he wouldn't see how much she was hurting, but it was unavoidable. "When you get emotional I want to console you, and when I console you I can't think because I'm too close to you, and being close to you makes me desire you."

"So what do you expect us to do, Soup?" she asked.

He wanted to look up at the sky, but only saw the underside of the overhang, so symbolic of the weight over them both. He wanted to see the peak, see the place he desperately longed to reach, with or without her. He interlaced his hands and placed them on the back of his head as he paced back and forth, kicking rocks down the hillside.

"Are you going to talk to me?" she said.

"Yes, yes, I'm thinking. I'm thinking and I'm not coming up with any answers. I don't know what to do, Gravity."

She was ready with a reply, "If two people love each other, have been happy together, and are willing to try, then hope should not be lost." She continued, "But I won't keep the flame going between us if I'm the only one making sure it doesn't go out. I'm not going to wait for you to figure it out. We have a strong bond, Soup. You know what I do when you're not home? I look through photos, memories of times we've spent together."

"And you know what I'm doing when I'm not home? I'm trying to be successful enough that we can have whatever we want, go wherever we want, and be whoever we want."

"I just want you to be you, and be here with me," she said.

Her point hit home, but he chose to ignore it. Soup picked up a rock that fit nicely between his fingers and heaved it as far as he could. "Just because I don't know what to do right now doesn't mean I don't love you anymore. Most of the time I don't know how to deal with you. One day you'll walk through the door and brush me off like a wayward bug, the next night you'll come home and yell at me for not greeting you when you get home. You can't have it both ways."

"I can work on that, but I want us to be able to listen to each other, reach an agreement, and move on," she said.

"It's not always possible. I'm a thinker, but I don't think that well on my feet. I need time to do the actual thinking."

"*Tell me* when you need to think, and tell me what you're thinking about so I can think about it, too. Don't just come back with a solution that I'm supposed to accept."

"I'm sorry. I know." He ran his hand back and forth through his hair making a mess of it. "It works both ways, though, when you react to something but don't tell me why you're reacting it just feels childish. As much as I dislike hearing 'I don't know,' I can deal with it if you're actively trying to figure it out."

No one spoke for a few moments, until Soup asked, "How many times are we going to have this conversation?"

"As many as it takes," she said.

"I don't know if I can keep doing it over and over again."

* * *

The movie preview ended. I put my arms atop the steering wheel and rested my head on my forearm until Promise said, *I don't think I want to see that movie.*

"I've already seen it," I said. "You can probably guess what comes next, right?"

You know, Soup, you both had valid points. Honestly, I think one could, and in fact you both did, argue for what you believed in. You both let some emotion into the discussion, which kind of clouded things, but unless you can see each other's side and meet somewhere in the middle, yeah, of course I know what's next.

"One of us had to leave the other. Look, we *did* try to meet in the middle, but every time we went out somewhere we barely interacted. At some point in the night we'd look at each other and signal that it was time to go home. It stopped being love, but it was still love. I mean, we *loved* each other, but we only loved each other when we were making love. That's what we kept gravitating back to."

That's not love.

"I KNOW THAT'S NOT LOVE!"

Okay. Okay. You don't have to yell.

"Then stop citing the obvious."

I can't tell if it's obvious with you. Would you rather I didn't say anything at all?

Promise had expertly used the recent scene with Gravity to make an extremely valid point. Soupy knew it, so he said, "Okay, I'm sorry."

Can we move on?

"Yes, we can move on."

What did you learn?

"Do we really have to do this right now?"

When might you expect to do it? Later?

"Alright, fine." I let out a sigh and gathered my thoughts before I spoke. "I learned that sex and love are vastly different. They each have their places in life, but they shouldn't be confused with each other. Gravity and I discovered how restricting sex was between two people who were struggling to find balance on a higher level. You know, like the wrong type of fuel for a fire?"

Sex can't nurture love.

"Well, when sex is the *only* thing being used or expected to nurture love. The fuel for the fire would smolder and smolder—like wet newspaper or logs—but never actually catch fire to keep us warm or allow us to cook a healthy meal. Honesty was all heart until my head interfered. With Gravity I was mostly in my head, not necessarily for the right reasons, and my heart wouldn't engage. But like I said, I kept coming back to her. I *want* to come back to someone and I want that same someone to come back to me, but when we get so far apart the nature of physics—you know, like, force equals mass times acceleration—brings us back together with a crash. I want gravity strong enough to let me grow and keep me close. We just had the wrong kind."

Promise could tell I was thinking, so she waited for me to continue.

"You know, Promise, this reminds me of something about relationships."

Go on.

"I have a theory. I call it the Pocket Theory."

Pocket Theory?

"Alright, think about a pair of blue jeans."

Okay.

"Jeans have two pockets on the back and two pockets on the front, right? The Pocket Theory is a way to categorize the relationships in your life based on the pockets on your jeans. First, you have Pocket One, also known as the Acquaintance Pocket. In this back pocket you put the people in your life who are your handshake friends. You don't often seek them out, and truth be told they're not really friends, you're just friendly to each other."

That needs to be a big pocket, doesn't it?

"Yes. The other back pocket is Pocket Two, a-k-a the Friend Pocket. These friends are easy to catch up with, as if no time has passed, some you go out of your way to keep up with and others you don't."

Another big pocket.

"Yes, and they're back pockets because the back ones are a little less personal than those in the front."

Okay.

"Every once in a while, a friend might sneak up to the top of a back pocket and jump into a front pocket I call the Dating Pocket."

Of course, because sometimes friends end up being lovers, temporary or long term.

"It's a temporary pocket. Why? Because no one really dates forever, the whole concept of dating is to evaluate whether you want to be in a relationship or not; it's a designated-for-pocket-reassignment pocket."

"The last pocket, the other front pocket, is the Family Pocket. No one is as dear as family, therefore they reside in a pocket that's close to you. The can also look across to the other front pocket to see who's jumping in and out of it."

Promise laughed.

"There's one more pocket."

That little pocket above one of the front pockets you can barely fit a finger into?

"Exactly. It's the True Love Pocket."

Ha! Since you can rarely find anything that fits in there, it's perfect.

"What *does* fit in there, anyway?"

Stop it. You're a believer and you know it.

"There's more. People don't just pick their own pockets, as I'm sure you can guess, pocket-jumping happens."

Pocket jumping?

"Yep. Pocket Jumpers are those you have trouble sorting or who refuse to stay in the pocket where they've been placed. They can be a real pain in the ass. I think this theory helps explain what was going on with Gravity and me. We were both Pocket Jumpers. We started as acquaintances and slowly worked up through the pocket levels. When we tried jumping from the Dating Pocket to the True Love Pocket, we kept falling back into the Dating Pocket, or even the Friend Pocket."

Maybe the two of you were never in the same pocket at the same time, so you'd both jump, at exactly the same time, and land in different pockets again.

"Timing—bad timing, actually."

I can tell you a little bit about timing; it's important, you know that. Love is about an ideal that can never be attained, but we all try to get as close to it as we can. We have to figure out what we need, but we rarely get everything, so we must determine a few things: what we need to live, and maybe more importantly, what we can't live without. Look, our imperfections are what make us unique, so expect them and accept them because we have to love each other for our benefits and our faults. A true love might have a little more of one thing you need or a little less of something else you need, but a real true love will help maintain balance. A lot of people think balance is a static state, but it really isn't; balance is only held temporary as you shift around on seeking your ideal stance together—true loves work together to make sure you don't lean too far in one direction or another.

"Yes, like standing on one leg. I'm constantly shifting my weight in my entire body trying to stay balanced."

Yes, she agreed. *Perhaps more relevant to what you experienced with Gravity, you two might have jumped into the True Love Pocket at the same time, but one of you wanted to be clipped to the lip of the pocket so you could see outside, and the other wanted to be tucked deep inside the pocket huddled together and sharing a warm embrace.*

'Within a pocket, there's constant movement! I never thought of that before, but it's most certainly true!"

She laughed. *I love seeing the light bulb over your head light up.*

It was an incredibly endearing statement.

"I've just experienced this intra-pocket movement," I said.

So we've just spent several years with Gravity, your second love. Think about the number two for a second. She came along at a time when you had to choose one of two paths, love or profession. It was a different choice than you made with Honesty, to love or not to love. With Gravity, the decision became much more difficult, two things you truly loved, but struggled to find enough time for both; one withered while the other flourished, right?

"Totally."

Two people are the minimum number needed to form a partnership; you can have a party of one, but you can't have a couple of one. So how did it end?

"I met someone else," I admitted. "It was far from pretty, in fact it was really ugly between Gravity and I, but it did the job. We fought for weeks about breaking up. Sometimes we ended up on top of each other and other times one of us stormed out of the house. It got to the point where it ceased being productive, mostly because I decided I wanted an experience with someone very different from her. I told Gravity I was leaving town and asked her to move out while I was gone."

How did that go over?

"By the time we got to that point we both knew it was over. She packed up a suitcase and took enough things to stay elsewhere until I left. I still loved and trusted her, but deep down we both knew something was wrong, and we obviously couldn't figure it out. So I made a choice to move on. Look, I'll show you." I pointed to the movie screen as another preview began.

* * *

There was a knock on the door. Soupy opened it to find Gravity standing there with a palm-sized rock, once more, in her hand. She was obviously nervous. Her brow glistened a bit with perspiration on an otherwise cool evening. "I know you're leaving town because you've met someone else," she said. Gravity exhaled deeply before adding, "I don't want you to go."

He shook his head fearing the same conversation they'd already had a million times before. He passively motioned that she was welcome to enter the house simply by walking away from the open door. She stood in the doorway contemplating what to do. She had a plan, but her fight or flight response stuck in neutral. "Come'on, Gravity," she whispered to herself. With a deep inhale of breath she found the courage to enter the house.

Soupy was pacing back and forth in the kitchen formulating words in his head for every possible scenario. When she entered, he said, "Gravity, I'm leaving. I'm leaving because I still have some things to discover and staying here with you doesn't allow me to do that."

She never stopped her walk once she entered the kitchen. With a determined look on her face she backed him up to the stove, straddled his legs, looked him in the eyes, and said, "How do you know you'll learn them with her?"

"Hey, I—"

Her hands moved to his pants where she deftly drew a reaction. The kitchen—and Soupy's world—was spinning out of control so quickly he felt light-headed. He watched her hands work his button-fly jeans. He could sense her intense desire. This determination from her had rarely before been seen, and it was intoxicating. She knew what she wanted, and she was being sexy and confident about getting it.

She looked up at him, her hands still quickly at their work, and whispered, "It drives me crazy to think about you with another woman when I already know what you need and how to give it to you." She reached into his boxer briefs causing his eyes to close as he reveled in her touch. Her eyes blazed as she found what she sought. "And I'm going to give it to you, give it all to you right now. Is that what you want?" Her other hand reached around his neck to pull his lips to hers, which forced him to open his eyes. He turned his head away at the last second, but she was kept expertly stroking him to rigidity. "I won't be denied," she whispered. "You want to learn something, well, I have something to show you." Gravity guided Soupy to the living room, stood him next to the couch, and pushed his pants down before shoving him just hard enough to make him sit. She climbed on his lap and sat in a sexual position she knew he loved. Soupy was at a loss for words; his head was a superhighway of emotion and reason radically racing each other to the finish line. As she unbuttoned her shirt to reveal a sheer, black bra, she said, "I bought this for you. You need to learn how to take it off of me."

They both knew sex prolonged their relationship; it'd been doing so for years. His head was arguing with his crotch as he tried to look away, but simply couldn't resist her breasts. He remembered all those times he coaxed them to grow, even knowing they were already the perfect size. *What an idiot I am,* he thought. *Why couldn't I ever just love her for her?*

Gravity fondled her breasts, coaxing her body to firm up as much as his, and moaned sensuously as she did so. "I know how much you love these. How do they look to you in this lingerie, Soupyheller? I know you want to—"

He gulped, closed his eyes again, and turned his head away from her. She was back to calling him by his first and last name as one word; it was playful and purposeful. Somehow he resisted her temptation despite the confidence she displayed, pushed her back, groaned, and said, "Gravity, I can't do this. Fuck. I'm leaving to go meet someone else, and I think there's something between her and I. What am I supposed to say if our conversation moves to one about intimacy? Am I supposed to lie to her instead of telling her I was with someone else, oh yeah, and she happens to be my ex, and we were together last night? NO. I can't—I WON'T DO THAT—to someone else. I'm sorry. You need to get off of me."

His words shattered her confidence and she backed away from him, but didn't leave his lap. Her chest heaved. Her hands went to her eyes. She looked to the ceiling, but her inner strength collapsed and she began to cry. When Soupy looked at her, like many times before, the unstoppable urge to console her kicked in, but she saw it coming and deflected it. He tried to console her with words, "Look, I can't stand picturing you with anyone else either, so I understand what it's like, but we have to stop this. It hurts right now, I know, but where do you think this will go? Someplace new? Haven't we exhausted this tactic?"

In the oncoming rush of emotion she could find no words, just the action of slowly buttoning her blouse. It pained him to see her put clothes on after all the years of watching her take them off.

"Stop," he demanded and held her by the wrists, shirt still slightly undone. "I will always care about you and want you to be happy," he told her.

She leaned in to kiss him and this time he didn't avoid her. It was a kiss that wasn't measured in seconds, but in minutes. As much as he'd recovered from the confusion formed from her initial erotic advance, he suddenly fell completely into her grasp, no longer able to resist—logic and the future be damned. She could have it all, whatever she wanted, whenever she wanted it, if she would just give all of herself to him now. He said, "Every time you kiss me, it drives me wild," and pulled her forcefully toward him.

She exhaled and twisted out of his grasp; it was a goodbye kiss, not a hello kiss. "Just not now," she added. "You made your decision and you're with someone else." She stood up from his lap, looked at him one last time, and walked out of the house, shirt tail trailing behind her.

All the air went out of the room with her, but the heat inside of him burned. He watched her go, heard her close the door, and slapped his hands to his forehead, "What the hell am I doing?" Soupy curled up on the couch in the fetal position until he cried himself to sleep.

* * *

Is that a preview to a sequel we've already seen? asked Promise.

"Coming soon to a theater near you," I added.

I'm not sure who won that round. Both of you, I hope. She threw herself at you and you rejected her. Women don't typically like that; it just took her a few minutes to realize it.

"Promise, in that moment it was the right decision, and in the end she helped me make it, but it wasn't easy, wasn't easy at all. I've played that damn evening over and over in my head for years wondering about the other option."

I guarantee you she's done the same thing.

"The way she came at me with so much confidence was incredible. For a moment I wanted to believe she became the woman I wanted her to be—because I desperately wanted to love a woman who had seen the world, knew exactly what she wanted, and had a plan to get there. But this was Gravity, and yes she was growing, but she was far from grown. As much as I wanted *that* kind of woman—the worldly one—people just don't change that quickly, and I knew she'd be back to herself…actually, *we'd* be back to our old selves tomorrow."

Good correction.

"Watching this story in my life, seeing it happen all over again, makes me want another chance. My heartstrings get yanked hard in her direction. And it's just as emotionally confusing now as it was the first time. That night changed the rest of my life."

And what happens when you feel that tug? You survive, right?

"Yeah, usually. At least, I'm trying to survive." There was a moment of silence before I added, "Promise, I need some fresh air and a bottle of water. Excuse me." I got out of the cab and walked toward the snack bar.

Chapter 24

I shoved my hands in my pockets and lowered my head, eyeballing every piece of gravel before it met my footfall, not as a means toward looking for something, but as a means to look for nothing. It was four parking rows from my cab to the snack bar, and I made a straight path toward it. Gravity had just been right there in front of me, again, practically close enough to caress. I was reminded of the way she smelled that night, how the world kept spinning while I was inside her embrace.

When I reached the snack bar, the line for service wound around the inside and out of the entrance door, so I kept walking toward the back of the drive-in parking area: head down, hands in pockets, simply walking. There was still so much to tell Promise, but I couldn't continue talking right now. I was out of energy. My battery was dead. The gears inside my head were about to seize up unless I could get some *me* time. At the back of the lot I found a fence with one bottom corner peeled back, and a path beyond, so I just kept walking. This theater was nestled into the mountains, and I had a mountain to climb, had to see the view, had to feel like I'd accomplished something other than what Promise said I should "learn" from every person I love.

My mind cleared a bit as the trail grew steeper, not that I could think more, but the mental smoke turned to fog, which turned to haze. I stopped to catch my breath and looked out over the drive-in theater, maybe two-thirds full, and some sort of intermission cartoon on the screen, nothing that mattered to me. The theater was the only source of light for miles. The land was dark, and quiet, but this was no time to sit on a rock and admire the view. After a few deep breaths, I continued my walk. Like I said, I had to get to the top.

The switchbacks upward covered maybe a third of its elevation. Beyond them the trail gradually spiraled around the side of the mountain. I looked over my shoulder one last time before the theater went out of view. My eyes had adjusted to the dark, which made it easy to see the light-colored trail amid the darker brush. Around the edge of the mountain there was a light higher on the hill than my current elevation. There was no going off trail in the dark, so I trusted the path to lead me closer to the light. I climbed, left after right, occasionally stumbling on a small rock or a root that had grown across the trail, but maintained steady progress toward the light. I could now see that it was a bonfire. The closer I got, the more I could see of it, but the colder the temperature around me. I rubbed my hands on opposite arms and picked up the pace.

I felt a presence behind me. Stopping abruptly, I looked over my shoulder, but saw nothing. Perhaps worse, in my head the fearsome, gigantic, invisible, imaginary hand from my childhood was behind me and maliciously drawing closer in the cover of the dark. "Don't be that character," I whispered, referring to the character in horror movies who runs from the murderer, looks back over a shoulder, trips over something, and then gets killed. But it was time to run. I had to run. It was coming. Ten strides down the path I encountered a rocky section where continued progress required leaping from boulder to boulder. As I jumped, using my hands to balance and catch my unbalanced landings, I kept my eyes on the worn places on the ground between the rocks that signaled the proper course. Upward was good, it was heading toward the fire I could now hear crackling. I grabbed a rock with my hand to pull myself upward, but it loosened from its position, leveraged the momentum I'd given it, and began its journey down the mountain. It narrowly missed me as I grasped for another handhold and slid to the side as it passed. I watched it go and was surprised to see it disappear into the dark a mere ten feet below my position. I had to climb faster, and stop checking the distance between the dark below and the light above. As I'd gone from a trail to boulders, I now went from boulders to huge slabs of rock. In the dark I found small hand and foot holds that helped me scurry up between the rock faces. I was almost there. As I held strong with my left side, I reached up with my right to find the next hold. A cicada walked across the back of my hand and down my forearm. I reacted both terribly wrong and incredibly right as I jerked my hand away and shook it to throw the cicada off. Luckily, my flailing hand grasped a shrub branch growing between the rocks that held me steady. The cicada took flight and buzzed past my ear causing me to wince in protection. Resisting the urge to look down—I didn't need to because I could feel my toes turning blue from the cold—I groaned and lunged for the top edge of my destination. *Got it!* Having reached it, I pulled myself over the edge. Sweat dripped from my brow as I thrust my right knee over the rock, scraping it in the process, and pulled the rest of my body up to the same level as the bonfire. I had no breath left in my lungs, but it was still several yards to the fire, so I rolled toward the heat and light. I caught my breath and trusted in the protection of the light from whatever had been trying to reach me below.

"Grandson," said Great Grandpa calmly.

I sat up abruptly and saw him sitting on a rock near the bonfire. He was working with his hands to make piles of small branches and leaves between his feet. "Grandpa?" I asked.

"Yes, Grandson, it is me," he replied and motioned for me to join him by the fire.

I got up, wiped the sweat from my brow, and approached him. Halfway there I checked behind me, just in case. Nothing. The fire radiated great heat; I raised my palms toward it.

Great Grandpa said, "Careful, it burns hot."

"I prefer hot after running from the cold," I said.

He chuckled and shrugged as if saying without words, "So goes life."

"What are you doing?" I asked.

"You must learn to burn," he said.

That got my attention, so I looked more closely at the piles at his feet: a bundle of grass, pile of leaves, and a few small sticks. He again motioned for me to sit next to him.

"Do you remember the fire?" he asked.

I knew he was talking about the first time he showed it to me, so I answered yes.

"Hold out your hand, palm up," he ordered. He did the same with his hand. The thumb from his left touched the thumb on my right and I immediately felt his heat. With his other hand he reached into the small pile of leaves and flung them into the bonfire. "Good journey," he said. The fire flashed brilliantly through the colors of the seasons and then returned to normal. Great Grandpa laid a handful of long grass on the palms of both our hands that bridged over the space between them. He said, "Hold steady," and then closed his eyes. "Watch," he added. I watched as he breathed slowly and moved his free hand as if he was conducting an orchestra. When he placed his hand over his heart, the end of the grass on his palm caught fire while the end on my palm smoked slightly. He leaned in and quickly blew out the fire on his palm before he said, "First lesson, fire is hot." Great Grandpa chuckled. "Remember, it is important to communicate with your fire. To do so you must understand what fire needs. What does fire need?"

"Air," I thought a moment longer, "and something to burn."

He smiled and said, "Yes, yes. You see, fire, it *wants* to burn. Do not misunderstand me, Grandson, for fire can burn for good or for bad. When it burns for good it gives light or warmth. When it burns for bad it destroys. Fire itself is neither good nor bad, it takes what it is given. You know exactly what you will get from fire, but you must tell fire what you are going to give it and what you expect from it in return. Be true to your words. What will you offer fire?"

"I'm offering this bundle of grass," I said.

Great Grandpa gestured for me to attempt lighting the grass on my own. I closed my eyes and imagined the dance of the flames in the fire. I remembered things that happened in my life: losing a fire truck and its men in an instant when a construction shed storing explosives exploded, a marshmallow that slid off a stick and burned a friend's thigh, a forest fire that leapt a highway and burned hundreds of homes, twin skyscrapers that melted under intense heat and collapsed—I grew angry at the dastardly things fire had done during my life. I thought, *I offer this grass to you, burn it*—I opened my eyes and the grass exploded. "SHIT!" I yelled pulling my hand away from the explosion. I shook it in the air until Great Grandpa grabbed my wrist, packed my palm with dirt, and then forced my fist closed around it.

"Just as I have always known," he playfully chastised. "It is in you, yes, but wrong. Tsk-tsk. Open," he said as he pointed to my hand, still holding my wrist, and then quickly slapped his palm against mine. The earth fell from it in a small cloud of dust. "Better?"

"Yeah," I admitted, "I think it scared me more than anything else."

"As it can." He tapped his index finger to his forehead and said, "Fire does not come from here. No. It comes from here." He tapped his heart. "Remember?" Grandpa did a few orchestral maneuvers replicating what he'd shown me earlier. I remembered his hand going to his chest right before the grass caught fire. "Do you know what I mean, Grandson?"

"Yes, I know her," I said, and then realized I'd appended the word "her" to my reply.

His eyebrows rose as he said, "Her?"

"Yeah, do you know—"

"No, no, don't tell me. Tell fire. Tell *fiiiiiiire*," he said and threw another handful of leaves into the bonfire.

I snapped my eyes closed once more and thought of the dream girl I'd missed all these years and how she had finally returned. She was back, and I'd spent most of this evening with her. We'd made up for all the years we were apart. And in this short night, I'd already wished for her to be there more often than not. I missed her when she was gone. We understood how to understand each other. I loved to make her giggle. I eagerly awaited her opinions. I knew I'd love her smile, and I knew she'd never use it against me because she'll know: my mission will be to see it often as I can. I loved her. *Loved her.*

With a deep inhale of breath, I opened my eyes and pressed my left palm toward the heat of the bonfire. I flexed it a few times by stretching my fingers outward as far as I could and squeezing them tightly back into a fist. On the last stretch I imagined a little spark of fire, and I asked it to join me. I asked it to take a journey with me, to rest in my fist, allow me to carry it to my heart, where it could feel the passionate fire inside me, and then, together, we would show the world an example of our passion, our mutual passion to burn brightly, which would send this bundle of grass on its own journey. Heat arrived on the palm of my hand, so I closed it gently and slowly moved it toward my heart. When it arrived, I opened my palm and pressed it to the center of my chest. My whole body tingled and warmed. My heart pumped blood in great gushing beats. The muscles in my right arm tensed and relaxed and the grass caught fire, just as it had in Great Grandpa's hand. As I smiled, I watched fire dance with the grass. I picked up the end that wasn't burning and held it out in front of me.

Great Grandpa patted me on the back. "Well done, Grandson."

As the grass began its journey, I tossed it into the air and watched it fully depart. "Good journey," I said to it, and then added, "Thank you, fire."

"Never a bad idea to thank the elements. They are under no requirement to adhere to your requests," he said.

I made a mental note of it.

"But now, Grandson, you must go. Do not take the path that brought you here; it will take you backward. You are the one, and you must go forward. Always forward." Great Grandpa pointed to the opposite side of the fire from where I'd first approached it.

"Thank you, Great Grandpa, as always," I said as I touched his shoulder.

"Always of great and honorable deeds," he replied, stating the Walker family motto.

I stepped past him and saw the downward path. It wasn't my day to reach the top of the mountain, not my day to see all I could see, but I'd learned an important lesson from Great Grandpa: I'd learned *fire*, and that would have to be enough. I jogged down the path, my blood still flowing and energetic from the experience. The sun began to light the sky as I descended, making it easier to see where to step. At the bottom of the trail sat my cab, idling in the middle of a dirt road, no passengers that I could see.

Chapter 25

I drove the cab around the base of the mountain on some kind of service road. As I rounded a bend to the left, the drive-in movie theater was just below me. Most of the cars had already left. A few stragglers remained, maybe those who'd fallen asleep during the show. *Yeah*, I thought and chuckled, *a movie about my life would put everyone to sleep.* A marquee sign on the concessions building flashed brightly in the pre-dawn light with a big arrow that pointed to the building itself, and letters that lit up one by one, P-R-O-M-I-S-E, and then flashed a few times, PROMISE, PROMISE, PROMISE. I hadn't seen that before, but it was as sure a sign as I'd ever seen pointing out my next stop.

I pulled into the theater and parked under the sign, which was pointing to a place at the back of the concession stand. A few moments later the back door opened and I felt my best fare sit down in the back seat.

Promise said, *Um, good morning?*

"Sorry about that, Promise. This isn't easy, you know. I guess it'd be one thing if I was simply talking to you about my life, but we're reliving it. I mean, I'm not just telling you about it, we're watching it happen. When I see those emotions on those faces, I'm transported back to those moments and I feel *all* of it."

It's genuine and I can see it, and it tells me more about you than if we were just talking about it.

"I guess," I added. "But I know what's coming and I'm not looking forward to most of it."

We have to do it. Remember, it's how we learn. If it's anything like what we've already seen, we'll continue to learn a lot from it.

"Yes, there is a lot of story left to tell, so I guess we better get on the road."

I believe in you.

I put the cab into drive and exited the theater.

So where'd you go for your fresh air?

"I walked toward the concession stand, but I could feel there was nothing there for me, so I put my hands in my pockets and walked past it. When I got to the back of the parking area, I found a hole in the fence and a path beyond that wound up the hill. It took me to my great grandpa."

Excitedly, Promise said, *You saw Great Grandpa?!*

"Yep."

And did he tell you a story?!

"Yep, sure did, but he did more than that: he taught me how to make fire."

Make fire? Like, by rubbing two sticks together?

"Nope, not like that at all, and I guess making fire is probably the wrong way to describe it; he taught me to *understand* fire—to know what it wants. By understanding it, when I tell it what I need, we can enter into a negotiation about what we can do for each other."

Interesting. What does fire want?

"Duh, it wants to burn," I answered.

I suppose it does.

"But that burning can be for good or bad, you know? Fire can lay waste to an entire city or it can warm a home; that's the negotiation."

Can it warm up this terribly-tasting cup of coffee? I'm guessing that drive-in patrons aren't much for coffee and it's been sitting on the burner all night.

"It might be better to offer the paper cup to fire instead of asking it to warm the contents."

Definitely, and I'm more of a tea gal than a coffee one anyway, so fire can have it.

I pulled the cigarette lighter from the dash of the taxicab and held it backwards over my shoulder.

Very funny.

I shrugged. "Can't fault a boy for trying. I think there's a coffee shop up here at the crossroads. How about we stop before heading to Possibly?"

Sounds like a plan.

I made the right-hand turn into the coffee shop, aptly named the "Dream Café." It was our luck; it had a drive-thru window, which helped us avoid unnecessarily seeing each other. What kind of tea do you want, Promise?"

"Hi, what can I get started for you this morning?" came the crackled voice over the loudspeaker.

Green tea latte, Promise said.

"Small green tea latte, and ummm, what black breakfast teas do you have?"

"English, Irish, Welsh, Earl—"

"Small Irish Breakfast tea, splash of skim milk," I added. The cashier repeated our order and asked us to pull forward to the window.

"Good morning, Sir," the cashier said. "One minute for your drinks." He leaned down to see for whom the second drink was intended, which caused a perplexed look on his face after hearing me carry a conversation over the intercom. When he returned, he handed the drinks to me one at a time calling their names as he did so. I placed Promise's drink between my legs and then sat my own in the aftermarket cup holder that had been wedged into the dashboard of this old cab.

"What do I owe you?" I asked.

"Oh," he waved his hand down at me, "The first customer of the day doesn't pay at the Dream Café."

"Sweet! Thank you! Have a nice day!" I said. Promise was holding her mostly empty coffee cup over my shoulder. "Oh, excuse me, can you toss this for us?" I handed the old coffee cup to the cashier and he feigned a smile as he took it. As I pulled away from the building, I handed the green tea latte back to Promise. "I might have to remember this place."

Yeah, me too, Promise added.

We left the parking lot, made a right turn, and immediately got into the left turn lane to head for Possibly. "Promise, do you think there's a formula for true love?"

Sure, I think there's a formula, but it's different for every person.

"So you're saying it's subjective?"

Yes. Some combination of important factors in the right portions for a unique individual. Otherwise, wouldn't we all love the same person?

"Yeah, I guess if there was one recipe for true love those ingredients would be pretty popular."

You are created from different ingredients than a friend of yours, so your ingredients likely fit with a different set of ingredients than he desires in someone.

"I've never understood the conversation that goes…a friend says, 'She's hot,' and I disagree and he says I'm crazy and then I follow up with something like 'Hey, then we won't have to compete for her,' and then he realizes that's kinda cool but completely misses my point."

Yes, I know that conversation. We ladies have it, as well.

"So I've been thinking about how to better understand myself, which is where I was going with the initial question. With Honesty and Gravity, I was pretty focused on their formula because I thought I'd done the work to understand my own—my thought processes, my feelings, my desires, dreams, goals, career, interests—but I was only just getting started. And for that matter, so were they as young as we all were."

That's the obvious starting place, since we know you can't figure out what you want until you figure out who you are.

"There was a time when I thought the important word in the phrase 'to better understand who I am' was 'understand.' Now I know the 'I' comes first. Understood myself more and I might be able to make a better 'we' someday."

Oh me, oh my, it's the I.

"That tea kicks in quickly for you, huh?"

Promise giggled.

"There were times when I was dating Gravity—or maybe that's better said: in those times when I *wasn't* dating Gravity—that I contemplated a life alone, without a partner. Because I was unwilling to settle, and every attempt I'd made at love, so far, had failed miserably."

But you were still so young, Soupy.

"I might have been young, but I felt older and wiser than everyone else around me."

Thank goodness you didn't settle; you were wise enough to realize that decisions have to be made with your heart and *your head, as we've discussed. True love isn't about one moment in time; it's about the rest of time.*

"Is it?" I asked.

What do you mean?

"Actually, I'm not really sure what I mean, but there is something about that statement that doesn't feel right. We'll have to come back to it someday. What comes to mind to me right now has to do with the formula. 'Formula' itself being a really brainy word. It's pretty head driven, isn't it? I mean, where's the heart in the head of science?"

You need a variable of magic.

"A variable of magic? I like that; it's the piece people guess at, figuring it'll all just work out somehow, sometime, somewhere."

And that's always *a good idea,* Promise said, sarcastically.

"So it can't be a magic *trick*, it has to be real magic."

No card tricks or pulling coins from ears. Yes, it has to be true magic.

"If it's true magic then how do you keep from guessing?"

If the formula is partly in the head and you listen to what your head has to say about it, and the formula is partly in the heart—

"Then you listen to what your heart has to say about it."

Both parts, head and heart, require you to understand the languages they speak in order to make a more educated guess about the variable of magic. You can only understand those languages if you know yourself well.

"So it's a pretty big variable?"

Sometimes. Not always. You still need to believe in magic for it to work, or even appear.

"Okay, to back up a little bit, I've been thinking about formulas like this: If there are ten important qualities I need, which of the ten are the most important? And secondly, once I've discovered these ten qualities, can a woman be strong in one category and a bit weaker in another and everything would still be fine for us? I haven't been able to figure it out. Like, there's no machine to spit out that answer."

The variable of magic.

"I needed another 'we' to better understand my 'I.' Enter Possibly," I said as we pulled into the town of the same name. "She roared into my life—no, that's not true—we'd been introduced to each other over email by a family member who thought we'd make a good connection. That was a year and a half prior to our meeting."

While you were still dating Gravity?

"Yes, but Possibly was half a country away.

Wouldn't you call that cheating?

"Cheating?" I asked, surprised. "No, at least I don't think so. Look, at the beginning of a friendship you have to first become friends, and based on how my family described Possibly, she seemed potentially a good addition to my group of friends."

Mmm hmm.

"I haven't dated *every* woman I've become friends with, so there's really no way to know where it will end up at such an early state. However, as Gravity and I began to waiver, Possibly was on my mind more and more often. She was young, beautiful, well-traveled, with a mind to change the world. Just like me, she was willing to ride opportunistic winds when they whispered to her. And having said that, as soon as I knew Gravity and I were done, I booked the opportunity to meet Possibly and help her drive across the country for a new job."

Across the country? I can only assume that would be in your direction.

"Sure enough."

How convenient.

"Indeed," I added.

I parked the cab in a long line of cabs at the Possibly City Airport.

Are we going to see your first meeting? Promise asked, giddily.

"Yes, we are. I was nervous as hell, just like I am now." I magically converted a side-of-the-road billboard into our personal movie screen, then added, "Once this plane takes off there's no turning back, Promise."

Awww Soup, like I said, I believe in you.

"You better."

Your nervous energy definitely tells me we're about to learn a lot!

"You have no idea," I said. "When we first met online we traded pictures, and as you know I was still occupied with trying to figure things out with Gravity. I didn't want to fall for someone else, but at the same time I was struggling and wanted the Calgon to—"

Take me awayyyyyyy!

"Exactly. Magic: the kind you want to believe in that doesn't actually exist."

Totally different from the variable of magic we were discussing earlier, by the way.

"Waaaay different, but what are ya gonna do? I showed Possibly's photos to some friends and they confirmed what I didn't want to feel: she was stunningly beautiful."

We both know that attraction isn't everything, but it sure is something, isn't it?

"Hell yes, it is, especially when it hits you that hard."

It's dangerous.

"You don't have to tell me," I agreed.

Someone like you falls head over heels in love every single time an opportunity presents itself.

"Not quite true. If I'm already in love, I don't swap it for a new love. But like I said, you really *don't* have to tell me. Not to take anything away from Gravity; she was beautiful, too, but in such a different way, a fun, cute, giggly—"

Gravity was a girl, Soup, and Possibly was a woman.

"Yes, yes, but…I can say that here, where we're just talking about looks, but that's not how it turned out." I paused for a moment before I said, "Oh, just roll tape." Our video screen showed Possibly standing among a large group of people waiting for friends and family members to disembark from their planes. I gulped when I saw her again. Sitting here, I now knew the outside *and* the inside of her, unlike when we first met. Perhaps I *was* learning something. "That's her with the straight, shoulder-length hair in the long, black coat."

Oh my, she is a looker.

I nodded my head. "I worked at saving my relationship with Gravity—it was too much work—and I needed to play in the worst way."

It's work, yes, but it's the type of work you should enjoy, but enough about that. Tell me more about Possibly.

"There were things about her—about the life she'd led—that fell into the realm of things I'd never experienced."

She had something to teach you *for a change.*

"YES! Gravity was so young when we met, physically and emotionally. Possibly had been around the block and wanted to keep circling it or exploring new neighborhoods. She touched my nomadic soul, my thirst for constant discovery. Honesty and Gravity were very wholesome, wonderful, caring women who held the goodness of others often above their own needs. Possibly was taking the world by the horns and wrestling out of it what she wanted."

On the video screen Possibly tapped her foot on the ground, inspected her fingernails, checked her phone, and looked around the airport.

"Like I said, I was nervous. I wanted to see her before she saw me even though I realized that the odds were in her favor; she'd be watching a string of passengers while I'd be searching for a face in a group of faces. This was an inflection point for us, our virtual relationship was about to end and our physical relationship was about to begin—it was about to get *real.*

My lovely Soup, the hopeless romantic.

"Seriously, on the Internet you can be anyone you want; it's the best place to lie."

Best place to lie?

"Yes, I could make myself out to be a twelve-year-old boy if I wanted. Meaning, maybe I only told Possibly about my best qualities…or maybe she'd done that to me. I needed to verify that Possibly was the person in real life she claimed to be online and over the phone."

So you just asked her for a background check?

"It would have been easier, that's for sure."

We watched the video screen together looking for Soupy to emerge from the airport's security exit. "Everything, and I mean everything, was awhirl. A dizzying mixture of lights and noise in a place I'd never before been. I had to remind myself to breathe, and then remind myself to breathe again. I fell into line with the other exiting passengers. The airport grew boiling hot, especially after the frigid air we'd all felt on the jet way. My hands were shaking uncontrollably. The public address system announced pages and arrivals and departures. I wondered, *Can I get out of line? Can I?* Suddenly, I stopped as nausea took hold and my stomach lurched."

"Excuse me," said someone behind me. I didn't give her any attention. She repeated more forcefully, "EXCUSE ME!"

"Sorry. Sorry," I said, waving a hand in apology. I leaned up against a wall and caught my breath. "I scanned the crowd ahead for Possibly, but I was still too far away. By the time I saw her she'd already seen me. The noise faded and my stomach settled. We were about to touch for the first time."

Dreamy!

"Cold," I corrected.

Cold?

"My first thought when she hugged me—a time when I wanted this incredible combination of warmth and comfort—was chilly. She was in and out quickly, a courtesy, two-pat hug while looking the other direction, like she was looking for someone else or had somewhere else to be."

Maybe she was really nervous?

"Maybe, but don't you believe a hug can really set the tone. I mean, after a year and a half of getting to know each other wouldn't a long hug with a deep exhale say a lot about finally being able to meet. Like, a comfortable relief, even if temporary, to mark the passing from one phase to the next?"

Yes, I agree that a hug can set the tone, especially when you were the one making the long trek into a place completely foreign to you. However, you also think too much.

"No argument there. I'd set pretty high expectations on us because I already knew what I wanted to discover, what I *needed* to discover. I guess I expected us to be on the same page."

And you weren't?

"I don't know that I'd say that; it's tough to say at all, really. It's easier to show you." I fast-forwarded the video. "We walked to her car. I was slightly behind her partly because I have a tendency to walk more slowly than others, but also because I needed to *see* her for the first time. And yes, she was more beautiful in person than in pictures."

I can see that, too.

Promise and I pulled out of the cab line at the airport and followed Possibly's car to a local bar. "We made small talk in the car while she drove us around town asking where I wanted to go, when it truly didn't matter. I would have gone anywhere that allowed her and I to be together. Being next to her in the car was infuriating because I couldn't actually look at her, but I could smell her perfume, which reminded me of the one question that had been burning in my mind since the day we decided to meet: would we kiss?"

Oooo, I LOVE that question.

"A kiss would say so, so much. I could read a kiss and all the body language that might come with it."

Do you—

"Patience! Possibly and I finally stopped somewhere and had a few drinks. I tried to look into her eyes, but she avoided mine. Our talk wasn't deep. She fidgeted in her seat and kept saying it was really weird to finally meet. I noted it, and tried not to let it worry me."

Her phone rang.

"Excuse me," she said, and got up to walk toward the bathroom.

Friend check-in call?

"Maybe, since when she came back she grabbed the check, paid it at the bar, and told me it was time to go somewhere else to meet her friends. I wondered whether surrounding us with her friends was a way to insulate herself from me or proof that I'd leapt the first hurdle."

Yeah, I see where you're coming from.

"So far, this wasn't the Possibly I'd expected. And as time passed, it was getting harder to chalk it up to her nerves. I was doing my best to keep a wait-and-see attitude."

Possibly and Soupy left the window table where they'd been sitting and walked back to her car.

"Possibly made small talk while she drove, mostly about the people I was about to meet, none of it I actually remembered. I need faces with names to have any chance of remembering who they are."

We watched Possibly park the car. She then bounced out with a huge smile on her face, ran her arm through Soupy's, leaned into him, and said, "I might get *really* drunk here since we're leaving town tomorrow." She smiled while latching on to his arm more tightly. "If I get too drunk will you drive?"

"Yeah, sure," Soupy replied.

She grabbed him by the hand and they jogged toward the front door of the bar.

I told Promise, "I was confused by the sudden affection. Was it to get something from me? Was she going to get drunk to make this night more bearable? As we entered the bar, I was nervous, confused and frustrated." I drew a movie screen on the side of the bar so Promise and I could watch what was happening inside.

We walked in and everything stopped but the music—a classic scene when the "in" crowd notices at once that someone unknown has entered the room. "It was hot and claustrophobic and I wanted to remove my pea coat, but I needed the armor it provided, especially if I needed to bolt. And I really needed a drink."

Possibly shouted above the music, "THIS IS SOUPY!" and everyone in the room yelled their version of, "HEY, SOUPY!"

"All the conversations then turned to a new topic: me."

Surely, but you look like you are holding your own, Soup.

"Thanks, love. As you can see, Possibly grabbed me by the hand after we hung up our coats and led me straight to the bar where several shots of tequila were already waiting."

Promise and I watched as Possibly kissed and hugged her friends between shots, handing one to me each time a new friend was willing to do one with us.

"The women wanted to know everything about me and the men, it seemed, measured me up as the new competition, which was fine. As you know, I prefer conversing with women more than men anyway. After each new person I met, Possibly would whisper into my ear who he or she was currently sleeping with, and then point out who they *used* to sleep with. I couldn't keep track of it, and I really didn't want to. Except, it made me wonder, if all of these people have slept with each other—"

How many had slept with her?

"Yeah, exactly."

Is there a number that would bother you?

I thought about that for a moment. "Yes and no. If she'd slept with every guy in the room I suppose that would be a lot to accept. So I don't know, is that something you think is important to know?"

Not so much the actual number, really. I think the question is more about the risks that you've taken with your partners than it is about the number of partners you've had. I don't want to teach my partner how everything works, and I don't want him to already know it all; I want us to know enough to have comfort in exploring each other."

"Well, that's just it, isn't it? You can learn from experience with someone else, but everyone in the bedroom is different, so even what you already know needs to be explored again."

Yes, and have fun doing so!

"Before we take the path down discussing our partners, how about we refocus on the story right in front of us?"

Promise replied, *Yessir.*

"The introductions only lasted so long, thankfully, since the tequila was quickly impacting my future ability to drive, and I was getting tired of answering the same questions. Possibly drifted off into the crowd and left me standing with the people I'd most recently met. It was cool, since I wanted to learn more about her, and part of learning is seeing her in a social situation. After my conversation group disbanded, I looked around to find Possibly, didn't see her, didn't see anyone I really wanted to chat with, so I headed toward the front door."

Let me guess, you wanted fresh air?

"Indeed, and to get away from the damn tequila. Don't get me wrong, I *love* good tequila, but I was starting to spin. And let's be honest, I felt like I was invading the herd to steal one of their females."

Promise and I watched Soupy walk out. He took a few steps away from the door and exhaled in the cold night air.

* * *

"Hey, man," a voice said from around the corner.

Soupy looked toward the voice and replied, "Possibly's…brother?"

"Yeah," he confirmed while shaking my hand for the second time. His other hand held a lit cigarette. "Bet you wish you were back in that warmer weather right now, huh?"

"Nah," Soupy replied, "I grew up in this stuff so it's nice to get back to it once in a while. Plus, there's that lovely lady inside I've just met in person for the first time."

He laughed, "Yeah, watch out for her, she's a handful, but she's been talking about you a lot, and look, you're here!"

"That I am."

At that time, Possibly leaned out of the bar and said, "Hey, there you are! Let's get out of here!"

"Grab my coat!" Soupy yelled back to her, and then turned to her brother and said, "Enjoy your night, man."

He motioned to the front door of the bar and said, "Yeah, you, too, but I don't think you're going to have any problem there." He followed his statement with a laugh and then added, "Hey Possibly, you take care of this guy. He seems alright!"

She yelled back at him, "Whatever, dork!" and then motioned for me to join her and the female friend whose arm she held as they walked toward the car.

Soupy threw his coat on quickly, grabbed the keys dangling from her hand, and slipped into step beside her.

Possibly said, "The three of us are going to the club, okay?"

"Sure," Soupy shrugged. "As long as you show me the way."

"Oh, I'll show you the way," she smirked.

Her friend added, "We'll show you the way," and they both laughed.

* * *

I backed the cab out of our parking spot and followed the threesome to Possibly's parked car.

Soupy unlocked the car and Possibly's friend opened the rear door to the backseat. Possibly turned to Soupy, grabbed his collar, looked into his eyes, and pulled him into her as she leaned back against the side of the car.

Promise yelled, *THE FIRST KISS!*

"Yeah, and pretty damn unexpected," I added.

It was the deepest and lengthiest amount of time that Possibly had looked into Soupy's eyes. Hers grabbed a hold of his, and her lips weren't long to follow suit after she said, "I like you."

"Any chill in my body evacuated immediately. She kissed me like she'd been fantasizing about it for a year and a half. It was everything I wanted our first hug to have: length, passion, comfort, and a lingering desire for more as soon as possible."

Soupy looked into her eyes and tucked her hair behind her ear when it was over.

Possibly said, "I like her, too," while pointing to her friend in the back seat. She ran a gloved finger over Soupy's lower lip and smiled. "Do you mind if I ride back here with her?"

Soupy leaned down to look into the back seat and saw Possibly's friend smiling back at him. She was incredibly beautiful, as well.

"I wanted an adventure," I said to Promise.

And it looks like you got it.

Possibly said to Soupy, "I'll reward you for it later."

He shrugged while he smiled, and then gestured for her to climb into the car while he held the door open.

"My mind was racing, Promise. We were coloring waaay outside of the lines. I don't mind doing that, but I've usually considered where and why and what the opportunity cost is for doing so. The tequila was warming my stomach. Her kiss had revved up my heartbeat. So I kept saying 'fuck it' over and over in my head, and smiling each time I did so, but there was a whole hell of a lot of risk here. I hardly knew Possibly and I didn't know her friend at all. Where was this going? I'd never done it before, but I surely knew the intimate tryst existed inherently on the thinnest of ice."

You lost control of this as soon as she kissed you.

"Pretty much," I agreed.

I tuned the cab's radio to a station that would receive the audio from Possibly's car in front of us. The girls shouted instructions to Soupy about radio stations and driving directions amid loud laughter and audible kissing.

What were you thinking while you drove? Promise asked.

"I was just trying to keep us alive. With the alcohol and the instructions, and I have to admit, sneaking glances into the rearview mirror to watch them kiss, that was about all I could process at once."

Not you, there was surely more going on in that mind of yours.

"I knew I was on a ride that I didn't want to get off of. I entertained the notion that this might be my first threesome, sure, and one that I'd definitely accept given how stunning these ladies were and how comfortable they seemed to be with each other. I mean, you want discovery and exploration? WHAM! Here it is."

But at what cost?

"Yeah, exactly. Would this night wreck a future relationship for Possibly and me? Maybe? Hopefully not. I figured if I let her lead, then she'd show me the way."

She's definitely leading now.

"And it was about this time that she showed me the path," I said.

We heard Possibly's voice on the radio, "Do you like watching us kiss?"

"Of course," Soupy replied.

Possibly's head leaned toward Soupy's and she nibbled on his ear before she whispered, "You can watch, but you can't fuck her." Possibly leaned back into her seat and both girls laughed.

At this point nothing she says is really going to surprise me.

"Her lead, as you said," I reminded Promise. "Who do you *really* think is driving that car? It sure wasn't me."

Obviously not.

"It gets better," I added.

Better?

Soupy's voice came over the radio, "Ummm, when you said 'club' I thought you meant dance club."

"Hell no," Possibly said, and then both girls yelled, "STRIP CLUB!"

That's what you call better?

"Not my ride," I said. "And this ride was spinning faster with each minute. You know that mare on the merry-go-round, the gray one with the flared nostrils pointing toward the sky that looks like it's all hopped up on performance enhancing drugs, front hooves all reared up and ready to run? That's the horse I was riding, and I wasn't about to let it buck me off because I knew, at this point, if I bailed out of the night that would be the end of Possibly and Soupy. And if there wasn't going to be a Possibly and Soupy anyway, then I might as well enjoy this ride as long as it lasted."

Did you believe there would still be a Possibly and Soupy after this?

"I did, maybe foolishly, maybe not. I accepted that she was someone who had explored things I'd never explored, and I was drawn to the teaching that she was giving me on the first night we'd ever been together. There was *something* to experience here, and definitely something to learn."

That's not the question I asked you. The question I asked was: how could you still think she's me?

Her question caught me off guard. "Wow. Good question. At that time, I don't know. I suppose I thought it was just an anomaly; one of those evenings of hellos and goodbyes that kick risk aversion to the curb. One of those nights when the spiritual, emotional side takes the night off and the physical side rules the roost—which is *really* atypical for me, but I guess with the recent feeling that I'd gotten it all wrong with Gravity, I simply found myself in this place of amusement: strapped in, slowly climbing the first hill—click, click, click—hands and feet inside the roller coaster until I'm ready to throw them sky high for the downward plunge. Hell, Promise, like I already said about this night, 'Fuck it.' I was ready to be led instead of doing the leading. And by that I don't mean, "Fuck it, I wanna get led to bed. No, I just wanted to see where this whole thing was going since I was sure it'd be somewhere I'd never before been."

We'd already parked at the strip club and I'd formed a video screen on the outside of the building. It flickered briefly, then showed the merry-go-round I'd just described.

"What the hell?" I asked.

If it's in your mind it can broadcast.

Possibly and her friend sat at the controls of the carousel, making out, yelling with amusement, and smiling at me when I passed by. As the ride increased in speed, I flew past and couldn't focus on her. I didn't want them to whiz by. I wanted to look at Possibly, to explore her, to understand her.

"Slow this thing down. I'm getting dizzy," I said to Promise, but the ride continued.

Nothing I can do for you, Soup.

With both hands, Soupy held tightly to the pole that impaled his gray mare and kept her firmly attached to the ride. His thighs squeezed her like a vice, but that only pressed her into greater fury. The stirrups got too small for his shoes, or his shoes too big for the stirrups, and his feet were left to dangle. Bareback and stirrup-less, he was convinced the merry-go-round was an experience, just no longer convinced that it was an enjoyable one.

Soup? Promise said. *SOUP!* she yelled.

I heard her, but I was losing consciousness.

Promise watched as Soupy was thrown from the ride. He landed where he couldn't reach the girls, but he could watch them in action together. Possibly was casting an intimate spell over her friend, and it was intoxicating everyone around them. The girls hit the "Stop" button on the merry-go-round, picked Soupy up, and all three walked into the strip club.

I opened my eyes to see the threesome walking into the entrance. "What'd I miss?" I asked Promise.

You got thrown from the ride. Are you okay?

"I don't know." I scratched my head, rubbed my eyes, and scrunched down into my seat. I let out a yell and shook my head back and forth.

Dude.

"Sorry, I just remember…remember this lair of sin. Look, I don't mind strip clubs, but I'd always been to them more for the male bonding than the boobs. This was a completely different experience. The graveled parking lot had welcomed our car. In fact, it seemed to take pleasure in our arrival, salivated in anticipation. The building, although foreboding in its lack of character, pointed brightly to its own entrance, which seemed to smile." I scratched my head again, sure my hair was standing on end. "Strip clubs. Darkness is complete in these places. Evil relaxes. Logic goes on vacation. Dollars stick to skin. A box has four corners and strip clubs are always square on the outside, but their insides ignore this geometric logic. Where there should only be four dark corners there are actually more than you can count. Patrons are over-stimulated by their drinks and the show, hence darkness needs not fear its normal protective sense; it can come and go as it pleases. No lock. No combination. No security alarm. No light swinging over an interrogation chair."

What the hell are you talking about?

"We entered a room of light, but it didn't wash away the dark feeling of the place. It was a world of music; a pulsating, hardcore, battering noise that lacked melody. The club smelled of lavender, or maybe sun-ripened raspberry, no that was a Gravity scent, and this is a Possibly dream. How do they pull off a sweet scent and a sticky floor at the same time? The girls sat me at a booth between them, the three of us in a booth built for two. Drinks all around. Possibly had her hand on my leg, but her eyes on her friend. Verbal conversation was difficult with the noise, but there was plenty of non-verbal communication occurring."

Soupy put his lips up to the friend's ear and said, "Kiss her some more. She won't mind."

Shyly, she leaned in closer and their lips touched briefly before Possibly looked at Soupy and said, "They frown on this type of stuff in here. Let's go home."

The movement never stops, said Promise.

"Look," I said to Promise as I pointed at the threesome leaving the club, "I could tell that Possibly had spent time with women before, it was evident in her way about things. She understood how to lure the desire, discovery, and curiosity out into the open. I knew her knowledge extended far beyond my own in that arena. That both excited me and scared the shit out of me."

Are you okay to drive? Promise asked.

I ignored her question and backed out of the parking lot to follow Possibly's car. "In today's world, you have to be careful about what you get into, literally, you know? That night, I watched Possibly run her hands all over her friend's body, face, and hair, and I wanted the same. I wanted to watch, but I wanted my turn. I didn't care what I was getting into as long as I was involved."

I don't think you want to get into this.

"*Now* you tell me? Gee thanks, Promise."

We rode in silence until we reached Possibly's friend's house.

"Possibly asked me to make drinks for everyone. The girls disappeared into another room and turned on some music."

Soupy brought three vodka tonics into the room before he said, "Hey, I thought you girls were going to—" He stopped his sentence in mid-flow because he'd found them locked into a deep, heavy kiss that had much more forward intent than any of their previous kisses. "Excuse me, girls. Sorry to interrupt, but your beverages have arrived."

"We aren't interested in those anymore," Possibly announced, breathily.

"May I ask what you *are* interested in?" Soupy replied.

"What are we interested in, sweetie?" she politely asked her friend.

"Going to bed," came her friend's reply. Possibly said nothing, simply got up from her friend's lap, pulled her by the hand, and caressed Soupy's cheek as she passed by before motioning with her index finger that he should follow them. She then shook her finger back and forth, and mouthed without saying, "No fucking her." Soupy slammed one of the drinks, left the other two on the end table, and followed them. He watched as they continued their make out session and slowly inched their way to the middle of the bed. Possibly motioned for him to join them. She put her hand around the back of his head to bring his lips to hers. Her friend moaned watching them kiss, signaling that she wasn't done kissing Possibly's lips. Possibly smiled, and then whispered to Soupy, "Be good." He nodded his head and watched them a few minutes longer, alternating between soft, loving kisses and furious, passionate ones, before he began to run his hands over both their bodies. He touched them gently, lightly running his fingers across their curves, through their hair, running the tips of his fingers down the length of their legs, and touching them in places that spurred on their kissing.

"I lost track of time, Promise. I was intoxicated from taking in this new woman full of so many things I'd never experienced. My mind floated slowly, weightless in this tangible vortex of intimacy, detached and isolated from everything real I'd ever known in the world."

I fast-forwarded the video until the sun came up and her friend left our bed.

Thank you, Promise said.

"Didn't see that coming, did you?" Possibly asked Soupy, a wry smile on her face.

"No, no, I sure didn't," Soupy replied.

"I like you," she said, repeating what she'd said the previous evening.

"I can handle that," he said.

"You sure?" she asked. When she looked into his eyes this time, it was a stare into his soul. All he could do was nod his head in affirmation. She pulled him toward her and their motion was purposeful. It only took a handful of seconds for them to be completely naked.

"This isn't what I came here to do," he said, catching his breath.

"Why not?" she quizzically, but confidently asked.

"This," he gestured around the bedroom, "is not who I am. I don't do this with someone I barely know."

"You know me, Soup. You *know* me," she said. It sounded as much a plea as anything else.

He moved between her legs and she opened them while pulling him as close to her as she could.

Nothing like jumping right into Possibly, Promise said.

"You don't know the half of it," I replied. "We got pregnant that night."

YOU WHAT?!

I sensed it before I felt it, so I winced in preparation for Promise to hit me upside the head, but she simply jerked back on the top of the driver's seat and—

Chapter 26

My jaw snapped shut and caught the edge of my tongue. Instantly I tasted blood, but I was still somewhat drunk and buried deep in an earthy tomb of semi-consciousness. Still, I winced and held my hand to the side of my face. Then, I noticed my wrist was sore from being cocked at such an angle under my sleeping body that it felt like it'd been pressed flat like a brilliant autumn leaf that had achieved scrapbook status.

How did I end up on my back? I don't sleep on my back. I don't even start the sleep process on my back. Why? Because my jaw falls open and my autonomous reflex is to snap it shut. Without fail, I catch the edge or the tip of my tongue in the action, and then enjoy the taste of iron as I recycle it back through my digestive system and into my bloodstream, which is then followed by days of having nearly everything I eat painfully irritate the healing region.

I thought, *What time is it?* I looked for the motel room clock as I rolled over, but couldn't find it.

Chapter 27

After I told Promise about the pregnancy, she disappeared. So I sat alone in front of Possibly's friend's house watching the events that happened a few years prior. It was an experience, yes, but one most likely to be discussed in a drinking game, like "I Never," than something I'd bring up out of the blue. In truth, it was debatable whether it was truly even a "threesome." If so it was the tamest threesome ever. Either way, I didn't care. There doesn't exist a check box on a bucket list of mine that says, "Have Threesome."

Sexual conquest, to me, isn't a conquest at all. I crave the emotional connection, not just the physical one. It's that passionate, breathy exchange of permission that happens in a moment, but lasts in the memory forever—that's the type of emotional wave I can ride and ride and ride. Like not being able to appreciate the peak of love without having been face down in the valley, there's a similar wisdom about emotional intimacy versus the simply physical kind that is only learned with experience—and even then not learned very often. The problem is: we crave the quick fix, that's the thing that's synonymous with fucking for fuck's sake, with anyone who will let you. The *bigger* problem is when the high departs just as quickly as the singular act itself.

It felt like that with Possibly—in the rapid nature by which I chose to be handcuffed to the reins of a wild horse—and just saying, "fuck it.". Even seeing it again, I'm in shock about how it went down, how I so easily *followed* Possibly after finding the strength to finally *lead* my life away from the magnetic force that was the constant return to Gravity.

The pendulum, when raised so high in one direction, does promptly swing far to the other end of its arc.

What did I get? A night like I'd never had in my life and will probably never experience again, and the fact that it may never happen again is fine with me. I thought I knew Possibly, given all of the time we'd spent talking, but as much as I'd gotten to know who she was online, I was rapidly learning that she was *much different* in person.

And so our road trip the next morning began.

Soupy and Possibly left the house in the morning. Possibly was moving to the west coast, closer to me not *because* of me, it was just where she wanted to be; a coincidental, fortunate happenstance that I lived nearby.

Turns out, the drive would be the continuation of the previous night's unexpected adventure.

The cab radio was still tuned to hear their conversation, but their banter didn't consist of much more than small talk. I remember being lost in thought back then, mainly about things I hadn't yet processed and didn't quite understand, things I was afraid to bring up for fear of hearing answers that would shatter the ideal image of Possibly I'd created in my head.

* * *

Before they jumped on the interstate, they stopped for refreshments. Soupy took the wheel, and their conversation waned. It wasn't long before Possibly ended the uncomfortable silence between them, "We're never doing that again, okay? We can talk about it now. I'll answer any questions you have, but after that I don't ever want to hear about it again."

"Okay," Soupy said as he pondered the invitation. "Truthfully, I don't have any questions. I don't know how it happened or why it happened and I don't need to know. All I know is that my batteries are fried. Last night wasn't my M.O. I don't just jump into the sack with someone, let alone some *ones,* plural, who I'd just met."

"I know that about you after everything we've discussed, that's why I knew it would be okay." After a moment's pause, she added, "So you liked it?"

Her comment before the question puzzled him, it didn't seem to make sense, but he let it go. "Yeah, it *was* pretty damn hot."

"It was, wasn't it?" she giggled.

They both spent a moment replaying their own favorite portions of the night in their heads.

Soupy finally ended the fantasies, "How far do we need to drive today?"

"As far as we can," she replied, suddenly sounding very far away. "I have some things I need to tell you."

* * *

"No! Not now!" I yelled at the radio and smacked the steering wheel. Suddenly, I wasn't anything *like* ready to relive this moment.

I shouted the word, "PAUSE!" while tapping my finger in mid-air on an invisible pause button, but nothing paused. "SHIT!" I tried it again, only louder, but the result was the same.

* * *

After small talk across the hours and miles, often staring at the passing countryside, Possibly finally said she was ready for a more serious conversation.

Soupy gripped the wheel and clenched his jaw. His eyes darted sideways to capture Possibly's body language. She sat Indian-style, visibly wringing her hands in her lap and periodically chewing a fingernail. Her words repeated in his head, *I have something to tell you.* In his experience, those words were rarely followed by anything he'd been dying to know.

"I know you're driving and this isn't the perfect time to talk, but I'm hoping it's a good time for you to listen," she said, and paused. "I have a lot of things to tell you about my life, just let me get through them because I can't stop once I start; I have to get it all out." She groaned nervously before continuing, "This is hard for me. I really don't know how to begin other than to just say it."

"Okay—"

"No," she said, holding her hand out to stop him. "It's not going to come out smoothly. It's going to come out in bursts. Just listen, and try not to hate me." Possibly visibly gathered herself. "I didn't have the best childhood. I was molested as a young girl and sexually abused as a teenager. I've been around drugs, even taken a few. Maybe you wouldn't expect those things because I didn't grow up in a bad neighborhood. Quite the contrary, I grew up in a really nice neighborhood. Nicer drugs. You know about it but you don't worry about it until it happens to you, right? We're kids, so we experiment and take risks and make stupid decisions. My decisions ended up being too much for me, all of this *stuff* that happened because of my choices, it was bad, *really bad,* so I repressed it all until maybe, like, a year ago."

Out of the corner of his eye he saw her look out of the window and chew her thumbnail again. This was *very* hard for her.

She mumbled because her thumb was pressed up against her lower lip, "And I don't like to talk about it, but I think you need to know." She pulled her thumb out of her mouth, took a deep breath, and continued, "Someone I really admired went through a terrible time in his life. He ultimately attempted suicide and failed, thankfully, so I took him under my wing as best I could to help him through his struggle. I didn't want to lose him and I couldn't imagine a life without him, so I gave him whatever he needed to get better. Well," she groaned, "he took *me*...whenever he wanted. He'd call me or come over in the middle of the night and tell me he was going to kill himself if I didn't sleep with him."

It was difficult for Soupy not to gasp, but he managed silence for a few seconds—seconds that felt like a decade to him.

Tears formed in her eyes. "What was I supposed to do? I didn't want him to die, so I let him have his way with me." She wiped the back of her hand across her cheek. "I'm not proud of it, and—," she sniffled, "I understand if you don't want anything to do with me."

"Hey," Soupy said as he started to reach across the car to caress her knee and then retracted so as not to violate her personal space. This moment had nothing to do with him; it had everything to do with her and because of that, his instinct was to console. "I'm sure it wasn't your fault, Possibly."

"I know, but that doesn't make it any easier."

Soupy thought for a moment as he stared at the hood of the car and tried to keep it between the lines on the highway. "You valued his life over your body. I can't begin to say I know what that's like, but I can try to understand." In truth, he didn't have the first clue where to unwind how something like this could happen between two people.

He started to pull the car over to the side of the road so he could look her in the eyes, or hug her, or whatever else she needed, "Hey, do you want to just sit and talk—"

"No, don't stop. We have to keep moving. I have to get farther away from it all," she pleaded.

"I can do that for you."

"Good, because I have more to tell you."

He hands gripped the steering wheel even harder, bracing for more.

"It's not really more, I guess, just how I'm trying to deal with it. My brain doesn't like it very much. Like I said, I repressed it once, but it's all starting to come back. The doctors think I'm bipolar because I have these massive mood swings. I go from happy-go-lucky to down-in-the-dumps in an instant. They gave me these meds to keep me mellow but I don't like them because I can't feel anything." She sniffled again. "I didn't take them before we met in person for the first time because I wanted to *feel* something.

He thought, *We definitely felt something.*

"But when I don't take my meds, bad thoughts creep into my head until—," her hands clenched into fists as she tried to fight the returning tears, "—until I don't want to live anymore." The façade of composure he thought she'd gained was wiped out with an avalanche of emotion. Words now came from her in bunches between sobs. "I would crawl…into my bedroom closet…at night… with a candle in one hand…and a…a gun in the other…searching for a reason to stay alive."

Soupy couldn't think of a single word to say, and ceased the typically autonomous act of breathing. It was all he could do to focus on driving and keep them on the road, alive, as his mind raced trying to figure out what it might be like to have been in such a state of despair. He dared not move a single muscle, as if every cell in his body had instantly transformed into concrete, and then every atom of air inside of the car had done the same. He wanted to unclasp the seat belt, open the door, and roll out of the car. He wanted to be invisible. Without moving, his eyes searched for the eject button and he knew—suddenly knew without a doubt—that *every* car should have one retro-fitted into it immediately. He wanted to be *anywhere* other than trapped in this heavy, suffocating coffin that was speeding down the highway, not to avoid the conversation, but to have it when he could focus on *it*, not be distracted by driving *and* listening.

Possibly asked, "Do you know what kept me alive?"

Her words snapped him back to their newfound reality. "No, what?"

"You."

"Me?" he replied, nearly swerving off of the road.

"Yes, *you* kept me alive," she said, now looking directly at him.

In a knee jerk reaction, Soupy returned her glance and it scared him. The weight of it was too much too hold. Staying fixed on the road ahead made him far less apt to drive the car into a ditch or slam on the brakes. Did he want to listen and learn, or run?

There was an intrigue about her, and that was the thing he knew would keep him out of the ditch. He wanted to understand the situation, understand what could make someone do those things or feel those ways or grasp on to someone like him as the reason for clinging to life. "Me? How?"

"I could always find you when I felt my worst. You were on instant messenger or available on the phone or I'd find an email from you. You saved me, Soupy. And the thought of meeting you someday gave me a reason to hide the gun in a shoebox, blow out the candle, and crawl out of the closet every night."

* * *

I was just as stunned hearing it the second time, as I was the first time. How was I supposed to respond to that? Our months of conversing had never provided one single sign that Possibly had such an incredibly sad story to tell, and that I'd been an unknowing character in it. For me, it'd been a process of exploration, making a new friend; for her it was life *or* death.

* * *

Soupy held his hand out to her, palm up, gesturing in a manner that asked her to hold it. She did, stared at it as if she was evaluating whether it was friendly before pulling it to her cheek. "Thank you," she said.

His hand gave her relief, but for him there was no such equivalent. He felt nauseous, like the gray mare from the strip club had strapped him into the saddle and the carousel was spinning faster than ever. The world wasn't right. It wasn't easy. This wasn't playful. Things were askew, cock-eyed, and a-kilter.

It started to snow. He knew he had to focus on the road. He could feel the slushy piles of dirty snow pull at the wheels each time he let his thoughts distract him. "If it's going to come down this hard we're going to have to stop," he said, meaning the snow, and not the conversation.

"Okay," she replied.

They pulled off at the next exit. Soupy wanted out of the car; he didn't care where, just had to put some distance between the vehicle and his smoking mental circuits. His route took him into the motel lobby. A clerk said he didn't think he'd ever seen it snow there in his entire life. Soupy thought, *And you don't know the half of it, Bub.*

Possibly and Soupy barely spoke except to determine which bags needed to come inside and which could stay out in the cold. She didn't leave his side as they checked in and carried their luggage into the room. It was like they'd just agreed on his undying, unspoken, and physically attached protection; she had bared all that she deemed ugly about herself, and he was still there. When they closed the door against the weather and the rest of the world, she pulled him into her personal space and whispered into his ear, "Not like last night." And as she coaxed him onto the bed, she added, "Love me."

* * *

I remember being happy to get out of that car. It had become her confessional—a place where she could safely say anything, where no one else could hear her, and where her priest couldn't leave. I hadn't planned to spend all day in a confessional, especially as the person listening to the confession, but at least I now knew she wasn't the Possibly I thought she was. *The Internet is the best place to lie. And lying in bed brought us peace.*

Was it fair to bare her soul to a captive audience? No, not really. I couldn't fully focus on listening to her, which made it harder to mentally record the important aspects of the conversation. On the other hand, she might not have been able to tell her story if I hadn't been so distracted by driving. She might not have been able to take the weight of my stare as she placed her heavy load on my shoulders. And the truth for me has *always* been: I'd rather know than not know.

I didn't let go of her all night. She was safe from everything in my arms. I was her superhero, and had been for quite some time. The role fit me.

* * *

Their lovemaking didn't last very long, they were too tired from so little rest the previous night, plus a full day of driving. When it was over, Possibly ran her finger over Soupy's lips and slowly traced it down his neck and laid her hand on his heart. She asked, "Is this real?"

"Yes, I hope so," he replied.

"If it's real can you promise that you'll never leave me?" She allowed the words to sink in before she added to them. "I can't love you unless I know you'll always be here."

He knew his response had to be immediate and firm, and there was nothing else—absolutely nothing—he could have said with all the recent miles behind them, if he wanted any ahead of them, except, "Of course, I promise."

Chapter 28

Possibly was a completely different woman on the second night of the trip than she was on the first. On the first night we had *sex*, and on the second night we made *love*: less primal, more vulnerable. We held each other gently, like we were breakable, and barely escalated or rushed the end, unlike our first occasion. On the second night, she was the woman I'd gotten to know online, the one I could easily fall in love with.

I sat in my parked cab staring at the curtains drawn over the motel room window where Possibly and Soupy had long ago turned out the lights. She'd shared difficult stories about her life that would take years for me to truly comprehend, if ever. My ability to understand was hampered by a fairly drama-free childhood; I don't recall any of my friends or family members who encountered the type of abuse that Possibly had experienced. Therefore, I had no idea how to process it. Could I bring it up in conversation? Point it out in an argument? Or would any allusion to her childhood heretofore stir the deep, dark emotions within?

The snowstorm had tucked the world in, making the parking lot quiet. That was, until a car drove up next to me and stopped driver's door to driver's door. The black cab. As I rolled down my window, so unrolled the window of the other cab.

Nectar said, *Ready for that ride?*

Soupy and Possibly were going to be out of commission for a while, so I rolled up the window of my cab, locked the door, and quickly slid into the back seat of Nectar's cab.

Hello, Soup, she said.

"Hey there," I answered.

Glad I got to you in time.

Confused, I asked, "In time for what?"

No way you want to relive that Possibly crap.

"Crap?" I sternly answered, perturbed by the ease by which she cast aside this time in my past. "It was rough, I admit, but there's bound to be something more I can learn from it."

Yeah, if you're crazy.

"Is this what you meant by 'ride?' Because if all we're going to do is bicker about my life then, honestly, I'd rather go back to my cab and sit in the dark."

That's completely up to you.

"How so?"

It's your dream, right?

"What?" I asked, but she didn't answer. I added, "You're going to bring me back, right?"

Nectar drove out of the parking lot.

"Okay, I guess not," I said, "How long is this ride going to be, then?"

Not long, she answered.

"Can you at least tell me where we're going?"

I'm taking you home.

"Home? No, I'm on the road for a reason: to learn from my past experiences. I can't go home yet."

Have you learned anything so far?

"Yeah, sure."

I doubt that…at least nothing worthwhile.

"How do you mean?"

You haven't learned anything from me. *You've been with Promise, yes?*

"Yes, I have."

She can't show you what I can show you.

The memory of having Nectar's scent under my nose and my hands on her body came rushing back so intensely I had to grip the back seat cushion in both hands to keep from losing consciousness.

I knew you'd like that, she added.

"How did you—"

I can feel *you, Soup.*

"What—"

I can love you now, not at some potential point in an uncertain future. I can give you exactly what you want: true love. Right here. Right now.

I imagined her pulling the cab over, getting out of the front seat and joining me in the back.

Did you hear me, Soup?

I had heard her. "Loud and clear," I replied.

Promise? She comes and goes. I've always been with you. We've driven these roads a countless number of hours, and over those hours we've learned who we are. When we're apart something draws us back together, so we're never apart for long. Soup, you already know me, and you know we're never happy when we're not together.

"I don't know you," I said as I struggled to comprehend her words.

Yes, you do.

Given what she'd said—that we'd been together all our lives—it seemed impossible that I *wouldn't* know her, yet I couldn't place her at all.

Those moments in your life when you've felt alone, you were never alone. I was there with you, helping you make the important decisions. Look inside your heart and you'll feel the truth in my words. You have faith. You believe that you can't possibly understand the dark without having experienced the light. Not until you've had them both can you understand where you are on the spectrum between light and dark, and once you've had them both you can't live without either one.

She had used a word that I still wasn't comfortable using, despite a conversation I once had with my dad about it: faith. It triggered alarms in my head.

I came into your life from across a crowded room, many years ago, drawn to you by something I couldn't define and neither could you. In fact, we were embarrassed in that instant because we saw our lives play out from beginning to end. We knew we only had to make the right decisions and we'd accomplish what so few ever do: truth in our love. In that instant, we found each other and our lives have never been the same. Once together, they will never be the same again. We're behind schedule; the longer you screw around with Promise the farther behind we fall.

I leaned in as closely as I could to the window that separated us and closed my eyes. As I listened to her words, I drew on all of my memories to picture this time she had described. The more I lost myself in her words, the more I wanted them to be truthful. I drew in deep, lung-filling breaths that took her scent into my body, and I began to recall…

And from that day, when we decided it was acceptable to share our lives with each other, never has there been a moment when I didn't know when you were thinking of me, and in every moment when I thought of you I know the world has tickled your heart, too. Over the past fifteen years, we've explored this spiritual connection between us with little attention to the powerful physical relationship that could have formed; it wasn't the purpose at those times or in those places, but it's here now. We will be stronger than we've ever been, which is what you want, what you believe, and what you desire more than anything else in the world.

On my lips sat a robotic response, "Y—," but I shook the fogginess and instead said, "I'm sorry, what?"

You believe that two people—the right *two people—together are stronger and able to accomplish more than they could ever accomplish alone, yes?*

"Yes," I replied, and I suddenly placed her scent and her voice; she *had* been with me for years, but only in my dreams. She's the woman who left a smile on my face in the morning when I returned from the dream world to the real. She's the fleeting dream that never attached itself long enough to memory to be memorable.

Then, this is truly the time for you to take this ride with me. You must see your truth; a truth that can only be found in true love.

Nectar said we were going home, and by "home" I anticipated she had meant someplace in the real world, but now I wasn't so sure. Home, to me, had always been wherever *I* am, but home could be, and perhaps *should* be, wherever *we* are: the place where two hearts meant for each other are together.

We've spent so much time talking, telling each other who we are and who we want to be. We've been dedicated to the background of us, chewing on it, kneading it in preparation for who we want to be in the foreground of our lives. Never have we gotten to where we want to be, despite always taking steps toward it by looking at the smooth and rough edges on each other, measuring them for fit like a tux and dress on a wedding day that we expect but have never actively planned. We've convinced ourselves that being together before now simply wasn't meant to be, but we own the responsibility for allowing life to make those choices for us. It's our time to make our own decisions, to choose each other. We're not the river that takes the path of least resistance; we're the boat showing the rest of the world how to navigate the waters safely. Isn't that what Promise has promised you at some point downstream?

"Yeah, at some point we're *supposed* to have an opportunity to meet if we both learn from our lives along the way."

Would you rather have what you want now…or later?

Our conversation and the inability to see where we were going had a sickening effect on me. And it was too much information too quickly. The pressure to make a decision was mounting at an unexpected time and place.

Nectar must have sensed my mental breaking point, for she said, *No need to answer me now. Our time in this moment is only just beginning. I guarantee we'll add to the wonderful memories we both have of laying in each other's arms, eschewing the rest of the world, listening to each other breathe, and creating more warmth together than we could create alone. We've not always known exactly what we have, but we always knew it was something unique and wonderful.*

I put my head in my hands and pressed on my temples.

We have *known that we* wouldn't *know what we have until we arrived here. By hard work, luck, faith, and the grace of love, we're here. Do you feel it?*

I nodded my head, hoping the answer would satisfy her *and* buy more time to think.

Are you ready to be in love?

The answer to that question was a most definite "yes," but by the time it got to my lips it was only a whisper.

Do you remember the promise you made to us?

I yanked my head from my hands in surprise. "Promise? No, what promise?"

You promised you would reinvent education. Remember? You touched my soul when you said it. I felt it ring unquestionably true. I knew you were talking about us. We're not going to listen to what everyone else has to say about us or follow the rules the world says we're supposed to follow—enough of that bull-shit—it's time for us to be together, and together we will show the world a new set of rules.

"I said that?" I answered, confused.

Yes, and it was beautiful to hear you speak so passionately. Sure, you've spoken to me that way many times, but to see you in action in the world doing the same, intoxicating.

The cab slowed and stopped.

We're home, Nectar said.

The rear door opened automatically, so I slid across the seat toward it. "Are you coming?" I asked before I stepped out.

No, not just yet. There's one small thing you need to do before we can be together.

My brow furrowed, "What—"

Don't worry. You'll know when you see it.

I stepped out of the cab, closed the door, and watched blankly as it sped off down the street. Nectar *had* dropped me off at home, my childhood home.

It was strangely humid for an autumn day, which I knew it had to be since I stood in a street gutter full of fallen leaves. A door closed across the street, and my neighborhood friends, looking like kids again, were walking toward me. As they approached they slowed, sly grins pasted on all their faces.

"Hey," I said to them, but they didn't answer. Instead, they circled me like villagers with stones. Another friend, a late-comer, jogged toward the group. As he approached everyone else took a few steps back to widen the circle. He reared back and hurled a football in my direction. Out of instinct I caught it. Suddenly, everyone hunched over and snarled.

"Oh shit," I said, and cradled the ball more tightly in my arms.

They shouted, "GET HIM! KILL THE MAN WITH THE BALL!"

I bowled over two of the smaller kids as the group converged on me, then executed a spin move to evade the grasp of another kid, the one who had tossed the ball. From the corner of the yard, which would have been a boundary back in the day, I saw my friends regroup to form one charging mass. Given the number of them and the size of the yard there wasn't a way through or around, so I turned and ran into the next yard.

"OUT OF BOUNDS!" one kid yelled.

"KILL HIM ANYWAY!" another screamed.

And the fastest kid in the group added, "I'LL CHASE HIM DOWN!"

I glanced over my shoulder as I ran, crossing into the next yard, and saw my pursuit roughly ten yards behind. I couldn't let him catch me, like my life depended on it. I entered the street on the other side of the yard and he yelled, "WAY OUT OF BOUNDS!" His voice trailed off behind me; he'd given up the chase. I lifted the ball one-handed over my head in celebration and leapt over a pile of leaves on the other side of the street.

"Yesssssssssss," the leaves hissed as my wake lifted a few of them from the pile.

I nearly tripped as I looked back to figure out who said the words. A gust of wind scattered the pile across the yard behind me. *Something invisible.* There was a feeling of an ominous presence. "Fuck this," I said and kept running. I hurdled bushes. I arced around trees and ducked under branches. The wind moved ahead of me and then changed direction in an effort to oppose my progress. It boiled clouds on the horizon that began to swirl angrily. It bent limbs and willed them to give up more of their leaves, they screamed as they went past, swirling all around me. I put my arm in front of my eyes, head tucked just behind the inside of my elbow, trying to keep my vision clear, but more leaves joined the attack. I dropped the football as an attempt to run faster, but the leaves reinforced their attack. There were too many of them, and they had no intention of being good leaves; no intention of evolving into trees as Great Grandpa explained many years ago. They were angry. Their points nicked at my skin.

"Yesssssssssss," they hissed once again.

The hissing of the leaves and the increased wind velocity combined for a deafening, howling sound. Leaves continued to prick at the exposed skin on my arms and legs, inflicting needles of pain. I brushed a hand across my face, grabbed as many leaves as I could, and tossed them aside. They audibly screamed in pain. The rest pinned themselves to me all the while interlocking with their mates—an attempt to entomb my entire body.

"WHAT DO YOU WANT?!" I screamed.

I fought them off with my hands, but the fight became fruitless. Their points struck at my eyes, so I closed them. In the visual darkness I immediately felt stronger. I saw the path. My pace resumed. I ran faster. Instead of trying to thrash my arms against the leaves, I put them to work on my speed, pumping in unison with my legs. And as my body's rhythm returned, the weight of the leaves dropped from my concern.

"Take us with you," the remaining leaves whispered as one.

I envisioned the houses on either side of me melting into a setting of blurry, horizontal streaks, as if the oil painting had suddenly turned watery.

"Take us with you," the leaves pleaded.

Why don't you evolve? I thought.

"Yessssssss. Evolve," they said. "You must take us with you."

"NO!" I yelled defiantly, and leapt into the air as high as I could.

Like a long jumper, I arched my torso forward and at the apex of my jump impacted what felt like a wall, one that I didn't see and couldn't describe since my eyes were closed.

Great Grandpa's voice boomed, "GRANDSON!"

I opened my eyes and saw nothing but brilliant whiteness. "Great Grandpa?"

I was floating. *Had he caught me?* I blinked. The act forced the light to turn dark and gravity to resume. Suddenly, I was falling. Another blink and I stopped, suspended in midair. "Grandpa?" The bright light turned from white to yellow to orange to red like the sky before a setting sun. A green flash exploded in the distance and sped toward me. I held my hands out against it as it approached, and then braced for its impact. The last of the sky's color departed as I closed my eyes to protect them from the flash. A great clap of thunder snapped across the sky, and I fell into the darkness.

As I fell, I heard Nectar's voice say, *Birth is beautiful.*

I couldn't see my falling motion, meaning I couldn't see that I was actually falling due to the complete darkness all around me, but I could feel the wind rushing past. My arms and legs flailed trying to stabilize the rest of my body.

Nectar's voiced returned, *Impact in three…two…one.*

I hit the ground with a dull thump, definitely not as hard as I expected from what seemed like such a long fall. I mentally checked my faculties to confirm that the landing had scared me more than hurt me. Except for my gasping breath, it was eerily silent. I rolled over onto my hip as I caught my breath. From underneath my body a leaf skittered off squealing happily.

"Hello?" I asked in the darkness. My senses weren't giving me much to go on. Senses in utter darkness, due to a lack of practice using them in utter darkness, were utterly useless. No one answered.

"HELLO?" I said more loudly.

Nectar said, *Welcome home, Soup.*

Chapter 29

The air was cold, damp, and entirely too quiet. With my arms I tested the circumference of my reach, and touched nothing. I closed my eyes and only imagined I could see my breath, nothing more. *Nothingness.* I began to feel dizzy with no reference points to determine which way was up, so I yelled, "HEY!" and heard the sound of my voice inside of a voluminous but enclosed space. No one answered.

I looked up as a large circle appeared over my head, an oculus. Its color turned from black to purple, from purple to red, from red to orange, and then from orange to blue. As it did, light began to fill the room, which I discovered to be a deep, spherical cave. I must have fallen through the oculus at the top of cave.

The sun was coming up, but it was coming up far more quickly than normal. As more light filled the room, I could better make out the cave's amenities. It was about fifty or sixty feet in diameter. One on each side of my seated position, parallel walls stood about ten feet apart, which framed a rectangular area across the middle of the circular cave. *En garde*, I thought.

The parallel walls were about four feet high, and made of rocks that were of a completely different composition than the cave walls.

As the sun continued its rapid path across the sky the circle of light that passed through the oculus created a spotlight that moved perfectly down the wall and toward the floor. I reached out to put my hand into the light when it drew near, but as I did so the light went dark. Ominous clouds like clenched fists suddenly filled the sky. I removed my hand and the clouds disappeared. I tried it again and experienced the same effect. *Put hand in light?* Clouds. *Remove hand from light?* Sun. Before the sun set, I walked the length of both walls analyzing the cave's floor and found nothing of use. Just as suddenly as the oculus had formed, it reversed its colorful spectrum from blue to orange to red to purple to black and was gone. It wasn't until my eyes adjusted to the dark that I noticed it had become a peephole into a universe of stars.

Nectar had welcomed me home. *Is this home?* No, this is not home—I need more light—but I was stuck down here.

I sensed no danger, so I laid down between the parallel walls and stared through the oculus into the night sky. I needed time to think about Possibly, to fully re-immerse myself in that time and learn as much as I could from it. The problem: I didn't *really* want to relive those still tender-to-the-touch, torturous days.

I'd gotten what I had asked for in her: a woman who had metaphorically been around the world. She hadn't hitchhiked either; she'd mashed the gas pedal to the floor and saw as much of it as was realistically possible in her lifetime. Some of it she wanted to see, other places she didn't. *Was her pace too fast?* Ours certainly started that way. Except, once we were alone together the speed melted away, instead of running a dash with everyone, we had a slow walk through the park. *Which tempo was her normal tempo?* I'd only relived our first two days—two *drastically* different days—so I couldn't yet answer that question.

Possibly moved into an apartment on the west coast, about an hour and a half's drive north of my home. Once settled, she set to the task of pursuing her dreams in the entertainment industry, where she learned less about her profession and more about aggression: overly dominant men in combination with excessive drugs and liquor—not a good equation for her. She was on her own, which made her feel alone and vulnerable. She called out to me at night, but I wasn't near enough nor could I throw on my cape and fly to her rescue. She needed the kind of help that could only come if one of us drastically changed life to be nearer the other. So I visited her more often and tried to decipher her days, to keep the pieces of them together, and to shield her from the world, not just the parts of it that were trying to kidnap her, but *all* of it. And the longer I kept her safe—kept her kidnapped for myself—the more it became a personal necessity; I fell in love with the idea of protecting her from the world.

I sang, "Here I come to save the day!"

While I was dating Possibly, I learned how to fly in my dreams. It had taken my entire life to learn the task, *years* of practice. Finally, I could fly. *Believe it or not, I'm walking on air! I never thought I could feel so free-ee-ee!* When I was a kid, my dreams allowed this goofy-looking ability to flap my arms rapidly and hover for a few seconds. As I perfected hovering, I could increase my altitude. With practice, I could ascend at will; I could reach rooftops and other vertical landings, places to rest, before hovering again. Landing, however, was a different story. In my teenage years, I leapt from great heights and tried to glide my way to a smooth landing; it was easier to imagine than it was to perfect, and once I'd started a descent it was very difficult to flap my arms hard enough to ascend again. On more than a few nights, I woke up completely drenched in sweat from the effort I'd put into flying. Possibly's presence in my life changed everything: with very little effort—a few great strides of my arms—I could take to the skies. I glided around the world, made sweeping turns, spun like a top, somersaulted and cart wheeled in midair; flying became everything I'd ever dreamed it would be. *You can fly, so what?* It was a good question because what did flying in my dreams translate to in the real world? *Nothing.*

Yes, there was still a lot to think about from my relationship with Possibly.

I also had Nectar to think about; she'd blown my mind purely by suggesting that the rules I've lived by aren't at all true. And I could have her *now*, she said so but what would I really have? What did I really know about her?

I slapped myself on the cheek and said aloud, "Don't get carried away." Learning from Possibly is important to help me understand who I am, and I need to know myself to know true love no matter which one I'm with.

As it became more necessary to be Possibly's superhero, those who often rescued me—the shoulders and rocks I'd leaned on in my life—slowly drifted away until I was alone. Possibly had me, but who did I have?

Nothing. No one. This was it. Stuck in a cave that seemingly had one way out, no walls to climb, no shafts to descend; a prison. *Or a crib.* Or a temple. Besides, it was nice to have silence so I could listen more to *my* thoughts than those of others.

I'd seen glimpses of incredible beauty in Possibly, but it scared the shit out of me to think of what was needed to help her out of her dark, protective closet. *With a candle and a gun.* The closet, minus the candle and gun, seemed a pretty safe place, but I couldn't keep her in there forever, that wouldn't be the right woman for me anyhow. Either I had to let her out or she was going to find her own way out. *Guns a-blazing!*

My relationship with Possibly became a disaster. The more I tried to help her, the less I could be me, and the more I needed help myself. The more I committed to the seemingly right decisions to put her back on the path to her dreams, and ours, the less possible they became. I thought those decisions meant we had a future together, and when that future arrived, all of my self-sacrifice would be rewarded. I wanted action to be *her* decision, though. I wanted her to feel as if she had played some part in improving her life, to own it. And that feeling of empowerment was meant to be her personal example of how she was strong enough to control her own destiny.

Hope for that dream took a major hit on the night she told me she'd ended up at home alone with a guy she met at a bar, and couldn't remember what happened, but physically felt like he'd had his way with her. *She escaped.* She didn't know his name, could hardly describe his face, and barely remembered the bar where they'd met. As angry and concerned as I was, there wasn't anything I could do to change it and she didn't want to track him down.

I did convince her, however, to go to the hospital for a medical check; that's when we learned she was pregnant, not by him, of course, we wouldn't have known that so quickly.

I sat up and buried my head in my hands. Those days with Possibly were a blur; the only thing that ran through my head over and over was the emotional and physical calculation of how we'd be as parents. I didn't care that I'd only met her a few months prior. I didn't care that we didn't live in the same city. I didn't care about all the questions we still needed to answer about our future. To me there was no choice, even if the baby was conceived from an affair that she'd had, one that she'd never told me about, I was in her life and we were working hard to build a future. We could do it, no questions asked—except for the multitude of questions that *had* to be asked. Possibly pushed me away, told me she would deal with it on her own, that she didn't need me. But I wouldn't leave her; she made me *promise* not to leave her on the second day we'd met, and I wasn't about to break that promise with a child on the way.

I stood up and paced back and forth in the cave, my hands clasped around the back of my head. I looked up through the oculus and saw the moon, mostly shaded by the clouds, providing me just enough light to see where I was going, as long as I stayed near the middle of the room, which worked until it began to rain. As the drops entered the cave, they dispersed into smaller droplets, creating a mist that swirled its way to the floor instead of falling like normal. I moved away from the center and toward one of the cave's walls to get clear of the moisture. As I leaned up against the cold rock, a difficult memory flooded into my head of the night I had to save Possibly's life.

* * *

"Whoa, we're heeling a little too—" the sailboat captain said, but it was too late. Soupy was on the high side of the boat, but as he looked over his shoulder he saw the boom hit the water. It wasn't too many more seconds before he hiked out higher on the starboard side and saw the top of the mast follow the boom. This was trouble, in the dark, in the middle of the bay with no other boats around. The passengers leapt into the chilly water, fully clothed in jeans, jackets and shoes, potentially deadly attire for swimming any length of time. Soupy looked for Possibly. She hadn't been sitting next to him because he'd been working the sails. His sight went from bobbing body to bobbing body until he finally saw her struggling, but with a few of his sailing friends near her he knew he had time to slide down the hull of the boat and into the water. In this situation a sailor should find the keel underwater, stand on it, and attempt to pull the boat back upright. Once that task is complete, swiftly bail the water from the boat to keep it afloat. If he could do that, with the help of a few others, they could avoid what looked to be a hundred-yard swim to the closest shore. Except, there was no keel to stand on. They looked at each other, confused, trying to paint the picture in their heads of a boat without a keel. Soupy and his friends reached up to the edge of the boat and desperately tried to pull her back to life, but she was already too far down.

"SWIM AWAY FROM THE BOAT!" the captain yelled from the stern. He rode her down until she burped and disappeared into the black water. Fortunately, no one was caught in the lines as she went down.

They suddenly had no choice but to swim to shore, which would be no easy feat. Soupy swam a beeline for Possibly. Of all the voices screaming, crying, panting, and gasping for air, he could hear hers above them all. Someone was already with her, which was good, and he was smartly keeping his distance as he urged her to keep dog paddling. He was the only one who knew she was so deathly afraid of the ocean.

"I'm afraid of the water," she said, panicking. "Soupy, I'm afraid of the dark water."

"You can do it, Possibly, I know you can. We aren't going to leave you," he replied, and his friend reiterated the same. "Focus on paddling, not talking. We're right here."

She let loose a fearful whine as Soupy looked toward the shore. They had to start making progress or they were going to run out of stamina long before reaching safety. Soupy pointed toward the rocky shore and said, "Possibly, we're going there, all of us, together. To get there we're gonna have to lose our shoes—"

A boat horn filled up the night.

A yacht had seen them go down and slowly idled closer. The horn blasts let the swimmers know they'd been seen. In the dark, the captain wouldn't be able to see all the bodies in the water, so he shouted at us to swim toward the boat. He'd cut our swim from a hundred yards to about twenty; everyone would take that trade, especially Possibly.

The swimmers made an about face and swam toward the yacht, but the weight of their clothes and shoes were tiring them out. Soupy paced Possibly, reminded her to keep moving. He kept telling her she could do it, and she did.

"GET HER OUT FIRST!" Soupy yelled at the passengers on the boat. They reached into the water and helped her climb. Once aboard, they whisked her away into one of the cabins. A few others climbed out of the water before Soupy really began to feel danger from exhaustion. It was far past the time when he should have ditched his shoes and pulled off his jeans to use them as an inflatable. Fortunately, he only had a few yards left to reach salvation. As he grabbed the rails of the ladder, the passengers pulled him by his weary arms and shoulders from the water. They supported his weight as they carried him upstairs into one of the upper berths. He saw Possibly on the couch as he passed and could think of nothing other than to check her mental and physical states. "Possibly?" he asked. He could see her shivering, she didn't respond.

"She'll be okay," someone said in his ear. "The girls will take care of her."

He knew that already. He knew how the girls would take care of her.

"Lose your clothes," someone said, and threw him a towel. "Drink this," he added and handed him a soda, "Unless you want something stronger?"

"Better not," Soupy said, there were bound to be some questions to answer since the captain would have likely radioed the harbor police once he saw our sailboat go down.

Soup stripped, dried off as best he could, then put his wet clothes back on and went in search of Possibly. He found her. The girls were on both sides of her trying to help her regain her warmth. She was scared, but alive, and probably in shock from the experience.

They needed the element of fire, but Soupy didn't have the capacity to create it.

* * *

I picked up a flat rock and pitched it across the cave. It bounced once and then settled into its new home. The best part about the sailboat story was that everyone lived. The worst part about it is the donation I made to the bottom of the sea: wallet, cell phone, money, keys. The second best part about the story is our brush with death demanded we do something to feel alive. When Possibly and I got home, we discarded our wet clothes in the foyer, lit the fireplace, and had an incredible, life-affirming love-making session right there in front of it, and then slept for about twenty-four hours.

A week later we sat with her mom, who had flown in to discuss our pregnancy options. Because of Possibly's past depression, we feared she might have irrevocable suicidal tendencies, which she said she was already combating. I didn't want to lose her and neither did her family, so we chose to abort the pregnancy.

I looked up at the oculus and closed my eyes. There have been few more difficult days than when Possibly and I went to the clinic. I waited for her to endure a procedure to end a potential life because we valued hers over one yet to be born. We silently walked back to the car. I took her home and tucked her into bed.

I wanted fire, but not for warmth. I wanted to *set* something on fire. I took in a deep breath of air to calm myself.

What if my first chance was also my last chance to be a father? I asked myself. It had been, maybe, a little more than a year since that had happened, and I was young enough not to worry, but the question still crossed my mind.

I didn't bother Possibly, simply told her I was there for anything she needed. She nodded her head, turned to her side, and curled up under the covers. I pulled them up to her shoulders, tucked her hair behind her ear to get it out of her face, and then sat in the other room listening for something, anything that might tell me what I was supposed to do.

After that, many things changed between us. Most significantly, Possibly was no longer walking slowly away from me; she was running. I'd promised I wouldn't leave her, which was meant to give her the ability to love me. She wasn't keeping her end of the deal. In fact, she was pushing hard to sever our ties. I told her she needed to move closer to me, find a new job, and simplify her life. And if she didn't, her and I were done.

We'd been working on a plan to get her out of her closet so we could truly be together. Instead, she broke down the door and disappeared.

I'd initiated the choice, should she stay or should she go, but I was still devastated and massively confused by her departure. I'd given myself to her completely. When she left, the emptiness that remained put me in a catatonic state. What had I done? I needed her to fix some things in her life, desperately needed her to fix them, but she refused. *She saved you.* What? *The carousel stopped.* I figuratively crawled into the closet she'd just vacated, where no one would find me.

I feigned confidence at the time, because there was no way I would beg for her to stay when she needed to fix so much. But I was truly torn between the seeming wisdom of separation and the hole it left in my life. For the first time since I'd known her, she was gone, leaving no trace or evidence of where she would go or what she would do.

I apparently wasn't enough. I couldn't protect her. I couldn't protect *us*. I couldn't knot the lines between us strongly enough to weather the storm—to be the shining example in the aftermath of disaster for everyone else in the world to see that truth *and* love were possible.

She was now alone in a world full of drugs and aggressive men.

Possibly went home to her own Bind.

Maybe she only lived in the dark because she couldn't remember the light. Was I naïve to think she could find it again on her own? Was I naïve to think I could help her find it again? I wasn't blind to the truth; I just didn't have the faintest clue where to look for it. I remember asking myself whether I was man enough to survive. I was spread so incredibly thin trying to be who she needed me to be. It was like we'd been playing a one-on-one game of *Risk* and she'd forced my army all over the globe with no real strait or beachhead where I could amass them to defend an attack. I was repelling her forces from all borders. I was divided and conquered. I continued the game because I felt it was worth it—who she *wanted* to become was worth it—but she'd never get there without finding her own answers; I knew that.

All this time I thought I knew, but it was clear now that I didn't know if she wanted to find her answers.

When I put my cards on the table and she walked away, a very small part of me knew it wasn't over; it was simply a strategic move that forced her to see the world without my protection. "Fucking games," I said, and I was the asshole playing them. It wasn't even *Risk*, it was more like Russian Roulette. What else was I supposed to do, forfeit? *Hell no.* I played to win. Either she never came back or she came back having made some good, confident changes in her life; both wins, or so I thought.

I shouted, "I NEED. A DRINK," and the words echoed off the walls of the cave. Some of the best, and worst, words I'd ever written down came when I was wasted. And now, just like when round one of Possibly and Soupy ended, I had nothing to do but wait. At that time, I drank. I saw nothing wrong with repeating myself…if only this cave had a bar.

Chapter 30

It sounded strange coming through the oculus, though it was easy to decipher: a car pulled up, stopped, and a door closed. A silhouette stood over the oculus and looked down at me.

Brought you something, Nectar said.

She dropped an object into the cave that landed with a clink of glass, miraculously not breaking as it rolled to a stop.

"Tough glass," I said as I picked up a wine bottle.

The toughest, she replied. *I opened it already, just stuffed the cork back in.*

"How'd you know—"

Woman's intuition.

I pulled the cork out with my teeth and brought the red end of the cork to my nose, it smelled amazingly good.

Go ahead, taste it. Some of my favorite stuff.

I brought the bottle to my lips, took a quick sip to wash my palette, and then a larger gulp that flooded my mouth until it dribbled down my chin.

Amateur, she chided.

I replied, "Thirstier than I thought." I wiped my sleeve across my chin. "Pretty good, though. Thanks."

Getting anything done down there?

"Just thinking through some things, you know."

Yeah, I know. The right things?

"Working through them one thought at a time."

She feigned a yawn by moving her hand back and forth in front of her mouth, then sat down on the ledge of the oculus, feet dangling into the cave.

"What is this place?" I asked.

A nice hiding spot, I'd say.

"Or a prison cell."

Oh, I doubt that.

"Depends on who's in control."

Truer words have never been spoken.

I could sense a smile on her face and knew she meant more than she'd said. "Sooooo?"

It's your dream, Soupy. Maybe this place is just what you needed.

"You mean *where* I needed?"

Where you needed to do what you need to do.

I twirled the cork on my fingers and then took another long pull from the tannic, dark liquid.

How long do you plan on staying down there?

"Umm, maybe you could drop a rope or something?"

Never mind, she added as she looked off into the distance like she wanted to be elsewhere. *Are you getting closer to what you came here to do?*

"It's nice to have a moment to think. You know, the world, especially the world in my head, is constantly being filled with incoming data. *All this stuff* that I'm trying to catalog, process, or expunge. What does it mean?"

The drink will help.

"It usually does, or doesn't, depending on how you look at it. The drink gives me focus, but focus on what? *Sex.* All the conversations happening simultaneously fade away when I drink, except for one: a singular focus on sex. And

I have to tell ya, from experience, decisions I make late at night aren't the best ones I make throughout the course of a day."

You're safe down there; no phone therefore no booty calls.

I thought but didn't say, *No need to call anyone with you sitting right there.* Instead, I said, "And that frivolous sex means nothing in the morning, just makes me miss true love more."

Is that what you're running from?

"Running from?" I paused for several seconds as I thought about what I might be running from, but could only think of Possibly. "Push and pull, I guess. I know what happens in the Possibly years and I don't want to relive them again, but being on the outside looking in provides a valuable perspective."

Possibly? Promise? Whatever. It's all in the past. Why are you wasting your time?

"Like I said, I believe there's something to learn...an important piece to the puzzle that unlocks another aspect of true love."

Do you know when to stop looking for something you've lost?

"When I find it?"

Yes, and do you know how to find it?

"When I stop looking."

Exactly.

"Oh, the conundrum. Hardy-har," I flatly replied. "I suppose, but first I have to know what I lost."

After a few seconds, Nectar said, *Interesting. Promise has given you a homework assignment to find something you've never experienced. You've never had it, so you've never lost it. Let me ask you this: how do you know what you're looking for?*

"I have faith that it exists."

Faith, huh?

"Ya gotta believe in something, right? Otherwise, what's life?"

Nectar pushed off of the ledge and fell into the cave. I jumped up to my feet as she landed, ready to run to her side if she was hurt, but she landed deftly on her feet. She walked toward me with a purposeful stride, then ran her hand along my arm and said, *You do have to believe in something, Soup. Yes, you do. Besides, I know what you're running from.*

I tingled at her touch. "What's that?"

Me. She put her hand on the back of my neck and pulled my lips to hers. We kissed, not a long kiss, but a deep, passionate one. When we separated, she lifted her head upward, eyes closed, and gathered in a great breath. I finally exhaled the one I'd been holding in.

Doesn't that make the world a better place? she asked.

"Yes," I weakly answered.

Then why run? What are you waiting for?

"A sign, I guess."

What kind of sign?

"I don't really know."

Then how will you know when you see it? Oh, never mind…faith…yeah, right, I know. She walked away from me and back toward the center of the cave. *You want to see a sign? I'll show you a sign.* She held out her hand to me and said, *Let's go.*

Confused, I asked, "You know a way out of here?"

Yeah, you can fly in your dreams, right?

"Awww shit, yeah." I laughed off the fact that I hadn't thought of that.

Then fly me out of here, Superman.

I wrapped my left had around Nectar's waist as she wrapped her hands around my neck. Her eyes were locked on mine as she stepped onto the tops of my feet and laid her head on my chest. She was close to me; couldn't get much closer. I looked up to the oculus, flexed my knees, and engaged in a slight jump that elevated us up into the sky.

"Afraid of flying?" I asked.

No, enjoying the moment.

Our ascent continued until we were a few hundred feet above the ground. "Check out the view," I said.

She raised her head from my chest and looked around. The desert mesas slept below us, but the sky stuck its chest out, brimming with brilliance. *Wow. Like I said, forget the past. This is your now…our now.*

With her words I looked into her eyes, and saw twin galaxies that would require a great explorer's effort to catalog, but her lips were in my galaxy, on my planet, in my arms, and with the last kiss still lingering on my heart, I lowered my head toward hers. As I approached she turned and said, *Not again. Not yet. I have to show you your sign.*

"You mean this wasn't it?"

Nope.

Nectar released her grip around the back of my neck and stepped off of my feet.

I reached to catch her arms, but I missed. "HEY! WHA—"

She waved and smiled at me as she fell to the ground. Just as in the cave, she landed expertly. Cupping her hands over her mouth she yelled, *YOU COMING?*

I descended slowly on purpose as a means to voice my frustration with her tactics. As I landed next to the black cab, I noticed the motor was already running. The rear door automatically popped open and I got inside.

"Very funny," I said as I reached for the door and closed it. She laughed.

The road away from the cave was really bumpy. "Can you fast-forward this?"

How many times do I have to tell you that it's your *dream?*

I reached up and slid my finger in the air from right to left. The bumping became frenetic, but ended after a few seconds.

Was that better?

"Not really," I replied.

Can I drive now?

"Who's stopping you?"

We drove at an increased speed, at what seemed like highway pace, until I heard the engine decelerate.

We have to pick someone up.

"What? Who?"

The cab slowed to a stop. When the right rear door opened, I slid across to the other side of the backseat bench. The sunlight that burst into the cab caused me to draw my hand over my eyes. For once, I was thankful that the windows were so darkly tinted.

A bundle of white jumped into the cab, bouncing a bit as she did so. It wasn't until the door was closed again that I recognized what had just happened.

"Faith?" I surprisingly asked.

"Hi, Soupy!" she giggled while gently tucking her wedding dress around her seated position, and then leaned over to kiss me on the cheek.

I touched the spot where she'd kissed me and then asked, "What are you doing here?"

She replied sarcastically, "Catching a ride to my wedding, of course, don't you see the dress?"

"Your wedding?"

"Yes. Big, white dress. Smile on my face. Wedding, you know? Two people in love making a proclamation in front of friends, family, and God about the love they want to share for the rest of their lives. You know, wedd-ing?"

"Yes, yes, I know what a wedding is," I said as I waved my hand at her, "Are you sure?"

"Yeah, well you never called me back," she replied.

Faith and I grew up in the same neighborhood, a wandering glance across a room that stopped when I saw her looking back at me. From that day forward we spent a lot of time together. Walking through the woods. Hearing songs on the radio for the first time. Seeing movies together. She was my first kiss. She was the first girl who sat around with me swinging or skipping rocks on the lake as we spoke about our definitions of life. And as time passed, our quick kisses periodically turned into passionate make-out sessions. We could talk about anything at any time, whether over the phone or in person. It was that strong pull toward conversation that kept us friendly over the years despite the many miles that were often between us. We never *really* dated each other, though we certainly created "the bar" for each other—that anyone else who entered our lives would have to meet, or exceed, if they wanted to love either of us.

Why hadn't we dated? More than anything else, because we had such conviction to our professional dreams, which kept us focused on our studies, extracurricular activities, and ultimately colleges in different parts of the country. I have absolutely no doubt we would have dated if we'd been in the same city once we'd grown up. Now, we were in the same cab, and it seemed as if the possibility that had been tucked away in a corner of our hearts all of these years was about to disappear for good. And she was right, I hadn't called her back, but she hadn't left a voicemail that said, "I'm getting married. Call me," either.

"You never told me about a proposal!"

"About a year ago. I called to tell you I'd gotten engaged because I wasn't sure if it was the right thing to do."

I remembered the call, of course, and there was a reason I hadn't called her back. On the last occasion we'd seen each other, I'd witnessed her swooning over the guy she was with, and to be honest I couldn't figure out why. With him, she wasn't the same person I'd grown up with, and the differences weren't for the better. She seemed to have been…kidnapped and held hostage. Like, she'd reached the age where it was time to get married, so said our culture, so she was over-the-moon committed to it, right or wrong. When speaking with her, in the boyfriend's company, she didn't use the same words she normally used, and the replacements didn't fit, like she was trying to plug square words into round holes. She was somewhere else, somewhere far away.

She continued, "When he asked me to marry him, the first person I thought about was you, so I called, but you didn't answer."

"Did you leave a voice message?"

"Yes."

"Did you tell me you'd gotten engaged?"

"No," she looked down as if she knew she'd made a mistake.

"You know I would have called you back if I knew you'd gotten engaged."

"I just told you to call me back. I'm sorry, but look!" She ruffled her dress for me.

"You look beautiful, Faith, as you always do." I could feel a disjointed connection, like it wasn't quite all there, similar to the last time we'd been together. I stared at her as she blushed. I wasn't ready to let her go again, not yet. "Why was I the first person you thought of?"

"I always imagined it would be you," she admitted. "And I wanted your input about whether I was doing the right thing or whether you thought it should have been us, too. But then, friends and family started to find out about the ring, and the excitement of it just took over. I accepted the offer, and of course the planning started and I buried myself in the decisions that had to be made." She'd said all of this while looking at the back of the seat in front of her, until she turned to me and said, "In all of that I discovered happiness."

"Happiness or acceptance?" I asked.

She frowned at me. "Not on my big day," she added before she continued to explain the plans she'd made for the wedding, her schedule for the day, and where they planned to visit for their honeymoon.

I was lost in thought trying to figure out the puzzle. Well, whether this *was* a puzzle, or a sign, and what I was supposed to do or learn from it.

Faith stopped mid-sentence just to look at me for a moment. She then added, "When I'm around you I can't stop babbling about insignificant things in my life."

"I wouldn't say today is an insignificant day in your life."

"No, of course not, but you know what I mean, this *is* a big day, but I'm babbling on about all the insignificant details when—"

I finished the sentence for her, "—when you'd rather talk with me about the important parts," and tapped my palm on my heart. "Yes," she said, and relaxed her head to one side.

"I know, and when I first get together with you I find it hard to focus on anything to say, so your babbling and my transitional silence kinda go together for a little while—"

"—while we get used to being next to each other," we said in unison and smiled.

The moment was one of millions we'd shared together; those moments when we were both in the exact same place at the exact same time and basking in the feeling of being completely connected to each other. "What do we do about this?" I said as I gestured to her gown.

"What do you want to do about it?" she replied.

I thought for a moment, suddenly fearful that the cab would stop and we'd arrive at Faith's destination. "Come spend the summer with me. Take a leave of absence from work, I don't care, do whatever you have to do, just come spend a few months with me and we'll see if what we've always wondered is actually true. Or," I reached across the seat to put my hand on hers, "ask me to move back home and I'll find a way to make money. I don't know, but I know we can figure it out. It's not too late. I know the cab driver, she'll do whatever we want."

Faith gulped audibly as she pulled her hand away from mine. She also attempted to look out the tinted window for strength, but only saw her face in the dark glass staring back at her.

"Look," I continued, "don't just rip the bandage off the whole thing. Obviously, you love him enough to consider marrying him, and that's something you'll have to deal with. You can't just run away from it all. You know what you get with him, I assume, and I'm a bit of an unknown quantity. You and I both dream about what we might possibly have together—always have—but the truth of the matter is *we don't know*. But I'm telling you, I'll do whatever it takes for us to find out, just give us a chance, Faith. Go to him and tell him you have one last question to answer before you can do this. Tell him you care about him, but it's important to know the truth in your heart before making a lifelong commitment."

"Don't make me cry, I'm about to get married," she replied, weakly. The cab stopped and her door opened. She looked at me lovingly, leaned in close to my face as if she wanted to kiss me, and instead placed the side of her head on my shoulder and gave me a hug. Faith brushed her right thumb across my cheek, which on any other day might have prompted me to close my eyes and focus on her touch, but today I wanted to grab her forearm to keep her from leaving. Her hand shook visibly as she pulled it away. She looked out into the sunshine and then looked back at me. "I—" she started.

"Don't," I said and reached for her hand again.

As I held it, she stared down at the floorboards of the cab searching for her words. "I don't have a choice."

"You do. You *do*," I pleaded. "You *always* do."

Her hand slipped from mine as she exited the cab. My hand reached in mid-air begging for her to return. In our past, we'd never wanted to let go of each other when parting, so we always tried to get it over with as soon as possible. But even though it ended quickly, we always, *always* looked back over our shoulders for one last snapshot. I didn't want this departure to end quickly, but I couldn't find the gumption to wreck her day. I watched as she pulled her dress out of the cab and gathered it up into one hand. Over her shoulder, I saw the aisle and the waiting groom, a path littered with flower petals that showed her the way. I waited for her to look back over her shoulder, but it never happened. With her dress in her right hand, she reached out with her left and closed the car door.

"NO!" I yelled as I slid across the seat toward her door and jiggled the handle. It was locked. I looked to the front of the cab and yelled at Nectar, "LET ME OUT!" I tried the handle again, but got the same result. "LET ME OUT, DAMMIT!"

I can't.

"WHY THE HELL NOT?" I screamed and pounded on the window that now separated me from my Faith.

I just can't.

Nectar punched the accelerator and the cab screeched to a start leaving tire rubber on the pavement.

"No-no-no-NO! WAIT! HOLD ON! STOP! I'M BEGGING YOU, STOP!"

She cranked up the music, obviously as a means to drown out my screaming.

"WAIT-WAIT-WAIT!" I furiously screamed, and thrashed about the interior of the cab testing every window and door and seat and any other options I could think of…until my hands were red from pounding, my throat hoarse from screaming, and my eyes spilling over with acceptance.

"Wait," I said as I fell back into the seat, beaten.

Thirty seconds down the road Nectar turned down the radio to see if I'd ceased my tantrum. *I'm sorry to ask, but you okay back there?*

"Not really," I mumbled. "I always imagined if I ever saw her in that dress she would be wearing it for me." I scratched my fingernail on the tinted glass.

"But I never did anything about it until now." I imagined Faith standing on the curb, the words she'd been searching for while sitting next to me suddenly finding their way into her head; words much different than the ones she'd actually used. "Where was I all of those years?" I asked aloud.

Soup, you're always on the go—either coming or going—do you really need to know more than that?

"What do you mean?"

If you really believed it, or if she really believed it, don't you think one of you would have done something about it. Because, it's not like your paths didn't cross a thousand times.

"I don't know." I wanted to beat my fists against my temples. "It feels like my soul mate just left the cab."

Can I try to make it better for you?

"Yeah, sure," I said not thinking she could actually accomplish that goal.

The cab stopped. I heard Nectar open and close her door. A few seconds later the back door opened and she reached in to offer me her hand. I grabbed it and allowed her to pull me into the night where a powerful wind blew across the plain.

Do you know this place? she asked.

A few charges of lightning struck far enough away to cause a delayed rumble, but close enough to light up the massive fig tree where I'd once conversed with my dad and great grandpa. Though surprised, I still said, "Yeah, I know it."

Come on, she urged, pulling me by the hand across the path as she led me toward the tree.

As I accepted her lead, she picked up the pace gradually until we were at a full run toward the tree's canopy. The wind howled, rustling the wheat stalks and tree branches. Frequent flashes of lightning helped keep us on course. When we reached the cover of the canopy, Nectar turned to me and leapt into my arms. I accepted her eagerly, and we turned in circles looking into each other's eyes until she dropped her feet back to the ground, pushed me gently by the chest, and backed me up to the trunk of the tree.

Thunder rolled across the ground, vibrating all who heard it.

Isn't this what you dream of?

"Yes," I groaned as I picked her up off of the ground once again, allowed her legs to wrap around me, and pressed her back up against the tree trunk. She moaned in anticipation. I dove into her lips, a passionate kiss that Mother Nature approved with a ferocious combination of thunder and lightning. Nectar's hair whipped in the wind. I collected it in my grasp as we kissed, which caused her to gasp longingly. "I must have you," I said with heated breath.

She reached for my shirt and pulled it quickly over the top of my head, and then pressed her lips to my chest. I did the same with her top, exposing a black, lacey bra in contrast to her milky-white skin. Her chest heaved as I examined her body, but she was in no mood to wait for my report, she reached for the clasp of her pants and urged me to do the same. Lightning followed thunder once more, a shorter time between them than before.

"Wait," I said, trying to catch my breath by sliding the tips of my fingers over the nook of her ear. "I don't want to rush. Not the first time."

Her surprised look turned to acceptance as she allowed me to take her hand and lead her away from the tree trunk, away from the protruding roots, and away from the protection of the canopy. I led her out into the elements, into the well-manicured grass and laid her down upon it. I pushed the wind-blown hair away from her face and resumed kissing her. Her hands wrapped around my neck, a guarantee that I wouldn't stop our passionate escalation again. Our hands explored each other, deftly maneuvering the clasps, snaps, and zippers that put up little resistance as a barrier between who we were and who we were about to become. And then, it began to rain. We both held our faces toward the falling precipitation, accepting it, like we were flowers in desperate need of water. With her hair wet, I no longer needed to keep it away from her face. The raindrops, warmer than I ever remember experiencing them, pooled around her navel. I drank from her, and she pushed the top of my head into her body, arching her back carefully so as not to spill the water. I filled my mouth, and swallowed visibly enough for her to know I accepted her, all of her and anything near or from her. The image of her hair, plastered around her shoulders and the upper reaches of her bare chest, drove even deeper desire. I rolled her to her side, then sidled up behind her. I held her head in my hands, locked in a kiss as I lifted her upper leg, and then gently felt the incredibly raw yet comforting feeling of being physically *one* for the first time in our lives.

Our lovemaking conducted a natural symphony that escalated and waned to the meter of our effort, making the weather equally unrelenting and subdued as it watched. And when we'd exhausted each other, the rain simply quit. Thunder's echo rolled off into the distance, I rolled onto my back and Nectar laid her cheek on my chest. My hands, wrapped around her, one at the small of her back and the other around her shoulder blades. Our lungs reached desperately for recovery, and slowly they found it as the wind dried our wet bodies.

We enjoyed the silence of our afterglow until Nectar pushed herself up to give me a soft kiss; it was all she needed to say about her level of satisfaction. She grabbed her clothes and started walking toward the cab. *Come on*, she said, *we gotta go. You can get dressed in the back of the cab. I have to get you to your next stop.*

"My next stop?"

Like you said, you still have something to learn.

I gathered up my clothes, ran back to the base of the tree to grab what we'd discarded there, and jogged to catch up to Nectar. By the time I reached her, she'd already gotten into the cab, naked I presume, started it, and left the rear door open for me. I pulled the door shut and we drove off into the night. As much as I wanted to talk about our experience, I didn't want to do it without being able to look into her eyes. She was whistling, which I interpreted as a good sign, so I happily got dressed to her tune.

A few minutes later the cab came to a stop. I could hear the transition of her body weight on the front seat as she turned around and said through the Plexiglas, *Thank you. Being with you means more than I can ever put into words. Now you know me, and that's enough to believe that you might someday choose me. I can't force you—at least that wouldn't be the right way to make you mine—but I can be confident that I've given you quite a story to consider.*

"I can't—"

The door opened while I was searching for the words to tell her I couldn't thank her enough, to tell her how amazingly incredible the experience with her was, but she either didn't want or didn't need to hear it.

Soup, no more words. It's time for you to go. When you step outside you'll see your cab. I know I'll see you soon. I love you.

I stepped out of her cab, pushed the door closed, and watched as she drove off into the night. I wondered if she knew how badly I desired for her to look back at me.

"I love you, too…I think," I said as I watched another woman leave my side with no promise to return.

Chapter 31

As I watched the black cab disappear, my phone vibrated in my pocket. I pulled it out, flipped it open, and saw a voicemail from Faith. I pressed play and listened to her say, "Just want you to know that many thoughts went through my head today, and I want you to save a dance for me when it's your turn. It wasn't the same without you there."

I couldn't think about the ceremony and the dancing and the toasts and the cake and the loss, just didn't have the space in my head to process anything about Faith after intimacy with Nectar. Plus, I still had to get through the Possibly story.

My cab sat in the small parking lot of a pizzeria. This night wasn't a good memory; one I'd rather forget than relive.

As I walked toward my cab I saw a silhouette sitting in the back seat. "Oh shit, it's Promise." I stopped in my tracks, spun around as if to walk away, just needing a moment to think. My head was spinning: I'd made love with Nectar, Possibly was about to beg for forgiveness, and Promise was waiting for me only a few steps away. The sight of her silhouette reminded me how abandoned I felt when I was twelve years old; a similar feeling I was having now since she'd missed the beginning of Possibly's story.

A rush of anger colored my vision as I became more frustrated about her absence. "Fuck it," I said as I stormed over to the cab, jerked open the driver's door, and slid into the seat. Angrily I said, "Where the hell have you been?"

I'm sorr—

"No. No. You don't get to leave me right when I need you the most. You did the same thing—THE EXACT SAME THING—when I was a kid. Do you have any idea how that felt? DO YOU?!"

Soupy, listen to me. I am *sorry. I lost you.*

Her words stopped my anger in its tracks. "You what?"

I lost you. I was with you, and then I wasn't, and I couldn't get back to you.

"Lost me? Are you okay?" My heart was racing.

Yes, I'm okay. I wasn't hurt. Just passed out, and when I awoke I couldn't find you. I tried everything I could think of, but you were nowhere to be found.

"But you're okay?"

Other than a small bump on my head where I knocked it against the back of the front seat, yeah, I'm okay.

"Wait—," I started and then thought for a moment to form my question, "do you take cabs everywhere you go?"

No, it was your cab…at least I thought it was your cab, and I was waiting for you to come back.

"Are you sure?"

I don't know, I thought it was. I waited for ages, where were you?

"I have no idea. I mean, I *can* tell you my world has flipped upside down since you left. I don't know where to begin; just wish you'd been here to experience it," I said while I tried to work out how to tell her about what happened minus the intimate moments—because it felt weird, just all around weird, like I was dating multiple women and had just slept with one of them for the first time. At what point do you tell the others, especially the one you'd never even seen or touched, but who felt like "the one?"

Believe me, I wish I'd been here, too.

I knew the importance of rehashing my life, and time with Promise could run out at any moment, especially now that it seemed something was working against us...*working against us? Nectar? Was she responsible?* No way, I'd been with her the whole time Promise had been gone, hadn't I? *No.* Couldn't be her, too coincidental. Could it?

Possibly's voice crackled over the taxi cab's radio, "Soup, I...I'm thinking about doing it."

Her voice scared me, prompting me to push aside all the other thoughts in my head.

Is that Possibly? Promise asked.

"Yes," I answered.

I think you ought to catch me up on what I missed.

I groaned and let my chin hit my chest in frustration. "I know it wasn't your fault, but going through this once sucked and twice totally blows. I don't think I can handle a third time."

Just the talking points, then?

"Fine. What happened before you left?"

Possibly was pregnant.

"Of course she was," I said in a defeated tone, since that memory was the most impactful punch in the belly our past could possibly drum up. "I helped her move to the west coast to pursue her professional dreams, but it was a difficult time for us both, starting with our choice to have an abortion because we feared the suicidal tendencies that arose from the hormonal imbalance caused by her pregnancy—"

Promise gasped, and I envisioned her hand cupping her mouth in shock.

"Exactly. It culminated with us breaking up."

Why the break up?

I groaned. "Ohhh, other men, drugs, unhappiness...nothing I did made her happy and all she did was continually test me to see what she could get away with."

How long were you together?

"About ten months."

And how long apart? I mean, before this conversation that must be nearby if we're hearing it on the radio.

"I'd say about three or four months. We're having this conversation in the pizza place right over there," I said as I pointed.

Soupy's voice replied over the radio to Possibly, "Okay. Don't stop there. Keep talking to me, Possibly."

I knew what Possibly wanted to do back then, but I also knew she didn't go through with it. "I have to be honest with you, Promise, the longer Possibly and I were apart the more I wished we were together. I still believed in the 'us' we *could* be, but I needed to recharge my batteries while, I hoped, she was finding her own place of happiness. Why? Because nothing, no woman, would have been greater to love if she became the woman we both wanted her to be—yet, neither of us knew the path to get there." I paused and then added, "You know how Gravity wanted to build a relationship and maintain a career?"

Yes.

"Well, at least Gravity knew what she wanted. Possibly still had no idea. She could talk about it, sure, but her words were vapor. In reality, she didn't know what she wanted, maybe didn't even know who she was. When we were still together, she was all talk and no action in the direction we both wanted her to go."

So in reality you didn't really break up with her, you let out some leash in the hope that she would make some quality discoveries about her life.

"Yes, exactly."

I see.

* * *

Possibly and Soupy sat on red plastic benches on opposite sides of a white, Formica, four-top table.

She said, "Yes, I need to talk to you. You're the only one out here I can talk to since everyone else is far away. As you know, I've been trying to figure out some things in my life."

Soupy nodded his head.

"But all I've been able to think about is how much fun we always have together, how much I miss you, and how sad I am that we aren't together. I know we've said we're going to date other people, but I've never been the type to just date around; I'm not a serial dater."

"Serial dater?" he asked.

"Yeah, someone who dates a lot."

"Okay," he replied.

Possibly added, "I'm a relationship type, but I try not to be because I think I'm supposed date around."

"Why?"

"To meet people? To know what I want?"

Soupy asked her, "Are you asking me or telling me?"

Her eyes narrowed, but she didn't answer. Instead, she said, "But dating around doesn't make me happy."

"You always have a favorite," he stated.

"Yes!" she exclaimed.

"You know you don't have to date to meet people."

"But isn't it unfair to simply enjoy someone's company when he thinks it's a date?"

This sentence from her, more than any other that he could point to, clearly defined how she thought of life: there are those who want her and those she doesn't want. "Possibly, that's why you have to be clear and honest about how you feel."

"Please," she said rejecting his point, "Guys just hear what they want to hear."

"No, they don't—well, maybe the guys you're used to—but okay," he capitulated. This was not the time to argue about it.

"So anyway, I'm a relationship person, but I think I should be dating, but that doesn't make me happy. And then I realized, I'm the same way about *everything* in my life and always have been."

She waited for Soupy to acknowledge that he understood, but he was still trying to process the way her mind was working through this conversation.

"Anyway, for the first time in my life, I'm beginning to understand that I need to do what makes me happy instead of worrying about what's right or what other people think."

To his knowledge and experience, she'd *always* done what made her happy without concern for other people, but he wanted to see how her logic played out. "Okay, but are the things that make you happy and what you consider to be right, different for you?"

Possibly answered, "I'm not sure what makes me happy because I've never stopped to think about it."

Surprised, he added, "*Really*? How old are you?"

She said, "Ha-ha," without the actual laughter. "Because of what I've been through, I know I'm never gonna be happy all the time."

"As terrible as your past may be, Possibly, it happened and none of us can take it back, but you can choose how it influences you for the rest of your life."

"I know. Some things in life are hard, like leaving my family to move to a strange city, and it just takes time to adjust."

"Yes," Soupy agreed.

"I'm unhappy right now because these changes are hard."

"Can I offer my thoughts?"

"Yes, that's why I wanted to talk to you."

"Why don't you make a grocery list of things that make you feel bad and things that make you feel good. Pin it to the fridge. You'll always have something to remind you of what you like and what you should avoid. Share this list with your friends and family so they can help you make better choices."

Her response came so abruptly it surprised him. "I'd put you on the list of things that make me feel good, but then I'd have to change the name of the list to 'Things I Love.'"

Soupy lost his train of thought while trying to visibly prevent rolling his eyes.

"I was so unhappy last night, I was in bed thinking about ending it all, you know, my life—"

That brought him quickly back to the present.

"—but then I realized that my emptiness disappears when I'm with you," she added.

This "you save me" story was too familiar to him. He was teetering on a fence post only wide enough for one foot and nothing but dark, bottomless pit surrounding him.

She asked, "Do you feel empty, too?" and then slouched back in her seat.

Soupy said, "Yes and no—now wait, allow me to explain. My heart wants you here, unbelievably wants you here, every single night. But I'm not—I mean, I can't be the reason you feel empty. You *must* be happy and full with yourself before you can ever be happy with me."

"I don't like your answer," she said, and looked toward the door.

He raised his hands from the table, a quicker and smaller shrug than using his shoulders.

"And what's that?" she said accusingly at his gesture.

"I—"

"No, I know what you're trying to say. I sometimes struggle to interpret your feelings, but I've got this one."

"You should—"

She raised her hand to stop him and then continued, "Here I am telling you how much I love you—how I've *realized* that I really love you, and you… you're *rejecting* me?"

"I'm not rejec—"

"YOU DON'T GET TO TALK RIGHT NOW!" she screamed and the whole restaurant stopped what they were doing to look at us. "I *usuuuually* keep my mouth shut when I get angry with you. I keep it all *bottled up* inside."

Oh, no you don't, Soupy thought.

"And then what I *didn't* say nags at me until I'm pissed about it. Well, let me tell you, I'm not doing that this time because I'm pissed at you *now*! You don't have to *wonder* about that!"

Possibly grabbed her purse and her phone, slid out of the booth, and stormed out of the restaurant. Soupy shook his head as she went. He knew everyone in the place was looking at them—at *him* after she was gone—but he wasn't interested in either smoothing the situation over or chasing her down. He wasn't the type to chase, which he'd learned from *her* since that's exactly what she always wanted.

Soupy thought, *If you want to discuss something with me, you don't fucking run away.*

She thought she was done talking to him, but he knew her better than that.

* * *

So much for the "let your loved one go and hope she comes back" cliché. I commend you for using a bit more of your head than your heart in this case, Soupy.

"Don't give me too much credit. I was still playing the game."

But were you playing with her life?

"I thought about it while I was speaking with her, but it didn't seem like her life was in the balance. She was just making a scene; testing me to see if I'd flop over like a good dog to let her rub my belly."

Talk about a game of Risk.

"I wanted her back in my life, badly, but not at the same price as before; not as the man keeping her alive so she could continue to make terrible decisions."

You knew you wanted Possibly to come back? Love really can be blind.

"You're right, but when you're down, you're down. An hour later my cell phone rang. It was Possibly, so I didn't answer it. Four calls and four voicemails over a fifteen minute span finally forced me to, at least, listen to her messages."

Guilt kicked in when you considered the possibilities?

"Right, and I didn't want *that* on my conscience."

* * *

Soupy drove home and collapsed in his bed before he called Possibly back.

"Why won't you answer your phone?" she asked.

He answered, "You stormed out on *me*. Why the hell would I want to talk to *you* now?"

There was a brief silence on the other end of the phone before she said, "I don't feel right. I want to kill myself. I can't take your rejection when I love you so much."

The words hit him harder than they did when she alluded to them in person. This was happening now, over the phone, and it wasn't a conversation right in front of him where he could measure her seriousness. "Hold on, Possibly, just hold on. What are you going to do?"

"Does it matter?"

"Yes, of course it matters."

"Why didn't you just let me drown?"

"W-w-what? Drown?"

"When the boat sank, why didn't you let me drown?"

"I love you too much for that," he admitted.

"No, you don't. You don't want to be with me."

"I do. I *do*. I want to be with you, but I want you to be happy with yourself first."

"How can I be happy with myself if I don't have you?"

His head was spinning and it felt as if there was no time for him to explain the answer. He'd *just tried* to explain it, and she wasn't interested in listening, but he couldn't help himself. "If you like yourself, you can have me. NO. Forget that. Never mind. I don't know what I'm talking about. Sorry, my head is spinning. Let's do this: Possibly, tell me what's on your mind. What are you doing?

Where are you?" He grabbed his shoes and his car keys as he prepared to race to wherever she was having such dark thoughts.

"I'm in the dark," she said. "I'm *really* in the dark."

"Listen to me, Possibly. Hear my voice. I'm right here."

"NO, YOU'RE NOT!" She began to cry.

Soupy felt like their time was slipping away. "Shhhh," he whispered trying to calm her down. "Talk to me."

"I don't want to," she mumbled.

"HEY!" he screamed in an attempt to shock her out of whatever dark thoughts were clouding her mind. "TELL ME WHERE YOU ARE!"

"I'm in your driveway," she replied.

"You're WHAT?" he ran to the window, peeked through the blinds, and saw her car parked in the driveway. It didn't take him out of total rescue mode, but he was relieved there wasn't so much distance, and time, between them. Soupy set his phone on the table and walked out to her car. She opened the door as he approached. With a tinge of anger in his voice, he said, "What are you doing?"

"I need you," she whispered.

"You just *told* me you were going to kill yourself and you're sitting here in my fucking *driveway*! What is that? What is that *all about*?!"

Her arms were crossed as she stood there, not like she was angry, but like she was trying to hold on to herself before she slipped away. "I...I...please don't yell at me...I left you and I started to think about what it would be like if you dated someone else and I...I just couldn't imagine you being with another woman. It didn't make me feel right, and not feeling right was far too familiar for me. I *did* think about it. I did, but I drove here instead. Missing you scared me. It *scared* me." At this point she finally brought her eyes up from the pavement. "After we broke up I realized what I needed to do to remove bad influences from my life and fix some things. I did them. It took me a few months and in those few months, like I told you, I thought about me. I took a new job. I made some new friends. At first, I resented you for kicking me out into the world all by myself, but some of what you said to me must have stuck because I *did* figure some things out. And then—," she started to cry again and stamped her foot on the ground in an attempt to stop it. "And then…you still wouldn't accept me."

It was like she had loaded up her fist with a roll of pennies and hit him in the gut; he never saw it coming. Her words took the gusto out of his anger, but he wasn't yet ready to let her simply waltz back.

Possibly continued, "I feel like you don't miss me nearly as much as you say you do."

Soupy shook his head and looked away. With a sigh he said, "Missing you is hard. I fear getting consumed by it, that's why you don't see it."

"I want to see it. I *need* to see it, Soupy."

"Then you have to wait for it. I don't mean you have to wait, like, days or weeks, but you have to wait for me to feel it and let me find the words to tell you about it. It's all there." He patted his chest and looked her in the eyes. "It's all right here."

"You tell good stories; it's your job. How do I know you're not just saying what you're supposed to say?"

He tapped his chest again. "When you learn your language, then you'll be able to understand mine."

"I want to learn," she said, and began walking toward him. He opened his arms to her and gently rubbed her back as she buried herself into his chest. "I want our old conversations back."

"Me, too, Possibly."

She added, "Those words weren't clouded by feelings and intimacy, and all this shit in my head. Since we started dating, they're all fucking jumbled up. Can't things be as easy as they were before we met?"

"I hesitate to say this, but I think you know the truth."

"I could tell you anything back then."

Soupy kissed her on top of her head. "You can tell me anything *now*."

"Seems like everything I tell you has to do with my problems. Why can't I be the normal one?"

"You can be. We'll get there together." Soupy pushed her away enough to look into her eyes before he said, "When I think about you, I don't think about your problems. I think about how beautiful you are and how hard you're trying to be who you want to be."

She laughed and said through tears, "Am I ever good to you?"

Soupy resumed their hug. "Yes, you're good to me. Of course you're good to me, and I never want to take the chance that I'll lose you."

"I know," she said. "I just don't realize when I'm going to be suicidal. All of a sudden I'm sitting in the closet, or wherever, and I don't see it until I'm there."

He whispered into her ear, "Look, if you're going to try and kill yourself, then I'll never let you leave my arms or this spot right here on the driveway."

She snuggled more tightly into his body. "I just need you to hold me for a second…just a second."

* * *

I said, "See why I never want you to leave again, Promise?"

Jesus, umm, yeah.

"It certainly wasn't the ideal way to start a new chapter with Possibly, but I wanted to believe that she really *had* taken some steps in the right direction. And truthfully, I didn't go back to her, she came back to me."

I don't know, Soup.

"I've never been able to understand what someone expects to accomplish by committing suicide. You've been in enough dreams, I'm sure, do you have any insight?"

Yeah, I do. It has to do with the amount of time you spend in the dark.

"What's that mean?"

It means you have no idea what the mind and the body can accomplish when they twist themselves up so tightly that, despite trying, there's no way to unravel the bind, so they just cut it.

"And then everyone blames themselves for not being there, for not being able to help, and they all feel like they should have seen it coming."

Didn't you see that you kept letting her out of the closet? What did you think was going to happen now that you'd "rescued" her again? Did you think she would miraculously become the woman you wanted her to be? Had you ever thought she might not want to be that woman?

"Wow, so many questions, Promise. I have answers, sure, and we're going to see how it all went down here in a few minutes, but look, knowing what I know today, would I have done this all over again? Hell no, but would I have done that moment in the driveway all over again? Hell yes."

She needs her closet, Soup. She cannot and will not accept vulnerability. When you let her out of the closet, you *become her protection!*

"Do you trust your intuition?" I asked.

Are you asking if I trust my own voice?

"Yes."

Yes, of course I do.

"Do you ever ignore it?"

Yeah.

"When you ignore it do you deny yourself an experience?"

Yeah, I suppose since you'd have a different experience depending on whether you ignored it or not, but both would be an experience.

"And how do you think your intuition was developed?"

It's me, and my experiences.

"Nature and nurture, yes."

Okay.

"And when we say 'experience,' we mean both times of success and times of failure, right?"

Yes, Soup.

"In other words, you need to fall flat on your face once in a while to understand what not to do. Then, the next time you're in that situation, you have a better chance of success."

If I can be honest here, Soup, you have a way of repetition without learning.

"Maybe, but there's no second chance after suicide."

Chapter 32

When I first met Promise on the eve of my thirteenth birthday, it was on the insides of a circular wall of rocks with a shorter wall through the middle; like a large, manmade "Do Not Enter" symbol if looking at it from above. I now found myself in this place again, sitting in the same position as I had at the first meeting, cross-legged on the ground.

"Promise?" I asked aloud, and then listened quietly for a response, but heard nothing. I got up from my seated position and walked around the semicircle exploring the black rocks and the Etch-a-Sketch tablets inserted into them. None of them created pictures or words, just scribbled. If truly an accurate depiction of my mind—as they were supposed to be—they were representing it well. As I approached the half-wall I asked once again, "Promise? If you're over there, say something. I don't want to destroy our future just because my curiosity drove me to peek over this wall."

There was no response.

What did I expect to see on the other side? Something different—a bent toward optimism, I suppose—but that expectation wasn't met, as the other side was an exact replica of my own. *And the grass was not any greener on the other side of the fence, old chap.* I put my hands on top of the wall and pulled the rest of my body up. With balance, I walked along the half-wall until I reached the larger boundary of the circle. I couldn't see over the top and it looked to be a questionable climb to do so. So I sat down straddling the half-wall and leaned my back up against the larger wall. Lightly tapping the back of my head on the rounded corner of a rock, I repeatedly thought, *What next? What next? What next?*

The Etch-a-Sketches closest to my ears changed audibly in pitch. What had been a uniform low hum of white noise now sounded more deliberate. I leaned forward enough to see a screen write the word, "have," and then it shook clean. Next, it wrote, "want," and shook itself blank. It repeated this two-word pattern.

Have and want, I thought to myself. You can't always have what you want. *True.* Was there a difference between what I had and what I wanted? There most definitely was. Neither Possibly nor I were in love with who she was. We were, instead, in love with who she wanted to be. But dammit, every single time she walked into the room I felt longing. *Why?* In that brief second, that second when I see her before she sees me, I want to believe that all the hard work had well, *worked.* That she had become the woman we both wanted her to be. Check please, happily ever after.

And then there's Faith, the woman I always thought I wanted, who became someone completely different when she started dating this guy she eventually married. Is it possible that in all those conversations we had, she never really told me want she wanted? Does what we want change who we are?

What Faith chose was close enough to make due, for *her*, which was in no way the same as the right choice. Or maybe Faith never really knew what she wanted, just followed that Mid-western inertia to marry at a certain age and on a certain plan, act out a couple of years of honeymoon bliss, make babies, and assume it would all work itself out. *Dumb idea.* Faith liked to be noticed for her successes, but never for her failures. She could spin a disaster into gold with the best public relations experts in the business. She hadn't yet learned that there was more to learn, more wisdom to be gained from failure than *perceived* success.

I had a dramatic reaction when Faith left Nectar's cab, even though her wedding was actually several years prior. I don't always think when I react, but who does? That's what all this hindsight examination is for, right? And when I say "training," I mean this process of dating, failing, and learning from each failure in order to avoid the same mistakes in the future—it's not that fun, so far, and I don't feel any closer to "finding" Promise.

In that reaction to Faith's wedding, I completely forgot she'd already been lost. The events in my life at that time were dramatically perplexing, but even so I knew on Faith's wedding day we weren't yet right for each other. If I had thought otherwise, I would have done something about it. I didn't, not then and not now either. And it was easier to let those events pass and engage myself in the fight to help Possibly find truth, love, and happiness, than it was to stand up and speak. *Easier?* I don't know if I would have lived through double the trauma of *not* holding the peace at Faith's wedding, and figuring out how to help Possibly, let alone the possible rejection from both if Faith would have gotten married anyway and Possibly learned that I tried to stop it. I'd have needed my own closet, for sure. Though, a dreamer can, and will, still dream. Apparently, dream and *still* do nothing different than he once did.

The Etch-a-Sketches furiously wrote the word "fire."

What was I supposed to do with Promise and Nectar? Why is my dream world more active and pleasurable than my real world? What the hell is going on with me? I bought into this process of learning with Promise, then, wham; Nectar revealed her aggressive and passionate plan. *Wham.* The "have," and the "want." I can have Nectar right now if I want her, so she says because she has "always been with me," so am I wrong to think I know Promise better than I know her?

"What the fuck is even real?!" I shouted.

The tablets responded by rumbling deeply.

"Okay," I said aloud, and then pressed my palms together and bent my hands back and forth to stretch my wrists; one of the techniques I use to relax. "Do I want Nectar?" I didn't know. Is that decision enough? Despite saying she'd known me forever, she still felt *new*. On the other hand, I felt a deep, aged connection to Promise. Yes, the same Promise I can't see, touch, or kiss.

And if I can't do those things, doesn't that make her an idea instead of reality? I *need* that physical touch; I don't feel loved without it.

"Hold on," I said to myself. "I'm in a damn dream, so what's the fuss?" I knew that the fuss was: the man, the mission, true love to save the world.

I know myself, at least I *feel* like I know myself, so why wasn't I able to choose? *Do I have to choose?* I shook my head and whispered, "Stop." I had to stop bouncing back and forth between the two.

I jumped from the half-wall, landed on the ground, and kicked a rock across the circle. I hadn't intended to launch it into one of the Etch-a-Sketches, but when it impacted the plastic screen, I felt an incredible pain in my head and crumbled to my knees. It was relentless. I winced and curled into the fetal position, continuing to repeat the word, "stop, stop, stop, stop, stop…"

The sky turned from night to day. *Relief*, I thought, but it turned back to night instantly. And like rollers in a slot machine that never stopped, it turned night to day, black to white, dark to light, with increasing velocity, until it was one continuous color: gray. I turned over onto my back, reached with one hand toward the sky, and gathering all of my strength, punched my index finger into the air and yelled, "PAUSE!"

The sky responded with the sun just the horizon; enough light to see.

My breath returned, slowly, as I rubbed my fists across my eyes, over my eyebrows, down both sides of my nose, and then, with the flat of my palms, wiped the sweat from my face from top to bottom until I finally laid my arms down at my side.

I smelled smoke. As I craned my neck upward, I could see it coming from the cracked Etch-a-Sketch. I rolled over, still spinning mentally despite having stopped my world from doing the same.

The smoke was mesmerizing. I stared at it, becoming more captivated as it wisped and twirled into nothingness. *Where are you going? Where are you coming from?* I got up and approached the dying Etch-a-Sketch. As I kneeled in front of it, I said to myself, "Remember. Remember what Great Grandpa taught you." A circuit wire from this broken, dream-world Etch-a-Sketch emitted a steady, bright glow.

Fire needs two things to thrive: air and fuel. To keep the ember alive, I lightly blew on it and it responded. "Ah, you're hungry. Good," I said. I needed fuel. The ember waned. I blew once more to buy myself time, but time wasn't on my side. "Think." I checked my pockets, empty. I looked around the rocky circle and there was nothing but rocks and dirt. "Think," I repeated. Was it really dirt? I reached down, grabbed a handful of dirt, and hoped it was some magical, flammable dust, or powdered leaves that still wanted to evolve. With my hand held open to the fire I said, "Fire, I give you this earth," and then I corrected myself. "No, not earth. Fire, I give you this, umm, FUEL!" My mind focused on the image of fire as I tossed the dirt into the Etch-a-Sketch.

The ember immediately ceased its glow.

"DAMMIT!" I shivered at the thought of receiving no heat in this cold place, and that was unacceptable. *This is going to hurt*, I thought. I chose an Etch-a-Sketch about three feet from the ground, turned my back to it, and like a fireman kicks open a door, thrust my foot backward into the face of the tablet.

On impact, I passed out.

Chapter 33

My headache was killing me, but at least I wasn't cold any longer; the air coming from my cab's heater was set on high. And fortunately, it hadn't taken ten minutes to warm up like it normally did; maybe it was the blue sky and the warm weather outside.

Are you feeling okay? asked Promise from the back seat.

"Not really. I have a terrible headache."

Do you have anything you can take for it?

"No, not much of a pill-popper. Never crosses my mind to take 'em, let alone buy 'em. You?"

No, not much of a purse-carrier. Never understood the necessity to carry something for everything.

I didn't recognize the setting: a small parking lot in front of a four-story office building. It wasn't until Possibly's car drove into the lot and parked next to us that I knew the exact moment in my past we were about to experience.

"Oh, okay," I said. "Therapy."

Yours, hers, or couples?

"Hers. After that near-suicidal night in my driveway, I made it clear to her that we had to actively work on finding happiness. Therapy was one of the ways, but she'd had an unsavory past with previous therapists and a disbelief in the benefit—or so she said—so it took some work to find one she liked. After a few months, she asked if I'd join her at a session. However—"

Possibly's voice over the radio interrupted my sentence, "You can't tell her anything about drugs or sex."

She had stopped Soupy as they walked toward the building. He replied, "Okay, but don't you think—"

"Nothing," she sternly cut him off and reconvened her walk to the front of the building. "Coming?"

I shut the heater off, as the cab suddenly felt like an oven. "As you can see, Promise, I initially thought she was making progress because she was able to tell a third-party the truth. But if she couldn't tell a therapist the truth—a person whose job it was to objectively understand her life and pose solutions—then who?"

It's exactly as I told you, she doesn't understand that opening herself up to vulnerability is the only way she'll ever understand how to rebuild who she is. She simply can't take the risk because it's fraught with the shame that she let it happen—though we both know that's not the case—all of these terrible things happened to her, so she thinks she must be a terrible person.

"I couldn't understand why she couldn't trust her friends, her family, her therapist; she couldn't even trust me anymore, so how could she get better if she wouldn't open herself up to those who cared about her the most, and accept that we were there to help?"

She needed her closet.

And I needed to hang up my cape in there.

We sat in the parking lot listening to my introduction to the therapist over the radio, but I turned it down to talk more with Promise. "There's not much to learn from this session because, really, the most surprising discovery was this grudge that Possibly was holding against me for breaking up with her."

Are you kidding?

"Not at all. You see, I'd promised that I'd never leave her, but I did."

So now she can't trust you?

"Yes."

Your strategic move backfired.

"I wasn't very happy about it because I could see the improvement between when she was catastrophically tumbling and now, when she seemed to be standing up straight again. I explained to the therapist that she had to change some things in her life—without mentioning the sex and drugs—and she'd changed them, much for the better. At the time, I didn't think she could do it if I was still in her life; we'd tried and failed at that already, and more than once. And the results were seemingly evident; she was much happier at this point than she was a few months prior."

Understanding her past is pretty important, not just for you and the therapist, but for her as well.

"Yes, I know the past is important. It creates a template for decision-making in the future, but her revisionist history for the therapist was bullshit. It was a story meant to make her look good and cast me into the role of blame."

Fair point.

"And shouldn't the focus be on where we are now, and where we're trying to go, rather than where we've been?"

Possibly was still trying to understand where she'd been. It was keeping her from being happy in the now and definitely prevented her from moving toward happiness in the future.

I groaned.

She just wasn't like you.

"I know. I get it, but it's still frustrating."

She told you what she went through, but that doesn't mean you can understand it.

"I'd never make that claim."

You focus on where you are and where you want to be, but you've always done that in your life; it's easy for you.

"I just wanted Possibly to see that my breaking up with her played a part in how she got here, this happier place, but she wouldn't see it."

Over the radio Possibly yelled, "But *you* broke up with *me*!"

Soupy replied, "But you are *so much happier now*!"

"We didn't get anywhere, and with the fact that Possibly wasn't telling the whole truth to her therapist, that feeling that we'd *never* get anywhere came charging back."

Did you ever see the therapist again?

"No, and we never spoke about the session either." I backed the cab out of the parking lot and drove with no intended destination.

Sounds like the second time around with Possibly was shaping up to be a lot like the first.

"She was happier, but we weren't. We had a trip scheduled to spend some time with her parents, but it took some serious discussion to decide whether I would actually join her, since things weren't going well between us. Ultimately, I did, and I was thankful because her mother was an important part of my support network. I could speak with her about things, get a deeper view into Possibly's past, and learn the reasons why she might act a certain way."

Mr. M-I-L-D, Mother In-Law's Dream?

"I like moms, what can I say? They're an important part of any relationship I have with a daughter. I'd been away from mine since I left the central states, so I hoped to find a woman who was close to hers. Besides, there's nothing wrong with having multiple places to call home."

There definitely isn't.

"Possibly and I didn't speak during the flight there. She was ambivalent at best, more standoffish than anything else. I asked her if something was wrong, and she simply shrugged, a sure sign that things were more amiss between us than I thought. It felt like she was doing me a favor the whole weekend, like, she was giving me the chance to say goodbye to her family before she broke up with me. We spent time together publicly, but not privately, if you know what I mean."

Intimately?

"There wasn't any of that going on. In fact, she was adamantly vocal about the fact that it *wouldn't* go on. She didn't touch me the entire trip. And you know when I say that, I mean she didn't hold my hand, latch onto my arm for an escort, cuddle with me in bed, hug me, or show affection in any way, shape, or form."

She was leaving you. She had to be because of the way she equates sex with love.

"You're killing my punch line, Promise."

Sorry.

"Damn, this is making my head hurt worse."

Sorry about that, too.

"I saw it, but didn't want to believe it, even when the weekend was ending and her parents asked if I'd like to stay with them a few extra days."

Oh dear, I'm sure that didn't fly well.

"Speaking of flying..." I tapped the cab's meter and it switched to a miniature video monitor.

* * *

"I CAN'T BELIEVE YOU LOVE MY FAMILY MORE THAN YOU LOVE ME!" Possibly screamed at Soupy in front of her parents.

Shocked, Soupy replied, "What?"

She stomped around the room and continued, pointing at him periodically, "I can't believe you—YOU—would take advantage of my family."

"Take advantage of them? What are you talking about?"

"Did my dad offer to pay for your room if you stay?"

"Yes."

"THAT'S EXACTLY WHAT I'M TALKING ABOUT!"

"Calm down, Possibly. I can pay for my own damn room."

"NO, YOU CAN'T!"

"Of course I can."

She put her hands on her hips and groaned loudly. "You don't have any idea what I'm saying, do you?"

"Obviously I don't, so why don't you tell me."

"WHY WON'T YOU YELL BACK AT ME?"

Soupy paused for a moment. It was a question he hadn't expected. "Because I see no reason to raise my voice, and you haven't expressed a valid reason why I shouldn't stay, and why, I ask, why the hell would I *want* to go home with this?" He motioned to the dramatic role she was portraying. "This is about the only emotion you've shown toward me the entire weekend. At least I know I still exist to you!"

She stomped her foot on the hotel room carpet. "Well, you don't get to see my family if I have to leave."

"That's ridiculous."

"I don't care if it's ridiculous."

"I can see that, but I don't see why it should keep me from doing whatever I want to do."

"YOU KNOW I'M AFRAID OF FLYING!"

In more ways than one, I thought, but it was true, she was afraid to travel by air. "Hey, okay, I *do* know that." Soupy rubbed his hands against his face and then capitulated. "Well, we're already packed and I don't think I can continue this argument in front of your family any longer, so let's go."

She said her goodbyes. He said his apologies. Her parents whispered to him that it was okay, a sure sign that this was normal behavior for her.

* * *

I fast-forwarded the video until we were waiting at our airport gate.

* * *

Soupy and Possibly walked through the airport. She kept looking at him, but his face told her all she needed to know: "Leave me the fuck alone. I'm pissed."

"Are you going to sit next to me on the plane?" she asked.

"Don't be ridiculous, of course I am."

"Are you going to talk to me? Because if you aren't then I don't want to sit next to you."

Suddenly Soup was the bad guy for not having spoken to her after she'd ignored him all weekend and embarrassed him in front of her family. Her attempt to assert blame on him only infuriated him more. "Grow the fuck up, Possibly. Look, you got your way, so fucking enjoy it. What you did to me back there—in front of your family, no less—was embarrassing to me, and it should be embarrassing for you, but you don't see it. Do you really think I love your family more than I love you? Never mind. Don't even answer that. I can't believe I validated it by asking it aloud." He looked at her and then looked away before he added, "I think *you* owe *me* an apology."

She mumbled an apology.

"Let's go home," Soupy replied, still visibly pissed, and they got up to board the plane.

* * *

Watching those scenes happen again had nearly the same impact on me as they had the first time around, which was becoming a regular occurrence. I was pissed, and I mashed the accelerator to pass traffic on the highway.

Whoa, Soup. Easy now.

"I'm tired of this shit, Promise. I don't want to learn from Possibly anymore."

I understand, but stick with me.

I drove the cab hurriedly onto the back bumper of a car in the fast lane, braking as I did to end up only a few inches away from it. I laid my hand on the horn and left it there until the car in front of me hit its brakes, flipped me off, and moved out of the fast lane.

SOUP! DO YOU HEAR ME? SLOW DOWN!

"No," I replied, calmly, and returned the finger to the driver in the other car as I passed him.

IF YOU DON'T SLOW DOWN THEN I'M LEAVING!

"FINE! FUCKING LEAVE! EVERYONE ELSE HAS!"

His words shocked her. *Soupy, no...that's not what I meant. I—*

"JUST! FUCKING! GO!" I turned toward the back of the cab to make sure she heard me, not thinking about jeopardizing our future. As I turned, she screamed, and then disappeared.

I never saw the back of an eighteen-wheeler. At eighty-plus miles per hour, there was no avoiding my fate.

Chapter 34

My eyes burst open as I woke in a dark, confined space that smelled of rubber and grease. I knew where I was just as soon as I awoke: the trunk of a car. Since I'd been in them before—the age-old "sneak into the drive-in movie theater without paying" trick—it didn't freak me out. However, the poor condition of the road didn't make for a comfortable ride. I groaned with each bump trying to find a more comfortable position on the metallic, lightly carpeted floor.

"HEYYYYYYYY!" I yelled as I pounded on the roof of the trunk.

The car slowed to a stop. A door opened and then closed. Another door opened and I heard the cushion springs in the back seat take on new weight.

I repeated my yell, "HEYYYYYY!"

Though muffled, Nectar replied, *You don't have to yell. I can hear you just fine.*

"If you can hear me then let me out," I ordered.

Not yet.

I groaned, "Okay, now what?"

What am I going to do with you?

"What do you mean?"

Nectar made a tsk-tsk sound and then said, *It's just so obvious, but you can't see it. What's wrong with you?*

I, of course, knew exactly what she was talking about: us. "Can you let me out of here so we can talk about it?"

Let yourself out, it's your damn dream.

I tried, both physically and telekinetically, but failed. Frustrated, I pounded my fists on the underside of the trunk.

That's gonna help, she said, sarcastically.

"I'd rather see you when I talk with you. I need the context of your body language," I pleaded.

Oh, you mean you want more than you have with Promise?

Shit. I walked right into that one, but it was true.

"I—"

You don't have to answer. I already know the answer. Why do you think I have you locked in the trunk?

"Kidnapper," I whispered.

What's that?

More loudly, I repeated, "I said, 'kidnapper.'"

Nectar laughed loudly. *You're acting the part more than I am, Soup. When you act like a kid—*

"I know. I know. I deserve to be treated like one. I know what you're saying, I just don't agree with you."

I'm not sure you do, understand what I'm saying, that is.

"Then tell me, oh wise one, why am I locked in your trunk?"

To keep you from killing yourself.

"What? I have no plans to kill myself."

Yeah right, I've seen the way you drive.

"Huh?"

I've also seen the way you live.

"What does that mean?"

You do the same stupid thing over and over, and continue to have this optimistic belief in a future that never arrives.

"I have to give all of myself to everything to truly know I tried."

Everything? Don't you mean someone?

"Someone. Something. Everything. Whatever."

No, not whatever. You see, that's the whole point I'm trying to make. What you want is this thing, this ideal that just doesn't exist. Believe me, there's a reason why you only find examples of true love in the arts and not the real world. It doesn't fucking exist.

"I disagree."

Disagree all you want, Soup. I'll just leave you where you are. She paused for a moment. *And another thing—this other stupid thing you do—this focus on the "something" more than the "someone." Your vision is so far forward that you miss what's right here in front of you.*

"In front of me?! In front of what?! Reality? What reality? It's my damn dream, like you said."

If that's your attitude, then this is going to be a long night for you.

"So what you're saying is, if I choose you right now then you'll let me out of the trunk?"

That would certainly be a start.

"How can you think I'd choose you when you're holding me hostage?"

The trunk popped open. My body was stiff from being locked up in such a small space, but I unwound and climbed out. As I brushed myself off, I saw the rear door to the cab standing open.

"Thanks…I guess," I said as I leaned my elbow on the roof of the car and peeked into the dark backseat where Nectar sat.

You're welcome.

I looked around outside, but only saw my own breath in the cloud-covered moonlight. Walking anywhere was out of the question, no lights could be seen in the distance and I had no idea where this road would lead.

You might as well get in; we're a long way from home.

Seeing no other choice, I did as I was told. The door closed behind me. Nectar snapped and a red hue of light illuminated the back of the cab.

So, she said.

"So," I repeated.

You know she's going to kill you.

"Who is?"

You know who.

"No, I don't."

Well, you better figure it out.

"Thanks for the advice," I sarcastically replied.

I don't want a front row seat.

"Then scalp your tickets."

I'd rather be in your corner.

"Yeah, I know you would. You take every opportunity to point that out without ever giving me a damn moment to think."

Why do you always think there's time?

"Why do you always think this is a game?"

Isn't it?

I simply shrugged.

You play the game. You know you do, and you play to win. Am I right? You shape up your opponent, figure out how to conquer her, and then fight to the death to win her as the prize so you'll be known forevermore as the champion of true love.

"Opponent? I'd rather think we're on the same team."

Red Rover. Red Rover. Send Soupy on over.

"What are you going on about?"

Let me ask you this: is death worth it?

"I won't give up on something if I think it's worth it."

Do you even know what worth is?

"I'm sure you're going to tell me."

Damn right I am. Would you rather die today or tomorrow?

"Tomorrow, of course."

And what if you do? Do you feel you would have lived in the moment today?

"I can't live that way. I can't make decisions solely in the moment. For me, there has to be some greater goal, or purpose. Something to achieve."

There you go with the somethings again, when my whole point is the someones.

"And you're someone."

Yes, I am. Don't you see that?

"I do. Believe me, I definitely do. You're so real to me that you don't seem real at all. That's why you have to let me breathe. Let me think."

Even if you're going to die tomorrow?

"Even if I'm going to die when I step out of this cab."

Even if she kills you?

"I won't give up on my dream."

It's my dream, too.

"What is?"

To be in love.

"Isn't it everyone's dream?"

Don't belittle it.

"You're right. I'm sorry. It isn't everyone's dream. I know that. And most who have the dream don't have any idea what they're dreaming of."

That's better.

"I'm learning."

Soup, I'm here to tell you this: You sound strong, but you're weakening by the minute. You've been lucky your entire life, and that's your biggest problem. The core of your fear is that you don't know how to win. I fear, even if you do win, you won't know what to do with it. You need someone who understands that about you.

"Maybe you don't know me as well as you think you do."

Think what you want to think, but if there's something I know, I know you.

"YOU KEEP SAYING THAT!" I yelled. "QUIT IT!"

Fine.

"Besides, I've won plenty of times. Sure, this is the greatest challenge in my life, but I'm winning the battles more than I'm losing them."

Promise has trained you well.

"Trained me well for what?"

To be this great glutton for punishment: stubborn, competitive, unwavering.

"Yeah, well I happen to believe in learning from my mistakes in order to reach my true potential."

What if you won the lottery tomorrow?

"I'd have to play first."

You're playing right now.

"The love lottery? That sounds like it's simply luck more than a skill to be learned."

Just entertain the hypothetical.

"Okay, fine, I win the lottery tomorrow."

What mistakes would you have made to earn it?

"I wouldn't have earned it. I would have just been lucky."

Would you choose not to accept your own luck?

"Of course not."

So you admit that not everything in life, or everyone you meet *in life comes from your hard work or learning from your failure.*

"Sure."

Then why are you looking a gift horse in the mouth? Don't you think you can be lucky in love?

I thought about it for a moment and she had a point. The question, really, was whether I wanted to concede the point because I knew where it led: Nectar was right there in front of me.

Before I answered, she said, *I'm in your corner. Right now.*

"I'm in the fight."

I know you are; it's killing you.

"I know. I'm losing myself." I lowered my head.

She doesn't keep you hydrated.

"I'm so thirsty all the time."

She stroked my head. *I know you are; so thirsty for love.*

"But I'm turning into this shell. THIS FUCKING SHELL!" I screamed in frustration.

Nectar comforted me while adding, *And you can't hear the ocean inside the shell any longer.*

"The ocean is just static."

Break the shell.

"I can't."

You can.

"I CAN'T!" I yelled and pulled away from her touch.

Let your guilt go, Soupy.

She touched on a nerve: guilt. I'd rather die than feel responsible for someone else's death, or the death of someone else's dreams.

She's killed everyone she's ever loved.

"I just don't believe that…yet."

Nectar opened her door, got out, tossed a six-shooter revolver onto the seat beside me, and said, *Then you might as well kill yourself, you're headed there anyway.*

She slammed the door, leaving me in the back of her cab all alone.

Chapter 35

I cringed when Nectar slammed her cab door shut. When I reopened my eyes, I was in the back of my own cab, not hers, and I immediately looked to the seat next to me, but found no gun. A sigh escaped my lips. I slouched in the seat. *What the hell?* My hands washed over my face as if they could scrub off the angst, confusion, and frustration. I counted to four as I exhaled, then counted to four again as I inhaled. Repeat. Repeat. Repeat.

As I regained a degree of calm, the sound of the ocean broke through the bubble of stale, dark air. From the depths of my slouch, I could see that my cab was parked in an alleyway that served as access between the houses for beach goers to reach the sand and water. It was weird to be in the back seat of my own ride, so I pulled the handle on the back door, rolled out onto the pavement, and meandered toward the ocean.

A voice behind me said, *Don't look.*

It was Promise. The door to my cab opened and closed again. I wasn't quite ready to jump back into conversations about my life, so I stared at the ocean a few minutes longer.

"HOOOOOOOOOOOONK!" The car horn scared me enough that I leapt into the air and clutched my chest. I purposefully didn't give her the pleasure of seeing the look on my face. Instead, I stubbornly continued looking at the ocean.

A homeowner leaned out over their balcony and tersely announced, "You can't park there. Don't you see the signs?"

"Yeah, yeah," I said as I waved him off, and turned to get back into the cab.

"I'm serious," he added. "I'll call the cops."

"In my dreams," I said, and waved him off again.

"Asshole cab drivers," he said as he walked back inside.

I see you're in a grand mood, but I am *glad to see you're alive.*

"Alive? What do you mean?"

When last I saw you, we were about to rear-end a tractor-trailer.

"Yeah, that's right, I guess we were. Well, I'm here. The cab's here. All must be well."

It doesn't sound like all is well.

"No, it isn't."

Why?

"I can't figure any of this out."

Do you still believe?

"Believe in what?"

If you have to ask that question, it doesn't bode well for the answer.

"Oh, believe in us, in true love, or whatever?"

Yes, Soup, in whatever. Disappointment was obvious in her words.

It also came across in my response, "I don't know."

A voice next to the cab yelled, "WHERE THE HELL HAVE YOU BEEN?!" I turned to it immediately recognizing at once that Soupy was yelling at Possibly. I hadn't recognized that we were parked next to the beach house I'd once rented with friends and family.

"Oh, great," I said to Promise. "We'd survived the plane ride home, spent some time apart and started a new routine far too similar to the one I'd experienced with Gravity: apart a few days, together a few days, apart a few days, together—"

I get it, but what's happening here?

"Possibly was supposed to join us for dinner but she went totally M.I.A. She didn't return phone calls or texts. I finally sent my friends off to dinner without me and said I'd meet them if she showed up."

Obviously, you didn't make it.

"No, and her excuse was the real killer. She was with a friend of her ex-boyfriend; someone she'd said to me many times before had made passes at her."

Does everyone make a pass at her?

"So it seems."

Was that true in reality or did she just think it was true?

"I never found out."

"That night she told me she'd ended up in bed with him, but stopped things before they actually had sex. It was a night that made me rewind all the other conversations we'd had about 'men' in her life and look at them with a completely different set of glasses."

What do you mean?

"I mean I'd never known her to say 'no' before."

If she did say no, might it have been an example of progress?

"You know, I would have been the first to believe that, or at least want to believe it, but the cover up around the whole thing was just too much. It reeked of lies. Her eyes darted everywhere and she fidgeted incessantly. She had pushed my trust to the limit. If she was going to be part of my life, she needed to spend time with the people I cared about. She *knew* about this night far in advance, and *still* put herself in a position to let some other guy fuck her. I was pissed."

Promise remained silent so as not to fan my flame.

"When Possibly saw how much she hurt me, she became very apologetic."

Of course she did.

"What do you mean?"

After all of this you still don't see it?

"See what?"

SHE'S NOT ME!

"NO SHIT!" I yelled. "Why do you keep reminding me of the same damn things over and over again? WHY? Do you ever think what you told me—this fucking fail-over-and-over-so-I-can-find-you crap—might not mean to fail with different women, but maybe to FAIL WITH THE SAME ONE? Maybe the greatest challenge I've ever encountered in my life—LOOK! LOOK AT THEM!—was meant to yield the greatest reward, too? DON'T YOU EVER THINK ABOUT THAT?!"

No.

"WELL MAYBE YOU SHOULD! 'CAUSE YOU MIGHT GET UP OFF MY ASS ABOUT HER NOT BEING YOU!"

It was silent for quite some time in the cab as we listened to the argument between Soupy and Possibly. At the end of the conversation, Possibly said, "I just don't love you like you love me."

Soupy looked at her and immediately knew his answer. "You've worked very hard to make that painfully obvious."

She glared at him.

He continued, "I think it's time for you to leave." He no longer had any interest in having her around family and friends. He walked away, grabbed a beer from the fridge and relocated to the porch to listen to the waves.

Promise said, *I'm sorry.*

I shrugged her off.

Soupy finished his beer and then, unprovoked, threw it against the beach wall smashing it to pieces. He walked inside the house and out of view, but I knew he poured himself a shot of tequila, pounded it, grabbed another beer, and went to bed.

"Fuck her," I said. "I didn't know where she went when I told her to leave, and at the time I really didn't care. I walked up to my bed and laid there in the dark." I paused for a moment, and then felt all those worries from that night come back to the surface. "Unfortunately, that was when the scary questions about her started creeping in. Where did she go? Who was she fucking now? Was she in a closet somewhere with a candle and a gun? Knowing and setting her schedule was how we tried to keep the dark out of her life, but I'd just severed the line that attached the boat to the anchor; she was free to float away and who knew where the tide and wind would take her."

Someplace dark?

"Yeah, you know the voice in your head that tells you to do bad shit?"

Yes.

"I'd just come to believe that hers was really loud."

So you started feeling guilty?

"You know me! What if I rejected her and she did something terrible to herself?"

It wouldn't be your fault.

"When the alternative could have been to let her stay, how can you say that?"

Have some self-respect, Soup. She treated you terribly and you stood up for yourself.

"It wasn't that easy, Promise. I never could shake the feeling that I was the only one looking out for her."

SHE made you feel that. Why would you want *to be her parent anyway?*

Her question silenced me; of course I didn't want to be her parent. She knew it. I knew it, but didn't want to admit it. Instead, I said, "I drank until my friends and family returned from dinner, told them the story as they shook their heads—obviously, they'd had enough Possibly Stories over the time we'd been dating—and finally crawled back upstairs to pass out in bed. When I woke the next morning, I knew what I had to do that day: talk with Possibly's mom. She was the only one I could speak with who knew enough about Possibly's past to help me make sense of her actions."

Could anyone make sense of her actions?

"You know what I mean."

A rare west coast thunderstorm rolled in over the beach and unleashed rain as I reversed out of the alley and drove away from the beach.

"The longer the day went on, the more I worried about her. Everyone had left town, and I was alone in my own home, curled up on the floor and shivering. In one hand I held a phone, the other hand was limp on the floor. I was strung-out on love, about to make a call to my dealer, Possibly. I just wanted to know if she was alive—*needed* to know if she was alive—but had to do so without allowing my compassion to let her off the hook for her behavior."

We've definitely seen you do that before.

"Yes, but Promise, I couldn't live with the chance—a chance that felt more real by the hour—that no one would ever hear her voice again."

Did you ever wonder whether those odds were greater in your head than in anyone else's?

"I'd known her for only a few years of her life, the last three to be more exact. There was a quarter-century of her life that was only a story to me, and I'd not had nearly enough time with her mom to determine what was real and what wasn't—shit, I had no idea how much of her story even *she* remembered.

I know, Soupy. I'm just making sure you see the other side of the odds.

We were heading toward Possibly's house. I fast-forwarded across the distance to get there in a few seconds, just as Soupy was walking to her front door. *You didn't?*

I nodded my head in affirmation.

Possibly opened the door as if she expected him. "I need to talk to you about something," she said and turned away without a hug or kiss. Soupy stepped into the house and closed the door behind him.

I created a video screen on her garage so Promise and I could watch.

"I was spent, Promise, but I would still get dizzy around her—because of the possibility of her—there's not a moment when I didn't light up when she entered the space around me. Even in the moment when she skipped out on dinner, I felt relief and my heart leapt when I finally saw her arrive...alive."

We'll have to talk about whether that's a good thing at some point.

"Yeah, I suppose it can really screw up my ability to think straight, but come on, who wouldn't want to light up when love enters the room?"

We can certainly debate whether this is love.

"Fine. I just wanted so badly to believe Possibly and I would succeed at some point. We *had* to. This endless falling simply couldn't go on forever."

Define forever.

"I know. How long is too long? I don't know. I just know that in this moment my mind raced between topics of pregnancy, drugs, guns, rape—we'd already been through it all, what else was there? I wanted *this* conversation to be the inflection point for us. We'd finally bottomed out. The sun would rise again."

And?

* * *

Possibly wore a short, white robe as she lit candles around the room and poured Soupy a glass of wine from the bottle she'd already opened. As she joined him on the couch, she pulled her wet hair from the small ponytail she'd tied. Soupy sipped his wine to distract himself from her presence; her body, fresh and clean, strongly drew him toward her, but she was sitting farther from him than she normally would. He knew, however, that if they were to have any semblance of serious conversation, she'd have to be out of his reach so he could discuss instead of desire.

* * *

I said to Promise, "I still believed in true love, that it could come from anywhere, even from the darkness that had tied Possibly's head into knots. Even after all we had been through, we could do this."

Promise didn't reply.

* * *

"I didn't expect it to happen," Possibly said, "but I've been seeing someone else."

Soupy's grip on his wine glass tightened. "You…what?" he said as his eyes closed and his face reddened.

Possibly took a long sip from her wine glass trying to think of what to say next. "I didn't expect—"

Soupy held up the index finger of his free hand and interrupted her, "I heard that part." With his eyes still closed, he was trying desperately to process this outcome that he hadn't seen coming. "How long?"

She looked down into her glass and admitted, "A few weeks."

"The guy from last night? No, I don't care." He breathed deeply trying to balance the anger and the…*emptiness* that came from the thought that she'd no longer be in his life. "Why am I here?" he whispered still with his eyes closed in an attempt to more easily see the right path.

She answered his question even though it wasn't intended for her. "You're the only friend I have here. I need you. And no, it wasn't the guy from last night."

Though he hadn't found the right path, he took the one that begged to be taken. Soupy sternly said, "You *know* I can't be your friend. That will *never* work for me. I've done everything I can to make you happy—to *keep you alive*—and you're off fucking someone else?" At this point, he stared at her waiting for an answer. No answer came. Soupy set his wineglass down on the end table, stood up, ran his hands over his face, and sighed. He grabbed his hair and pulled out the scream that had been building deep down in his now-volcanic core. *Where's the gun? And the candle and the closet?* In his head, Soupy imagined the scene like the prologue to a game of *Clue*, *Ms. Possibly in the closet with a candle and a gun.* "No," he whispered, and shook those dark thoughts from his head.

"He doesn't know me like you do," she added.

"Doesn't know you? Doesn't *know* you?" Soup turned to look at her and added, "No shit, Dick Tracy. I don't even know *you*!"

Possibly parried his anger by pursing her lips angrily before realizing that the moment wasn't right to counter anger with anger. "I've just been so confused," she said, and turned once more to the doe-eyed, innocent role she knew so well.

Soupy couldn't look at her. Instead, he stared at the mirror over the couch and saw his own tired face looking back at him. *What the fuck am I supposed to do now?* he thought. *Leave,* came the reply. *I can't,* he answered inside his own head. He imagined taking the first step toward the door, saw himself leaving it open behind him, not knowing whether she'd beg him to stay, just putting right and left footsteps together until he reached his car, departed, and found some breathable air again.

She broke the silence. "Will you stay?" she asked, tracing a line down her exposed inner thigh.

Soupy closed his eyes and walked to the bedroom knowing she would follow.

* * *

Promise asked, *What the hell are you doing?*

"I'm not sure I knew, but sex had been the language we'd spoken for a year and a half. We didn't know each other in the bedroom like I'd gotten to know other women—and, given her past, that may not even have been possible—but we communicated there better than we did on the couch."

So she tells you she's fucking someone else, after you got pissed that she was fucking—or almost fucked someone else—and you decide to screw her anyway?

"I admit, I never knew I'd be watching myself make that decision again someday, let alone here with you. It wasn't a selfish act. It wasn't an 'If I'm going out then I'm going out with a bang,' course of action. It was a last ditch effort to show her that I was the only man for her; that I could give her everything she desired and take her places she never knew she could go. Like, a last chance to bounce off the bottom and float through the clouds for the rest of our lives."

Last chance? I'd say your chances ran out long ago.

"It's easy to say that now, sure."

Did you not just watch all these scenes I've watched?

"Yes, I've watched. I've watched, Promise." With a sigh, I added, "I don't even know if I can explain anymore. That night, I didn't want to hear her talk anymore. I knew whatever story she would tell me about whatever had happened, it was a story I'd heard too many times already. And I didn't want to hear her beg me to stay, or use my words against me."

Because you were the one always saying that leaving means the conversation is over.

"If you want to talk, don't leave."

You couldn't leave.

"I promised I wouldn't."

Soupy stripped off his clothes as he walked from the living room down the hallway to the bedroom. As if drawn to the act, Possibly simply set down her wine glass, got up from the couch, and followed him. Her robe dropped to the floor as she crossed from the hallway into her bedroom.

Soup, Promise said, sternly and unhappily.

I knew Promise didn't want to see this so I shrugged and wiped my hand across the face of the video to move them to the next morning.

* * *

A light filled the room, evidence of a sun trying to rise, but still far from peeking over the horizon. Possibly and Soupy each had one leg uncovered on opposite sides of the bed. All the bedding but a single sheet had been thrown to the floor, evidence of the night's antics. A phone was ringing in the living room. Possibly leapt out of bed to answer it. Soupy groggily opened his eyes as he heard her answer; the first words she'd calmly spoken since they left the couch.

"You're on TV?" Possibly asked as she picked up her robe, leaned into her bedroom, and held her finger to her lips telling Soupy to be quiet. "Really? Okay, I'm turning on the TV now."

He crawled out of bed and grabbed his boxer briefs as he walked into the living room. Possibly repeated her motion for him to be quiet and then pointed to the television. Soupy pulled on his underwear as he watched.

"'The TODAY Show?' Okay. Oh-my-gosh! There you are! Hi, sweetie!" She got up from the couch and kneeled in front of the TV. Soupy looked around the room, scratched his head, and then sat down on the couch. He reached over to his glass of wine from the night before, sniffed it, tasted it, and grimaced after he took a big gulp from it.

Some guy was waving at Possibly through the television as he stood outside *The TODAY Show*'s studios.

"I'm waving back!" she said, excitedly.

Enough of this crap, Soupy thought, and got up from the couch to kneel down behind her. He pulled her hair back from her neck and kissed it softly. She pulled away from him and shot him an annoyed look. He redoubled his effort and ran his hands over the silky smooth robe on her back, she shrugged at first but eventually relaxed her shoulders. She was still talking on the phone, but Soupy wasn't hearing anything she said. He closed his eyes as he lightly expanded his touch from her back to her arms, over her shoulders, down her spine, and around her upper buttocks to her hips. She relaxed back into him. He focused his thoughts on what he was going to do to her; envisioned these actions crossing the inches between his head and hers. And as if naturally, his thoughts turned dark: *You must hurt her.* Soupy slowly nodded his head in acceptance. As he did, Possibly moved from her knees to a more natural seated position and leaned back into Soupy's chest. His legs straddled her body. She leaned her head back onto Soupy's shoulder while she spoke on the phone, and parted her legs to give him the nonverbal green light to touch her there. Soupy's hands inched their way toward her, teasing her with his touch until she pushed her hips up into his waiting hand. She accidentally let out a moan and clamped her free hand to her mouth as Soupy guided his fingers over her sex, the audible escape prompted her to open her eyes and seek an exit to the verbal exchange she was having with the guy who'd been on the television. The more firmly Soupy touched her, the more her body responded. She pulled his hand away, stood up, and motioned for him to sit on the couch. He obliged, pulling off his underwear in the process to reveal his own readiness. Possibly mumbled some affirmation to the guy on the phone as she undid the belt of her robe, walked over to Soupy and straddled him. As she guided herself down on top of him she held her hands over the phone to mask the gasp they both released. He pushed the sides of her robe aside and placed his hands on her hips while burying his face into her breasts. Possibly grabbed a handful of Soupy's hair to urge him on, and finally said her goodbye and tossed the phone toward the other end of the couch.

"You're bad," she said as she worked her hips into his.

"You like it," he replied as he looked up from her breasts.

"You're right. I do."

The dark voice in Soup's head returned, *You must hurt her.* He nodded his head unknowingly and grabbed a handful of her ass in each hand. She moaned and grabbed the back of the couch for leverage.

Say the worst thing you can possibly think of, the voice said. *Do it now.* Soupy was drunk from the motion that he and Possibly had found: rhythmic and forced. The sound of their bodies meeting each other pushed them to drive harder. *Say it.* Soupy ran his hand up her back, grabbed her by the hair, and pulled backwards. Possibly yelped in pleasure and then laughed. He then pushed the back of her head toward him and whispered in her ear between breaths, "Fuck me...you whore."

Possibly's eyes opened wide and she ceased grinding. With her hands against his chest she pushed away from him, turned, and walked down the hall to the bathroom. Soupy lowered his head to his chest. He didn't say anything as she left. He'd hit her as hard as he could with four simple words. And now, the unexpected counterpunch came not from her, but from the realization of what he'd done. It was impossible to fight off the guilty tears that welled up in his eyes.

Possibly opened the bathroom door and walked out fully clothed. She picked up Soupy's clothes that lay strewn about the hallway and threw them at him one at a time. "I. Can't. Believe. You. Would. CALL! ME! THAT!" she screamed between each throw.

* * *

I said to Promise, "I wanted to tell her I was sorry. I wanted to take it all back, maybe more than just those four words…maybe several months of words…that the voice in my head had pushed me to say such a thing…*that* she might understand…because she had the *same* voice in her head."

* * *

Soupy's guilt and confusion returned to anger. *Twist the dagger.* "You're fucking that guy on the television *and* fucking me. You're even FUCKING ME WHEN HE'S ON THE TV!" Soupy yelled as he pointed to the television where Possibly's boyfriend had been replaced by a celebrity interview. "HELL, YOU'D PROBABLY EVEN FUCK THAT GUY, TOO!"

Possibly walked over and slapped Soupy across the face. "GET THE FUCK OUT OF MY HOUSE!" she screamed.

He felt the dark voice careen away once her palm connected with his face, and his confusion returned. Suddenly, Soupy hardly knew where he was. Tears rained down his cheeks as he moved from the couch to the carpet. He pulled his knees to his chest and lost control of his building sorrow. "I'm sorry," he said, and kept repeating it inaudibly.

Possibly stomped down the hallway, paused with her bedroom door in hand ready to slam it, but instead turned back.

Soupy whimpered, "I…don't…want…to…lose…you. I never…wanted…to…lose you."

She walked back to him, ran her hand over his head, gently turned it so he would look at her, and said between clenched teeth, "Get. Out."

He saw her resolve. He *felt* her resolve. "I'm sorry," he said as he rolled away from her, gathered his clothes, and walked toward the door. He pulled on his shirt with no intent to look back.

And, as was often the case in their history, just as he hardened she softened. As he walked away, she said, "Soupy." She waited for him to turn back toward her. "I'm sorry," she said with sincerity.

* * *

"The image of her standing there with her arms crossed over her chest will be forever seared into my brain. Why? After everything else, she gave me the strength to forgive myself."

You hit her pretty hard given her sexually abusive history, Soup.

"I know; it was terrible."

But necessary.

"Perhaps. It was like she had a job to do—her dark voice had to teach me how to find mine—and the job was done."

Really? I don't see that at all. The way I see it, despite all the negative things that happened between you, it was in this final instant that she became the woman you both wanted her to be: compassionate, understanding, and real.

"I never saw it that way, Promise."

Do you now?

"No."

Why not?

"I haven't forgiven her. Even now, when I see her my heart leaps."

Where the hell does that come from?

"My heart?"

I sure hope so. I mean, I hope it comes from a good place and not a dark one.

"That's what it feels like, but—"

They can feel so similar.

"Yeah."

But that's why we're here, Soup. Look, her words gave you hope, not that you'd someday try again, but that she'd someday become the good woman buried deep inside of her. That's what you need to realize now.

"Okay," I replied.

There's something else we need to talk about.

"What's that?"

Who was that person? Where did you find those words? And how did you know exactly what would hurt her the most?

"Like she said, I knew her better than anyone else."

Promise grumbled as if she didn't accept that answer.

"They were just…there," I added. "You don't know what I mean?"

I don't think that's a good enough answer.

"Promise, it's all I've got right now."

We drove back to my house in silence, both thinking about what had happened.

I said, "I didn't sleep well that night, as I'm sure you can imagine."

If what we've seen so far is actually the true you, then we all know your guilt is going to kick your ass.

"Letting go is never easy, Promise."

That's true, for you.

"I needed to accept that I didn't want a life with Possibly any longer, didn't want to keep trying to save her. I knew I needed to call her mom. If Possibly and I were truly over, I needed to say goodbye and thank her for all the support she'd provided."

* * *

Possibly's mom's voice said hello over the cab's radio.

Soupy said, "I'm sorry to call you, but I don't know what else to do."

"You know you can always call me, Soup."

"Thanks," he replied, followed by a sniffle.

She said, "Tell me what's going on. I can hear the struggle in your voice, and given my daughter's past, it's worrying me."

"It's not her, it's me. I think it's over." Soupy began to cry, but he was resisting as much as he could. "I can't…I just can't take it if it's not."

"Believe me, I understand."

"I don't know what to do…and I can't fix it."

"No one can fix it but her, Soup. It's not your job."

"Nothing works. I can't love her enough for both of us. I just can't…and… what do I do? I don't know what—"

"Go ahead and let it all out," she said. "You don't have to explain it to me, I know what it's like. I've been here before and I know how hard it is. Let it all out. I'm right here."

Weep holes turned to leaks. Leaks turned to cracks. Cracks allowed the dam to finally crumble. He wept openly and severely while Possibly's mom listened. He managed to keep the phone to his ear as he fought for breath between waves of sorrow, and her mom kept repeating, "I know. It'll be okay. I know. It'll be okay."

* * *

Thunder rocked the cab and rain came down so hard Promise and I could no longer see more than a few yards.

* * *

Soupy finally gathered himself enough to speak. "I'm so sorry. I didn't call you to cry into the phone. I—"

"No, it's okay," she interrupted. "You needed it."

"I did," I laughed, a defense mechanism.

"Look, Soup, I know this struggle between the two of you has been incredibly difficult. I've seen it before. It wears out everyone but her. You've been so valiant; I admire the fight in you. My daughter—love her with all my heart—but she's a long way from healthy." She paused. "I want you to listen to me. I want you to hear me when I say this: leave her. If that's what you need to do for yourself, then do it. I'll understand—we'll all understand—we've seen everything you've tried to do for her and we thank you."

"I—," Soupy started but really had no idea what he wanted to say.

"We'll understand if you leave. We'll miss you, but we'll understand."

"You will?" Soupy asked between sniffles.

"Oh, Soup, yes, of course we will."

For the first time in a long time, he felt less alone, like a hand reached down into the dark hole he dug for himself to help pull him out.

She continued, "I've worried about you *because* you've tried so hard. I worry that you'll either go down with her or she'll leave you on the side of the road when she's done with you. I don't want either of those for you. You can't kill yourself trying, Soup, and now that I know you better—now that I've seen how loyal you've been to her healing cause—she *will* kill you if you don't leave."

* * *

The rain stopped and a ray of sunlight pushed through the clouds.

* * *

"Thank you," Soupy said. "You've always been so good at making me feel better."

"I've been at it for a long time," she said and chuckled. "Believe me, I try to find a solution for her every day, but we all need to understand that *we* can't fix her, she can only do that for herself. And maybe—I hesitate to say this because I know what loneliness can do to her—but maybe being alone for a while is the real therapy she needs. But that's not for us to decide. Soup, you can go on with your life."

* * *

"It was on the tip of my tongue to tell her mom that Possibly *wasn't* alone, but I realized it wouldn't do the conversation any good. Her mom would discover that on her own; I needed this conversation to be about her and I, not about Possibly and the guy on TV. There was nothing left for me to say but thank you, not just for the last few minutes, but for every moment she'd been there for me."

It was what you needed, so I'm glad you got it. Maybe what she needed, too. Her mom let you out of your promise. I'd like to thank her, as well.

I turned on the cab's engine and backed us out of the alleyway. "I took Possibly's mom's advice and left town. As it turned out, Grandpa Heller's health deteriorated at the same time my relationship with Possibly ended. I wanted to get home before he passed away."

Since we were still sitting outside of Possibly's house despite a few days having passed, we watched as Soupy considered leaving a note in her mailbox.

No, don't.

"I wrote it. It said, 'Possibly, I'm leaving town and I don't know when I'll be back. ~Soup.'"

Why the hell did you think you owed her that?

"Guilt? I don't know, but it's a damn good question, Promise." It was a question that stung, and I truly had no idea. Maybe I thought it might hurt her to know I was gone. Maybe I still had such deep belief that we could solve the puzzle. I don't know. Ultimately, I drove off without leaving the note. If there was anything fortunate about my Grandpa's deteriorated health it was that I had no choice but to leave. I'd been sitting around my condo on pins and needles waiting for the doorbell to ring; hard to overcome the way Possibly had conditioned me, I suppose. When I drove away from her place, it was pedal to the metal heading east."

This process with Promise had proven to be emotionally exhausting. I realized the potential benefit, but these memories were hitting me just as hard the second time around, and sometimes even harder as I began to see them through someone else's eyes.

"Promise, I'm sorry to ask this of you again, but I need to make this drive on my own. There are a lot of things I need to work out, not too dissimilar from back then, really. Can I drop you somewhere?"

Soup, I think—

I wasn't having it any other way. "No, Promise, I'll see you on the other side of the drive."

But Soup—

"PROMISE! PLEASE!" I gathered my patience before I repeated, "Please."

No need to drop me. I'll just go.

And she was gone.

Chapter 36

The mid-afternoon departure meant the sun was behind me as I followed Soupy's car east. It was an important day, meaning the sun was setting on a lot more than just another day, it set on a day that felt marked with freedom for the first time in months. Soup cranked up the music to keep him from dwelling on the distance he was putting between himself and Possibly, and I did the same. However, as the sun dropped below the horizon we both began to feel the weight of Possibly's chase—some mystical fucking force had given her the idea to reach out. Soupy's cell phone had several messages and texts from her; all of them had gone unanswered.

On the road I can think. Even more so once the light has turned to night; just me, my mind, and the lines that set the boundaries of the road.

Possibly was angry. I knew by the number of times she'd tried to reach me. The fact that I hadn't yet answered had only angered her more. I visualized her leaned up on the wheel of her car, accelerator mashed to the floorboard, brow furrowed into an angry "V," driving like a madwoman trying to track me down. I added another ten miles per hour to my own speed just picturing it, and with it came more energy for driving away from her.

A few miles down the road, I crested a hill and saw a plethora of flashing lights across the road, definitely a major accident. Soupy and I both slowed to witness the aftermath of a head-on train collision. "Damn, Possibly," I said aloud, wondering if she might have had some metaphysical influence on this event purely to slow me down. It was certainly an accurate depiction of the collisions taking place in my life, both then and now. Cars were stacked up on both sides of the track in a zigzag pattern spanning nearly a mile from the end of one train to the end of the other. When I got past the emergency vehicles, I punched the gas; no officers would be shooting radar for miles with that commotion behind me, so I could really put some distance between Possibly and me. But another few miles down the road I came upon a mandatory stop; an immigration checkpoint in the middle of the freeway. "Damn it," I said aloud. "Enough with the delays."

Soupy stopped at the guard shack. I heard him speaking with the officer over the cab's radio.

He asked, "Are you an American citizen?"

"Yes, sir," Soupy replied.

"I see," he said, then looked over the car from his perch, including a squat to see if there was anyone in the back seat.

"Have a good night," the officer said and waved him on.

Soupy's brake lights released and off he went. I pulled up to the shack expecting the same question.

"Are you an American citizen?"

"Yes, sir," I replied.

"I see," he said, and then looked over my cab from his perch, including a squat to see if there was anyone in the back seat. "Can I see your identification?"

"Yessir," I replied melding the words together this time, and reached into my back pocket to retrieve it.

"WHOA THERE!" he yelled, taking a few steps back and reaching for the handle of his gun.

I froze. "Just reaching for my I.D.," I said.

"Slowly."

I saw Soupy's lights disappear over the next grade in the road. Anxiety set in immediately.

With my I.D. in hand, the officer said, "Don't get too many cars out this way, and two back-to-back, well, that's just atypical. You know that guy?" he said as he pointed up the road.

"No, sir," I replied.

He stared at me over the top of my I.D. "Well, you sure look a lot alike."

I didn't reply, though he waited for me to do so. After a few seconds, he reached over to his desk and pulled out an 8"x10" headshot of Possibly. I tried desperately to hide the surprise on my face. "You know this girl?" he asked.

I squinted as if I couldn't make out the photo, so he pushed it a few inches closer. "Can't say that I do," I answered, "but she's beautiful, sir."

He smiled and replied, "Yeah, she is, isn't she? You probably wish you knew her, huh?" It stung me, but for him it was a brief moment of levity before his serious nature returned. "Where you headed?"

"Mid-west, sir," I said.

"You've got a long ways to go then, don'tcha?"

"Sure do, sir."

He handed my I.D. back and then said, "Drive safely, it's pretty dark out there."

"Will do, sir, you do the same—have a good night, I mean."

He tipped his hat and I left the shack. As soon as I was over the grade in the road, I pressed the car up over one hundred miles per hour in an attempt to catch up to Soup as quickly as I could.

I wasn't a fan of that little 8"x10" twist in my dream, so I blinked and caught up to Soupy's back bumper. With another blink, we crested a mountain and saw the beautiful nighttime glow of a large city. A third blink and the sun broke through the night on the eastern horizon to give us both the unexpected energy to continue. For me, it hadn't been too long, but Soupy had been driving for more than fifteen hours straight, aside from stopping briefly to get gas. The sunlight not only gave him the strength to continue driving, but renewed strength to resist Possibly's calls. She'd been unrelenting during the night, but he'd still not listened to a voicemail or read one single text she'd sent. In twenty-four hours, Soup had covered more than twelve hundred miles without being tempted by sleep. It wasn't originally his plan to make a kamikaze run from the coast to the Midwest; just sort of worked out that way.

Soupy ducked off the highway, and I nearly missed the turn to follow him as I was so deep into my own thoughts. We pulled into a gas station, the only two cars there. As Soup got out to pump gas I heard a payphone ringing in the near distance. The attendant moved to answer it, but I willed him not to do so. *Possibly.* He picked up the phone, looked around, and then shouted at us, "You Soupy?"

I shook my head and mouthed the word "no" to Soup. He was tired enough that I thought he might slip and nod his head in the affirmative, but he didn't even look away from the gas pump. It was then that I realized the attendant was looking at me, not him, so I shook my head back and forth. The attendant turned back to the phone, said a few words, and hung it up. As he walked back inside he gave Soup a friendly wave that he weakly returned. Possibly was on a mission to find me, even more so this time than the last.

After he'd filled up the tank, he only drove a short distance to a nearby park. He'd been driving long enough, and he felt far enough away from Possibly to see what the hell she wanted.

I listened in on the radio.

* * *

"WHERE ARE YOU?" she screamed as soon as she answered the phone.

He resisted the urge to simply hang up. Instead, he replied, "Screaming at me isn't going to get you any answers." She surprisingly found resistance and opted for silence until Soupy continued. "My grandpa is dying."

"You haven't answered any of my calls or texts since *yesterday*," she said.

"I'll say it again because maybe you didn't hear me, MY GRANDPA IS DYING."

"Why haven't you called me back? I'm all alone here and I'm—"

"Possibly."

"—not feeling right—"

"POSSIBLY!" he yelled to get her attention.

"WHAT?!" she screamed back.

"Whatever is going on with you isn't important to me right now. You're just gonna have to deal with it on your own. I'm twenty-four hours into a drive that I never intended to be nonstop; it just worked out that way. I'm headed toward a dying family member who isn't going to be with me much longer. That beats whatever you have going on in your head. And frankly, I'm too tired to deal with your shit. *And*, and it's a big 'and,' you have someone else for this now."

She was silent on the other end of the line.

Soupy continued, "Okay, then I'm just gonna go. Don't call me eight billion times. I'm busy driving and I don't need the distraction."

"NO! SOUP, I—"

Soupy closed his cell phone and then looked into the sky through his car's moonroof. It wasn't easy to tell her those things, but being tired made it easier to care less. He waited for her to call him back, but oddly she didn't.

Soup drove back onto the highway and I followed, but we didn't get very far before drowsiness set in. The phone call had taken a lot out of him, even as short as it was. We pulled off at a rest stop and parked under a big oak tree, its branches leaning out over the parking area. He released the seat back and tried to snare a few minutes of rest. I opted to do the same.

Chapter 37

A breeze blew across the plains through my rolled down windows. It was stiff enough to rustle the hair on my head and wake me from my nap. Groggily, I wiped my eyes with my fists. It was then that I heard Great Grandpa's soft voice, "Hello, my grandson."

I sat up straight, surprised, and shouted, "GRANDPA!"

He smiled, but held his index finger to his mouth to remind me that Soupy was sleeping in the other car, and then motioned for me to join him by the oak tree. I exited the car and followed him until we were both sitting cross-legged on the ground facing each other.

Great Grandpa asked, "How are you?"

"Tired," I admitted.

"You have had a long night. I can understand that."

I nodded my head in affirmation.

"Tell me, Grandson, have you practiced fire?"

"I tried, once, but I couldn't make it work."

"Tell me what happened," he said.

Without going into all the details, I mentioned the glowing Etch-a-Sketch ember that I'd found and how I'd blown on the fire to give it air, but didn't have any fuel. I tried to offer it earth. "Grandpa, I tried to think 'fire' as best I could to give the earth some magical incendiary property that would serve as fuel."

Great Grandpa laughed. "Do not fault yourself too much. First, fire is not at all fond of earth; it extinguishes the flame. Second, and perhaps more importantly, you said you *thought* about fire?"

"Yes, as focused as I could."

"That was your bigger mistake."

"How?" I asked, impatiently.

"The elements don't speak the logical language of your thoughts; they speak the language of your emotions."

I slapped my forehead. "Shit," I said, and then covered my mouth. I was an adult, but censoring myself in front of my elders was a habit hard to break. "You taught me that."

"Yes, I did, but sometimes it takes a few repeated lessons to learn."

"Don't I know it."

He leaned over and placed his palm on my chest. "Remember, you must *feel* fire here."

My chest heated up quickly. I replied, "Yes, Great Grandpa."

"Let us have another lesson," he stated.

Excitedly, I straightened up in my seated position, rocking back and forth a bit to get more grounded, and prepared to learn.

"Fire needs air and fuel, that much you already know."

I nodded my head.

Great Grandpa looked around and collected a few leaves that had fallen from the oak tree. "Find fuel," he said, and motioned for me to do the same, so I collected some leaves, too. He pinned the leaves in his open palm and then held it out in front of me. He placed his other hand over his heart. "This is advanced for you, Grandson, but I will first make fire and then you can speak with the fire I have made." He took a deep breath. His chest caved inward and then bulged outward as he did so. The leaves in his hand sparked into flame and burned very slowly. He nodded for me to proceed.

I pinned the leaves on my palm and held it close to his. With my other hand over my heart, I let my thoughts go and let my heart bulge with warmth. "Fire, I offer you these leaves that wish to burn and evolve." Like the circular burn from a cigarette, a hole burned in the top leaf, the flame barely visible. Grandpa blew on the spark and it replicated his inch-sized flame.

"Good, but needs practice," he said as he winked. "You have learned to burn. Now, you must know how to blow. What does the wind need?"

I thought about it, but couldn't come up with a great answer. "To blow?" I asked instead of answered.

"Obvious answer, Grandson, but not up to your standard," he said. "Stop thinking."

The wind increased, whistling across my ears and rustling the remaining leaves in the trees. I closed my eyes and listened, hoping that my other senses would enhance themselves. I heard a branch of the oak tree creak, a wind chime rattled in the distance, and a discarded paper coffee cup blew across the parking lot. "The wind," I started, "wants to speak."

"Very close and very good. You almost have it. The wind, itself, has no voice, therefore it can't speak, which is why it so desperately wants to be heard."

I repeated for memory, "The wind wants to be heard."

"Yes," Great Grandpa affirmed. "Now, open your eyes and watch," he added.

I watched as he inhaled while pulling his hand away from his heart and out to his side. As he exhaled, he swept his hand in the direction he wanted the wind to blow, ending his motion with his hand once more on his heart. The wind increased ever so slightly to fuel the burning leaves until they quickly lifted into the air and crackled as they burned away. "Good journey, dearest leaves," he said.

I knew it was my turn to try. I mimicked his motions by sweeping my hand straight out to my side and bringing it back in. "Wind," I said, "I offer you this spark." As I did so a memory blasted into my head of darting from a parked car to a culvert as a tornado roared overhead. Wind, eager to fan the flame, gusted so hard it whipped Great Grandpa's hair across his face, snatched the top leaf from my hand, and spun it into a miniature, swirling firestorm that, fortunately, burned quickly away.

"Shhh," Great Grandpa whispered as he made a calming gesture with his hands. He put more leaves into my hand and held his palm over them. Once more, he produced a small flame. "Wind wants to blow and be heard," he whispered. "It blows for good or bad. When it blows for good it powers the weather vane, fills the sails, or cools the warmth of the day. When it blows for bad it destroys: tornadoes, firestorms, hurricanes. Wind itself is neither good nor bad, it only takes what it is given. You know exactly what you will get from wind, but you must tell wind what you are going to give it and what you expect from it in return, just like fire."

I felt the heat in my hand and used it as a starting point to converse once more with wind. My hand repeated the pattern as I said, "Wind, I offer you this spark and these leaves so that they may sing your song." As my hand returned to my chest, I felt the love from a woman, who I imagined as Promise, intimately blowing into my ear and whispering her love for me. I let her breath blow past my ear, taking only a small piece of it to my heart as I let the rest take flight on the wind so the world could share in the sound of true love. The hair on my skin tingled and displayed my emotion by revealing hundreds of goosebumps. *I wish these words on the wind a good journey*, I thought. I didn't open my eyes because I could feel the increased heat in my palm and envision the evolution of the leaves as they burned and returned to the sky, where they would join the clouds, become rain, nourish the trees, and be born again.

Great Grandpa clapped slowly and quietly, which prompted me to open my eyes and smile at the absence of leaves in my hand. "Thank you, wind. Thank you, fire," I said.

He gripped my hand and motioned his head upward. We pulled each other out of our seated positions simultaneously and stood under the oak tree, a breeze happily blowing around us. Great Grandpa pulled me into an embrace and whispered into my ear, "You have gained some energy from the elements. Ask for more from the tree if you need it. You must hurry home, for there is not much time left and there is still so much for you to learn."

"Yes, Great Grandpa," I said as I patted him on the back. The sound of Soupy's car starting broke our embrace and I turned to see him signaling to reenter the highway.

"Go," Great Grandpa said. "Good journey, my grandson."

"Thank you," I replied as I hurried to the car, got inside, and followed Soupy down the highway.

Chapter 38

All told, Soupy made the trek home, driving practically non-stop, in twenty-eight hours. It wasn't his intent to tackle the distance in one fell swoop, but as he grew closer to home he felt a greater need to get there.

He was bedraggled and on fumes when he stumbled into the hospital. As soon as he arrived, he was told that Grandpa Heller had been calling for him. I remember sitting down next to his bed. He grabbed my hand with his dying strength and whispered that he wanted everyone else to leave the room.

* * *

When they were gone, he said, "Soup, it's supposed to be you."

"Me?"

"Yes, after your grandmother died, I did what I could to be a good Catholic by volunteering my time to those who needed it. I had to help the world heal for the greater good."

I squeezed his hand to show my admiration.

Though he didn't have much strength, he weakly chuckled before he added, "Your grandmother wouldn't let me into heaven if I didn't do some good before I died."

"You've told me that many times," I said, and laughed for him. Laughter was meant to hold off the tears, but it was having quite the opposite effect.

"If the Pearly Gates exist, she'll be standing there next to St. Peter. Even if I don't get in, I'll cherish the opportunity to see her one more time."

"I'm pretty sure she'll have some pull in that regard," I said and squeezed his hand once again, holding it for a longer period this time. I put my other hand on his forearm to signify that I was listening. Though I'd debated with others in my life for decades about the difference between religion and healing, there was no debate to be had at Grandpa's bedside. His true love was God, followed closely by his love for his wife; there was never a question about that. Right now, I could respect that.

"Soup, you must look more deeply into the healing history of this family. I never said anything to you about your choice to pull away from our religious beliefs, that was your grandmother's job."

"She prayed enough for all of us," I added.

"That she did, thank God." He squeezed my hand to show his humorous intent. "But listen, the role of religion in your life, or lack thereof, was purposeful. She *had* to pray for you every day because she knew being a beacon for religion wasn't part of your assignment. Religion plays a role in the pursuit of true love, it helps others understand faith, for one, but it's a different percentage of the whole for each person. We gave you the education you needed to understand our religion, and then allowed you the freedom to apply it as you needed."

I was surprised to hear that my grandparents had been so cognizant of my choices all these years, and so purposeful of not letting on that they understood why I had made them. One of the most grounded memories I have of Grandma is the question she'd ask each time we met, "Have you been going to church?" I always answered in the negative. She'd shake her finger at me and then reply, "I've prayed for you."

Grandpa closed his eyes, which reminded me of the short amount of time we might have together. "Grandpa, where do I look for more history?" I asked.

"Look no further than what you can see inside of yourself," he answered. "Though we haven't been as close as I would have liked, you are the one." Grandpa coughed roughly and seemed temporarily distracted. His eyes looked briefly to the baseball game on the grainy television screen in the hospital room before they closed again.

"Grandpa?" I squeezed his hand to bring him back to the present. "Grandpa, I feel like there's something more you need to tell me."

"Mother?" he asked. It was what he had called his wife.

"Grandpa, stick it out," I pleaded. "Stay with me a little longer."

His eyes refocused and his head turned toward me. "I've wanted to give this to you, but I never knew when the time would be right. Now, the time has to be right." With what life he had left in his frail and deteriorated body, he leaned forward to ask, "How is Honesty?"

"Honesty?" I was confused. The whole family had loved Honesty, but it had been years since we were together. "I'm sure she's fine, but I haven't spoken with her in a long time."

He gulped and shook his head as a sign that he was correcting himself. "Not Honesty...Promise. Have you met Promise?"

As my eyes opened wide in surprise, the bland four walls of his hospital room fell away to reveal a world of colorful clouds. The sun shined on us both as we ascended through the sky; his grip strengthened. His bed was no longer on a yellowed tile floor, but a lush golf tee box. His clubs and shoes awaited him, though oddly not the shoes he wore to play, but the white ones stained green from mowing his lawn, which always sat next to the back door.

He opened his eyes and smiled. I'll never know where he got the strength, but with a great clap of his hands he brought me back to the present. "Find Promise," he said, staring deeply and powerfully into my eyes. His left hand clasped tightly around my right forearm as he raised his hand for our secret handshake. With his remaining strength he executed our four-step shake that ended with a shot from my finger gun. I didn't want to pull the trigger; I knew it was the last time I'd fire at him. He pulled on my forearm, and I knew he was asking for the final blow. His grip gave me the confidence to complete the task. As always, his hand went to his chest and he fell back in his bed.

Even though the room had returned, the smell of freshly-cut grass remained. I sat there for a moment, not wanting to leave his side, not wanting to accept that this was the end, regretting that I'd not spent more time in his company, regretting that I'd always been a bit afraid of this firm-speaking, accomplished man. An emotional geyser sprang up inside of me. I slid my hand back into his grip, lowered my head, and said a few words. Nothing formal, just a few words to thank the spirits that he had been my grandpa. I watched in my mind as his light dimmed, like an old television after you turn it off; the screen faded to one line down the middle of the monitor that quickly shrank to a dot in the middle of the screen before it disappeared.

Suddenly, my body stiffened as if being electrocuted. I felt a shock of information travel from his soul, through his heart, and into my hand. The power of it broke my grip and sent me stumbling across the room. I ran into his untouched dinner and knocked it to the floor. As I leaned up against the doorjamb, my family came rushing into the room. "I'm okay," I said, and leaned my forehead into my hand as the message he transferred filtered its way into my mind. Their attention turned from me to him as they lamented his remaining few breaths. While their backs were turned, I righted myself and erratically walked down the hallway to the stairwell. I kept one hand on the railing and the other on my chest as I descended the few flights to the ground floor. I exploded out of the building gasping for air and let momentum carry me to the nearest tree trunk. I collapsed next to it, leaning my back up against it for support. In the sky, I saw white, billowy clouds screaming past before my eyes rolled back into my head and I fell unconscious.

His download whisked me backward in time, well past my birth, and anyone else's birth for that matter. At the beginning of time, in the Valley of Promise, there came a man to court a woman's family. Before such an act, life consisted merely of thought and action, not of feeling and emotion. He asked for her hand, which he was given, and together they requested a ceremony to announce their love for each other and the new direction the world should take from that day forward. A mere handful of people listened as these two true loves asked them to accept their example as the true way to bring light and goodness to the land. "We are simply your example," the gentleman said. "It is everyone's responsibility to love with truth, and to teach our neighbors and children to do the same. It will not be an easy task; you will fail repeatedly, but you must learn from failure and try again—always try again—until you discover the truth in love. Many of you and those in the generations who follow will lose their way, which makes it ever more important to accept and live with the desire to pursue this goal. Should we someday fail, the darkness will take over. We are the light. We are the beacon that must stay lit so others can find their way should they be brave enough to commit to this journey. Few will succeed, but we cannot accept dismay. We will tell the story of our journeys, whether they are of success or failure, and those stories will serve as lessons for our young and old. Should ever this beacon, this flame of love that lights the way, grow cold, a chosen one will be born into the world and given the specific mission to keep the flame lit. He or she will do this by finding Promise and becoming the example for others to emulate." He closed his speech by calmly saying, "For truth and for love."

My aunt shook me awake. I saw the look of concern on her face before I heard her voice. She mouthed words I couldn't hear, I was still traveling back from the Valley of Promise.

"Soupy," she said. "Are you okay?"

She held her hands on my shoulders to steady me and asked her question again.

"I feel drunk," I said, weakly.

"You look drunk," she said, chuckling. "Where did you go?"

Not quite understanding the question I replied, "Nah, I'm okay. I'm here." And then, I remembered that I'd been in Grandpa Heller's room before I bolted outside. "Is he really gone?" I asked.

"Yes, he is," she said and pulled me in for a long hug.

"I need to eat something," I said.

"I think we can handle that." She helped me up and we headed back into the hospital where we asked for directions to the cafeteria.

"Are you sure you're okay?" she asked again.

"I'm working on it, and…I'll get there." I said, and then added, "It's been a rough night."

Sarcastically, she said, "Rough *night*?" Meaning, she was pretty sure there had been more rough nights than solely the last one.

I chuckled. "Is it that obvious?"

"Duh."

We walked through the cafeteria and I grabbed the easiest thing: chicken noodle soup. After paying at the register, we sat down at a table on the outskirts of the cafeteria.

She started the conversation by asking, "What happened?"

I pointed upward with my finger and replied, "You mean…up there?"

She nodded.

I blew on a spoonful of soup, brought it to my lips, and closed my eyes as the warm liquid coated my throat. "I'm still trying to process it. Grandpa just…told me what he said he always needed to tell me."

"What was it? Do you mind me asking?"

"I don't think I can put it into words, yet. He took me someplace…someplace I'd never been before, and then told me I had to find someone…someone I've never met and haven't seen for a long time."

"Someone you've never met and haven't seen for a long time? You better eat more of that soup so you start making sense."

I smiled, but was then rocked by a strike of lightning in the form of a headache that made my brow crease. "I know. I know. It's a long story, longer than the few minutes I had with Grandpa before he passed."

"You'll have to tell me about it someday."

I nodded and pulled another spoonful from my Styrofoam bowl.

My Aunt leaned across the table, placed her hand on my forearm and said, "Did you *really* drive here without stopping?"

"Pretty much," I replied.

"I always thought you were a little bit crazy, especially after that day on the water. But now I know you *are* crazy," she said, humorously.

When I was a teenager she'd invited me out on the lake to paddle around in a canoe. We swam and conversed, and eventually for no particular reason I can define, I thought it would be a good idea to flip the canoe over. She didn't find it so funny. The memory of that day, fortunately, brought laughter to us both, and in that moment it worked to subvert my headache. Through my smile, I apologized, like I had so many times before, for tipping over the canoe.

She looked over my shoulder and said, "I think someone likes you." I turned to look, but she stopped me quickly, "Don't look."

"Well, then tell me about her."

"Cute, really cute. Eating alone. Can't tell if she works here or if she's visiting someone. Oh, wait. She's coming this way—"

"What?" I said.

I watched my aunt's eyes as she watched the woman approach. Once I saw her smile, I turned in my chair to see her for the first time.

She touched me on the shoulder and said, "I just want to tell you that you have a beautiful smile," she said. For a moment we shared smiles without any further words, and then she turned away and walked out of the cafeteria.

I whispered a "thank you" in her direction, but it fell on ears out of audible reach.

"Soup," my aunt said, "What are you doing? Go talk to her!"

"Nah, it wasn't about that," I replied. "She's not the one I'm supposed to find."

"How do you know?" she asked.

"I just know," I smiled. "She was sent to make me feel better. It's one of those things that just happen in my life."

"See. Crazy. Or Grandma sent her." We both smiled.

"Yeah, maybe Grandma *did* send her before she grabbed Grandpa's hand to lead him away," I replied.

"Let's get back to family," she said.

As I got up from the table, I looked in the direction that the young woman had gone, but she was long gone. She'd done her job, and it worked, too.

* * *

"Holy shit," I said as the story that Grandpa Heller had transferred to me came flooding back into my mind. I'd completely forgotten about the story, like it'd been almost instantly locked in a trunk in my attic only to be rediscovered when I needed it most.

Chapter 39

When Grandma Heller passed away, a few years before Grandpa, the whole family came home and took up temporary residence in the house where they'd been raised. There were more of us now than there were then, of course, since the kids also had kids. It made for cramped quarters; perfect for celebrating the life of an amazing woman. She had eight kids in twelve years. Her first came when she was thirty years old, a pretty incredible feat for the 1950s. I never knew how many lives she touched until more than five hundred people attended her wake. Though I knew very few of them, they all knew me.

When Grandpa Heller passed we all came home again, stayed in the house, and spent hours sharing stories while going through memorabilia that had been packed away in closets and drawers, some for several decades.

I followed the procession in my cab from the funeral home to the cemetery, and then watched as the family stood with their arms around each other in the warm June sun. My uncle, the firstborn, saluted a fallen veteran as a veteran himself, teary-eyed while Grandpa's casket was lowered into the ground. After that, as good German-Irish-Catholics do, we celebrated his departure for many days, tossing back several drinks while sitting around the kitchen table reminiscing.

I sat in the driveway watching the replay of those moments on the screen that I'd created on the garage door of the house. I mourned not only the loss of his presence, but also the loss of all the amazing stories he told about his life, and the lives of the children he helped raise.

In my pants pocket, now just as I did then, I felt heat radiate from the rifle cartridge that had been ejected during Grandpa's graveside gun salute. I pulled the casing from my pocket, twirled it in my hands, and winced from the sound of the gunshots as they replayed in my head.

Though Soupy had no plans to return to the west coast anytime soon—there wasn't anything to go back to—he understood that the irreplaceable moments generated when such a large family gathered would eventually run their course. And after it was over, he'd make his way slowly west, with the notion to see more of the country than he'd seen on his nonstop run to see Grandpa Heller before he passed.

When that day came, I stood leaning up against the front quarter panel of my cab and watched as Soup said his goodbyes to the family. He backed out of the driveway and drove down the street. I then walked around the front of the cab and got into the driver's seat. As I sat down I heard Promise say, *Large family gathering?*

"Yeah, Grandpa Heller passed away."

I'm sorry, Soupy.

"He was an important part of the family. Even so I felt like I didn't spend enough time with him."

Why didn't you?

"Honestly, I was intimidated when I was younger, and as I matured I saw him less once I moved to the west coast. He wanted someone to follow in his successful, professional footsteps, but none of us ever did. It wasn't until his deteriorating health made him frail that I sought him out for 'us' time."

I'm sure he appreciated that.

"As did I. The man was a tremendous storyteller, but how could he not be after playing baseball, surviving a war, raising eight kids, and staying married to the same woman for more than fifty years."

Promise sighed pleasantly. *Let's heal on the road*, she added.

"That," I paused, "we can do." We drove out of the neighborhood and onto the freeway before I continued the conversation. "I have a question for you, Promise."

Yes?

"Have you ever sent me an angel?"

An angel? What do you mean by an angel?

"I mean someone who, in my greatest times of sorrow, is there to brighten my day with a few words, nothing more."

I wish I could lay claim to such actions, but I can't.

"Who else could it be?"

Deceased, loving family member? Someone who prays for you constantly? A person of power? What makes you think someONE is responsible? Can it just be karmic?

"I suppose," I said.

This happens to you with regularity?

"Yes, well, it has happened a few times, I was in the doldrums when I kissed another girl behind Honesty's back. So I did what I always do when I feel terrible, I drove. I was out driving in my car and two girls I'd never seen before pulled up next to me at a stoplight. When I looked over at them they smiled and waved. I waved back, but as I did, the light at the intersection turned green and they sped off. I knew, just knew, they were only there to give me a touch of energy, enough to pick myself up off the floor and think about what was next. Still, I was a teenager, so I spent the rest of the night looking for them."

Did you find them?

"No."

Do you know the story of the guardian angel?

"Guardian angels are assigned to protect and guide people."

Right, but they do so as messengers from God.

"Messengers?"

Yes, what message have they given you?

"Smile. You're okay, Soup."

Is it that simple?

"Sure, why not?"

I'm not disagreeing with you. Was there an angel after Gravity?

"No, not that I can remember."

Maybe you didn't need one at the end of your time with her; you jumped right into the sack with Possibly, after all.

"I suppose," I said, and then added, "There was one after Possibly."

Oh yeah?

"Yes, she came up to me and said I have a beautiful smile, then walked away."

Pretty simple.

"But effective."

I find it interesting that your angels don't come to you when you're in the middle of a struggle; they come to you after you've completed it. Like, they avoid your strife so as not to impact what you were meant to learn.

"Sounds like us, you know? If I learn the wrong things about you now they might impact the strength of our love in the future."

Yeah, you could say that. Want to get back to that conversation?.

"Yeah."

Now that we're finally *on the other side of Possibly, what did you learn from her?*

"I learned a lot, but still in process, I think."

Makes sense, but you had to have learned something or your angel wouldn't have appeared. It's in your head somewhere, Soupy.

She was right, but it felt like a massive can of soda that had been well shaken. "It took me a long time to recover from that relationship; might still be doing so today."

You cleared the forest for new growth, by forest fire for sure, so you'll have to figure out where to plant your seedlings.

"Trial by inferno, for sure."

Are you over her?

"Now or then?" I asked.

Both.

I paused to organize my thoughts. "It's a difficult question to answer because I put so much into the quest, failed miserably, and did so more than once. I'm not used to feeling like a complete failure."

Yes, we all know.

After a chuckle, I jokingly asked, "You all know I'm a complete failure?"

No, no, no. We all know you failed over and over and over and over and—

"Yeah-yeah. At that time, I didn't want her in my life any longer, so in that sense I was 'over' her as a person, but definitely not over the ideal, or the woman she wanted to be."

I wouldn't expect you to be over your ideal woman.

"I was also sure that whether she became that woman or not, it was never going to be 'her' specifically. I learned, and am still learning more about myself from Possibly than from any woman before her."

In regard to learning, did she teach you or did you learn on your own?

"I'm not sure she *taught* me anything."

You learned it on your own, definitely, which is not what you expected when you started dating her, right?

"Exactly. I was excited about what she could teach me because she'd 'been around the world,' so to speak."

She was, at least, the spark that set your education in motion.

"She created ample opportunity to learn a lot about myself, yes."

Okay, so answer me this: why did you stay with her when all she did was beat you over the head?

I took a deep breath. "I believed...with hard work, and a little luck...that there was treasure to be found. That is, if I was patient enough to help her search for it, or do all the searching myself, we'd find that one little thing that changed everything. With all of the bad things that happened, there had to be—just had to be—some positive reward on the other side of it."

You are truly an optimist, Soupy, even when you've been run over by a truck every day, all day, for a year and a half.

I smiled, but it was a painful one. "It wasn't like that every day. There were days when I walked through the door to find dinner and candles and flowers and the biggest smile I'd ever seen in my life. I *lived* for those moments."

In my opinion there were far too few of them for the trouble you went through the rest of the time.

"I showed you the important parts of my time with Possibly. It's not like we have the time to sit here for a year and a half. But to get back to your question about why I stayed with her."

Yes.

"I promised from the beginning that I wouldn't leave her."

Soup, your word must be stronger than steel; it must be made of some hyper-alloy that Superman can't even bend.

"Yeah, maybe. Fool myself once, shame on me. Fool myself twice, shame on me."

You've got that cliché all screwed up.

"I think about it this way: I've had two serious relationships in my adult life now, Gravity and Possibly, so I can't help but compare them to understand more about what I truly want. I don't discount my time with Honesty, there were good learnings, but we weren't intimate. She played a role, sure, and I learned a lot, but it was…just…on a totally different plane than the other two. Anyway, Possibly was adamant about our sex being better than anyone prior, and at the time I really did believe it was. But *with* time, I discovered it was just sex and sex alone; there was little, if any, love associated with it. That's *not* satisfying to me."

That's not satisfying to me either.

"Given her abusive history, she was rarely comfortable with intimacy, which makes me more uncomfortable the more I think back on the intimate times we spent together. Do you know how stressful that is? Promise, believe me when I say I would never, never force her to have sex if she didn't want to do it."

Do you think that ever happened?

"Yes, of course it did, and I'm not proud of it, and thinking about it makes me sick to my stomach. There are two answers to your question. One, in that last moment together with her new boyfriend on the television, yes, I forced her. The ease by which she gave in was not something I'd experienced at any point in the previous year and a half—and we can, and probably should, talk more about that—because who knows how many other times in a year and a half, how little she resisted the advances of others. Two, if it had happened previously, then I was not at all aware that it did, and I never had any intent to do it." I took a moment to catch my breath before I continued. "With Gravity, love was *always* the main course and sex was the dessert we periodically ordered."

Yes, I'd agree with that learning.

"At the end of both relationships, Gravity and Possibly, sex was all we had left."

Our drive brought us to the start of an endless sea of red brake lights. I switched to the faster moving lane on our right, and of course the lane we'd entered came to a stop and the one we'd left started moving again.

"So to continue, what I mean is, Gravity understood that sex between us *was* love; she kept sleeping with me as a way to *show* me she still loved me. Possibly defined men by their physical attraction and engagement with her. She *had* to have sex to feel loved, but she didn't know the difference between sex and love. She kept sleeping with me because it was evidence, to her, that I still loved her."

Sex can't nurture love.

"Yes, yes, so well said, Promise. I couldn't say no to Possibly, but even more dangerously, she couldn't say no to anyone else. I couldn't stay in a relationship like that no matter how much I'd put into it or where I hoped it might someday go. How many times was she in an uncomfortable place with another man—especially the ones she never mentioned—coupled with an inability to say no? Or how many times with me? I can't think about that."

No, you can't. It'll drive you nuts, and there's nothing you can do about it now.

"I never slept around on her, no way, it's not something I do. I learned that lesson from Honesty. Possibly did it to me, and I don't want to know how often."

You did the right thing by ending it, Soup. Hold on to that.

"If she was lying to me about affairs, then what else was she lying about? Which *other* parts of our relationship were false? All of it? There's no way to know."

No, you were real in your relationship. You were honest and caring and loving and trustworthy, as much as you could be, so we cannot discount the reality of what you brought to it despite what she did or didn't bring.

"I guess."

Remember, Soup, you survived.

"Yeah, well, not without riding the roller coaster for a year and a half, but that's what you get when you try to find true love, right?"

Experience grants wisdom.

"So what did I learn? Possibly helped me understand my tolerance and my depth. She showed me how horrible a relationship could be, by constantly pushing my limits. She caused me more anger and frustration than I'd ever before felt, but by stretching those limits she forced me to understand my reservoir of passion, compassion, trust, faith and—let's not forget—love. I'm lucky I learned those things. I don't think most people ever get to know themselves this much."

These aren't the things most people just happen to learn. They're things you have to endure by resisting the easy path, and ultimately discovering your capabilities.

"I was listening to a radio show one night long after Possibly and I had parted ways, and the host told a caller that trying to fix a girl who had been through extreme sexual trauma was like trying to build a nuclear submarine out of kitchen utensils. I laughed aloud when I heard that; it was absolutely true. I couldn't be her superhero."

You sure gave it the effort, though.

"So I hereby declare: I'm done with the costume and fixing shit for people; it's not my area of expertise. I'm better at helping others realize their options, not solving them."

Declaration noted and believed.

"I don't always know what's best for someone, but I'm good at helping them see all the options."

You learned sooo much from her, more than you know. Your third love in life was one that invoked expression, but ultimately forced you to understand your limits, as you said. When you have one stick, you have a line. When you have two sticks you have a trough, but with three sticks you can form a triangle, which is the first number with which you can create a closed space.

"A triangle?"

Yes, a triangle. You've learned the boundary of your emotional limit. The triangle encloses all you can handle, which you didn't before understand. The number 'one' gave you direction. The number 'two' gave you choice. And the number 'three' gives you closure.

"Ah, I see what you're saying. I understand myself in a confined way now."

The number three also represents the past, present, and future. You took what you learned from your past, applied it to your present, and gained more knowledge for your future. You say you're good at seeing all the possible paths. Well, this is the time for you to leverage your expertise to make the right choice.

"I'm probably better suited to do that now than I was then. I say 'back then' like it was years ago, and it certainly does feel that way, but it was only a little more than a year ago."

Possibly gave you a great gift, the gift of knowing yourself. You'll lean on that knowledge for the rest of your life, Soup. I know you already know this.

"I don't know myself completely, but I sure know more than I did pre-Possibly."

Every person experiences a time in their life when they must change. Like a moth to a butterfly...a transformation...a metamorphosis...much like when you've been fighting to make it up a hill for so long and you finally reach the top, and when you get there everything becomes more clear, easier to endure. You begin to understand what really matters, what you really need to be happy, whether you're hardened, or understand that you don't need to care so intensely about little things that used to annoy you. Reaching the top of that hill reveals the view you never before had. It's a view of your surroundings, and those surroundings represent your life. No matter which direction you go from the top of that hill, every direction has the advantage of gravity; instead of sweating the incline, you're riding the decline. I couldn't pull you up that hill. I couldn't push you up that hill. I couldn't hire a band of men to carry you up your hill, only you can make that journey, and it's the hardest when you're in sight of the peak.

"Am I there? I'd sure like to be there because the climb is killing me."

There's no way for me to know, so I can't answer that either. You'll know when you know. But Soup, I have to tell you, I think you're looking in the wrong places. You are a light, a bright shining light, and the obvious place where a light is needed is in the dark.

Her words made incredible sense.

You won't find me in the dark. I won't be huddled, shivering behind a rock. You've been trying to discover something in someone that you can't visibly see. I'm your partner, your equal; I shine the same bright light. The women you're choosing may have the potential to shine, and you obviously see that, but when you shine your light on them they sparkle and you confuse that reflected light as a light they're shining. It's not. Possibly held you underwater to see how long you could take it. She'd let you up for a breath before pushing you under again…and again…and again. She left you for dead so many times, floating in her emotional tides, but you found ways to resuscitate yourself, to a fault. She was hiding in her closet because she had more control when she was in a space she knew so well. Her psychological challenges were another way of hiding—hiding from the real emotions buried inside her. I know for a fact this was her world. You know when I told you that I was lost and couldn't find you?

"Yes."

I found her.

I desperately wanted to turn around, look at Promise, and make sure I heard her correctly, but I caught myself before I finished the act.

I can see your surprise.

"How can you do that?"

You've shown me enough that I could focus my thoughts on her. From there, her signal was easy to find, and surprisingly when we connected, her signal wanted *me to enter.*

"Was she—no, I don't want to know, don't tell me."

I can't tell you much about her life, Soup, because I only saw her in her dream, and truth be told there isn't much to tell except, as I said, that I know her world is dark. It's like being in the middle of the ocean, deep underwater, at night, with no one else around, and it's not quiet. Voices don't heed to each other, they talk incessantly while Possibly curls up in a ball on the ocean floor. She kept pulling you under water because that's where she lives. It's easy to visualize the closet, and it worked for you, but in truth it was much deeper and much darker.

"Have you ever seen that before?"

Never.

But in the murky waters there was light, Soup. It wasn't always there, but when it was the light danced through the darkness as a beacon. I see what you saw in her, the potential is there, but she will have to swim to it on her own, and at least for now she shows no ability to do so.

"So I'm not crazy?"

You're still pretty crazy. In fact—"

"What?"

I have something to tell you and I don't know how you're going to take it, okay?

"Okay."

You didn't change the template between Gravity and Possibly; you just changed the name.

"What do you mean?"

You learned a lot from the experiences, but they were the same experience. You just paid more attention the second time around.

I suddenly felt like *I* was drowning. Had I wasted the last five years of my life? I couldn't find words, so my confused response came out as, "Wait. What?"

You met and fell in love with both of them through months of conversation. Eventually, you dated. When things didn't work out the first go-round, one of you left the other. And then, you got back together only to have the other one get even by leaving, so to speak.

Instead of resisting what she was saying or trying to defend myself, I replayed the words in my head to see if they rang true, but I felt my respiratory and pulmonary systems kicking into a gear normally reserved for fear.

After you'd broken up twice, you resorted to a relationship of sex until even that lost its appeal. But still, you kept trying to go back. Do you know why?

I didn't answer.

I'll tell you why, because your very first sexual experience didn't have anything to do with you. Desire came home from a bad date and healed herself by letting you screw her. To this day, you hold onto that memory as something very special. When she healed herself through sex, she taught you that life could be healed that way. It can't. Now, you keep trying to fix things with sex just like she did. Soup, listen when I tell you this: fixing things with sex doesn't work.

I knew what she was saying, and didn't know what she was saying all at once, but it *felt* true.

That's what I mean when I say you changed the woman but not the template. You might have learned a lot about yourself, but I don't see you applying it—you just keep doing the same things over and over.

It hit home, and I was flabbergasted. My forehead collapsed into my hand as I prepared to vomit all over my lap. My face turned a ghostly white and my lungs suddenly couldn't replace the breath they'd just expelled. I salivated in preparation for the worst, pulled the latch on the door of the cab, and fell out into the bumper-to-bumper traffic on the highway. The stinging, hot pavement on my hands and knees furthered my stomach's intent. Within seconds, I hurled uncontrollably, my body coiling like a snake and striking with each act, spewing everything that was inside me onto the concrete. Horns blared even though the cars in front of me hadn't moved an inch. I had nothing left inside, no substance or energy. I rolled onto my back next to the open door of the cab and covered my eyes with my forearm to shield off the bright sky. I attempted to tell Promise, "No charge for the ride," but my lips barely moved. "No charge," I repeated, more successfully the second time. On my third try, I found a reserve of energy; the fight or flight surge. "NO FARE CHARGE!" I yelled as I tried to get to my feet. "NO CHARGE!" I said, stronger yet again. "NO! FUCKING! CHARGE!" I stammered, finally rising from one knee and up to both feet. I screamed at the sky, the cars around me and anyone else who cared to listen, "NO CHARGE!" and pounded both fists on the cab. I sighed, and leaned face-first into the cab. "No charge, Promise," I said between heated, heaving, rank-smelling breaths. "You *do* know me better than I know myself."

Promise was no longer with me.

Chapter 40

The bumper-to-bumper traffic extended for miles in front and behind me. Horns honked randomly, but despite my meltdown not a single car's occupant heeded my dramatic state. *Now what?* I couldn't go anywhere and I didn't know which direction to go even if I could.

A nearby driver turned up a car radio:

"Never had a doubt,
In the beginning.
Never a doubt.
Trusted you true,
In the beginning.
I loved you right through."

I was drawn toward the source…so I could shut off the damn song.

"Arm and arm,
We laughed like kids,
At all the silly things we did.

You made me
Promises, promises.
Knowing I'd believe.
Promises, promises.
You knew you'd never keep."

As I walked among the parked cars trying to determine which one was playing the song, more switched their radios to the same song.

"TURN IT OFF!" I shouted.

A young mother rolled up her window, a disgusted look on her face.

The song was coming from everywhere.

"Second time around,
I'm still believing.
The words that you said.
You said you'd always be here,
'In love forever' still repeats in my head."

I labored to put one foot in front of the other as sweat gathered in my eyebrows and rolled down the side of my face. I used the side of my index finger to wipe it away before it dripped into my eyes. A car door opened in front of me as the owner stood up in an attempt to see the reason for the traffic jam. I executed a three-sixty and spun around the door without losing too much momentum.

"HEY!" he yelled, but I didn't look back.

"You can't finish what you start.
If this is love it breaks my heart.
You made me,
Promises, promises.
You knew you'd never keep.
Promises, promises.
Why do I believe?"

I kept jogging until I could see the reason for the traffic jam.

"Oh, fuck." A massive wall of shiny, black rocks—rocks that had no business being in this place at this time—had been placed across the highway, right at the peak of the grade. I walked up to the rocks, touched one, and immediately felt the heat in my hand…and in my pocket. I grabbed my pocket rock, held it up to the wall, and saw the similarity.

I pushed on the boulders at the lowest height of the wall to see if they were stable, and then climbed the wall. The black rocks were hot, maybe from absorbing the heat of the sun, maybe for some other metaphysical reason. It didn't matter, all I wanted to do was climb. When I reached the top, I slung a leg over and straddled the wall. The way I'd come was daylight. The other side was dark.

I see you're still alive, Nectar said, though the darkness.

Her voice surprised me, but I knew who it was as soon as she spoke. It also angered me because what I wanted the most was some damn privacy, so I could think.

When I looked back at the miles of parked cars, they'd miraculously been abandoned, no owners anywhere to be seen, as if they'd raced away from some approaching doom, leaving their car doors standing wide open.

About time you got here. Come on, she added.

Finally, I turned my head to look in her direction, but my eyes couldn't adjust very well from the light to the dark.

"Hey—" I started, intending to tell her that I needed a damn minute to think. What would make hundreds of people abandon their cars at once and run back the way they'd driven? The opposite direction I was heading, at that. *The Bind.* They don't want to be trapped. Yet isn't that what they already are? Isn't that why I'm so adamant about sticking to this journey; to *not* be like them? Of course they ran away, away from what they don't know, but need to learn.

Even though they were long gone, I cupped my hands around my mouth and shouted in their direction, "KA-KAWWWW!" Random, I know. "TOP-A-THE-WORLD, MA!"

Nectar started her cab. She honked the horn to hurry me along. *Fuck sake. Really?* I swung my other leg over the wall and eased myself down the drop to the highway.

Well? she asked when I got into the back seat.

"Well what?" I said, though I was fairly sure she was asking about my "choice."

She straightened out the cab and punched the accelerator. *Well, you're not dead.*

"Nope, but my grandpa is. Before he went he said something to me, and I feel I should pass it along to you."

Yes?

I looked for a seat belt and found none, so instead made sure I'd braced myself as best I could before saying what I needed to say. "He told me to find Promise."

Nectar slammed the cab's brakes, which threw me up against the back of the front seat, and we skidded sideways to a stop. She shouted, *THAT'S WHAT HE SAID, HUH?!*

I touched my temple, pulled my hand away, and saw that it was bloody. "Yes, he did, and I agree with him."

I felt the cab move with her shifting weight. *YOU AGREE? THAT YOU SHOULD CHASE AN EMPTY REALITY WITH, WITH THAT... LYING BITCH?!*

With the anger in her voice, I was happy to have the protective Plexiglas between us. "Nectar, I don't love you like you love me."

She laughed. *YOU DON'T EVEN KNOW WHAT THE HELL LOVE IS!* She slapped her hand against the glass, startling me.

I shouted back, "CALM DOWN! IT'S NOT YOU—"

DON'T GIVE ME THAT "IT'S NOT YOU, IT'S ME" BULLSHIT!

I hadn't, in fact, intended to say what she assumed I was about to say, so I simply shook my head in frustration.

WELL?!

"WELL, WHAT?!" I answered forcefully.

WELL WHAT?! WELL?! WHAT?! YOU GOTTA BE FUCKING KIDDING ME! WELL WHAT?! I SHOULD JUST LOCK UP THE CAB AND LEAVE YOU HERE. IT'D BE THE BEST DAMN WAY TO KEEP YOU SAFE!

"I don't think I'd—"

AT THIS POINT DO YOU THINK I CARE WHAT YOU THINK?!

I shrugged inaudibly.

WELL?

"I—"

DON'T YOU DARE SAY, "WELL, WHAT?!"

"If you'd calm the hell down for a minute, I'd—"

CALM DOWN?! CALM DOWN?! WHY AREN'T YOU SHOWING ANY EMOTION?!

"Because it doesn't help us reach a resolution."

She punched the Plexiglas, and it bulged.

"LOOK!" I yelled. "LET ME EXPLAIN!" I waited a few seconds and got no response from her, so I continued, "I've seen what happens when I choose the strong magnetism of intimacy; it clouds my judgment and...well...ultimately leaves me alone...in the dark...all by myself. I just did exactly what you're asking me to do—I *just did that* with Possibly. I can't do it all over again; can't do it to my family, can't do it to my friends, can't do it to myself."

Nectar said angrily between gritted teeth, *I'M. NOT. HER.*

"Maybe not," I said, "but you *feel* like her, and I don't *know* you. You tell me things like 'you've always been around,' and as much as I want to believe you, I also believed the things Possibly said about herself that simply weren't true. How do I know what you're saying is true, Nectar? Tell me that."

HOW DO YOU NOT SEE THE IDIOCY IN YOUR WORDS?! she screamed. *HOW DO YOU KNOW WHAT* ANYONE *IS SAYING IS TRUE?! SO YOU'RE NEVER GOING TO TRUST ANYONE AGAIN?! IS THAT IT?!*

"No, I—"

EXACTLY.

I fought off the boiling cauldron of anger that was about to bubble over because she was cutting off my words again. "Whatever," I said indifferently.

I couldn't see it, but I felt her stare through the glass in response to my indifference. *Whatever? WHATEVER?! I'VE GOT A WHATEVER FOR YOU! Whatever makes YOU think YOU can find true love by lumping EVERYONE into the same bucket as Possibly?*

"Because I have—"

She mocked my voice with her own whiny alternative, *Because I have. Because I—*

"BECAUSE I HAVE FAITH!" I screamed. "LOVE WILL WIN! IT HAS TO!"

Nectar laughed so hard the cab shook. Between laughs she asked, *Where... have you...read...that...rule? Love has to win? Oh, Soup, you're...a joke!"*

"I believe what I—"

Nectar's cackle switched back to a more serious tone. *Stop kidding yourself. Suddenly you have all the answers? You've been watching a movie about your life—you know that, right? A movie! And even though you've been watching, you haven't seen a damn thing at all. What is this word: Faith? FAITH?! You're not even a religious person!*

"You don't need religion to have faith," I said, trying very hard to remain calm.

You'd like to think so, wouldn't you? She laughed. *Keeps you from taking the blame.*

"Blame? Blame for what?"

Blame for wrecking all your relationships!

I shrugged her comment off. "What are you talking about? I haven't wrecked all of my relationships."

The hell you haven't, Mr. High and Mighty Who Has All the Answers!

"WHO ARE YOU TO JUDGE ME?!"

Maybe I AM your judge, you fool, ever think of that?

"No way. If you're the judge protecting the gateway to something, then I'm not interested."

Maybe you've ALREADY BEEN judged!

"What? At the end of my life, it doesn't matter if anyone judges me. I see the merit of doing good in life despite the reward."

And you've done sooo much good so far, leaving hearts littered on the road behind you. Come on, didn't you look down the highway after you climbed the wall? Nothing but broken hearts.

"Whatever."

You wanted it. I offered it to you. You accepted it. Besides, you have more proof that I exist than any God or Existence or Awareness or Promise or Universe or whatever you want to call it. Tell me, have you ever seen, heard, touched, or tasted Promise?!

Claustrophobia set in. I yanked on the handle of both doors repeatedly but they wouldn't open. With my fists pounding on the Plexiglas I shouted, "LET ME OUT!"

I'm not done with you, yet.

I curled up in a ball on the back seat with my fists on my temples, whispering, "It's just a dream. It's just a dream. It's just a dream."

Please, do you really think it's all in your head?

I didn't answer her question, only continued my desperate desire to be somewhere else.

You don't know shit. You're out in the world guessing—grasping at straws—just like all the other morons here. You're my fodder, Soup, and I've already molded you in my own image.

"NO!" I yelled and then returned to my whispering chant.

Would you rather I just left you here to die?

Weakly, I replied, "Out. I need out. If you're not going to let me out, then let me die."

Metal tapped on the Plexiglas. *Is this what you want?*

The image of the gun formed in my head and I nodded.

I'm not going to let you kill yourself; you're too important to me. Besides, who do you think helped you end the Possibly debacle?

"Possibly?" I whispered and then shouted, "NO MORE POSSIBLY!"

Yes, Possibly. Who do you think gave you what you needed to rid her from your life?

"STOP!"

You hypocrite. You're mine. You don't have a choice anymore. When Promise learns that you slept with me while you were pining over her, you really *won't have anyone else in the world* but *me. Might as well accept it for what it is.*

"What…did I do…to…Promise?"

Who fucked me while claiming this once-in-a-lifetime, the-universe-needs-it love for her?

"I didn't—"

YOU DID! DING-DING-DING! WINNER-WINNER-CHICKEN-DINNER!

"Stop. Please."

Your words are worthless right now. And just like every other person who enters the dark, you will break.

I feebly said, "I won't break."

Look at you! You're already *broken! You've felt my power—how desirable it is—and you struck Possibly with it perfectly. Bing. Bang. Boom. Knock out! Those were big words. Big ones. You liked it and you'll crave it. You'll lay in bed at night, unable to sleep, because your mind will be devising new ways to use your newfound skills. Drink it up. Slurp it up. Before long you'll be bathing in it, drunk on it, putting me on speed dial to get more of it..*

"LEMME OUT!" I screamed as I kicked at the door.

Oh really? How about, ummm, no?

I wrestled with the door handles again, only to get the same result.

Nectar laughed.

I turned onto my back, coiled my feet up to my chest, and kicked into the glass. Nothing happened.

Don't hurt my cab! Nectar laughed more loudly.

I kicked a second time, but the glass didn't break. "FUUUUUUUCK!"

So long, sucker, for now. Just know: this isn't over.

She opened and closed her door. I held my breath to ascertain whether she'd actually left or was still sitting in the front seat. The red lights in the back of the cab went dark. I pressed my face to the dark glass in an attempt to see into the front seat. *Nothing.* I tried to calm down by listening to my breath, but the kaleidoscopic patterns on the back of my eyelids made me dizzy. The darkness made me feel like I was floating, which was equally nauseating. And then, I heard the sound of trickling water. I stomped my feet on the floorboards and they made a splashing sound. "What the hell?" I reached down and found an inch of water on the floor. As soon as I made the discovery, the hydrant, so to speak, opened wide and water began flooding the back of the cab. The red lights returned, now illuminating the water.

All hands abandon sub! Nectar announced through a loudspeaker.

"Hey...hey...HEY!" I yelled as I realized this would eventually become a water-filled coffin. I checked the doors once more, but they wouldn't open. I banged on the front glass, but got no response. I turned to face the backseat and ran my fingers around the edges of it looking to yank it out, and possibly escape through the trunk, but it wouldn't budge. The water reached my stomach, and I began to move my arms through it like I was slowly walking into the deeper end of the pool. It was cold. My teeth chattered as my eyes frantically worked with my mind to devise a way out. I hugged my arms against my chest and rubbed my hands on my biceps in a fruitless attempt to warm up; that was when I noticed the angle of the water. Because the cab was sideways on a downhill slope, the left side was filling up more quickly than the right. It meant that the pocket of air would end up on the right side of the cab. With the water up to my torso, I maneuvered to the high side. The cab shook a bit as I moved. My eyes opened wide. I put my back up against the right window, took in a great breath, and then launched myself to kick at the left window. The glass held firm, but the cab rocked again. This time I placed my feet on the seat, my hands against the glass, and launched toward the left side of the cab. It rocked greatly with the incredible transfer of weight from the high side to the low side. "COME ON!" I yelled, and gathered myself for another attempt. I tried again, but it was still not enough to accomplish my intent. "Alright. Alright." I waited, taking in few deep breaths waiting for the cab to fill up. As the height reached my chest I lunged and the cab's rubber tires screeched as they slid down the hill. "AGAIN!" I yelled and recoiled for another strike. This time, the shift of weight set the cab in motion and rocked it up on two wheels. I screamed, urging it over on its side until I felt the peak of the parabola and gravity creating a new inertia. *An object at rest, will*—all four wheels left the ground and the cab rolled downhill, blowing out the windows and allowing the water to escape. Before the cab gained too much downhill momentum it crashed into the barrier between the northbound and southbound lanes. I gathered myself, damaged, but operational, and alive. The water had washed all the broken glass down the highway, so I simply had to crawl across the interior roof on my hands and knees to escape on the uphill side of the cab. I laid out flat on the highway, chest heaving, staring into the night sky, shaking my head, and wondering, *How long before these women are the death of me?*

Chapter 41

I don't remember how long I was on the pavement: minutes, maybe hours. Eventually, when I walked away, I walked downhill and into the quiet night.

A utility truck stood my hair on end as it passed by laying on its horn. I clutched at my chest and turned away from the road so my back would shield me from the wind that was surely trailing the speeding vehicle. A few seconds later, it was followed by a black Honda, Soupy's black Honda, and about the same time, the truck blew a tire, flipped on its side, and a ladder loosened from the top of the utility vehicle, bounced once on the freeway, and skipped right over the top of Soupy's car.

"Holy shit," I exclaimed. That moment came flooding back to me, rocking my memory, my life flashing before my eyes exactly as it did back then. By the time his adrenalin subsided and he was able to recognize his near-death experience, he was miles down the road. It took all of those miles for his heart to stop pounding against the inside of his chest, and those beats made him feel alive, more alive than he'd felt in some time…and more focused on paying attention to the road. With them came a sense of urgency about life; he'd been sitting still for too long. He made an important decision about his future; he knew who he wanted to spend the rest of his life with…before he had no life left to live.

The dark sky turned a paler shade of night.

A quarter mile down the road, I walked up to a rest stop where I found two empty, identical cabs in the parking lot. The difference being only in their license plates: DMORTIS and NXVITAE. *Vitae?* Life. *Mortis?* Death. *Life or death?* I chose life, so I sat down in the front seat, cranked the engine over, backed out, and headed for the still empty freeway. As I approached the onramp, I saw a man on the side of the road with a sign that read: "Tru Luv OR Busst." He wasn't paying any attention to me, but I pulled up next to him anyway, leaned over, rolled down the passenger side window, and said, "Need a lift?"

In a voice identical to Thomas Chong's, of Cheech & Chong fame, he replied, "Nawww, maaaan."

Confused, I asked, "Then, what's with the sign?"

"Siiign?" he replied, then remembered the sign leaning up against his leg. Slowly, he turned it around and mouthed the words. "Yeahhh, the sign. Some lady paid me five bucks to sit here with it, you know?"

I bet it was Promise. I *hoped* it was Promise. "What was her name?"

"I don't do labels, maaan," he replied.

"Okay. Then, where did she go?"

"Do you see a leash here? It's a freee country, brother."

I looked down at the seat of the cab in frustration trying to figure out the one perfect question that would unlock the puzzle. "You need a ride or something?"

"Wherever I go is where I am," he said. He pulled a small blunt of marijuana from his jacket pocket and held it up to me. "You wanna hit?"

"Nah, but thanks," I replied.

He lit the spliff, took a huge puff, and then said while he exhaled, "Maaan, when you're always in a rush to get somewhere, you never actually arrive."

"Okay?" I said wondering what the hell he was talking about.

"And you know what else?"

I knew I wouldn't have to answer to hear "what else," but I did anyway. "What's that?"

His hand holding the joint pointed off down the road, "Sometimes you're looking so far into the future that you don't see what's right before your eyes." As he brought his hand back to his face he said, "Hey look, maaan, opportunity." He laughed slowly and then took another long drag from the drug.

I couldn't help but laugh, as frustrating as it was, trying to figure out what the hell he was talking about. "You wanna do me a favor?" I asked.

"Oh, you wanna hit now?"

"No, nothing like that."

In that moment, I saw a dot of red fabric meandering toward us from the forest behind the man. It had to be Promise. I flipped on the cab "For Hire" light hoping she'd see that as a sign to approach. "Dude, can you count to ten for me?"

"Count to ten? Yeah man, I can do that for you." He started counting.

I put my face in my arms and leaned into the steering wheel like I was playing hide-and-seek.

"—two…three…four…fi—"

Hopefully, a ten-count would be enough for Promise to cross the tall grass and get into the back of the cab without seeing her do it. No big deal if not, other than I might have to explain why I wanted this guy to start counting again.

When he reached eight, the back door of the cab opened and I felt her sit down in the seat.

New friend? she asked.

"I might ask you the same question."

I can always use another friend.

"Another friend? No. Another *true* friend? Yes."

Fair enough, pessimist.

"Pessimist? What? I'm no pessimist, it's just been a rough night."

You been smoking in here?

I pointed out the window to the hitchhiker.

"Hey lady, youuu want the last hit?" the hitchhiker said.

Some other time, duuude, Promise replied, speaking his language.

"Thanks for your help, brother," I said.

"Help? What help?" He mumbled something I couldn't understand after that.

I asked, "You sure you don't need a ride anywhere?"

"Naaah, no place like the present. Peace, brother."

"Peace, dude," I said and put the cab into drive.

Promise gave me a few seconds to get up to speed on the highway before she said, *You were saying, it was a rough night?*

"Yeah, I almost died, what else is new? After you left I walked up the rest of the hill because I *had* to reach the top, you know?"

Yeah, I know.

"Then, the sun set and it was dark. "Nec—," I nearly said "Nectar," but heard her in my head screaming at me about cheating on Promise—*was that the truth?*—and remembered that I hadn't yet had a conversation with Promise about the other woman in my dreams.

Soupy? Promise prompted.

Hey, oh, sorry," I said, shaking those thoughts from my mind with little success.

You almost died?

I skipped telling her about climbing over the wall, getting into Nectar's cab, the water, and the escape. "As I was walking down the freeway, I found this rest stop and, well, here we are."

I think you skipped the part about almost dying.

"Ah, yes-yes, again, sorry. Well, truthfully, I was a witness to an event that I'd forgotten about when I made this drive many years ago—I was driving down the freeway and a utility truck blew a tire in front of me, lost a ladder, and that ladder bounced off the freeway right over the top of my Honda."

Holy crap! she exclaimed.

"I saw my life flash before my eyes—back then and here again."

I really shouldn't leave; your life is hard enough to follow in person.

"Exactly. Once I realized I'd lived through it, it really gave me some clarity."

The morning sky had a surreal look, like a daytime version of the Aurora Borealis. "Promise, can you see the sky?"

I imagined her leaning down in the back seat to better see through the front windshield. *Yes*, she answered.

"What day is it?"

What day is it?

I asked again, more frantically this time, "Yes, what day is it?!"

I don't know; it's your—

"Dammit, it's my dream! I KNOW!"

It's beautiful, though, isn't it? Did you do that? she asked.

"Me? Do *that*? HELL NO! Are you crazy?"

Crazy? I'm quite certain I have no idea where this is coming from, but that sky is surreal.

I heard my mom's voice in my head explaining what the sky looked like over the Mid-West on September 11, 2001. Because the FAA had directed all planes to land at the nearest airport they had to dump fuel in preparation for landing. The sky became an incredible canvas of colors. "Do you remember that day?"

Confused, Promise asked, *What day?*

"September 11th."

Who could forget it?

"Yeah, exactly."

What about it?

"I woke up that day, you know, the day the planes hit the towers."

I think we all did.

"No, I mean I *woke up*—sat straight up in bed—the moment the first plane hit, even though I was on the west coast. I turned on the radio, discovered what had happened, and ran downstairs to watch the news, like most Americans, and was transfixed for days."

I'm not surprised, but let me get this straight: you were asleep on the west coast, thousands of miles away from the event, and the impact woke you?

"I can think of no other way to describe it," I replied.

Not to take anything away from your connection, but that impact jolted a lot of people.

"I'd just been on the Trade Center a few weeks prior. Postcards I'd sent were still stuck to their recipients' refrigerators. Once I heard the news on the radio, I bounded downstairs in time to see the second plane hit the other tower live on television; it was terrible."

It woke your senses. There's some empathic ability in you.

"It was a day with too few miracles, you know? When there's a wreck or an earthquake or some kind of disaster, we watch because we want to see miracles, we want to see people walk away, we want to hear stories from the survivors, and how they have this new perspective on life because they survived."

Funny you should talk that way.

"Why's that?"

It's a miracle that you walked away from Possibly.

I hadn't, and probably wouldn't have ever compared my relationship with Possibly to an international disaster or a natural one, but Promise was metaphorically right.

With great emotion comes great volume. You tapped into something inside you that'd never before been tapped, Soupy. The attack on this country was your lifetime's Pearl Harbor. When so many people come together with such intense emotion, it's bound to trigger the metaphysical fire alarm…for some who are ready for it and others who aren't.

"I don't know if I was ready for *that*; it didn't have to be so horrific to wake me up. I could have done without the loss of thousands of lives, you know?

I know.

"It wasn't even the first time an indescribable jolt-like phenomenon woke me, Promise. When I was in high school, several firefighters were called to an early morning construction site blaze. They received no notice about explosives being stored on the site. They were victims of an unexpected explosion shortly after they arrived. The power of the explosion evaporated everything near it: trucks, men, and gear. It blew out windows nearly a mile away from the site. On that morning, more than three miles from the tragedy, I sat straight up in bed a few seconds before my windows rattled."

Maybe that jolt prepared you to receive the September 11th jolt?

"The Network."

The Network?

"Yes, I call those connections 'The Network;' an invisible switchboard that connects us to each other, some connections stronger than others, like my mom and the Little People who speak in her dreams. We connect to each other subconsciously at any time and from any place. It happens in dreams and in the real world, at least in my experience."

The Network. Yeah, okay, I can get with that name, but others might call it "empathy."

"Empathy. Check."

Another way of thinking about it is, as the highway system on which I operate, right?

"I suppose it is."

I'd even say the signal strength is hereditary, from what I've seen in dreams anyway. Everything else is passed from parents to children, why not the ability to connect?

"The Network *is* powerful; it has to be. There've been too many times in my life when it has connected me to someone or something, and made me realize how necessary it was in that moment to reach out in the real world. Do you think love strengthens the signal?"

And prayer, of course.

"Prayer? Prayer is lame."

Is that what you really think?

"I'm not one to seek assistance from an intangible entity; I'm more apt to reach for the people in my life who *can* provide influence."

Would it explain your World Trade Center experience?

"Prayer doesn't explain why or how it reached me. There wasn't anything I could do to influence it."

A flood of thought isn't choosy about who it influences.

"Exactly why prayer is useless. You're praying for one specific person, place, or thing. Specifically, you're asking some higher entity to influence the outcome of a specific thing. When I get a signal, it's not from someone's prayers, it's connecting to another person through The Network. It's person-to-person, not person-to-god-to-person."

Apparently, you've thought about this.

"Okay, topic change so we don't get sidetracked talking about prayer and religion. Do you think we dream about people because they're on our minds, or they're on our minds because we've been dreaming about them?"

Hmmm, maybe a little of both. We're obviously seeing the power of The Network in the stories you're telling me, which leads me to believe people are on our minds because we've been dreaming about them. But I'm not one to think our lives are resolved to fate. I'd like to think we also dream about them because they're on our minds.

"Or maybe, The Network is also a receptacle for dreams and thoughts; it doesn't have to happen in real time. When you dream about someone, it places inventory in The Network about that person. When the other person dreams, the same inventories are created. Once you've both created inventory about each other, The Network kicks in to deliver the messages."

The Network is phone and email with spam filtering!

I chuckled briefly. "I suppose. Look, I'm bringing up The Network now because it's pertinent to my next story." I paused. "But I'm fairly certain you aren't going to like it."

Where have I heard that before?

"I've had times in my life when I dream about someone every night for a week or two. When it first happened, I didn't pay attention, but then I started to recognize a pattern: I'd dream about people and then I'd learn that something terrible or wonderful had recently happened to them. So I began to pay more attention and reach out. More often than not, the hypothesis held true."

Since The Network is related to your next story, and that story has something to do with true love, and you haven't introduced me to a new woman, which former relationship were you dreaming about? Wait, Promise said, *I'm not even sure I want to know.*

"Wanna guess?"

Hell no. Just tell me.

"Gravity."

Of course, Gravity. Thank God it wasn't Possibly.

I rolled my eyes, but I did agree with her on that point. "I'd been dreaming about Gravity for weeks after Possibly and I split up. The dreams were so intense I was exhausted in the mornings."

What was going on in her life?

"After we broke up, she started seeing someone else, and eventually moved away with him. He wanted to build a career and maintain a relationship, while she wanted to build a relationship and maintain a career."

I guess someone else repeatedly doing the same things isn't unique to you.

I rolled my eyes and continued my story. "Her situation was worse this time around, because she was alone in a city with no friends, and this guy was one of those indifferent and verbally abusive types."

You mean the type who doesn't make her a priority in his life because he's too busy with work or school and friends and networking his way to the top?

I frowned at Promise. "Touché," I added. "At least I *knew* having a girlfriend wasn't a priority for me in college, and therefore didn't make a mess of it."

And, when you and Gravity lived together?

"I don't think I was *ever* indifferent."

I'm waiting for the punchline—the reason you're telling this story—so get to it.

"I reached out to her via email and explained the recurring dreams. And when I got her reply she unloaded to me as if we were best friends. She needed to get out of the relationship, and since we'd always been close she wanted my opinion."

Was giving her an honest opinion something you could actually do for her?

"I thought so. We'd been each other's longest loving relationship, so there weren't other people who knew us better than each other."

I see.

"The more we spoke, the more we remembered what we liked so much about each other."

Mmm hmmm.

"The more that wonderful, mystical, metaphysical feeling returned. That connection was really, really strong."

Immutable law of the universe.

"It was easy for Gravity to engage the magnetism whether she was trying or not, so I told her my feelings were returning."

How did she feel?

"I thought she felt the same."

But did she say so?

"Like I said, I knew her better than anyone else in the world. She was dealing with the same thing in her current relationship that we dealt with when we were together, and we were both coming out of abusive relationships. She was tired of it and depressed that she might have to start all over again. I was in the same place, Promise. How could I not want to see if our longing for the same thing might be the fix we both needed?"

If she was in the same situation as she was with you, then she should have known what to do.

"Really? I can't even fathom what 'known what to do' would mean in her case."

Yes, you do.

We sat in silence for a few moments.

"Close your eyes, Promise."

Closed.

I clapped my hands together and the cab's engine suddenly died. "What the hell?"

What do you mean?

"Hold on," I added. "I mean, sorry, this isn't what I expected." I shifted the cab into neutral and tried restarting it while we rolled down the highway. No luck. I managed the cab over to the breakdown lane before applying the brake and shifting into park. With my head on the steering wheel I mumbled, "That didn't work."

You killed the cab.

"Something like that. Would you be so kind as to mentally bookmark where we're at in this Gravity story?"

Yes, why?

"Because I'm going to pop the hood and act like I know what I'm looking at."

Promise giggled and said she could bookmark our conversation.

I reached under the dashboard, pulled the hood lever, and heard the latch pop. "Here goes nothing," I said as I grabbed a bottle of water on the seat next to me and exited the cab.

Good luck! Promise shouted.

Chapter 42

I looked aimlessly down the highway as I slid my fingers carefully under the hood. I might not have any idea what's wrong with the car, but I certainly knew I needed a moment to catch my breath before telling this next part of the story. *Take your medicine*, I thought.

After a few brief moments looking at the engine, I turned around and plopped down on the pavement to sit cross-legged.

Cars drove past. None stopped. *Who stops to help a cab?* No one.

I remembered hearing the words of a tow truck driver, who once told me, *You know anything 'bout magnats?*

"What was the rule? Opposites attract?" I said aloud, though no one was listening.

Cicadas in the brush on the side of the road began their song.

"SHUT UP!" I screamed at the insects.

I plucked some dead insects from the taxicab grill and flung them into the tall grass. "IS THIS WHAT YOU WANT?"

"Opposites attract. No, dammit, he said to *forget* that opposites attract. What the hell does that mean?"

An eighteen-wheeler blew past, scaring the shit out of me, and rocking the cab in the wake of wind it created.

"Rules. YES, RULES. That's it! Forget the damn rules!"

A heavy rain began to fall. I spread out my arms to accept it and looked to the sky with my eyes closed. I felt the cold droplets on my face and slowly forgot about the rules.

"Start," I whispered, but nothing happened. After a few slow, deep breaths, I made small circles with my hands to mimic the motion of "cranking" it over. Again, I whispered, "Start," and the engine made a bit of noise before it failed. "Believe," I said, and during the next few breaths I thought, *This story is almost over. I must push on...push through...and learn...as much as it might hurt, I must learn.* I imagined my heart beating fully, and in the next breath I gathered my energy, motioned circles with my hands, and confidently said, "Start." The engine roared to life. I smiled, jumped up from the wet pavement, let the hood fall closed, and made my way back to the driver's seat.

Chapter 43

You're all wet!

"I don't mind. Felt good. Cleansing, really."

You're going to catch a cold.

"No way, it's my dream."

Whatever you say.

"Ready to try this again?"

Always, that is, if you are.

I clapped my hands together and we moved from the highway to an oceanside pier. I parked the cab and pointed out Soupy and Gravity sitting with their legs dangling over the side.

"My relationship with Possibly taught me a lot about my capacity to love, I wanted to tell Gravity about all that I'd learned: how painful, eye opening, and educational it had been. I wanted Gravity to see and feel how much Possibly changed me for the better, because I now knew who I was."

How did she react to that?

"It didn't change anything."

Why do you think that is?

I shrugged.

Because you left Gravity for Possibly, Soup. Do you really think Gravity wants to hear Possibly's name? She doesn't care what you learned about love from her.

"But," I pleaded, "I explained to Gravity how my experiences put our past into a perspective I'd never before understood. When Gravity and I were together, we were young and foolhardy—"

We?

"Okay, *I* was certainly young and foolhardy."

Better.

"I struggled to get Gravity to comprehend that Possibly forced me to understand that Gravity was someone I *should* consider spending my life with."

She's a woman—a woman you scorned—she'll never hear it. She'll have to see it, and even then she'll only see it if she wants to.

"She was willing to talk with me, as you can see." I pointed toward the pier. "I hadn't slept the night before, my mind was too busy trying to figure out how to convince her that my renewed feelings were real." I watched them for a few seconds. "I remembered how Gravity was so incredibly of the earth; so good in her heart, so desperate to be grounded and nourishing. Possibly and Gravity were *so* different—water and earth don't get along, one serves to erode the other—so how can they be of the same 'template' as you said?"

Because, like you *said, it's the verbs that matter, not the nouns. It doesn't matter what element you put into the template if the template itself is broken.*

"Ungh. Yeah, yeah, thanks for the reminder."

Anytime.

"It was a huge relief to be near Gravity again. I was nervous at first, of course, but it wasn't long before we settled into our normal chatter: warm, thought provoking, and friendly. I knew, if there was an opportunity for me to say something about us, this might be the only chance."

I turned up the volume on the cab's radio.

* * *

"Gravity, are you okay?"

"I don't know, Soup," she replied. "The man I thought I was with, isn't the man he turns out to be."

Soupy looked down and picked at the edge of the pier's wooden decking, "There seems to be a lot of that going around, eh?"

They both smirked and she said, "I guess there is."

"What are you going to do about it?"

"I don't know," she paused and looked out at the ocean. "I just don't know."

"You have another option," Soupy nervously said. He waited for her to turn and look him in the eyes. "Us," he added. "We could try again. This time with all we've both learned from our recent failures."

She looked down at the space between them and said, "I don't know much about my life right now. It's hard to think about *that* without having figured out *this*. I've had a hard time getting over the fact that you left me for *her*. You rejected me. I didn't win."

"Not to keep score, but I *know* how that feels between us; you chose another man over me when we were in college. It hurt me so much I dropped out of school and left town, but it didn't stop me from eventually giving us another chance."

A slight breeze brushed the hair away from her face. "Are you trying to say we're even?"

"No, I'm just saying we have a history of learning and coming back to each other with the knowledge gained while we were apart."

"You might be right, but you hurt me, *really* hurt me. I don't know if I can open up to you again."

Soup had an immediate response because he'd thought about this very question for hours on end. "Believe me, I know what you mean. Remember how *done* you were with your boyfriend while he was studying overseas, so done with that relationship that we used to burn the letters he sent you?"

She giggled and said, "We *did* do that, didn't we?"

"Yeah, we did. Imagine the pain I felt when you suddenly decided he was a better choice for you than me."

She placed her hand on Soup's thigh, looked at him, and said, "I'm sorry."

They stared at the ocean for several seconds. Soup wanted to reach out and touch her, to let her feel how much he wanted her in his life again, but he respected her current relationship; though ragged and likely to fail, it kept him from doing so.

"How do I know you're not all talk?" she asked, breaking the silence unexpectedly. "You're so damn good with words. How do I know you're not just saying what you think I want to hear?"

"I can't convince you of that, only ask you to see it in my eyes and heart."

"My heart doesn't like you," she said. It was difficult to tell if she was being sarcastic or serious.

"I understand. I do. I really do. I'm not saying it starts right here and now. I just want you to know I'm here hoping you want to walk next to me again."

"This is *so* similar to how we met," she said. "I was dating someone else and you were there for me."

Soupy nodded his head.

Gravity continued, "And from that point so much has happened between us." She looked at him and shook her head. "I don't know, Soup."

"Please think about it," he said.

They got up from the pier and walked back to their own realities.

* * *

"You've been awfully quiet back there," I said.

I can't believe you did this. I know it's silly to get angry with you about it now since it's in the past, but I'm having trouble resisting that emotion.

I sat there silently.

You're not learning. How can I expect you to find me if you keep doing the same damn things with the same damn women?

"I'm not sure."

What do you mean you're not sure? Have you already forgotten how it made you feel when I told you you're not changing the verbs, only the nouns? Gravity is the same noun and you're gravitating back toward her again.

"She was hard to resist."

RESIST? SHE DIDN'T CALL YOU! BREAK THE PATTERN!

"Would you rather we didn't review this part of my life? Would you RATHER NOT KNOW?" At that point, I'd reached peak frustration. WHAT DO YOU WANT ME TO DO, PROMISE?!"

LEARN!

"I'M TRYING! BESIDES, HOW'S IT ANY DIFFERENT FROM US?!"

What on Earth are you talking about?

"YOU KEEP COMING BACK TO TALK TO ME! HOW'S THAT ANY DIFFERENT?!"

Frustrated, Promise said, *I have half a mind to leave, simply to preserve our potential future, before I say something I completely regret.*

"Leave if you want to, I'm used to it; Possibly did it all the time. Or stick it out, say what you have to say, and we'll work through it like adults."

You don't have to lecture me, and I'M NOT POSSIBLY!

"WELL, THANK GOD FOR THAT!" I yelled back.

After a moment of silence, she said, *I don't think I've ever heard you say the word "God."*

"Then that must tell you how mad I am!"

You bring God into the conversation when you're mad?

We sighed at the same time, then chuckled. The only time God is part of my life is when I'm pissed.

I'm sorry.

"Me, too."

Virtual hug?

"Virtual hug."

We both hummed out loud to note that a virtual hug was in progress.

"So are you going to stick with me for the rest of this story?"

Yes, Soup.

"Okay. I spent the rest of the day thinking about the spark I felt when Gravity and I sat next to each other. Could we turn that spark into a fire again? It wasn't just going to happen on its own this time; there was work to be done."

Oh, dear.

Promise and I pulled into the parking lot of a Mexican restaurant where we could see Soupy through the windows sitting at a bar table by himself. Over the radio, we heard him order a shot, a beer, and a plate of chicken nachos.

* * *

"You're not messing around, are you?" the server asked.

"Nope. I've got something I need to figure out," Soupy said as he tapped the point of his pen to his notebook. He clapped his hands together, kneaded them, popped his knuckles, and got to work.

"Here ya go," the server said as she laid the first drink on the table.

Soupy thanked her, dropped a bit of salt on the webbing between his left thumb and index finger, licked it, and threw the first shot of tequila down the hatch. The server looked over her shoulder from the bar and he motioned for another.

"What do you like about her?" Soup whispered to himself, then wrote a few things in his notebook. "Pro or con?" he added, then drew a line down the middle of the paper dividing it into two columns.

* * *

What did you write? asked Promise.

"Ummm, something about how well we know each other, I think."

Was that a pro or a con?

"A pro. I'm a complex person, so getting to know me can be difficult."

No way, Promise sarcastically said.

"Indeed. Fortunately, for Gravity she'd already endured the learning process." Soup wrote a few more things in his notebook. "I added bullets for her beauty, inside and out, how she's not trying to be anyone other than who she already is."

Those are pros, definitely pros.

"Yep. I also noted how I thought she'd be an incredible mom. I saw her interact with kids when we were together—she just gets them in a wonderfully loving way."

Pro, for sure. What else?

"Well, our sex life was...phenomenal. I don't mean just physically, though that's part of it, we fit together in that emotional way you and I have already discussed."

Pro, Promise said in a deep, sultry voice.

"I added trusting, dependable, thoughtful, caring, faithful, and then the bullet that had, to a degree, driven me away from her and toward Possibly."

What's that?

"Silly."

And, you thought you'd like that more this time around?

"After such a massive dose of seriousness with Possibly, a lifetime of silly sounded great."

Silly is good; too silly is bad.

"Yes, agreed."

Were they any cons?

"Yes."

Soupy took his second shot of tequila and ordered a third.

"She hadn't been as introspective as I had."

Was that really a con?

I thought for a moment before I answered. "Good question. What I was trying to note were her knee-jerk reactions to things; answers without reasons, you know?"

I mean this in a loving way, but does anyone dive as deeply into questions to discover reasons like you do?

"Few that I've met, I guess."

Soupy's third shot arrived and he slammed it.

"Back to the list. I didn't have a great relationship with Gravity's mother. We got along, but we weren't close."

Like with Possibly's mom?

"Yes, exactly. We weren't even that close in proximity, but we had a relationship that was close enough for me to call her just to chat. I would never have done that with Gravity's mom."

What else?

When Gravity and I dated, she never had her own life. I mean, she had work and she had me, but rarely did anything with her own friends."

She smothered you?

"Yes! Exactly! Much better way of saying it. I can't breathe when I'm being smothered."

Gravity was different than Possibly. Possibly had friends, but she drowned you because she'd swim into the deep end without knowing how to swim. Gravity buried you because she was all around you.

"Gravity hadn't ever been alone. She started dating in her teens and had a boyfriend ever since, and I need—"

You need to be with someone who is happy alone because you like your alone time.

"I *love* my alone time. So I had a good list about Gravity's pros and cons; good enough that I knew what I was going to do next."

What's that?

"You'll see."

Promised sighed.

Soupy walked out of the restaurant and across the parking lot to his hotel.

I tapped my finger in midair and watched as the stars quickly traveled across the sky then yielded to the sun. "I'll never get tired of that." I said, and smiled. "I slept with a smile on my face that night. You've spoken in the past about how I 'go for it' when it comes to love, which is true, but it's not without having first thought about all the different outcomes. I'd spent a lot of nights thinking about Gravity—even made a list, as you saw. Today, I was going to change our lives."

Soupy bounced out of the hotel and into his car. We followed him.

Where are we going?

"You'll see."

A few blocks down the road we pulled into a jewelry store parking lot.

YOU DIDN'T?! Promise yelped.

I nodded my head and said, "I did. It was an easy decision to make."

Soupy walked into the store.

"I was nervous because I didn't know the first thing about buying a diamond, but I did know Gravity, so I could make an educated guess about what she would like. I told the friendly salesperson my story, admitted I had no idea what I was doing, and he taught me about clarity, cut, color and carats."

I pulled my favorite black rock from my pocket, held it between my hands, and turned it into a 1.5 carat, princess cut diamond mounted in a solitary setting of white gold.

I accept, Promise said.

Soupy walked out of the store with a smile on his face, but he knew there was a difficult task before him, and it wasn't one that could be helped with tequila.

"Now, I had to call her father and ask for permission...and do so completely out of the blue."

Uh-oh.

"Making that phone call was one of the most difficult things I'd ever done in my life."

* * *

"Okay, Soup, you can do this," he said to himself as he took a series of deep breaths.

He dialed Gravity's parents' number. Her mother answered after only two rings.

"Hello?" she said.

"Hi there, it's Soup."

Slightly confused, since she hadn't heard his voice for a few years, she answered, "Hi, umm, Soup. How are you?"

"I know we haven't spoken in a while, so I'm sorry to bother you."

"It *has* been a long time. I'm surprised to hear from you."

"How are the both of you?" he asked.

"We're good."

"Well, I don't want to take up too much of your time, may I speak with your other half?"

"You have a car question?"

She was probing, which was a sure sign that she'd already figured out why he'd called.

"No."

"Okay, but he's not here right now. Busy weekend, you know how he is?"

Nervously, Soup added, "Busy is good."

If Soupy was going to have this conversation, then it was going to be with Gravity's mother.

Soup continued, "I admit, I didn't just call to chat. I called for a specific reason, so I'm not going to beat around the bush."

"Yes?"

"Your daughter and I have been talking a lot about what we've learned from our most recent relationships. In fact, we sat together yesterday trading stories about our lives. You know, we've really learned some very valuable lessons about love, and—"

"You're *there*?"

Her question caught him off guard. "Yes, I am."

"I see," she said, sounding very surprised.

Soup continued, "Our conversations have been about whether these valuable lessons are a good reason for us to try again, so—," he paused to catch his breath, "—I'm calling to seek your blessing when I ask for her hand in marriage."

The sun was beating into the car with intent, heating it up until it felt like an airless, glass coffin. He'd never wanted it to go down this way; asking the person he'd never connected with for her daughter's hand in marriage, and doing so *over the phone*. His hand shook furiously as he held his breath and waited for her answer. Time seemed to stop altogether.

"I see," she said with a pause for thought. "I'm going to be honest with you, Soup. I don't think that's what my daughter wants."

Soup had anticipated a negative reaction, but it still caught him completely off guard. *What?* Suddenly, time caught up with itself and pushed its pace. Clouds ripped past. His eyes darted back and forth looking for the proper response. Tears welled up in his eyes. He stiffened in an effort to hold them back. He still needed to fight; an emotional collapse would weaken his attack. *Crass*. Crass or protective? *Fuck her.* Anger gave Soup energy. She hadn't been privy to his conversations with Gravity. And she certainly didn't have an excuse to sucker punch him in the gut.

Soup said, "My conversations with her suggest otherwise, and if she agrees with me I'd like to ask for her hand in marriage. I'd sincerely like for you to reconsider my request."

"Well, like I said, I don't think my daughter is interested in this, and I think I know her better than you do."

It became a waiting game. Soup held his ground silently.

Gravity's mom then surprisingly added. "If she agrees with you, then we'll support you both."

It was a rubber stamp, a split-decision in the bout.

Soup said, "I know this has been a difficult call and I apologize for springing it on you like this, but I hope you hear how much I respect you and your daughter."

"Good luck," she said, but he could tell she didn't mean it.

"Thank you and goodbye," Soupy said and ended the call.

He broke into a fit of crying. There was no point holding back, no trying to straddle the fence by letting one or two tears roll down his face. His body jerked with great hulking sobs. Soupy needed this cry; it was part joy at having come this far in his journey and part sorrow at always being on the brink of success *or* failure. He whispered to himself, "Why is it always so hard?" He had no tissues, so he wiped his face with his shirt; the right sleeve for the right eye and the left for the left.

Eventually, with a big breath of air, the crying ceased, and he knew it was done.

A stranger knocked on the glass scaring him out of his wits. "Are you okay?" she asked.

Soupy nodded and said, "Yes."

She walked off to her own car with a concerned look and a wave.

He watched her go and whispered, "I will be, anyway."

* * *

"The fight was a struggle, but I didn't go down. I was happy enough with her mother's promise of support."

If you can call it that.

"I hear ya, but what else was I supposed to do? Even if she didn't give her approval, I would have moved forward because it's what I believed in."

I'm proud of you for putting yourself out there, for making that phone call, despite what happened.

I gathered my emotions quickly. "Between the decision to buy the ring and the phone call with Gravity's mom, I was spent. I told myself to sleep on it one more night before arranging a time when Gravity and I could talk again. When I got home that night, I looked at old photos of our first relationship. It was *so* easy to feel love for her again. Is that normal?"

You shared a lot together. I think it's normal.

"Is it measurable? I mean, is there a way to tell if *this* amount of love or *that* amount of love are enough?"

We sat in silence for a moment, thinking.

“Loss can be measured,” I added.

There are a million reasons why I love you, but I only need one reason to hate you.

“Or, there must be many reasons in order for me to love you, but I only need one reason to hate you. We work really hard to find a reason to hate, and not hard enough to find new reasons to love.”

Yes, of course we do, and it's a problem. Once we've found love we take it for granted, expect it to be omniscient, and then prickle when it isn't.

“I must be the unluckiest at love the world has ever seen.”

Hardly. I'd say you've been pretty damn lucky.

“How so?”

You're lucky that your loss is always followed by a gain.

I slipped the ring on my left pinky finger and created a video screen on the side of the hotel.

* * *

The call from Gravity, identified by caller I.D., freaked Soupy out; it felt wrong. *Her mom.* He was sitting on the floor and leaning up against the wall in the darkness of his hotel room thinking about how he might say what he wanted to say. For a moment, he considered letting it go to voicemail, but then realized that would have been the chicken shit decision; there were big moments occurring in his life and he needed to address them.

“Hello?” he said.

Gravity didn't return his greeting, and instead led with an angry response, “I heard you called my mother.”

“I did.”

“What's the matter with you? Why would you do that?”

“After our conversation, I—”

She cut him off, “Don't bother me. I don't want to see you. I'm done talking to you.”

He had no answer for her. The hotel room suddenly felt like a closet. *Where's your candle? Where's your*—the tears flowed instantly. Soup held the phone away from his face so she wouldn't hear his emotion.

"Do you hear me, Soup? HELLO? Do you hear what I'm telling you?"

He was fighting tears so desperately he couldn't answer her.

"SOUPY!" she yelled. "DO YOU HEAR ME?!"

A barely audible, "Yes," escaped his lips.

"Why do you *always* do whatever you want without considering what I want?"

Her words confused him. Was it a fair question? If what she'd told him all summer was the truth, then his assumption that they might try again would have been valid. If not the truth, then he was way off course.

Soup said, "I didn't mean to do anything other than continue this conversation with you. And I wanted to be ready to deliver more than just words."

"So you bought a *ring*?" she asked, with great emphasis on the final word.

"Yes, it's a symbol that supports my words of love; proof that I'm more than them."

"Why did you call my parents?"

"I'm a traditional guy. Before I'd get down on one knee I'd want permission from them."

"Really?" she asked.

"Yeah, why wouldn't I?"

"No, you're right. I know you're a thoughtful, respectful person."

"Well, that call wasn't the most pleasant thing I've ever done in my life. Your mother very simply said she didn't think this is what you'd want, and…I guess she was right."

After a short pause during which it seemed Gravity was gathering her strength, she said, "Soup, I have something to tell you."

He had no idea what to expect at the time, but those words so specifically called back all the moments with Possibly when she revealed terrible news.

"I'm seeing someone new already."

Soupy fell over from his seated position to the floor. *How? What? Who? I just saw her and asked what she was going to do and she already knew? There's someone new?* The phone slid off his ear and he stared blankly into a cold, lonely future that could only muster a frail response, "Oh."

She kept talking, but he couldn't hear what she was saying. Defending herself perhaps. He wouldn't have remembered it anyway. He'd heard what he needed to hear. He thought he'd considered all outcomes, apparently not.

* * *

"I didn't sleep in the bed, just stayed right there on the floor, and that's about all I remember from that night."

I'm sorry, Soup.

"All because of you." I winced as a sharp pain entered my head and the words from Gravity's mother repeated, *I just don't think that's what my daughter wants.*

Soup, are you okay?

"Yeah," I grimaced, "just a sudden headache."

It looks like more than that.

Gravity's words were also in my head, *I'm seeing someone new already.* I hunched over in the seat and buried my face in my hands.

Soup? SOUP?!

The pain whisked away with their voices. I leaned back in the chair and opened my eyes wide. "I'm okay, Promise. It's gone."

What was it?

"Migraine? I don't know."

I don't like it.

"Believe me, I don't either."

I don't like that you're hurting, now and throughout your life, I never wanted that for you.

"I know. There's a reason why things don't go right, and it must be because they weren't right to begin with." I saw the pain returning like the shadow of a cloud as it swept across the land, up and over the houses, and consumed the yard across the street, sucking away the sunlight. The headache was twice as intense this time. Gravity's mother screamed in my head, *I TOLD YOU, I JUST DON'T THINK THAT'S WHAT MY DAUGHTER WANTS!* The volume of her scream caused my hands to clench and the blood vessels in my neck to surge. *AND I TOLD YOU I'M SEEING SOMEONE NEW ALREADY!* Gravity yelled.

Promise leaned forward, very close to my ear it seemed, and yelled something I couldn't understand.

My vision went dark. I shook my head back and forth in an attempt to clear it.

Promise screamed again. It was indecipherable again.

I reached for the door handle of the cab and mumbled, "Must...go... home." I swung my leg out onto the pavement and let my body's momentum roll with it. As I stood up, I fell back into the cab.

This time I heard Promise yell, "SOUP! COME BACK!"

I pushed away from the car with my hands and stumbled onto the hotel's lawn. Somehow, I maintained balance as the voices returned, tackling me into the grass. I rolled onto my back. The grill of the cab stared at me with open eyes and a pursed mouth. On its lips it held the license plate, NXVITAE.

A hallucination or a memory—I wasn't sure which—of Nectar began. I could smell her scent under my nose and feel her breath on my neck. She whispered slowly into my ear, *Night of life,* and her lips closed around my earlobe seductively.

The world rushed back quickly as the sun warmed my face. Scared, I jumped to my feet and ran down the sidewalk away from everything: Promise, Gravity, Possibly, Nectar, love, loss, dreams, truth. I shook my head, trying anything to get the words—these words that represented the recurring failures because I never had all the information or never said the right thing or was never in the right place at the right time or never loved as much as I was supposed to—out of my life, out of my head, out of me so I could do something, anything else.

I ran carelessly off the sidewalk, into the street, and—

Chapter 44

The pavement was hot; it was all I could feel as I laid there on my back. I raised my head only to see the reflection of the sky in the dented front bumper of a car. I spelled its license plate in my head, D-M-O-R-T-I-S.

"Die mortis," I whispered, channeling some formerly forgotten Sunday school service vocabulary. *Day of death,* I thought and began to ask aloud to no one in particular, "Why—"

A figure stood over me casting a shadow that shielded my eyes from the sun.

In her distinctive voice, Nectar said, "You need to get rid of that ring before it kills you."

I raised my hand to see the diamond ring on my pinky, then my world went dark.

Chapter 45

Frantically, I sat up in my motel room bed. Dream over. A sliver of morning light pierced the thick wall of curtains. Audible, and annoying, static hummed in my head, which was a nuisance, but at least it wasn't throbbing. I was groggy, not rested. Stumbling to the bathroom, I expected the light over the toilet to feel like a zillion suns being flipped on at once, but the yellowed, old fixture and a low-watt bulb hardly forced a squint. After evacuating my bladder, I splashed a few handfuls of cold water from the sink onto my face, rested my elbows on the vanity, and took a deep breath.

I'd had a night of dreaming with Promise, for the first time in twenty-something years, and I was happy for that despite the challenges of our time together. But it was still just a dream. *She* was still a dream. There was a lot to process from the night's dream, and it was important to learn, but this wasn't a textbook that needs reading and highlighting, it was a life lesson—a lot of them—they would take time to sink in.

I heard Promise's voice in my head, *Learn, Soup.*

I packed everything except the clothes I needed to complete my task, threw them on, and walked toward the door. Before passing through the threshold, I looked back into the room. It was an attempt, and maybe a feeble one, to record the place where Promise returned to my dreams after so many years away. Important, indeed, but feeble because the room looked exactly like all the other forty-odd, or so, rooms in this two-story motel.

I drove through town in my Honda, found it weird not be in a cab, and slowly took in memories. On the west side of town, the road dropped into larger, ranch-style residential plots, which gave way to agricultural land, and eventually ended at the ocean. Not far out of town, I turned off the road into a dirt parking area. The goal: climb a mountain and cleanse the soul. It wasn't a technical peak, just a long uphill walk with a few small boulders to hop up and over. From the peak, I'd be able to see a line of volcanic peaks poking up across many miles.

I'd spent the entire night looking into my past. Today, I would admire geology's past.

I got out of the car, tightened the laces on my boots, and tossed a backpack full of snacks and water onto my shoulders.

A car pulled up next to me, but I didn't pay it any mind until I heard a voice emerge from it. "You going or coming?"

I turned around and leaned down enough to see the driver, who I didn't recognize. "Going," I said, and then added, "You?"

"Going," she replied.

We looked at each other for what should have been an awkward amount of time, but oddly wasn't.

I looked up at the hill and then leaned back into her window. "Enjoy your hike," I added with finality, and then set off down the slight incline to the fence, not waiting for her response.

"HEY!" she yelled. "Is that it?"

It caught me off guard, but I expressed a playful confidence, "It doesn't have to be."

She gestured from her window, "How about I drive around to the other trailhead. First one to the top buys the other a drink?"

"Deal," I smiled and then pointed at her. I knew nothing about her, other than she'd easily made my day more interesting.

She checked her rearview mirror and punched the gas, leaving a trail of dust behind as she made for the mountain's other access point. I didn't have much of an advantage because her drive would take her to a higher elevation and a shorter walk to the beginning of the climb. But there was a new pep in my step, the low-level hangover now long gone.

I stretched out my steps to cover as much distance as I could. The exercise felt good, like blowing the dust out of a hot rod carburetor that'd been sitting in the garage for too long.

After fifteen minutes, I could see the sign that marked the beginning of the climb only a few switchbacks ahead. She wasn't there. I picked up the pace, pulled down hard on my backpack straps, and jogged up the rest of the trail. Breathing heavily when I arrived, I grabbed a water bottle, took a few gulps, and caught my breath. It was then that I noticed a piece of paper attached to a clip on a post titled "YOU." I pressed open the clip with one hand and pulled the paper from it with the other, opened it, and read, "You're just a train stop on the way." I flipped the paper over in my hands again, held it up to the sunlight, but saw no other words on it.

"On the way to where?" I mumbled to myself. I looked up and down the trails again. Seeing no one, I shouted playfully, "ON THE WAY TO WHERE?" Only my own voice came back to me, echoing from the face of the mountain.

I shrugged, tucked the piece of paper into my shorts pocket, took another gulp of water, and returned the bottle to my backpack. This day wasn't about chasing down a woman I barely knew, not even to leave a note on her parked car; it was about me and no one else. With a big intake of breath, I set out for the beginning of the climb.

My Grandpa Heller used to tell a story about his perfect day. He'd rise early to take care of whatever chores his parents had laid out for him, pack a sack lunch, grab his gear, and start walking to the park. If he happened to be the first to arrive, he'd simply toss a baseball up into the air as high as he could, and make dramatic catches when gravity brought it back to earth. When a second person showed up, they could play catch. With three, hot box. With four, they could start a narrow-field version of Over the Line. Eventually, since they lived in a neighborhood full of kids, enough of them would arrive to field two full baseball teams and they'd play until sunset, stopping only to nibble on their lunches, and even that could be done when it was your team's turn to bat.

My perfect day is vastly different from his. I preferred to spend most of mine alone, with nature, on a process of thought and discovery, attaining some goal at the end of it, either physical, or mental, or both. And after that, a nice bath and a few bottles of wine with friends as we discussed whatever pertinent worldly or intensely interesting matters needed to be discussed. As I leapt into the empty creek bed from the trailhead, I thought, *Pretty good day, so far.*

There were seven small climbs to reach the top of the mountain, each one a dry waterfall, unless it had recently rained. I hopped from boulder to boulder in the creek bed until I reached the first climb. It wasn't a difficult climb, so I spied my foot and handholds, and jumped into the ascent. A few seconds later, I was staring down at the creek from the center of what would have been the waterspout. I already felt a sense of accomplishment, but nothing like what getting to the top would give me.

A cute, random stranger had put a smile on my face. Maybe she was another angel, like the post-Possibly "you have a beautiful smile" one. It had worked then *and* now, for sure, but this time her message was a lot more complex than just a compliment. A "train stop" on the way? On the way to where? I'd asked myself that question already, even asked it aloud, but hadn't come up with any answers. If I was a train stop, then she was on a journey to somewhere else.

I stopped in the middle of the path and stared at the ground.

She was on a journey somewhere else. She only stopped to be with me for a short while, but to what end: bathroom break, snack, stretch, add coal and water to the steam engine? For her it was a matter of seconds, but for me it, quite possibly, made my entire day.

If I'm truly just a train stop on the way, then that might change how I look at my past relationships. Honesty, Gravity, Possibly, even Desire, they were all on their own journeys, on the way to somewhere else—trying to stay in a place they were destined to leave. I wasn't a destination for them. *You're just a train stop on the way.* Am I?

If I *am* just a train stop on the way, it wouldn't just be for those in my past, but also for anyone in my future.

Given my belief in Promise, that certainly *can't* be true; couldn't be true.

The creek bed between the climbs wasn't difficult to manage. Periodically, I encountered a standing pool of water, but on the whole it was fun to skip across the rounded rocks making my way up the mountainside.

The second climb was a lot more difficult than the first. The waterfall had carved out an overhang that provided twelve to fifteen feet of shelter beneath it, which was too high to reach with my hands and pull myself up. In addition, the rocks on both sides had fallen together in a way that stacked them very steeply on top of each other; I couldn't just lean into them and belly snake my way up. Fortunately, the cracks between the rocks were wide enough to easily fit hands and feet, so it was merely a matter of finding the right holds and transferring weight properly between them as I climbed.

I was temporarily gassed after I made the climb, so I flopped down on the ledge, let my feet hang over it, and proceeded to take several drags from my water supply.

The view through the canopy of trees was already remarkable, and I'd barely achieved any elevation, the low-lying fog had yet to fully give way to the morning. This town was quite a paradise for almost a decade of my life, much longer than your run-of-the-mill train stop. But what amount of time determines the difference between a stop and a stay? A few hours? A day? A week? So despite the fact that the women in my life have only been at my stop for a little while, relatively speaking, we could still have moments of paradise, and I think we have.

When things enter my head they take up space. In order for new things to get in, old things must be taken out. If an artistic image appears, it's best if I walk straight to the drawing board, and at least sketch out the piece. There are files upon files of Word documents on my computer made up of thoughts, dreams, paragraphs about love, emotional tirades about past relationships, and heartfelt poems about romance, all meant to get things out so that new things can get in.

I know Promise. That's not to say I've met her in the real world and our timing hasn't yet been right. That's also not to say we've passed each other in the night going opposite directions on the highway. But I know Promise. She's innately familiar, like old souls from previous lives who haven't yet met in this one. If we're meant for each other, then I have to believe we're meant for each other in *this* life...and every other life from this one forward. And if by some chance we never meet, despite which one of us has failed, I have to believe there will be another chance in a later life. There has to be...unless love dies.

Sweat covered my brow. My shirt was showing wet regions as a result of my effort. Forcing myself up this hill was good penance for the sins of the previous night. Sweat it out. Sweat it *all* out.

Reenergized, I jumped up from the ledge and made my way to the third climb. I had faith that I'd conquer this mountain in more ways than one. The Bind is dark and Promise is my light. There may be times when she's the most distant, tiniest speck of light in the deepest region of my mind, but she's there. Faith is part of what we covered last night, a big part: faith, timing, trust, respect, knowing thyself, and realizing that when I do the same things I get the same damn results, that is, until I evolve.

I'm sure I'll see Promise in a lot of women. I'm in love with love, after all. But how quickly will she reveal herself? Will there be a discovery process? Maybe I'll only see a piece of Promise in a woman and I'll have to explore for the deeper reveal. There have certainly been pieces of Promise in the women I've dated, but to this point none met all of the promises for us to achieve those great and wonderful things in life we could never do on our own.

Next time, change the template, and not the girl. Or next time trade the girl for a woman who knows herself. That'd be a start, wouldn't it? Shouldn't true love be a journey that requires incredible effort, near catastrophic failure, and immense education in order to reveal such an amazing reward? I already had scars from this journey, and I was sure there were more to come. I quoted Keanu Reeves in *The Replacements*, in a Keanu-like voice, of course, "Pain heals. Chicks dig scars. Glory lasts forever." Exactly, man.

The third climb is the granddaddy of all the climbs on this trail as it takes the longest and requires the highest ascent, around forty feet. I knew my normal route and I started by stepping up on a boulder near the right side of the creek bed, and then hugged the face of a rock before slowly scooting my way up the front of it. From there, it's ten to twelve feet of crawling back and forth over boulders until reaching two great slabs of rock with a mere three or four feet between them. This vertical chasm allows me to shimmy my way up to a ledge, but it's about fifteen feet of shimmying straight upward.

I stretched my arms and legs out and then clapped my hands together to indicate a state of readiness. My starting hand and footholds were there, as usual. Halfway through the climb, I still felt good, exhaling a deep breath and replacing it immediately as I sought the next hold. As I looked up, a few specs of dirt fell into my eyes causing me to reposition myself so I could clear the debris with a finger. A voice in my head said, *I just don't think that's what my daughter wants*. "WHAT?!" I asked aloud. It distracted me so much that I slipped a few inches down the rock. My hands pressed against the inside of the opposite rock, same one as my feet, while my back straightened against the opposite wall. "What the fuck?" I whispered and looked upward once more. A small rock bounced off my forearm. Suddenly, I feared the worst. Another rock followed it, passing between my arms and catching me on the thigh. A scattering of noises occurred above me, so I shielded my face as I looked up once again. A rock roughly the size of my head blocked my view of the sky as gravity brought it directly toward my face. Luckily, my arm caught enough of it to change its trajectory—a direct hit would have likely knocked me out—instead of catching me between the eyes it glanced off the side of my face. My foot lost its grip and shot out the face of the chasm. "Shit-shit-SHIT!" I mumbled as I began to lose control and realized I'd have to make a leap. With only a small ledge to catch me, the odds for a successful landing were little to none.

In that instant, I strangely remembered the words of a Navy pilot who once said during a television interview, "Landing on an aircraft carrier is like climbing up on your couch and diving face-first toward a postage stamp on the floor, and trying to land on it with your tongue."

There was little to grab as I landed. The instep of my right foot caught the edge of the ledge and slid out from underneath me. Although the ledge provided some braking to my acceleration, my ass bounced off of it, and the boulders below offered no flat footing to control my fall. I rolled my right ankle on the first step. That error shot me to the right where my arm took a blow from the face of the rock. I tried to hug that rock with my left arm and felt its rough kiss across my right ear. My twisting motion caused a sudden life or death panic, which wrecked the confidence that I would actually emerge from this unscathed. I careened head over heels until my right knee landed hard on a boulder only a few feet off the ground and stopped most of my falling speed. My left temple slammed against the mountain—

* * *

When I came to, I wondered how much time had passed, the sun hadn't moved in the sky. Afraid to move, I surveyed the damage in my head. Another earthy rumble above caused panic and I felt compelled to painfully scoot on my back into the brush and away from falling rocks. My back felt wet. *Is it blood?* I remembered having water. It must be water. The plastic bottles surely didn't survive the fall.

Great Grandpa once spit into my hand when I was a kid and then placed my palm in the grass. "For your thirst," he said as he offered the nourishment to the plants. I was thirsty. I whispered weakly, "For your thirst," and hoped for the burst of energy I felt when I was a kid, but I didn't have the strength to spit into my hand. I was tired. I was in pain. I had no idea what to do, so I whispered to anyone who was willing to listen, "Save me."

* * *

"GRANDSON!" Great Grandpa screamed.

His voice woke me, but it was too dark to see, and I was too tired to answer.

He yelled at me again, but this time added, "LISTEN!"

I tried to open my eyes, but with no success. The only thing I *could* do is listen.

"TO THE ELEMENTS!" he continued.

I was so tired. Sleep sounded perfectly good; a long, long sleep.

"GRANDSON!" Just as soon as his voice appeared, it left again, farther away than the previous shouts.

I heard the ocean. There wasn't a conch next to my ear. *The ocean? It couldn't be the ocean.* I smiled. The sound of the waves relaxed me even more.

There was something else. I crawled a few small steps out of sleep to concentrate ever so slightly. Over the sound of the waves I began to hear a whisper. It repeated itself as it grew louder. Five syllables. Repeating. And suddenly, I knew it.

Burn. Blow. Nourish. Grow.

I remembered the mountain, momentarily…and the fire.

Burn. Blow. Nourish. Grow.

The fire.

Burn. Blow. Nourish. Grow.

An intense sensation struck my thigh. It woke me from my sleepy state more so than my recognition of those memorable four words. I frantically brushed my hand against my hip as if to clear the pain like a stray bug, but it didn't recede. I reached into my pocket and felt my black rock, practically burning to the touch. With it in my hand, the desire to sleep slowly returned. The warmth of it seeped through my body; a comfortable, soothing feeling that—

Burn. Blow. Nourish. Grow.

Wait. Burn. *Burn. BURN!* The word escalated in my head, but I could only muster a whispered "burn" aloud. What does fire need? Fuel. And air. I shook my head slowly back and forth. In the dark I heard the rustle of leaves, and leaves are the perfect fuel. I reached behind my head, grabbed a handful of leaves from the brush, placed the rock into the center of them, and then wished for fire. Nothing happened. I was too desperate. I needed to focus on the emotion, not the logic. My emotion was fear; I needed love.

I heard Promise say in my head, *I love y—*

"NO!" I shouted at myself. Out of the falling and into the fire? That image was too strong; I'd fry myself on the spot. *What else do I love?* I remembered the safety of the canopy under the great tree on the plain; how I felt so relaxed as the wind gently rustled its dark green leaves. I remembered leaning into the large exposed roots of the tree, allowing it to hold me while I cuddled up in its presence. I imagined this comfortable, secure Place of Power and warmth, and then whispered, "Always do great and honorable things," as I closed my hand more tightly on the pouch I'd created for the rock inside the leaves.

I took in a slow breath, pursed my lips, and then blew softly, and steadily, into the darkness…and there I began to see a light.

Epilogue

My eyes struggled to open, like I was falling asleep with a book in bed at the end of the day, but I didn't have a book and I wasn't in bed. And in this case, my eyes weren't transitioning from awake to asleep, but asleep to awake.

"AWAKE!" came an unfamiliar, booming male voice.

I kept my eyelids from closing more than halfway, which was progress. Numerous brilliantly, red-leafed trees encircled me. The wind casually passed between them, which caused them to dance briefly. The grass was yellowed and dormant, well on its way to a nap. The sky was high, blue and cloudless. A low wall of gray boulders formed a circle around me. I was leaning up against one end of the wall in a seated position with my legs straight out in front of me. At the other end of the circle sat three figures. I couldn't make out their faces, only that they sat in tall stone thrones. I tried to rub my eyes to help them focus, but I couldn't move my arms.

"He will wake up in his own time," Great Grandpa's voice added. His voice gave me more motivation to do so.

"Our time is dire," the male voice replied.

A third voice, a female one, chimed in, "If we don't have time to do this right, then when will we have time to do it over?" There was silence for a moment. "Be patient," she added.

Great Grandpa said, "He has been in the dark for a long time. Give him a moment to return to us."

I tried to say, "I'm awake," but no noise emerged from my lips.

"You see," Grandpa said. "Soupy, my grandson, there is no need for you to speak here."

I wanted to nod my head, but that task also failed me. I blinked and hoped Grandpa knew I understood.

The male voice continued, "Soupy Robert Heller, you have been brought to Autumn for evaluation. We are here to judge your ability to keep the promise you have made as The Chosen One. I am Truth."

"And I am Love," the female voice said.

"Your great grandpa is here to speak on your behalf. As he said, there is no need for you to speak in this court."

"Twenty years have passed since you were made aware of your mission, but we see that no progress has been made to become the beacon of light we need you to be," the female voice said.

The male voice added, "And you refuse to learn from your mistakes; it jeopardizes my faith in you, which jeopardizes the future of our people and the world."

Great Grandpa began, "I think if you—"

"One moment, Walker," the male voice interrupted. "This tribunal asks all parties present whether Soupy Robert Heller should be allowed to continue his mission. Walker, you may now make your case."

Great Grandpa winked at me before he lifted his left hand, which coaxed a light source from the middle of the circle to produce a video screen. I watched as he made his presentation, as if I was watching a movie from behind the movie screen in a theater instead of in the crowd.

"I have taught this man to understand his mission and the tools he has available to achieve it. As you both know, these tools take much of a lifetime to develop. In fact, most never acquire them."

On the video screen, I saw Great Grandpa telling the story of Leaf to the kids in my neighborhood.

He continued, "He has blossomed much since the day I showed him the strength of the elements. In our practices together, I see a great reservoir of power inside him, often too strong for the practice routines I have given. But he is learning, and he learns quickly."

The video screen showed us practicing fire.

"I do not fear an inability for him to learn in his real world relationships. In fact, he has taken his first step out of The Bind after a very long stay. None before him have endured the length of time he has spent there; none ever returned who have. He is wiser than he has shown. I have faith in his future."

My most recent memory appeared on the screen causing my eyes to open wide; I lay broken at the base of the mountain.

"He has fallen from the tree. He has accepted his failure. He has been burned."

On the screen, my body slumped as my eyes closed. It was an obvious sign that I had accepted my own death and failure of my mission. But then, my eyes reopened.

Grandpa smiled, "He found strength in the knowledge I have helped him learn. He was resilient in the face of failure."

I wanted to protest. Wanted to tell the tribunal that it had been Grandpa who wouldn't allow me to die; that he was the one who deserved the credit. I *had* given up, accepted my failure, and my own death.

Grandpa continued, "He asked the elements to help save his life. This is why I believe he can save our world. He will heal, and then he will evolve."

When the video screen disappeared, I saw the regents of love and truth staring at me. Truth had his chin in his hand, contemplative. Love looked at him before she spoke to me, "Mr. Heller, do not speak when I ask these few questions of you, simply nod your head in the affirmative or shake it in the negative."

I nodded my head to show I understood.

"Do you feel that Promise has been a suitable match for your mission?" she asked.

I nodded my head up and down four times in an attempt to strenuously show my agreement.

"I see. And do you wish to continue your mission to find her?"

I considered the alternative briefly, but feared the unknown. Or even worse, a life of indifference or hate without love? I definitely preferred an optimistic present, and hopeful future, and nodded my head to show it.

"Your best path hasn't been the one you've seen first; I think you understand that now. Your best path will always be the one to teach you the most about who you are, despite the outcome."

I nodded my head while I thought how much Possibly fit that "despite the outcome" scenario.

"Very well," she replied. "By nodding your head, I ask you to now reconfirm your commitment to your mission to find Promise, and give the world the example of true love we so desperately need."

I felt her belief in me; it gave me warmth. I nodded my head confidently knowing I was in her good graces. She smiled at me in return.

"I concur," the male voice agreed. "But I certainly wish for you to cease the insanity," he added. "You may return to your mission, Soupy Robert Heller."

Grandpa said, "It was not your time to die yet, Grandson. Old souls do not die tragic deaths. Know this with truth and love in your heart; together they will act as your guide."

I nodded my head one last time.

"Of great deeds for the state," Great Grandpa said, and my eyes closed once more.

* * *

I heard my mom worriedly say, "Put these on him. He had surgery once and the recovery nurse said he was singing when they wheeled him out of the operating room, so she put headphones on him, and he loved it."

I felt an ear bud go into my right ear and then another in my left. I could smell the nurse's perfume as she inserted them.

Slightly muted from the headphones, I heard the nurse ask Mom what kind of music I liked. "I don't know; that eighties stuff?" she replied.

"No problem," she said. Several clicks passed from her music player to my ears as she searched for her eighties playlist.

The opening notes of "Promises, Promises" by Naked Eyes played through the headphones and my eyes shot open. "Promise?" I said.

Mom jumped up from her chair and wrestled the earbuds from my ears. "Soupy?" She looked tired, like she hadn't left my side for quite some time. "SOUPY!" she yelled, obviously happy to see that I was awake.

"Hi, Mom," I replied.

Other family members walked into the room and surrounded my bed to offer affection, which was nice but caused me to wonder how long I'd been asleep. The hustle and bustle went on for a few minutes before my sister walked over to me, held the ring in front of me, and asked, "They found this on you; we all want to know the story."

My throat was still dry, but I eked out a response, "You'll have to read the book after I write it." I smiled.

She laughed and said, "We'll see about that."

The noise in my room from the various joyful conversations was loud, but I could still hear a cell phone ringing. "Will someone answer that?" I whispered. Mom heard me, but didn't understand what I said, so I mimicked a phone with my thumb and pinky finger and held it up to my ear. She leaned down close to me and I said, "I think my phone's ringing."

"Quiet everyone," Mom said loudly. With a quiet room it was easier to find the source of the ringing. She picked it up, answered, and said, "Yes, he *is* awake." The obvious look of confusion about the room was due to the fact that no one outside of it could have known I was awake these few minutes since I opened my eyes. She handed the phone to me.

"Hello," I said, weakly.

Faith was crying on the other end of the line. Through her tears she said, "I need you to come home." I motioned for everyone to give me some privacy and they left the room.

"How did you know—"

"The Network," she said before I could finish my question.

Afterword

Grandma Heller once told me, "Our ability to heal doesn't come from a magical elixir or a pill of any color. Hellers carry only what can be found on or within their person." And what I've learned since then is that we heal by helping others think about all the possibilities present before choosing the path best suited to them. Therefore, the tools of our trade are our ears, eyes, and experience. Our calm in the midst of chaos can feel cold, but our capacity for caring is unmatched in the world. We have a great passion to help others resolve personal conflicts, troubling group dynamics, and community unrest.

We've traveled millions of miles over the course of our family's generations. Our trade hasn't changed much over that time, but the world has changed dramatically. We've seen assassinations, catastrophes, coups, miracles, and the change of many, many seasons, but it's been a long time since we've seen the beacon of true love the world so desperately needs. It's not just those of us who are looking for it, and too few are, but the entire world has lacked love leaders for many generations.

Anything good in the world must be earned; that's why we haven't seen true love in hundreds of years. Anything truly great must *truly* be earned, but the concept of earning has been lost. As children, we can get a movie, song, or a toy instantly. No longer must we save up the money or sit poised with one finger on "Play" and one finger on "Record" waiting impatiently for our favorite song on the radio. If we're hungry, we have a multitude of options that can be retrieved or delivered at a whim. When we want attention or conversation, we can find it online, twenty-four hours a day. We make "friends" in minutes through any number of social networks.

This instant gratification flies in the face of earning and makes us lazy. When you can have something so easily, you're likely to toss it aside just as easily. We'll throw out moldy cheese just as quickly as a cheesy spouse, when maybe all that's really needed is to trim away the moldy fringe to reveal more good, edible cheese.

Healers must learn from their own experiences while helping others make decisions with theirs. Fortunately, we believe relationships are understood through action, or inaction, not material. In other words, understanding how people relate to things is more important than the things themselves. For example, whether you use a bowl or your hands in the shape of a bowl is irrelevant. It's the nourishment you get from the soup that defines your relationship with it; the actual utensil or serving mechanism is of little importance. This is the concept we Healers apply to the entire world: relationships between things. The source for knowledge or guidance comes in many forms: friends, lovers, parents, strangers, books, and dreams, to name a few. The presence of these sources is an important part of life, but what's transferred from them to you is of much more significance. What fills in the spaces between persons, places, and things defines how strongly we feel about them, not the persons, places, and things themselves; in the space between things we find the stomping grounds of emotion.

Friends are always present and integral in life, but they aren't always the same persons. If we focus on why certain types of people are constants in our lives, then we'll be more likely to understand what role they play, no matter who they are or where we are. If we focus on why we are attracted to certain kinds of significant others more, then we'll eventually understand the relationship connections that work for us. This introspection helps us build the successful template, no matter what homework assignment we've been given in life.

We must remember: it's the verbs, not the nouns, which define us.

Acknowledgments

In 2007, Laura F. walked (with intent) around a bookstore asking if I'd read this, that, and the other. "Oh my, you haven't read this? And this?" She guffawed at my having never read a few books; books that would ultimately change my life. Thank you, Laura.

I blew through them over the next few weeks—and two years later I woke up so many times in the same night with the idea for this novel, I finally just got up and started writing.

It took me ten years to write the first book of this series, in addition to the hundreds of thousands of words waiting in the next three books and an outline for Soupy's journey, and it might never have happened without the support of so many wonderful people, like Jay Rubin, Will Fogel, Joe Rollinson, Tracee Knight-De Souza, Elizabeth Higgins, Mark Mattison, Courtney Pesek, Naomi in California, Heather Magee, Karen Batcher, Jennifer Boerger, Kelvin Blunt, Sylvia Tran, Charity Sherwood, Kurt Kemper, Craig VanderZwaag, Dan Berkeland, Matt Dromi, Susan Choudry, Roxselle Edwards, Tess Cameron, Joey Nelson, Jennifer Osborn, Eileen Everett, Sheila Peterson, Robyn DeuPree, Alwyn Leyland, Sandy Hill, Tammy Byergo, Jerry Osmus, Andres Gomez, Sam Taylor, Kevin Vento, Laura Sei, and a family member who wished to be an influential, but unnamed contributor. Your donations through a successful Kickstarter campaign paid my mortgage for a few months, which allowed me to keep writing. I'm so very thankful. Love you all!

Over the years it took to write this, I spent a lot of days and nights without showers, but in the company of friends-turned-family who were happy to leave me to my writing while periodically reminding me to eat: Bob and Darcy, Alicia and Charles, Willy Jo Smith, Laura T., of my California framilies, and Jeff and Sheila of my Illinois framily, Cynthia and Charles of my Honduran framily. I suppose, on that note, I also need to thank their animals who warmed my feet or forced me out for walks: Corbin "Multi-Pass" and Leelu "Bada-Big-Boom" Dallas, Cecil the 5-Toed Diesel, Molly-Molly In Come Free, Truman 2xDoodle, Whiskey Biscuit, The Brown Dog Newton, Tobe-Toby-Tobin, Chloe and Leo (who I called Cleo and Theo the first three days after I met them), and dos gatas bandidas, Picasa y Diego, as well as Jazzy Sizzle and Pupa, twin pups from different mamas.

Finally, there were a few workhorses who kept encouraging me to write by providing feedback, begging for more to read, and at times playfully threatening me for the next chapter, challenging my assumptions, and reading (and reading and reading and reading) the various drafts multiple times over. If y'all can handle it, we'll be doing it many more times in the future as we complete the rest of the series: Jenn "Did You Eat Today?" Everett, Shelly "Beanie" Ryan, Patty "No Canoe For You" Redman, Charity "Forest For the Trees" Sherwood, Michael "Mumbo" Roth, and Haydee "Send Me More Pages" Deupree. Thank you. Thank you. Thank you.

More love.